"If the oh-so-glorious Arthur Pendragon, Hero of Battles and High King of all the Britons, needs a fawning chronicler, let him find one elsewhere. When the worm feast comes, he won't lack for chroniclers, will he? There'll be scribes and bards aplenty struggling to wring meaning from his life. But what of the others who shaped me? How much shrift will they get from the weavers of glorious legends? Who will tell their story if I don't?"

"This won't be Mordred's life of Arthur, but Mordred's life of Mordred."

MORDRED'S CURSE

IAN MCDOWELL

AVON BOOKS • NEW YORK

MORDRED'S CURSE is an original publication of Avon Books. This work has never before appeared in book form. This work is a novel. Any similarity to actual persons or events is purely coincidental.

AVON BOOKS
A division of
The Hearst Corporation
1350 Avenue of the Americas
New York, New York 10019

Copyright © 1996 by Ian McDowell
Cover art by Lars Hokanson
Published by arrangement with the author
Library of Congress Catalog Card Number: 96-96182
ISBN: 0-380-78195-6

First AvoNova Printing: October 1996

AVONOVA TRADEMARK REG. U.S. PAT. OFF. AND IN OTHER COUNTRIES, MARCA REGISTRADA, HECHO EN U.S.A.

Printed in the U.S.A.

RA   10 9 8 7 6 5 4 3 2 1

For my parents,
Donald McDowell and Rosemary Campbell McDowell

and my friend Anne Abrams,
pretty damn close to family herself

Acknowledgments

With special thanks to Richard Curtis, for believing in me; eluki bes shahar, for her invaluable editing; the magian Neil Gaiman (whom I'd want to be when I grow up, if it wasn't too late), for generously letting me use the Castle of Teeth and getting me over a major hump; and Poppy, Poppy, burning Brite, for needed encouragment and ego-salving praise, so rewarding when it comes from someone of her gifts.

At the risk of sounding like an interminable awards speech, I must also express my gratitude to and affection for the following people: Lee Ramey, who got me off my bum and back to the keyboard a few years ago; Fred Chappell, for long ago but never forgotten tutelage; Kelly Link, for being brilliant and wonderful and a better writer than me (and whom I forgive for the llama fetus); Michelle Mouton, for keeping my life from being boring and much else; the Raven Ladies, Jenn and Linda Ingram, for more than just the stylish cloak and hat they made for my iguana; Andrea Fullbright, for friendship and favors; those phosphor goddesses Sunshine Ison and Gwenda Bond, whose e-mail always brightens my inbox; and the lovely and amazing Go-Go Max Bernardi, for proving that one can meet terrific people even at lousy conventions.

Finally, a tip of the iron helm to the Fabulous

Lorraine Garland and Emma Bull, and to Ms. Tori Amos, two friends and a stranger whose albums sustained me in the face of the wordless void.

BEGINNINGS

I remember the very things I do not wish;
I cannot forget the things I wish to forget.

Cicero, *De Finibus*

One

I DON'T care what Guinevere and Gawain say; this won't be Mordred's Life of Arthur, but Mordred's Life of Mordred. Fuck them; *they* can chronicle my sanctimonious progenitor's exploits if they've got the stomach for it. I love them both, more than I've loved anybody except my mother, and once, maybe Arthur himself, and with Gwen and Gawain there isn't any hate mixed in. Love, however, goes only so far, and they're pissing me off with their constant admonitions to write the marvelous history of my father's reign.

If the oh-so-glorious Arthur Pendragon, Hero of Battles and High King of all the Britons, needs a fawning chronicler, let him find one elsewhere. Hell, if Gwen, Gawain, or anyone else wants the full tale told, they ought to seek out little Merlin in his Caledonian exile. That way, this story can be written by someone who knows how it's going to end, as folk say that Merlin can see the future. I wouldn't know; I only met him once, and on that occasion he seemed solely interested in the moment. At any rate, he's barely in my story. Sorry.

Back to Guinevere and Gawain, and their well-meant but infuriating advice. Gwen, as usual, has an ulterior motive. She wants Arthur to make me Regent whenever he goes off on his proposed "rescue" of what's left of the Roman Empire. Truth to tell, he just might do it; I've had an honored place at court for quite some time now, and he's long acknowledged my parentage. Even so,

3

making him the hero of some puffed-up piece of official hagiography won't put me any closer to the throne. You don't get anywhere with Arthur by flattering him.

Guinevere knows that, if anyone does, which makes her insistence puzzling. Possibly, she also believes that writing such a history will help me find peace of mind. Spare me, Gwen. Yes, perhaps my soul would be more tranquil if I acquired some perspective about my father's life. First, though, I think I need some perspective on my own. Know yourself, Socrates said. I've been working on that. Besides, the tale of Arthur and me's not done yet, and won't be, I fear, until we're both provender for worms.

When the worm feast comes, *he* won't lack for chroniclers, will he? There'll be scribes and bards aplenty struggling to wring meaning from his life. He doesn't need me, or this testament. But what of the others who shaped me? How much shrift will they get from the weavers of glorious legends? Who will tell their story, if I don't? I don't mean to make grandiose claims for all of them; far from it. Lot of Orkney, the man I once thought my father, deserves to be nothing more than a footnote in our royal history. If I were honest with myself, I might even say the same about my dear, dead, loved, hated, and never-once-forgotten mother. However, I don't want to. It's been a long time since I spoke to her, or touched her lips to mine, and even longer since she died, but she haunts me still, and now, a decade since I last beheld her dead or living face, I've but to shut my eyes and there it is, her Breton features flat and swarthy as any Pict's, all wide cheekbones and black commanding eyes. For the first few years that Gwen and I were lovers, I'd sometimes wake in the cold dark and think my dead mother lay beside me, instead of my father's wife. Isn't that a pretty thing to put in my history? Posterity will be edified, I'm sure.

Don't think this will be just a litany of dirty secrets. There are marvels here, as the credulous reckon them, and even a soupçon of glory. In my not uneventful life I've slain two monsters and rescued a fair queen from an enchanted prison, which tempts me to call this history the Three Deeds of Mordred, making it a modestly prosaic Latin elaboration on the traditional Bardic Triad. Oh yes, were I less likely to be eclipsed by my pious King and father, I'd say my tale contains fine grist for the legend-makers once I'm safely dead. Which is my point, really. I'm less interested in what I did than what I felt, and they never get that part right. I'm no paragon, surely, weighed down with flaws and more than half a fool, but my own self just the same, and not just another star in Arthur's heroic firmament. At six centuries and a continent's remove, I can read Catullus and briefly think: I *know* that man, he died long ago, but I know him now; I've shared the sharp-edged particulars of his daily life. Maybe someday some unimagined you will read these words and think that you know me, and then I'll be reborn inside your head. Everyone has his or her own scheme for cheating death; this poor testament is mine.

I equivocate and explain myself at such tedious length because I really don't know how the hell to begin. Where *do* I start, with all the bloody history of Britain, dating straight back to storied Brutus? Should I include the Last Legions, the Decline of Albion, Vortigern and Hengest and Horsa, Ambrosius and all that? Honestly, I'd rather give myself an enema than write that sort of tedious chronicle. Let dickless monks like Gildas make our past a stick to beat us with; I've got better things to do. Not that Gwen would ever want me to be like Gildas.

The wind has shifted, and I smell apple blossoms through the open casement. Somewhere above me, a lark is singing in the eaves. *Don't worry,* say wind and birdsong in harmony; *let it come as it comes; it will find its own best shape.* Good advice, I think, for life as well as Art.

I suppose I could begin twenty-eight years ago with my quite ordinary birth in the far Orkneys, those barren windswept islands of my youth, or start even farther back than that, with the less mundane details of my conception. The former, alas, is rather dull, and while the latter is not, it's something I'd prefer to describe as I myself found out about it, in teasing scraps and pieces. No, dammit, it's Arthur after all, for I must start with our first meeting, the day he officially became King. It was a day of some importance to another Mordred, my long-dead younger self, and to the other principals of my early history, to my mother and most especially to her husband, sour, pickle-faced Lot, the man who taught me how to hate.

God, but I've been thinking of *him* quite a lot lately. I'm not sure why. He wasn't the first man I killed, just the first one I knew by name. I never thought of him as my father, even when I believed myself his son, for I hated him long before I knew the truth. Why, at this point in my life, twenty-eight years old and possessed of the nearest thing I've ever known to peace of mind, do my thoughts turn toward the old lamprey? Is it an omen, then, something to do with patricide? No, for although I've slain a giant and been to the Otherworld, I don't believe in omens, and I'll not be giving that sneering prick more importance than he deserves. It's quite odd, though; he's been dead so long, I wouldn't have thought I could still hate him, but now it all comes rushing back, a veritable cataract of bile. Or maybe it never went away.

All of this is why my most vivid early memory is of one fateful day, when Lot's dreams of ever being lord of anything more than his bare islands were finally and irrevocably dashed. It's Arthur's coronation I'm speaking of. Always the last-minute opportunist, Lot had insisted on attending, hoping to sound out or even instigate opposition to Arthur's claim among the assembled Kings of Britain. Mother had simply wanted to visit my brother Gawain, and brought me along, too, saying I was old enough, and it was time I saw something of the world. I've forgotten most of the magically short but still-tedious voyage down the Irish Sea, but I vividly remember the wet worn stone quay, bone pale Cornish cliffs, white inland clouds, salty wind, our creaky ship mooring under a vibrant blue sky turning muddy dark on the horizon, the burns on my thighs I got from shinnying down the rope to the dock, and the expression on my brother's face as he came running to meet me, with Arthur right behind him and grinning almost as broadly. Yes, that's it; I've but to let twenty years come rushing back and I'm in my eighth summer again, and setting foot in Britain for the first time.

All right then, I begin with Arthur, though only briefly. Just remember; this is my story, not his.

Two

"**O**UR WARS are done!"

That's what Gawain said as he bounded along the quay to sweep into his arms the cheering bundle that was me. My brother spun me around, his broad face buried in my chest, while I laughed up at the churning, cloud-streaked sky. Then he put me down, and gestured at the man beside him. Reeling with dizzy joy, I got my first good look at Arthur in the flesh.

Not big, though he seemed it at the time. Broad shoulders, barrel chest, eyes the color of the sky above our heads. He had worry lines at twenty-four, but laugh lines, too, and his brown hair was cut short in the Roman fashion, exposing ears like jug handles. His leather jerkin and doeskin boots were rather the worse for wear, and he smelled like a horse.

"Hello, Mordred," he boomed in a voice that was all rough campaign music. "Your brother's the best man I have. Will you be my man, too?"

"Always, my lord." Impeccable manners, even then.

"Don't 'lord' me, laddybuck," he said as he lifted me into the air. "It's 'Uncle Arthur' from now on!"

If the young *Artorious Imperator,* Hero of Battles and the Chief Dragon of the Island, wanted to forgo formalities, that was fine with me. Now level with his prematurely craggy face, I looked down beneath his chin, to the thing that hung around his neck. It was not flashy gold like I would have expected, but plain, ugly wood, no

more than a big splinter, really, with a hole drilled
through it so it could hang from a leather thong.

"What's this, Uncle Arthur?" I said, fingering it.
Always the bold one, despite my manners.

"I've been told that it's a piece of the Cross Our Lord
died on," said Arthur. "I'd like to think it so, though that
may just be my sinful vanity. Bishop Gerontius says I
should have it encased in fine copper, or even silver and
gold, but no, I wear the raw old wood plain and simple,
like my faith, for I don't believe Our Lord well served by
fancy ornaments."

I thought it ugly compared to Mother's jewels, but
even then had some inkling of diplomacy. "What
Lord?" I said, letting go of it lest I get a splinter.

Arthur held me at arm's length with seeming ease, no
effort evident in his sinewy arms, but there was an
undercurrent of tension in his voice. "You've not heard
of Our Savior, lad? Jesus, who died that we may live?"

"The god Mum calls the dead carpenter?"

Honestly, I think he almost dropped me, but then his
composure came back, settling like a veil across his face.
Swinging me up onto his shoulders, he turned to Gawain.

"You've not told him, then?"

My brother scuffed algaed stone with his booted toe.
"Ach, it's not been easy. Our house is not a Christian
one, as you know. I've been away from it some time.
Mordred has not. He's only eight, and has not lived
outside of Orkney. You know there are no priests or
churches there. Your sister is our mother; would you
have me tell her how to raise him? There's enough
problems when I go back home as your envoy, without
me trying to do that."

I could not see Arthur's face, only the top of his head. I
was bemused by how much more hair he seemed to have
there than my father, though I'd never seen the top of
Lot's scabby pate so close as this. "True enough," he
said, and I felt the strong shoulders under my thighs
shrug off their burden of distress. "It's hardly the lad's
fault, is it? We must work to save him, but now isn't the

time." He craned his head up to squint at me through his own bangs. "Come on, Mordred. You jumped off that ship nimble as a cat, but I think your father and mother will need some help."

And so we set off down the dock, a dozen armored warriors tramping at our heels. I looked back at them, their spearpoints glittering to prick heaven, their ring-mail coats and conical helmets a shining contrast to their master's much abused leather, and found myself suddenly, inexpressibly happy. It seemed a new emotion.

I remember it clear as glass, all so particular and bloody perfect—the particular salty brightness of the air, the particular sweeping blueness of the landward sky, the particular cries of the particular gulls coasting on a particular breeze. Moments of ineffable happiness are like that, so sharply defined you stab yourself on them, and laugh with joy at the way they hurt. It was a trivial thing, maybe, but for me it was like a second birth, the moment at which I first became aware, not just of the world beyond myself, but of myself *as* myself, someone with a newfound capacity for transcendent joy. There was a high shining place beyond the cliffs that surrounded Lot's dank Orkney palace, and suddenly, for just an instant, I was part of it.

Arthur set me down on the dock and turned back to Gawain. "You best go see to your father," he said quietly.

Several of Lot's warriors were helping him across the crude gangplank that connected our ship to the barnacled stone embankment. As usual, the King of Orkney had been drinking, insisting that inebriation was the only true cure for seasickness. Now, as he stumbled onto the battered wharf, he reeled and vomited all over the red beard and brown tunic of Beortric, the big walleyed Jute who commanded the royal guard, leaving his own fine purple robe relatively unspotted. That seemed to sober him, and he straightened up and came lurching toward us, looking not a whit ashamed. The air around us seemed darker and danker, and when I looked up, I saw that that the muddy clouds were no longer lurking on the sea rim, but were almost overhead, blotting out what had only just been blue and white.

Gawain intercepted him and tried to take his arm, but Lot shook him off. "I'm fine, dammit," he said, wiping his mouth on his already-stained sleeve. Steadying himself, he gave Arthur what might have passed for a token bow. "Hail, O Dragon of Britain. Congratulations on your good fortune." His tone was mild, but something about his bloodshot eyes suggested a man speaking through clenched teeth.

Arthur nodded back. "I'm glad you arrived safely, lord of Orkney. Is my sister with you?"

"Of course," said Mother as she appeared atop the gangplank, raven's wings of black hair framing her olive moon of a face. Gathering her black wool robe up about her legs, she clambered nimbly to the dock, ignoring Beortric's proffered arm. "I wouldn't have missed this occasion for the world."

Arthur gave her a diplomatic smile. "You honor me, my lady." Despite the polite facade, they did not embrace. Gawain, however, stepped forward and received a hug. "It's good to see you, Mum," he said, in a tone that suggested he really meant it.

A smattering of droplets hissed across the water toward us. "Ach, but did you have to bring bad weather with you?" chided Gawain.

My mother's smile was secretive as always. "I brought us wind to fill our sails, and rain often comes with that. It's easily gotten rid of, though." She fingered a tube of bone that hung on a cord around her throat. Mother had few secrets from me, and even at that age I knew it had come from the tiny thigh of one of my other brothers, all of whom had died in childbirth or shortly thereafter. Of her five children, Gawain and I were the only ones to live, and I'd come at the end of a semibarren period, in which her womb produced one sickly, ill-fated infant after another, which is why Gawain, her firstborn, was a decade my senior.

She raised the bone whistle to her lips, but Arthur reached out his hand and stopped her. "No, sister," he said softly, but with frost in his eyes. "I'll have no magic here."

She nodded her head, the half smile never fading from her face. "As you wish, my brother. But you may have a sopping coronation."

"I'll chance that, Morgawse. If the Lord wishes to baptize the event with rain, he will do so." He bowed again, more stiffly this time. "I'm sorry if I appear a bad host, but there's much to do before this evening, and I need Gawain's help. My steward Kay will see you to your quarters. Perhaps we'll have the opportunity to speak further after tonight's ceremony." With that he waved his hand and turned back toward the palace, Gawain and his other soldiers falling in behind him. I watched them tramp up the pebbled beach, still giddy as if Jupiter had just welcomed me to Olympus.

"Bastard," said Lot, kicking the royal trunk so hard it nearly went off the side the of the dock. "Bloody, shit-eating bastard. And he's got my own son to lick his arse for him!" His eyes were redder than before, and a vein stood out like a purple worm on the pale dome of his forehead.

"Such a tantrum is unseemly," said Mother mildly. "Especially since none of this was a surprise. If it bothers you so much, why did we come?"

Lot sat on the chest, hiked up his robe, and scratched a skinny red-and-white ankle. "I don't have to explain myself to you, Morgawse. And if I want to have a tantrum, as you call it, I bloody well will, so you can just piss off."

"As always, your manners are as refined as your intellect," she retorted, a gibe which pleased me with its cutting tone, even though I didn't understand the irony. Depending on one's definition of intellectual refinement, Mother's quip may have been unfair. Despite his boorishness, Lot was seldom a fool.

He must have noticed my smile, for he lurched to his feet. "What the hell are you smirking at, you insolent brat? Is there another Arthur-worshiper in the family?" He started to reach for me, but Mother's strong hand shot out and closed on his thin wrist. "There'll be none of that," she said so quietly I almost couldn't hear her. "We should see to our quarters."

Cursing under his breath, he turned away. "You can see to our fucking quarters. I'll not wait on the dock like some lackey." He motioned to Beortric, who got the royal guard into rough formation. "Come on, you dogs; let's see how things fare in the palace. I want to find out if the other lords of Britain are really as content with Arthur's coronation as is claimed. If they are, this is going to be a bloody short stay."

They went tramping off down the quay and up the pebbled beach, leaving me and Mother and a handful of servants standing in the rain, which ceased when Mother put the bone whistle to her lips and blew a short, sharp note. "Your uncle may want his coronation drizzled on," she said, "but I prefer to stay dry."

Stopping rain was nothing special to me, for I'd gotten used to Mother's arts long before she summoned the wind that had allowed to us to sail from Orkney in scarcely a day, a trip that later in my life took the better part of a week.

"Why doesn't Uncle Arthur like magic?"

She shook her head like a dog, only more gracefully, and her long tresses were no longer wet. When she ran her fingers through my own hair, it dried, too. "Christians are funny about that, and much else. I expect he shan't get on well with little Merlin."

"Who's Merlin?"

There was a look on her face I'd never seen before, not just distaste but something approaching trepidation. "Your grandfather's . . . magician. With Uther dead, I suppose he's Arthur's magician now, though I doubt Arthur will want him, especially considering what else Uther used him for."

Before I could ask what she meant (and probably be told to never mind), we were hailed by Arthur's steward Kay, a broad black-bearded man with a squashed nose, who escorted us up the beach and through the broken maze of fortifications that were the grounds of Uther's old summer palace. At Mother's whistling command, the wind had changed direction, sweeping the rain clouds back out to sea, and the sky was all blue and white again, with the afternoon sunlight gilding the broken ramparts. I was amazed by how big everything was, and how much of it was made of stone, although today I'd find it shabby enough. We passed weed-choked courtyards and dead orchards, crumbling limestone walls and cracked plaster facades, skirting the main hall and threading our way through half-collapsed colonnades and dilapidated out-buildings. Mother dryly commented on just how far our lodgings were from the restored inner palace, but she did not seem offended. Thinking on it now, I imagine she considered it more of a reflection on her husband than herself.

As for Lot, he eventually rejoined us, apparently having met little success at stirring up discord among his fellow petty kings. In the bare chamber where we lodged, he snarled and cursed, and would probably have kicked the furniture, if there had been any, and even muttered about not attending the ceremony that evening. In the end, of course, he did. More to the point, he allowed me and Mother to attend with him.

I felt joy again that evening, when I stood between my brother and my mother, the former in burnished ring-mail and the latter in fine red linen, and watched Arthur pull the old sword of Maximus from its brass scabbard that had been in set in a block of polished black stone. "*Ave Imperator!*" yelled the throng, with enough force to gutter the torches in that smoky, high-timbered hall, and if the assembled Kings of Britain were not cheering as loudly as the warband that had protected them for two decades, they nonetheless did cheer. Except the man I thought my father, who stood slightly apart from us and muttered in his beard.

"*Ave* my arse," said King Lot. "He's come from nowhere and taken everything. Bloody peasant soldier bastard."

"I'd not say that too loudly if I were you, husband," said Mother. "I doubt many of those present would care to hear it." She gestured at Arthur's soldiers, hard-eyed battle-worn men who looked at their chief with an expression close to awe. Lot snarled something inaudible and kept his peace.

I'd say disappointment soured him, but Lot was always sour. His face was a pale, indignant mask in the fire-thrown shadows of the hall, his pursed mouth, long ascetic nose, and perpetually startled eyes all giving him his usual look of sanctimonious hauteur mingled with righteous indignation, like a prelate who's just been buggered by a Jute. This coronation had been inevitable for many weeks now, and he should have had time to come to terms with his disappointment, but Lot rarely came to terms with anything.

It had all been set in motion over a year before, when Uther sat up on his deathbed and declared a young squadron commander named Arthur both son and heir. Ordinarily, such a proclamation would have gotten nowhere without the support of the more powerful local kingdoms. However, the Warband of Britain, the mobile cavalry force established by Uther's brother Ambrosius, did not wait on any petty king's approval before declaring Arthur the *de facto* High King, calling him the heroic Defender of the Britons so long rhapsodized in Bardic prophecy. Some challenged the claim, but the Battle of Celidon, where Arthur's troops smashed the forces of Hueill and the other Northern Brits and united the rebellious frontier tribes with the South, put an end to any real dissension. Lot once considered siding with Hueill, which would have made things very difficult for Gawain, who was even then serving Arthur as a Master of Horse, but the King of Orkney had ultimately known better than to join a lost cause, and our islands remained neutral in the conflict between the mainland North and South. Arthur would most likely have been crowned that year, but the Saxons hadn't proved so obliging, and only the desperate action waged by the British forces at Agned had kept them from making further incursions toward the West. (Lot's warband sat out that campaign, too, which accounted for the cool reception our party got from Cador of Cornwall and the other southern kings, although Arthur's indulgence and Gawain's heroic reputation prevented any active discourtesy.) Now, after a season of uneasy peace, things had settled down enough for the lords of Britain to gather and officially submit to the man whose forces and tactics had kept them from becoming Saxon thralls.

Pardon the digression, for I know that if this is to be my story, it can't also be the whole bloody History of Britain. Yet some overview is required, along with more than a little hindsight; I can't just capture things the way the boy I was then saw them. Telling this tale is going to be enough of a pain in the arse as it is, without trying to bring *him* back. At eight, he was still incredibly empty in his innocence. Ultimately, I must see his story through my present-day eyes and tell it in my adult voice.

That point made clear, let me return to the coronation.

Arthur still wore his scuffed campaign harness, but he looked magnificent as he held the short, broad old Roman sword high above his head, the jewels in its hilt glinting in the torchlight. "One Britain," he said, seemingly softly, but his voice carrying above the crowd. "One Britain under One God and One Law. I take up this sword for us, for all of us, for all of the kingdoms of the Island of the Mighty, all the kingdoms that are one kingdom now. In your names I hold it, my lords, and in your children's names, the children who are our future and our hope." He looked at me then, or I thought he did, his eyes blazing like the jewels in his sword. He kept speaking, but I don't remember what he said, just what I felt swelling inside me.

His men felt something, too, for they shouted as one, drowning out whatever else he'd meant to say, and then they surged forward. Forgetting all ceremony, they bore him on their shoulders, him laughing as much as I had earlier, his pomp and fine words forgotten, and carried him out into the courtyard, where a huge bonfire was burning.

I was almost caught in the rush for the doorway, but

then Mother grabbed me and hugged me into the shelter of a column, while men in iron and leather surged around us like the sea. Then they were all outside, even the assembled Kings of Britain, and dancing around the fire. Other than our own men-at-arms, Mother, Lot, and I were alone in the hall.

Picking up a flagon of ale that had been left behind on a table, Lot came forward and took Mother by the arm. "We're not part of this, and will need to rise early. We're going to bed." He snapped his fingers for our soldiers, who still seemed nonplussed by what they'd seen, as if they couldn't imagine hoisting *their* king that way, and they were slow in coming to attention. "Dammit, Beortric," snapped Lot. "Don't tell me he's bewitched you fools as well!" He cocked a thumb at one stupefied-looking warrior. "Get your arse down to the dock and tell Nadog my bloody ship better be ready to sail at first light."

Before anyone could respond, a broad figure appeared in the open doorway, silhouetted by the bonfire. "Father, Mother, come outside!" Gawain reeled closer, his brown hair tousled and spilled wine gleaming like blood upon his harness.

"To hell with that," said Lot. "My ship leaves with the dawn tide."

Gawain swayed, and leaned on a table for support. "Leaves! You mean you're not staying?"

"For what?" snapped Lot. "I've had my fill of this."

"But there's more ceremony tomorrow. The High King will be anointed in chapel by Bishop Gerontius. After that, there's new postings. Arthur's making it official. I'm to be commander of a hundred horse."

"A hundred horse!" I said in astonished wonder. "Oh, Gawain, can it be true?" I imagined him riding before a forest of mounted spearpoints, hoofbeats drumming like thunder, the red dragon unfurled as a wedge of horse and iron swept down on the hapless foe, a vision with all the pomp of Rome and the heroic splendor of ancient Albion. I started toward him, but Lot took me by the shoulder and shoved me back into Mother's arms.

"I don't care if you're made commander of a hundred whores. It's equal shame."

Gawain's confusion looked so out of place on his usually confident face. "Shame! What shame? You yourself sent me to serve here. Arthur thinks I've done so with great honor . . ."

Lot nearly choked in his fury. "I don't give a fart what Arthur thinks. I sent you here to serve Uther, to speak well of me, and be my eyes and ears in Britain. But no, you stupid git, you were always off somewhere, fighting one of Arthur's battles, and now Uther and Ambrosius are dead, and Arthur sits upon the throne. There's nothing for me here, or for any son of mine that truly loved me. You'll come back with us, if you're worth your salt."

No one bullied Gawain, not even his own king and father. Though his eyes were downcast, he stood straight and tall in the flickering light. "I gave the Pendragon my oath," he said in a low, even voice. "I won't break it."

"To hell with you then!" Lot clapped his hands, and his men surged forward, escorting us outside. Mother didn't say anything, but paused to hug Gawain, then followed her husband, pulling me gently with her. Looking back at my brother, standing there like a dejected bear, I remembered my earlier joy, and wondered, in my childish way, where it had gone. *No,* I wanted to scream, *we can't go! Don't take me away from Arthur!* But I kept silent, as I knew Mother would want me to, though my eyes stung with more than just the smoky courtyard air.

That, I think, was the first time I knew I hated Lot.

Skirting the revelers in the courtyard, we made our way to the outbuilding where we housed. Here and now, as I sit writing this memoir in a high room with a fine window that looks out on the sighing Usk, I find it hard to remember the days when there were relatively few multistory edifices in Britain. Uther's "palace" actually consisted of many squat, thatched or slate-roofed buildings linked by enclosed walkways and courtyards, a stone-and-timber labyrinth that sprawled over several acres, incorporating the remains of a villa and an ancient hill fort. We were lodged near the northwestern corner of the palisade, in a low timber-and-plaster structure with two rooms, a small inner one floored in cracked flagstones and a larger outer one floored in earth and straw, which is where our soldiers and attendants bunked.

That night, I lay wrapped in a blanket on the stones of the inner chamber, while Mother and King Lot rustled in the straw of their crude bed and murmured to each other, sometimes angrily, until the talk gave way to Mother's shallow breathing and Lot's loud, gurgling snores. Trying to sleep despite those sounds, I found my thoughts returning constantly to Arthur. Not even the troubling discord between Lot and Gawain could blot out the wonder of my new-met uncle. Shutting my eyes, I could still see his face. Maybe that's how Christians see Jesus, when they close their eyes to pray—not the scrawny carcass on the cross, but a man proud and alive, with something good burning bright inside of him. When I think back to the boy I was, I can almost understand such worship.

Three

SLEEP NEVER came. I lay in my scratchy blanket, wide-awake, my mind racing. If we were truly sailing in the morning, then I'd not be seeing Arthur again, at least for a long time, and that prospect was suddenly unbearable, like seeing sunlight after living in a cave, only to be told you can't look at it anymore. If Gawain could stay on his service, why couldn't I? The fact that Gawain was an adult and I was not did not seem a fair objection. Surely, if Arthur were to request that I remain behind, Lot could not gainsay it. I wasn't sure he'd want to. Even then, he was not the most affectionate of fathers.

No, I told myself, *I must find Arthur.*

Sitting up in the chilly dark, I tugged on my boots, then groped my way to the door. Finding the bolt, I pulled it slowly, slowly back, trying to be as silent as possible. Despite my efforts, there was a metallic creak, and behind me I heard Lot stir and grunt, but he did not wake up. Neither, apparently, did Mother. Holding my breath, I eased the door gently open and slipped out.

There was no door to the outside, just an opening in the wall. Our warriors were huddled together in their cloaks for warmth. None stirred as I picked my way between them, even at that age as light-footed as a cat. Outside, I saw shadows folded upon shadows, dark walls, the glow of a distant fire, the bright points of torches on the outer earthworks, and above all, the fainter torchlights of the stars. I skulked across the courtyard, scaled a low wall, and slipped through a large hole in another one, where rotted timbers poked out through patches of ruined plaster and broken dry stone. Uther had restored the outer defenses well enough, but much of the inner complex remained in disrepair, leaving plenty of gaps through which a boy my size could slip.

Eventually, I found myself in another courtyard, one enclosed on three sides by the central hall. It was darker there, and even my sharp young eyes could spy no egress in the gloom. I walked to the nearest wall and touched it, but felt nothing but cold, rough, crudely dressed limestone. Arthur's chamber was somewhere inside, but I had no idea how to reach it.

"What do we have here?" said a soft, high voice very near my left ear.

I jumped back with a wordless cry and spun around, to find myself facing a dim figure scarcely taller than myself, muffled and shapeless in a hooded cloak. "Who's there?"

"I might ask the same thing of you," answered the fluting, insinuating voice, that of a child with a naughty secret.

"Mordred Mac Lot, Prince of Orkney!" I said, trying to sound older than I was. My heart was pounding, but I quieted it by telling myself that Gawain would not have been afraid.

"Ah, the younger son of King Lot and the beautiful Morgawse. Brother to the much-vaunted Gawain." The accent was very strange, almost affected-sounding. "I thought it might be you. Come inside with me, boy, for I should like a better look at you. I deserve as much, considering that I helped bring your mother and father together, just as I helped your grandfather and grandmother before them." A hand no larger than mine closed over my own, and I found myself being pulled forward.

"Wait, I'm looking for the King!"

The voice laughed, a high, childish giggle. "Which

king is that? We've plenty here. Tonight the palace is well stocked in kings."

"*Artorious Imperator,* King of all the Britons," I said, impatient that someone wouldn't know who *the* king was.

"Ah, Arthur. Yes. The new Pendragon. It's funny, he doesn't much care for his sister, does Arthur, but he dotes on her son Gawain as though he were his own. Does he dote on you, as well? That would certainly be fitting. Should I take you to him, little Mordred?"

"Yes, please."

"Well, follow me then. Keep hold of my hand, and soon we'll be there."

I was silent after that, as I was led to the opposite corner of the courtyard, where now I could see a short flight of stairs leading down into the darkness.

"Where are we going?" I motioned over my shoulder. "Arthur's back there, somewhere."

The covered head turned back toward me, though I could see no face beneath the shadowed hood. "We go to my quarters, first. Like a badger, I lair underground. Come into my hole, little Mordred."

I followed him gingerly down into the darkness, where I could hear our breathing, and the echoes of our feet on stone. "But how will going down here get me to Arthur's chamber?"

A soft chuckle. "Silly boy, there are more tunnels beyond my lodgings, connecting almost every building on the grounds."

The stairs leveled out into a narrow corridor. I could see nothing, but when I stretched out my free hand, I felt rough, damp walls. There was nothing for it but to be led through the confining darkness, with no sound but our breathing.

Finally, there was a glimmer of light ahead, reflecting off the wet tunnel. Those walls became higher and farther apart and more regular as we approached the source of light, the stones drier and better fitted. Suddenly rounding a corner, we stepped through an open wooden doorway and into a large, well-lit room. It came as quite a shock. Remember, royal though I was, I'd been born in the decidedly rude splendors of Lot's Orkney palace. During the day we'd been in Britain, we'd been treated to precious little luxury. For me, the contents of this new chamber were as strange and wonderful as the interior of a fairy hill.

Fat red and yellow candles were everywhere, in little brass holders that hung on hooks from the plaster walls, on row after row of scroll-covered shelves, on two low tables, one of variegated marble and other of some dark, ornately carved wood, and on several large, iron-bound trunks. There was a luxurious Roman-style couch with stuffed scarlet cushions and a gilded armrest, as well as a more homespun but equally comfortable-looking wicker chair. The furnishings were impressive enough to someone accustomed to more spartan accoutrements, but the decorations were even more dazzling. The entire floor was an intricate tile mosaic depicting a naked woman borne on the back of a rampant bull, partially obscured by several sheepskin rugs and the pelt of what must have been a truly enormous bear. Two of the walls were also decorated. On the left-hand one was painted a naked youth, bent over in front of a bigger, bearded man with a large erect penis, while on the opposite one, a blood red dragon emerged writhing from between a supine woman's splayed legs. Having seen precious little art of any kind, let alone the pornographic variety, I would have been intrigued if the figure in front of me hadn't been so extraordinary as to command my full attention.

Stepping out of his heavy, hooded robe, which I now saw was dyed scarlet and lined with otter fur, he tossed it on the wicker chair and turned to face me. At first I thought he was a boy, only a few inches taller and no more than a couple of years older than myself, with very ruddy skin and fair hair, a boy wearing nothing but a green tunic that left his slender pink arms and legs bare. But no, the short, soft-looking hair that covered his head like downy fuzz was not blond but white as snow, and there was a delicate tracery of wrinkles around his small, mischievous mouth and large wet eyes, eyes that on closer inspection appeared yellow and rheumy and flecked with spots of red. He wasn't a dwarf, for I've seen dwarves since then, in the courts of the Summer Country. He was not stubby or foreshortened, but slim and graceful and delicately boned, with small hands and narrow hips, and a high-domed, narrow-jawed head.

"Hello, Mordred," he said in that strange accent, which I did not then recognize as being that of someone who spoke pure continental Latin. "Will you give Merlin a kiss?"

"I want to see Arthur!"

"Of course you do. I can take you to him. I was his father's wizard."

As I've already demonstrated, at this time in my life I'd not heard of Merlin, the prophetic boy who became Uther's pet seer after foretelling the downfall of his predecessor, the traitorous Vortigern. But I did immediately know that he was someone whom it was unsafe to be around.

"You said you'd take me to Arthur."

He bowed, a movement as graceful as a dancer's. "And so I shall. But I thought you might want to rest first, here in my chamber. Would you like some wine?" He motioned toward the marble table, where dark red liquid filled a wide-mouthed enamel bowl.

I shook my head. "Mother doesn't let me have any."

He clucked disapprovingly and then giggled. "Well that's Northern provincialism for you, isn't it. Here in the South, we let babes drink wine as soon as they're weaned. Try the wine. I'll even give you some bread baked with honey, for dipping in it."

At any other time, such a treat would have been very tempting, but I shook my head again, more adamantly this time. "I don't want any. I just want to see Arthur."

He walked toward me and reached out with one slim pink hand. "Ach, everybody so loves the shining Arthur. I'd love him, too, if he'd let me. But he won't, and I fear I'll not be long remaining here. I'll miss my comfortable lair, though not the miasma of piety that's hung over the palace since Arthur came back from the North."

His fingers tingled like icicles when they touched my face. "Please, I must see Arthur," I said again.

"And maybe I'll bring you to him once I'm done with you," he said softly as he stroked my cheek. "Maybe I'll even tell him who you are. That would serve our Christian Highness right, wouldn't it, to know the truth? He'd likely be too shocked to even punish me for having had my fun with you."

I had no idea of what he was talking about, but I recognized danger. I backed away, but he'd somehow gotten between me and the door, and further retreat was blocked by the painted wall. Merlin giggled as I sidled along the plaster, only to find myself trapped in the corner of the room.

"Now, now, pet, don't be frightened of old Merlin. You're such a pretty boy. All I want to do is kiss you. At least, that's how I want to start."

At that moment, Mother stalked through the open doorway behind him. "Get away from my son," she said in a low, dangerous voice.

Merlin turned and gave her a courteous bow. "Good evening, Morgawse," he piped. "The past nine years have been kind to you. You're to be congratulated on having borne such a lovely child."

She was clad only in her linen shift and her long, unbound hair, but none the less regal for all of that. "Don't play with me, Merlin," she snapped in the ominous tone of voice that I'd seen make Lot quail. "Or with him. I know what you wanted to do. Your years may lie lightly upon you now, but I can change you into the wizened ancient you really are."

Merlin smiled boyishly and balanced on one foot, while scrabbling idly at the tiled floor with a dirty pink toe. "Oh, Mistress, I doubt that, I truly do. All right, so you've managed to spoil my fun. Now be wise and leave it at that. Take the brat with you and go, before I set a dragon to hatching from your cunt, as in this lovely fresco here."

I darted around him and ran to Mother. She held me to her, gripping my shoulder so tightly I nearly cried out

in pain, and said five or six low guttural words. My scalp
tingled, and I felt the hair on my arms and the back of
my neck stirring. Looking up, I saw Mother's tresses rise
in a tangled halo about her head, making her look like a
beautiful Medusa. Our shadows danced on the obscene
wall as the candles guttered in an impossible wind, and
many of them went out. However, it did not get darker,
but brighter. Above me, Mother's upraised right hand
was burning like a torch, with a silent blue flame that did
not harm her flesh. Her fingers clenched and unclenched,
as she gathered power that I knew she would momentar-
ily be throwing in Merlin's face.

But he only laughed and waved languidly, and the
wind stopped, the extinguished candles springing to life
again. Mother's hand burned less brightly, but did not go
out. Clucking softly, Merlin padded forward, his eyes
locked on hers the way folk credulously think a snake
fixes its gaze upon a bird. When he was close enough, he
reached out and took her hand. She hissed, and I felt the
tension surge through her body, but she did not move as
he pulled that burning hand down toward his face. It was
impossible that she, who'd never been this docile with
her own husband, would allow this creature such familiarity, but she made no apparent resistance. When he
stuck her index finger in his small red mouth, the blue
flames went out. Mother's hair fell back limply about her
head, and she stood there, breathing deeply, suddenly
drenched in sweat and looking pale and drained.

He released her limp hand and bowed again, his pink,
infantile face still a mask of courtesy. "Ah, dear Morgawse, you needed my help almost nine years ago with a
simple spell of seduction. Do you really think you can
threaten me now? I could explore your son's sweet body
in front of you, and you couldn't stop me."

"I'd die trying," she said, the words whistling through
her teeth like the winter wind through a cracked wall.

He stepped back, his arms outspread. "No, you
wouldn't. But we won't put it to the test. Have you ever
wondered why I helped you?"

"Let Mordred leave," she said. "We can discuss this once he's gone."

He sat in the wicker chair, one slim leg over the other. "No need. You'll both be going in a moment, and quite unharmed. But you've not answered my question."

I wanted her to smite him with her power. I wanted Arthur to appear out of the darkness, the sword of Maximus gleaming in the candlelight as he swung it to cut off Merlin's head. I wanted Gawain. Hell, I even wanted Lot. Anything to end this excruciating standoff. I'd never seen Mother's power checked so easily before, and had never feared anything other than Lot's temper, and that only when Mother was not around. Maybe there was value in Arthur's carpenter god, if he really didn't allow things like this to happen. I wished I knew how to pray to him, but all I could do was press my face into Mother's left arm, and clutch the hand with which she still gripped my shoulder.

"All right, I'll play your game," she said finally, in the easy tone that she used when humoring Lot. "I'll even admit I've wondered. Why did you help me?"

Merlin drew his legs up in front of him and rested his chin on his knees, looking more like a mischievous boy than ever. "In a week Arthur will banish me. I helped Uther build everything that Arthur has inherited, and loved him enough to help him wet his dick in his vassal's wife. Like all fools for love, I got what I deserved, when he decided he liked her cunt better than my arse. Now, because the illicit fruit of that union does not wish to be served by his father's catamite, I'm going to lose everything. And do you know what? There's nothing I can do about it. It is still Arthur's time to be borne upward on Fortuna's wheel, and there is a power in that upstart god he swears by that really does protect him. Because of this, I'll trudge back to the Caledonian forest where my faerie father sired me, and where the Myrddin-spirit tried to overwhelm me when I was very small, only to find me mastering it instead." He shifted his legs and I could no longer see his small and hairless manhood, which was a blessing. "One thing I wrested from the Myrddin was my gift of prophecy. I knew this would happen when I met you, and I knew what consequences our little subterfuge would have for the man who would one day exile me. Nine years ago I began my revenge for what will happen to me next week. Now that you know that, you may go. Mordred there won't understand a thing of what we've been talking about. Don't fool yourself into thinking that explaining it will make any difference."

"I'm going to kill you for this," said Mother, her voice still calm and soft.

"No, you won't," said Merlin. "There is much I do not understand about the woman who will someday kill me, including just who she is, but I know that she's not you. So take the boy back to bed. Unless you want me to take you both to Arthur. Mordred was seeking Arthur when I found him."

Mother looked down at me, and for an instant I saw a glimmer of what might have been fear cross her face. "Mordred, why were you doing that?"

I stared down at the polished tiles and did not answer her.

"There are certain facts about Mordred that might interest Arthur," continued Merlin, "facts that might interest your husband, too. Perhaps I should have King Lot awakened, and we could all discuss this together. Would you like me to tell your husband and your brother who your son really is?"

Mother said nothing. *Let's go,* I said inside my head. *Please, Mother, let's go now.*

"But I'm too tired for that," sighed Merlin. "Nor would it change anything, even if I wanted things to change. So be off with you, before I start feeling nasty."

Pulling me behind her, Mother backed toward the door, then hustled me out into the dark corridor. She did not say anything to me, as she led me along, as apparently at home in the darkness as Merlin had been. My heart was still pounding, but things Merlin had talked about had been so far beyond me that they meant almost nothing, and the main thing I felt was disappointment, for now there was no chance I'd be seeing Arthur before we left. Of course, I don't suppose I really understood what had almost happened to me, there in Merlin's chamber, but I was greatly shaken by seeing Mother faced down. Certainly, I'd never known her to retreat from anything before.

A courtyard away from our lodgings, I hung back and made her stop. "I just wanted to see Arthur again," I said. "Before we leave. Please, Mother, can't I see him?"

She hugged me to her flat stomach, her breasts a comforting shelf above my head. "No, love, I'm afraid not. Even kings need their sleep."

"But it's not fair, for us to be leaving so soon."

She knelt down and kissed me, but when she spoke her voice was steely. "Don't start talk of things not being fair, Mordred. I hear enough of that from Lot. Things are as they are, and you must accept it. My husband is enough of a burden. Don't make me ashamed of you, as well."

I dabbed at my eye with a forefinger. "I'm sorry."

She lifted me in the air, for she was very strong, and held me tight. "That's all right. You've not had a good night, have you? If I'd not followed you, that little monster would have . . ." Her voice trailed off.

"Would have what?" I asked through a mouthful of her hair.

"Never mind. We need to go to bed."

The men-at-arms did not stir as we crept back to our chamber; it was a good thing we weren't assassins. Of course, for all I knew, Mother was seeing to it that they did not awake. Instead of climbing back into bed with Lot, she curled up with me on the floor, with her arms around me and my head upon her breast. Comforted by that pillow, I slipped my hand up her sleeve, and fell asleep feeling the smooth softness of her bare skin underneath my fingertips.

Four

UE ROSE and dressed before dawn, and trudged through drizzly fog to the docks, where a ship waited to take us back to Orkney. I stood wrapped in oily sealskin in the creaking darkness, while Lot's men stowed our gear aboard. I was too dazed and inside myself to ask Mother why she did not improve the weather. Nobody else broke the silence, either.

Until, finally, I did. "Where's Gawain?" Oh, I knew he wasn't coming with us, but I thought he'd be seeing us off.

Mother was a cloaked shape looming at my right, a warm hand squeezing mine. "He's staying with Arthur, love. He's Arthur's man, now."

"I wish I could be Arthur's man, too."

The blow came out of the darkness to my left, spinning me around and knocking me onto the wet, salty-smelling planks, where a splinter was driven into my cheek. Then I was grasped by the sealskin where it bunched at my throat and hauled up, to stare into the dim oval that was Lot's ale-stinking face.

"Then stay here, you whelp, and be damned to you!"

He cast me away from him and I reeled, feeling empty space and water behind me, before I regained my balance. Then a gust of wind swept over me, and I heard Lot make a sound like he'd been struck, and a shrill, keening cry that was Mother, chanting in some old

Breton tongue. Blue fire crackled in the dank mist, and I smelled something like rotting eggs.

"No!" cried Lot, "I didn't mean . . ."

But I was already running away, recklessly down the dim pier, leaving him to face Mother's rage. In the predawn glimmer, I could see the pale expanse of beach, dotted with black lumps of rock. I leapt from the pilings and ran along the shingle and wet sand, finally stumbling to catch my breath in the deeper darkness of the cliff.

The rain had stopped, and light was seeping into the sky. I huddled against a weedy outcrop, my face buried in my knees, sobbing deep, racking sobs. Here was something I wanted to be part of, and I was being taken away, just as soon as I'd found it. As disturbing as Merlin had been, I still wanted desperately to be with Gawain and Arthur, but had no idea how to find my way back to the great hall, which was at least half a mile away. So I just crouched there and continued to cry, hoping, if I was formulating any thoughts at all, that Lot's ship would leave without me.

Then Mother was holding me, though I'd not been aware of her approach. "It's all right, Mordred, it's all right. I've dealt with him. He'll not be doing that again." Beneath the soothing, there was steel in her voice, like a dirk hidden in a fine linen sleeve.

"I don't want to go back. I want to stay," I said at last.

"I know. Me too."

That took me aback, somehow. Even so young, I didn't know what there could be for her here. What was Arthur to her?

"Please, can't I stay?" I said finally.

"No. Merlin is here. Harm might come to you."

"Arthur would protect me!" Oh yes, I was very sure of that.

"No, Mordred. Your place is in your father's kingdom."

At that, I started to cry again. "I wish he weren't my father."

She didn't speak for a long time, but just sat there, on

the damp rock, me in her lap now, holding me, while
dawn broke over the cliffs. No one came looking for us.
Finally, she nuzzled my cheek and whispered in my ear.

"Mordred, I'm going to tell you a secret."

"Yes?"

"You must swear, though, not to tell anyone. Or to ask
me more than I tell you. Not till you're a man."

"I swear, Mother. By Lugh and Jesus." An oath I'd
picked up from Gawain, who'd adopted some slight
trappings of Christianity.

She seemed to flinch at the Carpenter's name, but
accepted the oath. "Mordred, Lot is not your father."

"Who . . . ?"

Her hand was at my mouth. "Shhh. You swore. Now
sit here a while, and cry if you must, and then be done
with it."

That's what we did. At least, I think she was crying,
too, as she held me and rocked me. At length, she dried
my eyes with her cloak and we trudged back to the ship,
neither of us speaking. Lot was huddled on the deck in
his sealskin, also not speaking, nor meeting his wife's
eyes, or mine. He was very pale, except where several
livid boils had sprouted on his face and hands, and bent
over, as though he were in pain. Probably he was.

Of course, I couldn't understand then, how it must
have irked him. It wasn't just losing the throne, either; I
can't be so uncharitable as that. It must have eaten at
him that Gawain was staying behind. It would prove to
be another eternal thorn in Lot's side, the fact that his
firstborn son had sided with his brother-in-law, had
never once suggested that Lot might have a better claim
to the throne. From the first, the Heir of Orkney had
forsaken his birthright to be the right-hand man of the
Dragon of Britain.

I love you, Gawain, and I hated him, but one could say
you did him wrong.

Who could blame you? Our kingdom wasn't much to
come home to. Lot's grandfather had been one of the
first Scots to leave Ireland and carve out a realm for

himself among the Brits and Picts. But he'd never gotten a real foothold on the mainland, and had been forced back to these harsh islands, all peaty windswept hillsides rolling down to the cold and churning sea. His grandson had until recently dreamed of better things.

Now, so long after, I can almost pity Lot Mac Conag, King of the Orkneys and thwarted would-be king of more than that, the father of my brother and lord of the house where I was born. I pity him even though it was me who killed him, with Mother's help after she was dead. As I've already said, it feels strange to me to consider these memories now, after so many years. It's been so long since I last thought about the crafty old turd.

His craft never paid off, nor did his marriage prove to be as lucky as he'd hoped. He'd wanted much more than the bare kingdom he'd been born with, and had come so close, but Fortuna proved as fickle as they say she is. Think what it must have been like, to have a common soldier turn out to be your wife's long-lost brother. When Arthur turned up to catch the falling crown, all of Lot's royal ambitions proved worth less than a crofter's fart.

That draught would have been bitter enough, but the very man who'd so thwarted Lot also turned out to be the incestuous father of Orkney's younger son. My da, I mean. Our family history does tend to sound like something out of a complicated bawdy joke, doesn't it?

And Gawain thought our wars were done.

Son of the Morning

To love our parents
is the first law of nature.

Valerius Maximus

Five

I'LL SPEAK now of Orkney, and then of the two people who intentionally helped make me what I am, my mother and Gawain. Arthur shaped me, too, but only through negation, by refusing to let me be what I so desperately wanted to become. I'll write of that later. I suppose I could also consider Lot a teacher, and if he was my real father, I would say he taught me patricide. But I'm getting ahead of myself again.

First, my homeland, such as it was. Imagine a landscape forever defined by the ocean and the sky, of earth and stone bounded by water and wet air. Imagine low hills blanketed with peat, bracken, and scrub grass, rolling down to pebble beaches or falling away into sheer cliffs, where the surf has cut stacks of black rock from the jagged shoreline, and over all of it the cold, colorless cloud-and-bird-filled vault of heaven. Imagine that sky, now like iron, all gray and hard and pressing down with unthinkable weight; now closer still, and black and roiled with heavy storm; now, though a rarer now, deep and blue and so far away you fear one slip could loosen your grip on earth and cause you to fall forever upward. Imagine the sea, and all her myriad faces—foam and wave and swell, blue-green and blue-gray, shading to black at storm time, or touched with blood at sunset. Imagine the wind that knifes in off her, and stings your cheeks, and makes your clothing smell of salt. Imagine waves booming on rocks, the cries of shags and shearwaters, wind in the bracken and rain drumming on the eaves. Imagine a land of broken cliffs and peaty hills, where the air is as full of turbulent motion as the sea. This, the largest of our islands, a narrow strip of ragged sea-bound moor which Orkneymen perversely call Mainland, was my bare playground and stark school-yard, the rocky, salt-soiled garden where my spirit first took root.

Scaling the wet crags in search of plovers' eggs taught me agility and endurance and strength of limb, and gave me what I can only call a sense of perspective, an appre-ciation of the delicate equilibrium necessary when one hangs between twin voids. Navigating the waves below those cliffs in my bobbing coracle taught me about the hidden currents that exist beneath the calmest swell, and of the dangerous whirlpools and eddies that could lurk unseen around every twist and turn of the broken shore. Looking out on a low, treeless, sea-and-sky-rimmed horizon taught me to look past that horizon, past the encircling confines of my senses, with that mind's eye that looks inward or outward or both at once, but always sees beyond the Here.

Mother encouraged such vision, showing me what lay beyond the commonplace, introducing me to magic and the powers of the Otherworld, as well as that scarcely less fantastic other world we call the past. I remember being very small, and sitting with her before the fire, both of us half-sprawled on the warm flagstones, her gown hiked up and her strong brown legs stretched protectively around me, while she ran her long fingers through my hair and murmured gently of the glorious old days before the Romans left, and the even older days, before they ever came. As she spoke, the hand that wasn't stroking my head made a languid motion in the air, creating visions in the burning peat, so that the sparks became the gleam of sunlight on bronze, the flames unfurled into red banners, and suddenly antlike legions were tramping across black hills, leaving straight roads and walled towns in their wake. Like so many women, Morgawse of Orkney was full of contradictions, and I've never understood how the classical Roman strain in her could be so intertwined with her wild, dark mysticism. Whatever the paradox, one thing is clear: she should have been either a Roman matron or a Druid queen, not the wife of a petty island warlord with thwarted designs upon her father's throne. But then, how many of us are lucky enough to live the lives to which we seem best fitted?

Born of an Armorican princess and unwanted by Uther (for he cast aside offspring like old shoes), Morgawse had been raised in the proper Latin household of her uncle, Ambrosius Aurelianus. The two strains, Roman and Breton, did not mix well in her. Believe me, I should know; I suffered the discomfort of her attempts to raise me in both the heritage of Greece and Rome and the old ways of earth and fire and blood. She did her best to teach me how to command wave and storm, to speak the language of the animals, to read the future in the cooling guts of a sheep or a servant, that sort of thing. Some of it took, but not much as she would have liked. Truthfully, I never had more than a dilettantish interest in her arts. By way of illustration, this anecdote should suffice.

Like many petty lords, Lot was fond of ostentatious displays of what small power he possessed, and one manifestation of this was the gibbet his guards had erected near the palace's landward gate. It was nothing more than a heavy timber laid across two standing stones, but in wood-starved Orkney even that was an extravagance. Of course, he could hardly string malefactors from the nearest tree like the mainland nobles did.

It was a lot of trouble to go to for a mere crofter caught stealing a lamb from the royal sheepfold, but there he hung, his hair and face the same ashen shade, his eyes open, his mouth a toothless hole. He wore a dirty wool tunic with no breeches, exposing pale skinny calves, knobby knees armored in purple scabs, and big blistered feet, swollen even larger with settled blood. Hiking up her robe, Mother dismounted from her big black horse as easily as a man, leaving me in the saddle. That was no matter; even at eleven, I was a better horseman than many in Lot's warband.

I thought she was going to scramble atop one of the menhirs and cut the body loose as she'd sometimes done in the past, but no, she simply crouched at its feet, stirring the black earth with one finger. Flies buzzed there, where his bowels had voided. Drawing a silver dagger, she poked through the mixture of loam and dung.

I looked around, feeling vaguely embarrassed by this. It wasn't seemly, that my mother should be mucking about in filth. Well, at least she hadn't asked me to do it for her. A quarter mile behind us loomed the stone and earth wall that encircled the royal palace, sentries on the rampart pointedly looking the other way. In the opposite direction, Mainland Orkney's one dirt road wound its way over low, peaty hills, past turf cottages and sheepfolds bounded by crude dikes of rough red sandstone. The sky was low and gray, shading to black near the horizon, and the wet salt wind was heavy with the promise of rain.

Mother was scooping damp black earth into a small leather pouch. "They spill their seed when they die," she explained. "Mandrake may grow here, if my husband hangs enough peasants."

"Is that what we came here for?" I asked, trying to hide my boredom. "Some twisty old root?"

She looked up, her hair a shining black veil over her face. "No, Mordred. But dead man's seed is useful for many things. Weren't you paying attention to my lesson yesterday?"

I bowed my head. "Sorry, Mother. I guess I was thinking of something else."

She stood up, wiping her hands on her wool gown. "And I can guess what that was. Arthur and his battles."

I didn't deny it. "When is Gawain coming to visit?"

She put dagger and pouch away and climbed easily back into the saddle. "The next time King Lot's taxes are due, I suppose. It will be too soon for Lot, I'm sure."

Taking the reins, she turned us back toward the palace. "When he comes, don't talk of this."

"Why not?"

"Because he might tell Arthur, and my brother would not approve. Christians don't like magic."

It wasn't the first time she'd said this, and I'd seen evidence of it three years before, but I still didn't understand it. "Their god came back from the dead. He turned water into fishes . . ."

"Into wine," she corrected.

"Water into wine, yes. That's magic, isn't it?"

She laughed, a full, throaty sound. All my life since, I've liked women who laughed that way, and have had no time for gigglers. "Yes, but they don't like it when other people do it."

It was very puzzling, I thought, but I knew she wasn't the right person to explain. Maybe Gawain could, or even Arthur, when he came. I knew Arthur would come here someday. He had to. I'd dreamed of it and hoped for it so long, it had to come to pass, for if Mother's arts had taught me anything, it was that, despite truisms to the contrary, wishing can indeed make it so.

Later, in her chamber, I watched as she opened the pouch of earth and poured it into out in a copper bowl. Then she sharpened her dagger on a whetstone and heated it over her brazier.

"I need blood, Mordred," she said, like a cook asking for butter. "Might I use a spot of yours?"

I sighed, wishing she'd be done, so I could run off and play. "Yes, Mother. Please don't cut too deep."

I needn't have worried. The sharp tip of the knife drew a line across the palm of my hand, but I didn't feel a thing. Then she pulled my bleeding hand to her lips, and sucked on it. As she did, and I felt her wet mouth on my skin, a tingle ran through me, a stirring of excitement. I didn't understand it, but it embarrassed me, and I looked away.

Her mouth left my hand, and I heard her spit into the bowl. When the mixture of her saliva and my blood hit the earth that had been dampened with a dead man's semen, it sizzled, and a small plume of gray vapor uncoiled above the bowl.

She gripped my hand tightly. "Repeat after me, love." There followed a string of very old words, ones I don't remember now. I said them with her, or slightly after her, my lips struggling with the ancient syllables.

"There," she said, "that wasn't hard, now was it?"

I looked in the bowl. There was a dirty white spot, no bigger than my thumb, sprouting from the wet dirt like a clump of lichen, or some oozing fungus. I heard a tiny, wet whistling sound, which seemed to emanate from the yeasty little globule, its pitch rising and falling with the blob's pulsations.

"Listen," she said. "He's trying to talk."

"What is it?" This was disgusting, but more interesting than I'd expected.

"His name is Gloam. He's a lesser earth spirit, what my brother would call a demon. He'll grow with time, and become quite useful."

"Really?" I couldn't imagine any possible good use for the slimy little thing.

"Yes. Simple oracular pronouncements, mostly. Revelations about the past and future. That sort of thing."

"Ah." Better than sheep guts, I supposed. "May I go play now, Mother?"

She nodded without looking up. "Yes, love, but be careful. It looks like it will soon be pouring, and I'm too tired to send the rain elsewhere. Healing is not my most practiced skill, and I don't want you to get a fever."

"Don't worry, I won't," I said as I headed toward the stairs. Behind me, the thing in the bowl whistled like a tiny kettle. I wondered what it would look like when it was bigger.

Although sometimes tedious, such morbid exercises were far preferable to what felt like years of poring over my Donatus, mastering the Trivium and Quadrivium, and memorizing the appropriate quotations from Cicero, Ovid, Juvenal, and all that lot. It's an irony, perhaps, that the remnants of one of the finest libraries in Roman Britain should have ended up here, in what to Rome was Ultima Thule. Apparently, no one else had wanted Ambrosius's books, after he died.

Guinevere calls me the best-educated man in Britain, aside from monks like Gildas, who have no use for any history and learning but that of their constipated church. If that's true, it's a measure of this benighted age, for I was dutiful enough in my studies, but less than inspired. I could quote from *De Oratore* well enough, and had slogged through most of *De Republica,* but found no joy in Cicero's windy sonorities, and Seneca and Lucretius generally put me to sleep. On the other hand, finding a tattered roll of Catullus tucked away on a high shelf one rainy afternoon when I was twelve proved a revelation. Here was a Roman who spoke to me as a living man, not stately phrases on a faded strip of vellum. I can still quote his little ode to Ipsitilla:

> *Ipsitilla, sweetest sweet;*
> *I cannot wait till next we meet.*
> *This afternoon, my darling whore,*
> *I'll plunge between your thighs once more.*
> *So let no client bar my way;*
> *Let me in without delay!*
> *And then, in thanks for all my rhymes,*
> *Fuck me six or seven times.*
> *Yes, seven, eight or even nine!*
> *I've eaten and I've drunk my wine;*
> *My cock is hard, so please be mine.*

Mother was less than pleased the first time I recited *that* out loud. Nor was she happy with what it awakened in me. Catullus got me to thinking about women. His easy talk of whorehouses (a civilized extravagance in which Orkney was sorely lacking), of Lesbia's burning kisses, of passion and regret and then more passion, stirred my heart and loins, and I descended upon the female slaves and serving girls like a one-man, or rather one-boy, Saxon raiding party. Mother did not approve, but said little, and did nothing, at least at first, other than scowl, or allow a slight quiver to linger upon her upper lip, each time she called me away from my pursuit of some fair-faced, soft-bottomed kitchen wench, and silently handed me a stylus and wax tablet.

Queen Morgawse was anything but a prude; I'd heard her swap bawdy jests with the palace guards, and in a rage, match Lot obscenity for blistering obscenity. She remained the hot-blooded Briton, for all her sometimes pitiful attempts at a Roman matron's stoic hauteur. Yet it clearly bothered her, seeing me take an interest in the flesh. Most mothers are like that, I suppose, at least to some degree, but it was worse in her. It would be a while before I realized why.

Lot remained a glowering presence on the periphery of my life, like sullen clouds on the horizon. We stayed out of each other's way, for the most part, but of course there were times when our paths had to cross. I remember one such occasion in particular.

I was thirteen or so, and was groping in the hay with Moira, an Irish kitchen girl with wide hips, big strawberry and cream breasts, and freckles everywhere. We lay spoon fashion on the straw of the royal stable, spent and sweaty, our feet beside each other's heads, with her shift and my cloak as a blanket. I turned on my side and ran my hand from her sturdy ankle to her upper calf, idly trying to catch a mite that scurried through the thick red hair of her leg. Trapping it under one finger, I crushed it against the relative hardness of her knee. An observer might have thought me comically small and dark, next to Moira's ruddy bigness.

"You're getting better," she said.

"Practice makes perfect," I replied, still feeling enough postcoital euphoria that I didn't mind having my performance judged by a kitchen girl. "It's good to practice something besides magic and Latin."

Moira snorted. "It's not right, her bringing you up like that. She scares me. I don't like her much."

I sat up. "Don't talk about her like that, Moira. Say

what you like about the King, when there's no one around who'll have you flogged for it, but Mother's not for you to judge, not ever. I'll whip you myself."

She looked pouty and rolled away. "I'm sorry, my lord. I forgot my place." There was bitterness in her tone.

I lay back beside her and stroked her tangled hair, feeling guilty. Well, she was my first girl, and I was young enough to be sentimental. "There, there, it's all right now. I didn't mean it." Though still turned away, she snuggled closer to me, and as her plump cushion of a rump pressed against my hips, my erection sprang to life.

Suddenly, she rolled away from me and pulled my cloak about herself, leaving itchy straw pressing into my flank. I looked up. A dozen feet away, Lot leaned against a stall and looked at us, his face impassive. My erection shrank under his fishy scrutiny.

"I wonder if his cock was that small," he said idly.

"Whose?" I found enough self-possession to ask.

"Your real father's. Whoever he was." With that, he turned and stalked away. I never found out how long he'd been watching us, or what he'd been doing in the stable. That was the first time he ever admitted to knowing I was not his son.

Lot gone, Moira sat up and brushed straw off herself. She stretched, then bent over, her breasts soft against me, and nuzzled my chest, but I did not respond, only stared up at the rough ceiling beams.

"He was just being mean," she said. "It's not small."

"Bigger than his, probably." I said, imagining Lot disemboweled, his eyes plucked out by ravens, drowned and fish-eaten, a thousand lovely deaths.

"Is he really not your father?"

I kneaded a nipple between thumb and forefinger, a bit hard, as I was angered by the question.

"Of course he is. Like you said, he was being mean."

She tried to draw back, but I didn't let go, fascinated by the way her breast stretched as it pulled away from my hand.

"Ouch! That hurts."

"Good," I said, releasing her nipple. "Who are you to ask me about my parentage?"

She hugged her knees to her chest, straw in her hair. "Sorry, my lord." The bitterness was back.

I sat up and stroked her knee, her hurt look making me feel tender again. "Ach, Moira, it's all right. Just treat me like the Prince, all right? The King doesn't, and that's bad enough." I bent to kiss her ankle, then moved my mouth upward on her leg, where the hairs shone golden in the shaft of light from the open barn door. Shaking hair out of her eyes, she parted her knees, and I crawled in between them.

At least I had that solace, the knowledge that he'd not sired me, and I owed him nothing. You may think me thick for not realizing who my real father was, what with all the hints Merlin had dropped, but after five years that night in Cornwall seemed less real than a dream, and sometimes the most obvious things are what we find hardest to see. Does it seem incredible that I was only mildly curious as to who my da might be? Credible or not, that's the truth of it. Mother would tell me soon, now that I was nearly a man, and that surety was good enough. I doubted he was anyone important, but knew he must have been a better choice than Lot.

Actually, I did try to bring the matter up that evening, as I sat on the floor of Mother's chamber, wrapped in my cloak against the cool air from the open window and practicing my Latin script by the light of a flickering lamp. "Lot said something nasty to me in the stable today," I said idly, as I scratched away on my wooden-backed wax tablet.

Mother sat on a three-legged stool, polishing a small piece of dark crystal. "Yes. He found you there with Moira."

I paused, stylus in hand, and didn't say anything. Was it embarrassment I was feeling?

"Did you come inside her?"

Oh, shit, I thought, *I really don't want to have this*

conversation. Something strange was happening inside my head these days. When Mother and I talked of private things, I found myself naked, without the invisible armor I wore against everyone else. Had she been watching me from her room, seeing our coupling reflected in a bit of polished stone or shining in a dancing candle flame? Hell, she probably knew the answer to her question.

"Mother, I don't think that's your concern."

A gust swept in the open window, guttering the candles. Mother stood up, seeming taller than her usual height.

"Yes, Mordred, it is very much my concern." For a moment her voice had the same steely edge she used on Lot, then it softened. "Please understand," she said, as she crouched down beside me, to run long fingers through my hair. "I will not forbid you to take such pleasure, although it does not please me very much. What I will not have is grandchildren sired on palace servants."

I didn't want to look at her, but she tilted my chin upward. I felt so much younger than earlier in the day, when thrusting my way into Moira made me sure I was now a man. "What would you have me do?"

A look of distaste flickered across her face, before smoothing itself out into concern. "Pull out before you come, that's all. Moisten the place between her thighs with your own spit, or with the white of an egg, and come there, or in her hand, or between her breasts. Even up her backside, if that's what you like, and she doesn't mind. But not if she does, even if she's just a kitchen drab, because that makes you no better than a beast. The important thing is to be careful not to remain inside her. Pull out, no matter how good it feels. Do you understand me?"

"Yes, Mother," I murmured, my face feeling as if it were on fire.

She continued on in her dry, pedantic tone, like a tutor lecturing a slow-witted pupil. "If it pleasures you to pleasure her, then learn to use your tongue. It's good to develop such skills, wasted as they may be on her sort. Someday, you'll have a lover more suited to your station. It's bad manners not to make her come, too. Don't end up like King Lot."

I struggled out from under her caress and headed for the door. "Yes," I said through clenched teeth. "Thank you for the advice."

"Heed it, Mordred," she said. "I'll know if you don't."

I fled down the stairs, aghast at the thought of her being able to watch me from afar, something that had never bothered me before, that had instead proved comforting. Christ and Mithras, but it would be a miracle if I ever managed to get it up again. Of course now I can't help but wonder if that wasn't what she'd intended all along.

There is another relationship I have not yet touched on, that between myself and Gawain, who was such a god to my younger eyes, and a good friend later. The only thing that bothered me about not being Lot's son was the fact that it made him only my *half* brother, and not a full sibling. There was no halfheartedness in my love for him.

Gawain was almost twice my age, and as wonderful as the sun. His visits were infrequent, but treasured, although not by Lot. Indeed, if Gawain had not needed to come here regularly on official business, I don't doubt that King Lot would have forbidden him to set foot in Orkney. It must have galled Lot that Arthur was always finding some pretext to send Gawain our way. Generally, it involved reconnaissance and other military exercises in the Pictish domains across the firth, for which Gawain had the authority to muster levies from Lot's warband. Of course, Arthur also sent his nephew to keep an eye on Lot himself, for Arthur surely knew that it was his northmost subjects who bore the most watching, as they were the least tied to the High King. And once a year, there were taxes to be collected. That must have been the ultimate humiliation for Lot, to have his own son be his liege lord's tax collector.

Not that I cared about any of that. If Mother had tried to show me the splendors of the past, Gawain proved that the present could be just as wonderful. Each time my impossibly grown-up brother visited our islands, I had him regale me with tales of the court Arthur was building at Caerleon, of old campaigns against the Saxon foe, of the grim but glorious days of battles. Disdaining a chair, he would squat bearlike before the fire, coppery hair falling across his face and hiding his mischievous eyes, and tell me fabulous tales of his and Arthur's exploits.

If the evenings were for tales and wild boasts, the days were for practical lessons. As I said, Mother was not my only teacher.

Six

"**G**O ON," said Gawain. "She won't bite you."

Actually, the mare looked as if she might. She was small and wiry, though sturdier than a normal highlands pony, with a shaggy coat almost the color of a wolf's pelt, and equally wolfish eyes that gleamed with feral cunning. Her saddle had four low horns, two in front and two behind. Gingerly gripping the stitched leather, I accepted my brother's offer of a hand up. The mare snorted and shifted her weight, but made no attempt to buck. Between my calves, her flanks quivered with restrained energy.

"Not a proper cavalry mount," said Gawain, referring to the big horses Arthur had imported from across the Channel. "But you're not ready for one of those yet. Don't sneer at this one, though; she's proved herself in battle."

"Really?" I stroked her coarse peppery mane, then sniffed the rank, wild odor that lingered on my fingers, so much stronger than any equine smell I that was used to. "Are the Picts riding horses, now?" I asked, jokingly. She seemed the type of steed a Pict would choose, if such a wild man ever went to battle mounted.

Gawain laughed. "Right idea, but wrong savages. I got her from a Gallic horse trader, who got her from some Franks who'd skirmished with Huns, and lived, and even taken some booty. Damned lucky, they must have been. Generally, it's the Huns who do the taking."

I looked down with wide eyes, and would have levitated out of the saddle, if I could. "Huns? This is a *barbarian* horse?" The mare seemed to sense my discomfort, and turned her head around, as if she was going to snap at my leg, but Gawain caught her bridle.

"Ach, see now, you've upset her," he said as he calmed her. "*Barbarian,* is it? That's Mum talking. In the eyes of Rome, boyo, we're barbarians, too. So's Mum, with her Druid ways. She likes to think herself a Roman lady, but all a real Roman lady would do is sneer at her, and maybe slip her a few coins to curse or poison some rich husband or unwanted lover."

The derisive way in which he liked to speak of our mother had long upset me. "Gawain, don't say that. Have respect for her that raised you." I must have sounded ridiculous, a green boy chastising a man who was already a hardened veteran.

If he thought as much, he did not say it, but then, he'd always treated me as an equal. Spitting on the dusty ground, he tried to make peace. "Let's not be starting this again. What, are you telling me you don't like your present? It's Arthur himself who wanted you to have her."

Now, I think maybe he stretched the truth a little when he said that, in order to prevent another argument about Morgawse, but I believed him then. "Arthur? Arthur wants me to have this horse?"

Gawain thumped me on the knee with one big, raw-knuckled hand, an affectionate tap that nonetheless smarted like hell through my cowhide riding breeches. "Take my head if he doesn't! 'Gawain,' he said to me, 'does your brother get to ride much, out there on his islands.' 'He can sit a horse well enough,' says I. 'That's not what I meant,' says Arthur. 'I want him to master a warhorse, so one day he can ride for me.' 'That's a fine thing,' I says, thinking of your safety, 'but these big horses we use, he'd kill himself for sure, trying to master one of them. He needs something smaller.' Just then, Arthur spots this wild beauty in the corral. 'Ach,' he

said, 'there's just what I mean. When next you go to
Orkney, take her to your brother.'"

I ran my hand through her oily mane and felt the
rocky muscles of her neck. This put the shaggy, rank-
smelling little mare in an entirely new light. "Lugh and
Jesus, if Arthur wanted me to ride a pig, I'd do it. Of
course I like her. She's a grand present."

Gawain laughed. "I thought you'd change your tune.
But there's more." Walking to the side of the barn, he
picked up the lance which rested there. "I had it made
especially for you," he said, hefting it easily. "It's lighter
than the ones we use, and a little shorter, but close
enough."

I took it from him, and nearly overbalanced. Over
nine feet long, it was of smooth ash, with an iron head
the length of my forearm. Resting the butt of the lance
on the ground and holding it vertical, I saw the head was
like a high, narrow pyramid, with a square base as big as
my palm, and a sharp point. The butt and lower part of
the haft were sheathed in lead, and wrapped in leather
strips. I tried hefting it overhand, like a spear, and again
found myself nearly tipping over, no matter how tightly I
gripped the mare's sides with my knees.

"Not like that, now," said Gawain, slipping it under
my arm. "Couch it like this. Let the weighted butt stick
out behind you, to give it balance."

It worked, and I could shift the point around without
becoming unseated. Taking the reins from Gawain, I
dared to urge the mare forward. She proved marvelously
responsive, not balking at the strange rider, or the lance
which swung so precariously above her head. "Jesus," I
said, "I could almost steer her with my knees."

"Aye, that's what the Huns do, right enough. It took
some doing to break her to the reins, and even so, she
turns quicker if you put your legs into it. Now get down
and look at this."

He helped me from the saddle. More at ease with my
new mount, I actually dared stroke her narrow, shaggy
head, and she whinnied in what might have been appre-
ciation. Gawain squatted, and throwing his dirty orange

cloak over his shoulder, began to sketch with one blunt finger in the dust of the courtyard. The result looked something like a child's drawing of a hanged felon.

"Make an upright post with a crossbeam," he said, "then take a cowhide, and cut out two pieces in the rough shape of a man, front and back. Stuff them with straw, weight the bottom part with sand, and sew them up with horsehair. Then hang the man-shape from the crossbeam like so. Can you do that?"

Of course I could. "Looks easy enough. But why?"

He stood up and gave me a gentle cuff that set my ears to ringing. "For practice, laddybuck. You think the Saxons and Picts are going to just line up and let you ride at 'em, until you're used to sending your lance point home? Practice sticking this target, at least an hour a day, every day. Once you've gotten somewhat good at it, strap an old shield to it, the way a man would hold the shield in front of his body. Practice getting the point over the shield, to stick it where a man's head or neck might be, or below that, in the groin or thigh. Practice putting your point in the center of the shield, so you'll know what it's like, when it sticks or when it glances off. It's no substitute for a killing a man, of course, but I don't think you're ready for that yet."

That smarted. "How the hell old were you when you first killed one?"

He cuffed my head again and laughed. "Not much older than you, maybe, but somewhat bigger."

"I may be small, but that doesn't mean I can't swing a sword! You want to try me?" On his last visit, Gawain had given me both a good regular sword and three practice ones. Two of the latter were of wood, with lead rods down the middle for weight. I used these to spar with the household guard, or anyone else I could press into service. The third was entirely of lead, and very heavy. Every morning I worked out with it, swinging it through the air to develop the muscles of my sword arm.

"Later, wolf cub, later," he said laughing, as he ambled back toward the bundle he'd left beside the barn. "I've something else to show you now." Squatting, he unwrapped the bundle and pulled out a short, recurved bow, made of lengths of some dark wood fitted together with strips of horn and dried sinew.

"Archery practice is dull as dung," he said. "Not like banging some obliging partner on the head with a wooden sword, or galloping around on horseback sticking a lance in things. What's more, there's plenty of fools out there who think it's unmanly, that a true warrior stands toe-to-toe with the enemy. That's bullshit, let me tell you. Some day you may find yourself crouching behind a row of stakes, you and your troop pinned down by more Saxons than you can count, and all of them closing on you and screaming like banshees. You'll be glad of your bow then, and count every arrow precious."

"I can shoot well enough," I said, thinking of the stiff yew bow in my room. "I've brought down heath hens on the wing."

"That's a good enough start," he agreed, "but you'll do better with this. When next I come here, I want you to give me a sack full of feathers, with each feather from a different bird, and all of them killed with this bow. Can you do that?"

"Oh, yes," I said through clenched teeth, as I tried to draw the bow.

He laughed. "Don't strain yourself. You'll get the knack of it in time."

"This isn't what I want for Mordred," said a voice from behind us. We turned, and there was Mother, in a green linen robe and red shawl. "He should be a scholar, not a soldier."

"Ach, Mum," said Gawain, "there's no reason why he can't be both. Arthur has need of enough learned men, especially ones who are neither unworldly prigs like Gildas or just plain unnatural, like that creature Merlin."

Distaste briefly registered on her smooth face. "I take it he still languishes in his Caledonian exile. I wish my brother had been astute enough to have him killed."

Gawain shrugged. "I wouldn't like to have been the one to try, from what little I saw of him. You knew him

better than me, apparently. At any rate, Arthur's not one
to kill somebody who served Grandfather for so long,
even considering what services he performed."

Mother's eyes bore a frosty glimmer of the icy visage
she reserved for Lot. "At any rate, my brother is well rid
of him."

Gawain shrugged. "No argument there, but I wish we
had another wizard in our service, despite all I share of
my uncle's faith. That's why Cerdic tried to sell us out
last year. He and a few other lords thought Merlin had
been the real power behind Uther's throne, and that
being king had made Arthur forget how to be a Warlord.
When it didn't work out that way, they tried aligning
themselves with the Saxons, and it took the Siege of
Badon to teach 'em all that the Dragon was just as fierce
as ever. If Merlin had still been in the South and on our
side, it might never have happened to begin with. Not
that I ever cared for that smirking, wrinkled boy."

Mother nodded, her face more serene now. "I can't
imagine Arthur accepting the help of any magician, even
though without one he would never have been born.
Maybe that's the reason why. Ah, but life is a complicated thing, and sometimes as ludicrous as a comedy by
Plautus."

"I wouldn't know about that," said Gawain. "Mordred here's the scholar. Anyway, there's things I need to
talk to Father about, in private, so he can't raise a fuss at
dinner. Is he in the hall?"

Mother shrugged. "My husband's whereabouts are of
scant concern to me, but you may find him there. I take
it you're dining with us, then."

Gawain nodded, making a face. "Yes, once again, I get
to share the magnificence of my father's table." We all
smiled at that, for Lot was never the best of hosts, even
when the guest was someone more welcome than Arthur's ambassador. After bowing to Mother, Gawain
squeezed me on the shoulder. "There's plenty of daylight
left. Maybe you'd like to take your new steed out for a
ride."

"That I will," I said, observing the dogged set of his

shoulders as he went off in search of Lot. Even after so many years, these visits must have been uncomfortable for him.

"There is indeed much sunshine left," said Mother, once Gawain was out of earshot. "It's a bright afternoon, and good for reading. Gawain's ship brought books as well as weapons, all the way from Gaul." As if books could have come from any place nearer.

"Fine," I said, walking back to the horse, whom I'd decided to name Moira, for some perverse reason. "I can look at them tomorrow, after Gawain is gone. For now, though, I want to please him, and show him I appreciate his gift."

"And what of me? You don't want to please me, also?"

Damn it, I thought. I hated it when she spoke to me with that tone of voice. "Of course I do, Mother. Don't say that."

She came to me as I turned to face her. There was a rueful smile on her face, and the afternoon sun highlighted her shimmering black hair. "Then why make me unhappy?"

I reached out and took her hand. "Ach, Mother, what of my happiness? *You* love *me,* don't you?"

Her face softened, and I felt a certain selfish power, knowing as I did that I was the one thing in the world that could hurt her. "Of course I do, Mordred, more than the land or the sea or all the stars."

She only talked like that when she was being maudlin. "In that case," I said as I gently squeezed her hand, "you'll want me to be happy. Right now, it will make me happy to take this fine horse Gawain has given me and go riding on the moor. Can you really begrudge me that?"

She laughed, and stooped to kiss me on the mouth. "Of course, not, sweets, I begrudge you nothing. Take your fine new horse, and be off with you."

Scrambling into the saddle, I guided Moira toward the open gate. "I'll be back before dinner," I shouted as I rode toward the treeless horizon.

Seven

FROM THAT day forward, I paid less and less attention to my studies, to Mother's greater and greater displeasure. It was summer, when I could look out the window and see red clover blooming on the slopes beyond our palace, and ache for more freedom than all the Orkneys could afford me. Reading some torn scroll or scribbling away with my stylus and wax tablet only increased my sense of confinement, and so I practiced Gawain's lessons more than Morgawse's. Though I loved her as much as ever, I was thirteen and almost a man, and so the prospect of her disapproval was not as daunting as it once had been, especially now that she was so quick to disapprove of everything.

Mainland, the largest of our little islands, is about fifty miles long, although no point is more than five miles from the sea. I ranged the length and breadth of her on my new mount, the heavy lance tucked under my arm, or more comfortably, stuck upright into the leather socket that hung from one of the saddle's four horns, where it bounced against my thigh as I raced the incoming tide across the shining sands, or galloped Moira over cliff-bound flats that swelled up into waves of moor. As I rode, I imagined that my island embodied all of Britain in miniature, and I all of Arthur's horsemen, charging the length of the country to fight Saxons wherever they made landfall.

In truth, that's how I found my first real foe, and killed

him, with no help but my horse and weapons. It was not a particularly glorious encounter, but then, I'm not writing this history in order to flatter myself.

Surprisingly, considering what a bitch the thing had been to draw, I became quite a good shot with the wicked little Eastern bow Gawain had given me, and had already killed enough birds to stuff a pillow, even though I only took a single tail feather from each one. I'd also become proficient enough with the lance, and could stay in the saddle while impaling the dummy I'd built to Gawain's specifications. That target grew quite perforated, and I found myself hoping one of the household slaves would die, so that I could use his (or her) corpse in its place (assuming Mother didn't claim the body first) and thus get a better feel for ramming my lance point into flesh and bone.

That opportunity eventually came, though not in the way I'd expected. I was riding on the south shore, where the highest cliffs looked out across the sighing firth to Solway and the Pictish territories of North Britain. It was an unusually bright day, with sunlight reflecting off the white sand and dancing on the waves. Rounding a tumbled pile of basalt, I sighted a solitary figure dragging what appeared to be a dead pig across the pebbly beach, to a small curragh moored just above the tideline. The pig was big and fat, and leaking blood from its apparently freshly cut throat. The man was small and swarthy and clad in a sheepskin vest and cowhide breeches. His bare arms were covered with writhing blue tattoos, and when he looked up at me, I saw that even more intricate designs decorated his face. The Dobuni and some of the more backward Southern Britons still tattooed their arms, but only the Picts tattooed their faces.

Dropping the pig, he turned and sprinted for his little boat of hide and saplings. Without thinking, I drummed my heels against Moira's sides and urged her after him. That wasn't as foolish at it might seem. The beach was empty of any other sign of life, so I surmised he'd come alone, especially in such a tiny craft. Lot's warband, and the ease with which it could mount reprisals on the mainland, meant that our neighbors across the firth contented themselves with slipping over in ones and twos, to snatch livestock from outlying farms. For many of their young men, it had become a rite of passage, to sneak over in a bobbing curragh, cut some farmer's throat, and go back with a hog or a goat or a brace of chickens. Nothing like the bloody raids of the old days, of course, but annoying enough for all of that.

Pulling my lance from its socket, I steadied it as best I could underneath my arm. The salty wind whistled in Moira's mane, and pebbles crunched under her drumming hooves. The distance to the Pict had already been cut in half, but he still did not turn to face us. Either he was very inexperienced, or his tribe was one that had not learned the futility of trying to outrun horsemen over level ground. I caught up to him just before he reached the boat, and should have skewered him like a pig, but he ducked under my point and I went charging past. By the time I'd wheeled around for another charge, he was waist high in the surf, dragging the curragh behind him.

My first impulse was to plunge the horse into the waves after him, but better sense prevailed. Instead, I steadied Moira, slipped my lance back into its socket, and pulled my bow and an arrow from where they hung beside my right leg. Testing the wind and drawing smoothly as I could, I sighted on his broad-shouldered back and tried to keep my hand from shaking with excitement.

My first shot went high, but my second one caught him below the right shoulder just as he tried to heave himself into the curragh. Yipping like a dog, he fell back into the water, and a wave went over him, lifting the curragh on its swell. His head reappeared a dozen feet away from the boat, his arms flailed, then he went under again. I nocked another arrow and waited, but he did not immediately reappear.

Jumping from the saddle, I dropped my bow and waded into the surf. That was stupid, yes, but all I could think of at the time was that I wasn't going to let the bastard drown on me. Few Picts can swim, but then, a

lot of Orkneymen can't, either, for all that we're islanders and descended of pirates. Being royal, I'd had time to
learn a few exotic skills, and could manage it well
enough.

I was lucky in my naive eagerness, for there wasn't
any fight in him when I found him, and I was able to get
him back to the shore without him putting a knife in
me, although I had to pull him out of his waterlogged
sheepskin to do so. He was about my size, bigger-boned
but not as well fed, and I didn't have much trouble
dragging him up onto the beach. He lay there, gasping
like a landed fish, his eyes closed and blood running out
from where my arrow pierced his shoulder. I pressed on
his muscular, almost-hairless chest until he coughed up
the water he'd swallowed, then rolled him on his side.
After shoving the arrow through his shoulder until
enough of the shaft emerged, I broke off the head, then
grabbed the fletching and pulled it the other way. It came
out of his flesh with a sound not unlike a sloppy wet kiss.
He shuddered at that and kicked spasmodically, but his
eyes did not open.

I used the dagger that hung from his belt to cut strips
of linen from my undertunic, then did my best to
staunch the wound with these, drawing on the surgical
and anatomical skills I'd learned from Mother. I'd just
finished my ministrations when he opened his brown
eyes and looked at me, and said something in his
language which I didn't understand.

I stood up. His face was young and unlined, and
though I couldn't tell his age, I guessed that he wasn't
much older than me, for he did not have the lime-
stiffened mustache typical of Picts, just dark fuzz on his
lip and chin. Along with the tattoos, he had tribal scars
on his cheeks and forehead, the decorations making his
swarthy but round and quite ordinary face seem fierce
and alien. He wore an old Roman coin on a leather
thong around his neck, along with bears' teeth and a
fresh-looking human finger.

I drew my sword and backed toward Moira, who still
waited patiently where I'd left her (damned if I've owned

as good a horse since). His teeth clenched in what was either a grimace or a snarl, but certainly not a smile, he sat up, then rose most unsteadily to his feet. I kept my eyes on him while climbing into the saddle. He just stood there, feet spread apart for balance, looking like he wished he had a weapon.

I lifted my lance from its socket. "I'm sorry," I said to him, doubting that he understood me. "But I really need the practice, and if I took you back to the palace, they'd just hang you, anyway."

I reined Moira down the beach until we were far enough away to get up a good charge, then swung her back toward him. Nowadays, if I wanted to go at an individual Pict from horseback, I'd use a javelin or some sort of light spear I could thrust overhand, or even a long cavalry sword, rather than a heavy, hard-to-maneuver lance, and if he'd been older and more experienced, I'm sure he could have eluded me, despite being wounded and nearly drowned. But no, he was young, and probably as green to combat as I was, despite the finger he'd taken as a trophy, for he just stood there, swaying, watching me come.

The iron head of my lance took him in the chest and I heard his collarbone break. It wasn't anything like sticking a dummy, and I was nearly jolted from the saddle, but I kept hold of the lance and managed to tear it out of him as I swept past. When I wheeled Moira back around, I saw he was down and splayed out on the sand like spilled laundry. He was still twitching a bit, and blood came in bubbling spurts out of the diamond-shaped hole my lance point had made in his bare chest. I slipped from Moira's back, drew my sword, and hacked at him until he stopped moving.

Looking down, I wondered why I did not feel more elated, for I'd killed my first man, a deed that brought me closer to being the sort of warrior Arthur would welcome at his court. There was no revulsion or guilt, just a sort of distanced numbness, and a feeling of looking down at myself from far away. Gawain later told me *he* got so sick when he killed his first man that he vomited, on both himself and the corpse. Arthur, too, once indicated that his first bloodletting had been similarly queasy. Well, maybe they're better men than I, for I felt no immediate nausea or disgust. That's ironic, really, when you consider that they've both killed more men than I probably ever will.

There remained the matter of a trophy. Even today, I can't decapitate someone with a single cut, and neither can anybody else I know, despite what you hear in stories. Weary as I was, and as heavy as my sword arm suddenly felt, I had to hack at him another four or five times before I got his head off, but at least my swings did not go wild, and it came away pretty much unmarked. Tying it to my saddle horn by its long, wet hair, I galloped along the strand, feeling the salt wind in my face and my prize slapping against my knee. Remembering an old Irish song about the triumphant warrior bearing the heads that are the fruits of his valor, I tried to whistle it, but kept mangling the tune.

Rather than immediately returning to the palace, I reined Moira inland, toward the farmhouse I knew to be nearby, for I doubted that the Pict had come upon such a fine pig wandering freely on the beach. The small farm, consisting of two squat buildings and a turf-walled pen, proved to lie just beyond the next rise. Nothing stirred in answer to my shouted greeting, and I found the farmer dead in his little hut of peat-roofed stone, his throat cut and his right index finger missing. All his swine were dead, too, even the white and pink piglets. "Idiot," I said to the head that hung from my saddle, as I held Moira's rein and peered down into the bloody sty. "You could have bundled them all up in a sack and gotten them into your boat alive, and then you'd have been a richer man when you returned to your tribe." Well, no one had ever accused the Picts of being overly practical.

Back at the palace, Lot was not impressed when I showed him the head. "Cut if off a drowned Pict, did you?" he asked dryly.

"Drowned, hell!" I said, trying to sound proud of myself. "I killed him with my bow and lance."

Lot took another swill of ale. "Oh, I doubt that, and I don't appreciate your interrupting my dinner with the sight of that carrion." Burping explosively, he turned to his wife. "Really, Morgawse, where are the goddamned Roman manners you've been drumming into the brat's head?"

Mother's face was serene in the firelight, for she was used to this sort of conversation. "Don't be a hypocrite, husband. Mordred is only following the customs of your people. Your father took more than a few heads in his time. Have you forgotten the ones that hang in the outer hall?"

Lot burped again. "It's not the bloody same. King Conag was a great warrior. He didn't hack his trophies off corpses he found washed up on the beach."

Her eyes flashed at that. "And neither did Mordred. If he said he took the head in single combat, then that's what happened. Or do you demand proof?"

Even when he'd been drinking, Lot was quick to see which way the discussion was heading. "No magic!" he barked. "I'll not have magic at my table!" Lot was, of course, no Christian, and in fact professed no faith other a sour pragmatism. I suspect his protest stemmed from a simple distaste for being reminded of his wife's power, though he certainly had no objections to her skills when they brought him some advantage.

"Too late for that," said Mother lightly. "You should have accepted the truth with better grace. Give me the head, Mordred."

Enjoying Lot's dyspeptic expression, I handed it to her. She held its face level with her own. Her features contorted for a moment, as if she were chewing a particularly tough piece of meat, and when her tongue appeared between her clenched teeth, it was raw and bloody. Making a gurgling sound in the back of her throat, she spit into the head's open mouth. I was used to this sort of thing, but Lot looked like he was about to gag. "Lugh's balls, Morgawse," he said thickly, covering his face with his hands.

Mother ignored him, and proceeded to address the head. "With this blood I bind your spirit to your flesh," she said. "Speak on my command. Tell us, in a tongue that we can understand, how you met your death."

The head blinked, and its glazed brown eyes focused dully upon her. Its lips twitched back from its yellow teeth, and a dry rasping sound emerged from its truncated throat. Finally, it began to speak, not in Pictish, or even North British, but in Latin, albeit with Mother's own Southern British inflections.

"The boy killed me," it said in a muddy, toneless voice.

"What boy?"

It rolled its eyes toward me, exposing the whites. "The one who stands before you."

"How did he kill you?"

"He shot me with an arrow, speared me on his lance, and cut my throat and chest with his sword." The voice might have been that of a man describing what he had eaten that day.

Morgawse nodded. "Good. You have told me the truth as I commanded you. Return now to your rest." She smiled at me. "Arrow and lance and sword? I only wish you were as thorough in your studies."

Despite the gibe, she actually seemed proud of me, for all the disdain she'd exhibited toward warlike pursuits. Well, I've said she thrived on contradictions. Part of it, I think, was her natural inclination to take a stance opposite of Lot's. And there was the fact that she genuinely loved me and liked seeing excel at something, even a craft distasteful to her.

She clapped her hands for a steward. "Take this fine head," she said with a note of pride, "and have it preserved in the traditional manner, then hung with the other heads in the outer hall. Let it be known that my son is a credit to the spirit of his warrior ancestors. Let no one gainsay this." She gave Lot a penetrating glare, as if to say *and where are your trophies, little man?* He

picked at his stewed dogfish and looked away, mumbling
something too low to be heard.

Ultimately, of course, I had taken the Pict's head not
to please Morgawse, or even to gall Lot, but to show to
Gawain, in the hopes that he might mention it to Arthur.
Indeed, on his next visit, my brother seemed genuinely
impressed.

"Ach, it's a fine head," he said, standing in the outer
hall and looking at it where it hung from a carved
timber, along with half a dozen more ancient trophies.
"Arthur doesn't really approve of taking heads, you
know, and he calls it a barbaric practice, but I think he'll
be impressed just the same. I can't wait to tell him that
my lessons were put to good use."

"As was Moira," I said. "Be sure to tell him I thank
him for the horse."

"Oh, I've told him that already," he said dryly. "I told
him he should have seen your face light up when I gave
her to you. A fine Gallic stallion could not have pleased
you more, I said."

I laughed. "Right. Well, it was kind of you to lie like
that. Now come inside, and tell me of how things go in
the Southern kingdoms."

Things, it turned out, had been going quite peacefully
of late, for which he was grateful but I was not, as it
meant that he had no exciting stories to tell. Indeed, it
seemed that Arthur's dream of a united, strife-free realm
was close to becoming reality, with the Saxons under
heel, the Picts not daring to cross the Wall, and even
the Irish more interested in settlement than piracy. I
feigned sulkiness, and said I was irked to find, now
that I was just about old enough to take a place at court,
there looked to be no adventures left for me in Britain.
Gawain laughed, and said he'd try to stir the Saxons up
again, just to keep me from being bored.

Actually, we both knew that things would not be so
stultifying as that. Human foes may have been temporar-
ily scarce, but this only meant that, like the champions
of ancient times, Arthur and his warband were free to

turn their attentions to marauding dangers of the nonhuman variety. Huge worms still churned their way through the waters of the northern lochs, the occasional dragon still gorged itself upon sheep and unlucky cottagers, and there were even a few giants about, the first of their race seen on British soil since before the days of the Roman occupation. The heroes of Britain have always warred against the Huge Folk, since the time of Bran the Blessed, and now another Heroic Age was dawning. Why should Arthur have been any different from his ancestors? A hero needs to slay monsters. It was because of this need that his life again touched mine.

Eight

A YEAR after I killed the Pict, and two months after I turned fourteen, I was riding by the sea. Very bored and needing the illusion of not being confined, I saddled up Moira and went charging out the gate, whooping inanely in the halfhearted hope that something exciting might happen. Well, there wasn't much else for me to do, and as Lot wasn't about to dispatch the royal ship to take me to Britain so I could serve his hated brother-in-law, I had to wait for Gawain's next visit, which of course would not be until after the harvest. Never had "mainland" Orkney seemed so bloody small.

My boredom was no doubt increased by the recent demise of the other Moira that I liked to ride, the kitchen wench after whom I'd named the horse. Dammit, now, fourteen years after her unfortunate death, I can no longer remember its exact cause, though I do recall that I believed myself heartbroken for a week or so. None of the other palace girls had caught my fancy, and the days were past when we could expect to be taking Saxon wenches in raids. My studies seemed more of a prison than ever, and there was no acre of even the smallest island that I'd not explored many times over, and those explorations had yielded no more Picts. Still, there was nothing for it but to ride, and pretend I was going someplace new.

Spurring my mount, I rode over peaty treeless hills

and down sand and shingle beaches, over low walls and into pastures filled with sheep and shaggy cattle, past the sod huts of crofters and through muddy yards full of squawking chickens. Eventually, I passed all signs of human settlement, and there was only the occasional bit of old Pict or Fairy stone peeking out from under a blanket of peat and heather to remind me that men had ever been here. I'm not sure how long or how far I rode, but I remember where I ended up.

I was down by Scapa Bay, leagues from Brough's Head and the royal hall. Guiding my dappled mare across a stretch of speckled sand festooned with green clumps of salty-smelling weed, I rounded a stack of wave-worn basalt, landlocked now at high tide, and saw it.

It was a like a huge bowl, thirty or more feet across, constructed of pitch-soaked hide stretched over a sapling frame. It took me a moment to realize it was a curragh, not unlike the one that had brought my Pict of the summer before, but immensely larger. Was it a whole raiding party this time? Surely they'd not have left their craft untended.

The crude boat stank something awful, and flies buzzed about it in a black cloud. Where a large hole was gashed in it, I could see that the hides were pink and tan on the inside, apparently lacking their outer coating of pitch. What sort of workmanship was this? It was a miracle the thing had proved seaworthy.

My mare didn't want to get too close, so I left her back atop the rise, her reins pegged to a clump of scrub grass, and approached it on foot. It was propped against a rock, that apparently being what had torn the hole in it, and I couldn't see over its rim. Instead of climbing the rock, I pulled back a flap of the pink tear. The untreated side of the skin was freckled and decorated with a plate-sized patch of red, curly and distinctly human hair. Gagging, I forced myself to stick my head through the flap.

I'd seen strips of human skin before; Mother had entire scrolls written on it. But unlike those, these were more or less whole, flat man-shapes reminiscent of the target dummy I'd cut from cowhide. Some had been sewn into the curragh with their scalps and birthmarks and scars all turned outward, so that the craft's owner had presumably sat on them. Others had been sewn the other way, creating raw pink human silhouettes decorated with blobs of greasy yellow fat. Flies and crabs swarmed over these.

And over the carrion strewn across the bottom of the stinking boat, adding to its stench. I saw scattered feet and hands, forearms and calves, the bones of thighs and upper arms, cracked ribs, gnawed-looking vertebrae, and pelvises with the buttocks stripped away but the genitals still intact. And not a single head. Something had made landfall upon our shores, and had eaten the food it had brought with it before it left its craft behind.

I scrambled back atop my nickering mare and reined back the way I'd come, my heart pounding like a kettledrum and piss trickling down my thigh. It was low tide, and I kept the horse to the surf line whenever I could, steering away from the gorse and bracken-carpeted hills, where anything might lurk over the next rise. Monsters were a fact of British life in those days, but there hadn't been one in our parts since before I was born. That had changed now.

Cado had come to Orkney.

Nine

THAT WAS the beginning of an eventful summer. I arrived back at the palace to find it in an uproar. A delegation of crofters was huddled in the mud of the courtyard, clutching each other and muttering prayers, while Lot's soldiers strapped on extra armor and milled around looking scared—even big, tough Beortric, whose face normally bore about as much expression as a piece of driftwood. While I was away, an entire steading had been found ransacked on the other side of Scapa Bay, the family and their sheep both reduced to gnawed and scattered bones. The slaves and servants were hysterical, and in truth, even Lot's supposedly seasoned warriors weren't much calmer.

After much debate, Lot rode out to view the wreckage, taking all his men with him and keeping snug in the middle of them, leaving the serfs of the palace feeling woefully unprotected. Mother stood on the battlements all the time they were gone, an oakwood staff in her hands, her face hard but calm. I wondered if Arthur looked like that while waiting for the Saxons to charge at Badon. Some things ran in the blood.

Lot and his warriors were back well before dark. They all looked very pale, with their king the palest of the lot. No one suggested they try to track down whatever was responsible for the carnage. Nobody slept very well that night. Mother wanted me to sleep in her chamber, but I refused, feeling it was unmanly. A bucktoothed kitchen girl with a nice backside ended up sharing my bed, but although I wasn't as frightened as my nominal father, I was too nervous to take pleasure there.

And that's how things stood for the next few weeks. Mother spent the better part of a day and a night in her tower, calling on spirits and elements, burning powders and boiling liquids, and consulting scrolls and oracles. Eventually, she came dejectedly down into the great hall and said she could do no good, that whatever had come to Orkney had some power guarding it. "You'll have to take matters in hand yourself," she told her husband, "or send to Camelot for help." Despite her dejected state, there was a certain note of triumph in her voice. The thought of Lot having to rely on her hated brother for aid clearly gave her pleasure.

The monster destroyed another steading and must have eaten half a dozen crofters and twice as many sheep before Lot let me write the necessary letter that his ship would take to Arthur. Doing so must have surely hurt his pride. Less than it would have hurt to ask his wife to write it, though.

To Artorious Imperator, Most High King of all the Britons

Greetings, Uncle:

One of the dreadful monsters that you and your warriors have so diligently driven from your shores has turned up seeking refuge here. Many sheep and cattle have fallen victim to his terrible appetite, as well as no few of our precious subjects. I take it that the creature is called Cado. At least, that's the name that King Lot and his warriors found on the wall of one demolished steading. It was written in blood and excrement, but rather good Latin. Above his signature was scrawled the words, "this island is mine now." Unlike King Lot, this monster can apparently read and write.

Help us, Uncle. We can do nothing but remain

barricaded in the palace, and pray for swift deliver-
ance.

Your nephew,
Mordred Mac Lot

By the time I wrote the letter, our daily situation felt
less dire than I'd made it sound, for Cado confined his
depredations to lonely farms and pastures, and eventually a sense of normalcy returned to the palace. You get
used to any danger, especially if there are thick walls
between you and it, and other people are the ones dying.
I'd taken such a grim tone in my letter because I wanted
to be sure that Arthur came himself.

I should never have worried on that score.

Ten

I SAT on the cold cliff and stared out across the water, absentmindedly trying to drop rocks on the heads of the squawking terns that nested on the tiny beach so very far below. I'd been waiting a long time—my nose felt full of icicles, and my buttocks were almost frozen numb. Ignoring the chill wetness seeping through my woolen breeches, I dangled my heels over salty emptiness and squinted at the gray horizon, scanning it for some sign of Arthur, Arthur, Arthur. He would come today. He must come today.

That was an idiotic certainty, ocean voyages being what they were. I knew the sea well enough to know he might not make landfall for the better part of a week. Still, he was coming today, I knew it, and it was my letter bringing him. My first brush with the magic of the word.

Yes, Arthur would be here, and soon he'd be dragging Cado's head triumphantly behind his horse. I wondered what the head would look like? Was he a manlike giant, or one of those who were said to have the heads of animals? Perhaps he'd had three eyes, or six, or maybe only one, like the Cyclops of the Greeks. Mother would want the head, probably, so I'd get to examine it at my leisure, in the tower that was her sanctum, the place that Lot never entered. Lot, on the other hand, would not be wanting the head, or anything else to remind him that he'd been forced to call on Arthur's aid. I'd be almost sorry to see Cado slain, for I'd truly enjoyed seeing how

73

each additional bit of news about the monster's depredations had left King Lot looking as though he was about
to take a particularly painful shit.

Yes, I'd be sorry to see Lot's discomfit end, but even
then I knew all pleasures were transitory. And I did very
much want to see Arthur. He had to come today.

And that was when I spotted it, the tiny speck that
could only be a distant ship. I rubbed my eyes, but it
stayed out there, not wishful thinking but the hoped-for
reality. Beyond the toylike sail, dark clouds tumbled
low across a sky like unpolished iron. The ship seemed to
be riding before a storm. It was a wonder they'd decided
to chance the weather and make for Orkney, rather than
turn back to the mainland coast they must have been
hugging during their long trip up from Cornwall.

I leapt to my feet with a whoop and started scrambling
back away from the cliff. The jagged stones, wet and
black and speckled with bird shit, gave me poor footing,
and I stumbled and fell several times before I reached
the sand and turf. Over the rise loomed Lot's palace,
squatting in the lee that gave it some scant protection
from the sea and wind. It might not have been much by
mainland standards, but it was the grandest building in
all the Orkneys. A twenty-foot ditch and two reinforced
earthworks surrounded a horseshoe-shaped two-story
stone-and-timber hall. I dashed across the plank bridge
that spanned the ditch and waved at the soldiers manning the outer earthwork. Those not too busy sleeping,
gambling with dice and bones, or relieving themselves in
the shadow of the rampart waved back.

Mother's tower was on the opposite side of the inner
courtyard from the great hall. Kicking and shoving my
way through a mass of chattering serfs, grunting pigs,
squawking chickens, honking geese, and other livestock,
I carefully skirted the deepest mud and the steaming
piles of fresh excrement until I arrived at the tower's
slab-sided foundation.

The stairs were steep and winding and another reason
why Lot never came here, though they didn't bother
Mother, who had the constitution of a draft horse. The

room at the top was high and narrow and all of gray stone. It had one window, large and square, with an iron grille and heavy oak shutters. A ladder connected with a trapdoor in the ceiling that opened onto the roof. In one corner was a brick hearth with a chimney flue, not so much a fireplace as an alcove for the black iron brazier that squatted there like a three-legged toadstool. Flanking the alcove were imported cedar shelves that were lined with animal skulls, a few precious books, rather more scrolls, netted bunches of dried herbs, and small clay jars filled with rendered animal fats and various esoteric powders. In the center of the floor was laid a tile mosaic in the shape of a circle lined with runes and astrological symbols. Off to one side of this was a low marble table where Mother sacrificed white doves, black goats, and the occasional slave who'd grown too sick, old, or just plain lazy to be worth his keep.

Today it was a goat. Mother stood over the spread-eagled carcass, absorbed in the tangle of entrails that she was genteelly probing with the tip of her silver-bladed sacrificial dagger. From her expression, I knew she'd found a particularly interesting set of omens in the cooling guts.

"He's come," I said, trying to sound calm.

She looked up, straightening to her considerable full height. I may have gotten her black hair and dark eyes, but the impressive stature had gone to Gawain, though he was beefy where she was willow slender. Today she was dressed in the usual manner for her art, an ankle-length black gown that left her strong forearms bare. On her head was a silver circlet, and her long, straight hair was tied back with a blood red ribbon.

She put down the knife. "Arthur, you mean?"

"Yes. I saw the ship."

She nodded, frowning. "The augury was correct, then. And me such an untidy mess." She wiped her bloody hands on the linen cloth she'd laid out under the goat. "Do me a favor, love. Clean this up for me while I go change to greet our guests. Do you mind?"

"No, Mother."

"Ach, that's a good lad, then." Giving me a quick kiss on the cheek, she hurried down the stairs, leaving me alone in the narrow room. I bundled the goat into the stained cloth and staggered with it to the window. The rectangular tower was built into the earth-and-timber wall that formed the fourth side of the courtyard square. With a heave, I got my burden through the aperture. It landed on the other side of the wall. Immediately, a battle for possession of the meaty carcass broke out between several of the serfs who had hovels there and a pack of the palace dogs. The barks and curses continued for quite some time.

A wet whistling sound came from above my head. "Hello, Young Master. Please give me something to eat."

I looked up at Gloam, where he clung directly over the magic circle. "No, I don't have time. Arthur's coming."

Gloam resembled nothing so much as a pancake-shaped mass of dough several feet in diameter, his pale surface moist and sweaty with patches of yeasty slime. Offset from the center of his flat body was a bruiselike discoloration about the size of a head of lettuce. Only when a round mouth puckered open and wrinkled lids parted to reveal eyes like rotten oysters did it become recognizable as a face. Gloam wasn't much to look at, but few people call up demons for their beauty.

"Arthur," he gurgled, "oh, yes, I know all about Arthur. More than you do. Give me food."

"Oh, right," I sneered. "What would you know about Arthur?"

"He's your father." Gloam darkened to a deep purple, and then faded back to his usual pasty hue, always a sign that he was enjoying himself.

My first reaction was that Gloam was honestly being stupid. "Piss off, you slug. He's my uncle."

"Yes, that too. He sired you on your mother fifteen years ago, before he knew she was his sister."

I was too stunned by the content of what Gloam had said to be affected by his sneering tone. Briefly, I was eight again, and sobbing in wet darkness with Mother's arms around me. Arthur, my father? Could he be? I remembered little Merlin's veiled hints, hints I'd so stupidly never really thought about, but which seemed clear enough now. Oh, but it would be good, so very good, for it to be him. I sat down on the cold tile and hugged my knees to my chest, while Gloam festered and bubbled above me. *Please let this be true,* I thought, *oh please, and not some stupid demon's trick. I must ask Mother,* I told myself; *I must remain calm until I can ask her. She'll tell me the truth.* Hell, she'd promised to long ago, once I was a man. Well, I was fourteen and a half, a man now, had been for a while. Oh, yes, I told myself again, I was definitely a man. So why did I feel so much like a very little boy?

Finally, I was able to look up at him and speak. "Tell me more."

The eruption that was his face flushed from dark purple to bluish green. "I've said too much. The Queen will be very angry."

"I don't care. If it's supposed to be a secret, you've told me too much already."

"Give me something to eat, then." Such creatures are like that, all appetite, with no surcease while they're encased in flesh. "An infant would be nice. A tender little milk-fed babe."

"No, but I'll give you something."

Moving dazedly, I went downstairs and caught a rooster, getting rather muddier in the process. Around me, the chickens seemed to be clucking *Arthur Arthur Arthur* in an inane barnyard chorus that was echoed by my footsteps on the stairwell, the hiss of the air outside Mother's window, and Gloam's bubbling exhalations. Tying its legs together with a strip of cloth, I tossed the squawking cock into the center of the tile circle. Gloam detached himself from the ceiling and fell on it with a wet slapping noise. For a few moments he was just a featureless, quivering ball of flesh, then his mottled face erupted again from his outer surface.

"Another one?" he asked in his wet, plaintive whistle of a voice.

I was tempted to light a torch from the brazier and

make his blotchy stain of a face look even more like a blister. "All right, Gloam, but first you must tell me what you know."

His lipless mouth pulsed like that of one of the small, shapeless sea creatures I sometimes found in tidal pools. "Mistress will be so angry with me . . ."

I nodded. "True enough. I expect that what you've told me already is enough to make her melt you into slime. Your only hope is that I'll say nothing about this. Now, are you going to tell me the rest, or do I go find her and ask her to do so?"

"It happened at the Yuletide feast at Colchester, when the King and Queen of Orkney were paying their seasonal visit to Uther's court. Arthur was just a landless bastard of a soldier; your mother knew no more of his real parentage than anyone else did, but she fancied his looks. The magic of the carpenter god was not so strong in him then, but it was growing, and Morgawse needed Merlin's help to cast a spell, much like the one he cast for her father Uther, so that Arthur would not know that the woman who came to his tent was the Queen of Orkney. Humans are like that, fools blundering around in the dark. She had another spell ready to make him want her, but it proved unnecessary. The carpenter's magic isn't much good against lust, which is one reason why it upsets his followers so much."

It could be true. Gloam, like all his kind, was prone to lying, but it could be true. Arthur could be my father.

My head hurt. It was dizzying, sure enough. Almost half my life, I'd known I was not the the son of my cold island's colder lord, but that was a simple negation, nothing to prepare me for the heart-thumping wonder at the prospect of being sired by the best man in the known world. He never knew, Gloam said. What would he say if he did? Could he embrace me as his son? Some spark of hope had been kindled here, and with it, the chance of sharper pain and disappointment. Would he acknowledge me? He loved me as a nephew, I was sure of that, but could he do so as a son? Yes, I was getting ahead of myself, being tormented by possibilities when I didn't even know what the truth was yet, but I couldn't hold back the rush of hopes and fears. I felt like I was balancing on a precipice. For me, who could scale sheer cliffs as easily as a spider scampers up a wall, suddenly all was vertigo.

Don't think me thickheaded. My understanding of Christian morality was dim at best, and the incest taboo was not the first thing on my mind. I'd no formal schooling in any religion, and no real idea of what the followers of the crucified carpenter might think of this. I now know that the pagan Romans despised incest nearly as much as Christians do, but that was one part of her uncle's heritage that Mother had not passed on to me, and of course the Druids had no such qualms. Despite the conversation I remembered from my boyhood visit to Orkney, Gawain said that Arthur seldom spoke directly of his faith, dear to him as it plainly was. That was understandable, for he'd come to power in a realm that was more than half what he'd call pagan, and no doubt that had forced him to learn a certain amount of tact. Could I have seen the future, I would have known that the High King of all the Britons would lose this easy way of living with his Christos because of what I will soon relate; but I was no Merlin, and such gifts were beyond me. I did know that Arthur had never tried to suppress the worship of Mithras, the Roman soldier's god, among his mounted troops. But did this tolerance mean he'd welcome an illegitimate and incestuous son with proverbial and literal open arms?

He might. I didn't know, I couldn't know, but he might.

And he might have welcomed Merlin to his service, some small voice should have whispered in my brain. *As he might have offered your mother a better place than these empty islands. Aye, and the sheep in the barnyard might start shitting rubies.* But no, there was no tiny voice of wisdom to counsel me that mights are often less than nothings.

The sound of a sudden commotion outside broke my reverie. "That would be Arthur's arrival," commented

Gloam wetly as he flopped over to the wall and began to climb it, leaving a sluglike trail across the tiles and flagstone.

I was out the door and down the steps in a trice, for at least action would keep me from having to think. The yard was a confusion of babbling serfs, barking dogs, and clucking fowl, all frantically trying to stay clear of the muddy wake churned up by the two dozen riders who came pounding under the fortified gatehouse. A trim man on a magnificent black gelding rode at their head, snapping off orders with a practiced ease of long command.

Arthur was dressed for rough travel in an iron-studded leather jerkin and knee-high doeskin boots. His head was protected by an iron-banded cap of padded leather, lighter than the conical helmet he'd wear on campaign, and a sopping cloak draped around his shoulders, back, and saddle like limp wings. Obviously, his ship had passed through the storm I'd seen brewing. There were more lines in his clean-shaven face, but the short bangs that projected from under his cap were still light brown. With his sharp gaze and imperial, almost beaky nose, he looked like a Caesar on an ancient coin.

Until he smiled. Vaulting from his tall horse, he clapped me on the shoulder, his crooked grin and easy manner still, after all these years, marking him as more the soldier than the king.

"Hullo, laddybuck; no need to bow; we're all bloody royal here. You've grown more than a bit since I saw you last."

Trying not to think of what Gloam had told me, all I could do was reply to his compliment. "I wish I'd grown more. It looks like Gawain got all the height, and I'm to be the puny one."

He laughed. "Does it now? Well, a lad's growth is measured in more than the distance from his head to his heels, and that's the truth of it."

I saw no sign of Gawain. "Is my brother with you?"

He shook his head. "His squadron's manning the Wall, keeping an eye on our Pictish friends."

I could only stare at him there in the courtyard, directing the actions of his dismounting men while he scanned the crumbling fortifications with a critical eye. His hand was still on my shoulder. What could I say, with my new secret swelling inside me?

Lot's acid bark cut through the brouhaha. "Mordred, get the hell out of the way, you're filthy as a fucking Pict! Change before supper or eat in the stable. I'll have no mud-splattered brats at my table, by Mannanán and Lir."

I turned to see his thin, stooped form come stepping gingerly through the clinging mud. Arthur's formal smile was as cold as the sea wind. "Give you good day, my lord of Orkney." He winked at me and motioned me away. "Run along now, Mordred. We can talk later, out of this forsaken gale."

"Gale, hell, this is a slight breeze for this place," grumbled one of his captains.

While Arthur exchanged formalities with Lot, grooms led the horses to the stables and Arthur's men slogged toward the barracks that stood beside the great hall. I scurried through the crowd until I reached the hall's massive doorway, shut the heavy oak portal behind me, and crossed the huge, smoky room to the stairs that led to the raised gallery and then an upper landing. Bounding up the steps two or three at a time, I narrowly avoided a collision with my mother.

"Ach, you're all over mud," she commented mildly. "I do hope you're planning to change for dinner." She already had, and was wearing a samite gown the color of fine ash.

"Mother, I want to know all about Arthur," I said as she started to pass me.

She paused and looked me in the face, her own darkening like a storm-pregnant sky.

"Is he my father?"

She just looked at me.

"Answer me, Mother. I know I promised I'd not ask, but I'm a man now, or almost one, and I have to know. Is Arthur my father?"

"Why do you ask that?"

"Gloam told me that he was."

Her face darkened more, which did not bode well for her familiar, not that I cared about that. "And you believed him?"

I matched her stare. "All these years, I never thought much about what Merlin said. Maybe because he scared me, and because I love you, and didn't like seeing him dismiss you so easily." Oh, yes, some part of me was angry, that she'd hidden it so long, for me to be saying this. "He sent you away like a whipped serving wench, when I thought you as powerful as one of the Ladies of the Sky. So I tried not to think about it and succeeded very well. But now it's quite clear what he was talking about. So don't try to tell me that Gloam lied."

She looked away from me, and when her eyes met mine again, her face was calm and resigned, and I could barely refrain from shouting in my joy, for that meant it had to be true.

"I'm sorry, Mordred. I should have told you long ago."

I shrugged. "It's all right."

"No, it's not, not now or ever. But it's done, and we can but make the best of it."

This was too easy. I'd anticipated more argument, more drama, more something, not this quiet admission. I sat on the stairs and looked down at the torches guttering in their brackets. "Does Arthur know?" Merlin's taunts had implied that he did not, but who knew what had changed in the years since then.

She didn't answer at first, and when I looked at her, her smile was bitter. "No. Not him. He was just a handsome young commander, sick with his first taste of battle, and drinking too much because of the sickness. Our eyes met across a table in Uther's hall, and he raised his goblet in salute. I liked the look of him, and was very tired of my dry little stick of a king. With hindsight, I doubt I really needed any magic to seduce him, either Merlin's or my own. Like all men who are usually moderate in their drinking, Arthur had no idea how to pace himself when he decided to indulge, and I could have gone to him with no glamour and no clothing but my crown, and handed that crown out the tentflap to Lot, and I doubt he'd have known me for his king's daughter. And, of course, sly little Merlin gave no inkling that he knew what Arthur and I really were to each other. I'm sure it amused him to no end. You can imagine my surprise, much later, when I found out who and what Arthur really was."

She sat down beside me and put her arm around me. "He's a strange one, my brother is. I can't say I've grown to know him, in the years he's been king. But maybe I see things you don't. For all his free and easy manner, he's as shackled by his faith as any tonsured monk. Christians make much of guilt, and the thing they call sin. You love him, don't you?"

I was as sure of that as I was of anything, so why was the question so hard to answer? "Well, yes. He is a great man."

Her laugh was sardonic. "Your father—I mean, King Lot—does not share your good opinion. But enough of that. I am thinking, Mordred, that it would not be wise to tell Arthur of what you know. He loves you very much, but he loves you as a nephew. I am not sure how well that love would fare if he knew the truth. I'm sorry."

With that, she kissed me on the forehead and stood up again.

"Poor lad, you've had no father at all, and far from the best of mothers. Soon, perhaps, we can talk of this more freely. For now, I must see to our guests." Her face was beginning to brighten into a mask of hospitality. "Now run and change for dinner, or you'll miss the first course. I've made Lot set aside his stinginess for once, and we shall have a proper feast."

And so, my head aching with the weight of these strange and unexpected matters, I continued up the stairs, walking carefully, as if the world were about to tip beneath my feet.

Eleven

NOT KNOWN for the generosity of his table, Lot usually served visitors niggardly meals of boiled haddock, salt herring, smoked eel, and the occasional bit of mutton stewed in jellied ham hocks, leading Mother to remark sarcastically that we'd be better off as Christians, as they at least only observed Lent once a year. Even high lords and petty kings could expect to be guested in such a stingy manner.

Tonight, however, was different. The hall itself was tidied up, with newly laundered banners hung over the crumbling frescoes and freshly strewn rushes covering the shit and food scraps on the floor. The hacked and chipped high table had even been spread with that ultimate luxury, a clean linen cloth. Arthur's officers and the household guards sat together on sturdy, rough-hewn benches, quaffing tankards of ale and wine while the household dogs and pigs milled about, waiting patiently for the tidbits they knew were coming. To emphasize the refined and fastidious nature of the occasion, every person was provided with a clamshell of salt and a bowl of liquamen, the expensive sauce made from aged salt fish. In those days, you could still get liquamen.

The food was varied and abundant: dogfish pies, stewed seal and otter, smoked plovers and cormorants, shags and shearwaters spit-roasted with their guts inside, salads of watercress and red fennel, heaping piles of raw leeks and onions, and a whole roasted ox. The latter indicated that Mother had foreknown the time of Arthur's landing, as she must have ordered the cookhouse servants to begin preparing it the day before, although she'd said nothing to me about expecting her brother to arrive today. Individual servings of each dish were served shoveled onto trenchers of crusty bread, and most of the guests respected the pristine tablecloth and wiped their hands on their clothing or on the backs of passing dogs.

Lot sat at the head of the table, his back to the roaring hearth, Mother at his left and Arthur at his right. The King of Orkney had dressed for the occasion in a purple robe trimmed in ermine fur, and there was fresh black dye in his thinning hair. The beard that scarcely concealed his weak chin was more clipped and clean than usual, but the barbering only emphasized its sparse inadequacy.

By contrast, Arthur's garments were of plain wool and bare of any fashionable embroidery at the neck, sleeves, or hem of his surtunic. His brown breeches were cross-gartered with undyed strips of dull leather, and he'd changed to a plain but far from new cloak that was fastened at the shoulder with simple bronze brooch. He'd never learned to dress like a king and wouldn't until after he'd married Guinevere; but despite the severity of his clothing, he looked magnificent.

Lot was actually trying to put up a polite facade. "Tell me, good Artorious," he said, his use of Arthur's Latin name only just masking sarcasm with obsequious formality, "what do you know of this monster that has been eating my sheep and crofters?"

For a moment I thought Arthur might actually spit, so acute was his look of fierce distaste; but his manners were better than that. "Cado," he said in an even voice, "is an abomination and pestilence."

"We're aware of that, brother," said the Queen. "But where did he come from?"

"Brittany, or so it's said. Legend has it that, over a hundred years ago, the wife of the commander of one of the Armorican legions went riding too near Saint Michael's Mount, and that the giant who lives there, ah, well, had his way with her."

"Raped her, you mean," said Mother.

"I'm not sure Mordred needs to hear this."

Lot snorted in his cup. "Oh, him, don't worry about him." He then mumbled something about me having had my way with half the palace wenches. Fortunately, Arthur didn't seem to have heard.

"No, don't worry about me," I said, smiling calmly at Arthur while wishing I knew enough of Mother's magic to make Lot's head very small, so I could squeeze it between my thumb and forefinger like a pimple. "I've heard much worse, living here, in such a refined kingdom." Lot and I glared at each other for a moment. It was a tribute to Mother's attempts at civilizing me that I could sit there calmly and engage in barbed dinner conversation like the smoothest Roman while my head was spinning with wonder and apprehension.

"Well, anyway," Arthur continued, "she survived the experience, miraculously enough, and somehow managed to keep it secret from her husband. The boy born from that union seemed normal until his tenth birthday, when his growth increased alarmingly. Realizing that Cado was not his son, the legion commander killed both his wife and himself. The monstrous youth escaped that fate, but not the wrath of the local peasantry, and he was driven into the wilderness by an angry mob. There, he swore vengeance on humankind and began to live as a ravening beast."

"And who could blame him," said Mother dryly. "It was hardly his fault. Or the woman's."

"It's always some woman's fault," muttered Lot.

Arthur continued his story. "Perhaps we should pity the miserable creature. But whatever sins had been committed against him, he paid them back many times over in the following decades. From his father had come an inhuman life span as well as inhuman size. He stalked men as if they were deer, and ate their flesh and took their heads as trophies, and for nearly a century none in the Frankish or British settlements dared try to hunt him down. You know what Gaul was like after the Empire fell."

"But that changed, apparently," said Mother.

"Yes. In time, the Franks and Bretons prospered, their towns grew larger and more fortified, and their war-bands stronger and more disciplined. Four years ago, they finally drove him from Less Britain."

I imagined the monster swimming the Channel like a ditch. "And that's when you began to hunt him?"

"Not at first. He first ravaged the steadings of the Saxon Shore. Though they've been my nominal subjects since Badon, their kings were not likely to invite the aid of the British crown. But when his depredations spread to Dumnonia, I had to take action. My men and I hunted him from Winchester to Strathclyde, driving him before us like the stag before the hounds. We even crossed the Antonine Wall after him, and harried him among the Picts. That was uneasy hunting, you can be sure, us never knowing when blue-painted savages would come screaming out of the gorse."

"Ah," said Lot, "that was when you turned back, and let him get away."

"No," said Arthur, coldly meeting Lot's eye. "We almost caught up with him on a barren spot of beach, under cliffs even Cado couldn't climb. From the top of the cliff we could see someone at the edge of the surf, a cloaked form with long gray hair; tall, but not tall enough to be Cado. Something bobbed on the waves a few hundred feet out, something like a giant upturned leather basket with a huge manlike form crouched in it. When we picked our way down the one path to the beach, it was just a speck on the horizon, riding in the middle of a storm that had come pounding out of nowhere."

"But who was it on the beach?" I asked.

"I don't know. When we reached it, there was no one there, just a bird flying away. There was magic in the work of that, I'm sure. There's another thing I fear I may need to root out when I'm done with the giants and the dragons."

I remembered what Mother had said, about some power guarding Cado. I looked at her, and saw that she in turn was giving her brother a cool stare.

"Careful, Arthur; remember where you are a guest. Am I to be 'rooted out,' as you put it?"

Arthur dipped his head in apology, but his voice remained stern. "I'm sorry, sister. You are my kin, and I honor you, but I cannot condone the arts you practice. You know that."

She reached out over the silver candelabrum at the end of table, winding the flames around her fingers like red cloth, until her hand seemed gloved in fire. "Ah, yes. My arts. The same arts once practiced by Merlin, who brought our father to the throne."

Arthur flushed, and his voice softened. "I am a guest here, sister, and would not make unreasonable demands, but I must ask you not to speak of Merlin. I do not pretend to know how My Lord works His will, but it shames me that the man who sired me was ever in league with such a creature as that."

The flames on Mother's hand winked out, leaving her flesh untouched, but her eyes still shone like ice. I had to end this confrontation. "Well, you've got Cado now," I said, desperate to keep the peace between those I loved and worshiped. "He can't go farther."

"No, not even he could swim to the Zetlands, or bob there in a curragh."

One of Arthur's men laughed. "Aye, sire, we'll do the job these Orkneymen cannot."

An angry mutter came from the other end of the table, where big, walleyed Beortric sat with the elite of Lot's warband. Arthur turned toward his man, frowning. "Enough of that, Corum. We are guests here. I suggest you retire to the barracks and contemplate how best to improve your manners. Take some food with you, though."

The chastened warrior silently rose and left the hall. Lot hiccuped and changed the subject.

"So, you want to fortify the Northern coast."

Arthur nodded. "Yes, and I'll need Orkney's help for that."

Lot look pained. "Will the Picts consent?"

Arthur looked thoughtful while a steward refilled his cup. "I hope so. I need them, too. They may be half-naked savages, but they're British ones. I could use their help, if the Saxons rise again."

"But you beat them!" I protested. "Surely Badon ended all that."

Arthur shook his head. "Not by half, boyo, not by half. Do you know what my loyal subjects on the Saxon Shore are calling us now? *Welsh-men*—their word for foreigners. Foreigners, in our own forsaken country! I fear a time will come when either Briton and Pict must stand together, or go down separately under the English yoke."

Lot sipped his wine. "No doubt the *Sassanachs* will always be a threat. Of course, as someone who's had need of their service as mercenaries, I can see certain virtues in them that your folk can't. For instance, their kings are very brave."

Arthur looked at him very sharply. He knew full well that the King of Orkney wasn't one to be praising foreigners, or anyone else, without some ulterior motive. He stared at Lot for a long time, smiling but his eyes cold; and when he spoke, there was steel in his softness. "I came here to rid your land of a menace, Lot Mac Conag, not hear you sing the praises of my enemies."

"Well-spoken," replied Lot easily, "but I was simply remarking on a fact. Take old Beowulf Grendelsbane, for instance. He took on the monster that was menacing his people alone, and bare-handed at that. Tore its arm off as easily as I pull the wing from this bird's carcass."

"I am familiar with the story," said Arthur dryly. "For what it's worth, Beowulf was a Geat. What's your point?"

Lot smiled. Wine had made him very bold, to be playing with Arthur like this. Mother and I exchanged a pained look.

"Just this. You've never said as much, but I do believe
it would please you to see my islands converted to your
faith."

Arthur nodded, warily. "Yes. I'd have you all come to
Jesus, if I could."

Mother cleared her throat, but said nothing. I looked
down at my trencher and prodded a plover's thigh with
my knife, pretending I wasn't hearing this. Pagan or
Christian, it was all the same to me, but I knew something tricky was up.

"But you must understand," continued Lot, "Orkneymen are simple folk. They find it hard to be impressed
by your faith when you must bring with you over a score
of armored men to do what a pagan like Beowulf did
with his own strong arm."

One of Arthur's men spoke up. "Sire, this is boastful
nonsense. No Saxon oaf could ever had done such a
deed."

Arthur silenced him with a gesture. He turned back to
Lot. "King of Orkney, if I go after Cado all alone
tomorrow, taking none of my men with me, and if I
bring you back his head, will you, your household, and
your people, all consent to Holy Baptism?"

Lot nodded. "If you manage that, I will build a church
on every island!"

There was a fire burning behind the ice in Mother's
eyes. "Husband, we must speak of this," she said softly.
"Do not be so eager to pledge your people's and your
family's faith."

Lot slammed his cup down on the table. "Who is
master here? You were right to call them my family and
my people, and I will do with them what I please!" The
vein stood out even more prominently on his temple,
and his face was very red.

They sat like that, eyes locked, his forehead throbbing,
and then, under her cool stare, he wilted like a flower.
With a gasp that was half a sob, he sank back in his chair
and motioned wearily for more wine. "Don't do that to
me, damn you."

Arthur spoke then, smiling, easy humor in his voice,

and I saw another reason he was king. "It's all right, sister, I'll have no forced conversions, here or anywhere. But if I can provide an example that will lead even one person to the faith, I must do it."

I could scarcely believe I was hearing any of this. "Uncle Arthur, you are the greatest warrior in all of Britain, but is this wise?"

He looked at me solemnly. "I would show you the power of the Christos, Mordred. I doubt you've had much education in it."

I felt uncomfortable under his gaze. "I was thinking of your people. Such a risk puts them in danger, too."

He grinned his lopsided grin. "Well, they'll just have to cross themselves and hold their breath, won't they? I do know what I'm doing, Mordred; I'd not be King today if I was a complete fool. My God defended Padriac against the serpents of Ireland, and Columba against the dragon of Loch Ness. He protected Daniel in the lion's den and gave enough strength to Daffyd's arm to drive a small stone deep into Goliath's skull. He'll not fail me, not if I'm half the man I must needs be to call myself a king."

Arthur's soldiers, who'd been marveling silently at all this, broke out in spontaneous applause. He looked at them with good-natured affection. "Come now, you lot, I know half of you are pagan."

"After tonight, I'm not!" shouted one, a strapping fellow with a beard and a broken nose. Many others joined in shouting their agreement. The palace guard looked shocked at all this rowdiness, not used to seeing soldiers address nobility in such a familiar manner. Only Beortric remained impassive, but he studied Arthur coldly, as if he was sizing up a potential enemy.

Oblivious to that, Arthur grinned even more broadly. "You louts are just glad to be off the hook. It'll be me alone out there, slogging through the muck looking for a bloody monster while you keep your duffs warm in Orkney's cozy barracks."

There was general laughter at this, from our men as well as Arthur's. I looked carefully at Lot. Despite his fixed smile, I wasn't sure that he was entirely happy with the way things had turned out. Had he really thought Arthur would refuse his challenge? For all his craft, he seldom counted on people being able to rise above his expectations.

Mother had sat stony-faced through all of this. Now she stood.

"Brother, if it will please you, Cromach, our court bard, is ready with a song in your honor. Will you listen?"

Arthur nodded. "Yes, good sister, if it pleases your household to so honor me."

Mother clapped her hands, obviously glad of the change of subject. At her signal, Cromach came strutting out. He was a compact little Leinsterman, a flashy gamecock of a man with blue ribbons in his red beard, dressed in a splendid ensemble of crimson tunic, purple breeches, and green leggings. Bowing so low I feared his curly head would pick up scraps from the floor, he addressed Arthur.

"Oh, Great King of all the Britons, I apologize in advance for my poor, unpracticed song. I can only hope what little skill I have serves to bring you some small pleasure." With that, he plucked the strings of his harp and began to sing, not in Irish, or the impure Latin that passes for court speech, but Arthur's native British. The song was called *"Artos ab y Cyfddyd,"* which means Arthur, Son of the Morning.

> *As night falls hard, and thick with rain,*
> *I stand beside the moaning swells*
> *And shiver in the sharp-edged wind.*
>
> *Beyond black waves and blacker shores,*
> *Upon the mainland's rolling green*
> *A candle burns against the storm.*
>
> *I see it is the light of men*
> *Standing in their polished mail*
> *And something brighter than themselves.*

At their head, a warrior bold,
A Dragon King with upraised sword
Stands shining like the rising sun.

The night rolls round them like the surf
Breaking on the jagged rocks
But they stand fast against the storm

The song ended, but Cromach kept playing, his notes mingling sweet loss and bitter hope. A cynic might call it music fit for Brits, those self-consciously melancholy folk who embrace lost causes like a drunken lover (and are we Scots any better?), but no cynics were present while Cromach plucked his haunted strings. The notes echoed in our heads long after his fingers were still.

Mother was the first to speak. "I've not heard that song before, Cromach. Is it yours?"

He smiled and looked at me. "It comes from you, lady, in a sense."

One part of me wanted to hide under the table, but another was grinning in anticipation.

"From me? How is that possible?"

"Easily enough. Your son composed the words. As they come from him, and he comes from you, they are your words, too." Cromach's attempts at courtly wit were often just this feeble.

"That song was really yours, Mordred?" What, did she expect me to deny it?

I fingered the fragments of my trencher, soggy with stew and meat juices. "I just composed the words. The tune's an old one, Cromach says, from the days of the Tuatha Dé Danaan."

Finally, I looked up. Everyone was staring at me. Well, not really—many of the soldiers were too drunk to focus on anything. But Arthur's eyes were on me, and there was pride in his wide grin.

"Your son has the bardic gift, Lot Mac Conag. If he were mine, I'd be very proud."

And then, they applauded, everyone, the whole bloody room. I remember that sweet moment—the fire chuckling in the brick hearth, the shadows dancing across the tapestries, the satisfied dogs lounging in the dried rushes underfoot, Mother's gleaming eyes, and most of all, Arthur's approving pride. For once I felt fine and decent and part of something better than myself.

Lot, of course, simply had to break the mood. He'd listened sourly to Arthur's praise of me, his normally pale face red and crumpled-looking from too much drink. "You are too generous. The whelp does little that becomes a man, and that's the truth of it." He punctuated the statement with a loud burp.

For once, his sarcasm bounced clean off my shield of self-esteem. Arthur had been impressed, and that was enough. Mother gave her husband a look that would have knocked a raven off its roost at twenty paces and changed the subject.

"Tell me, brother, how are you finding kingship; is it a bore yet?"

Arthur had been giving Lot a rather cold stare of his own. Managing a polite smile, he turned back to his sister. "Ach, it's far from dull. When I was a soldier, I thought it would all be over once we beat the Saxons, that I could sit in my hall and grow fat, larky as that sounds. Then the man I'd never known was my father made his fateful deathbed revelation. For a while, it looked like every local king with half a cohort to his name might challenge my right to rule, and I'd be old and poxed and dying like Uther before I got it straightened out."

"What now, then? You've had six years of peace."

He looked thoughtful. "Has it been that long? Well, there's still much to be done. I'll die happy if I can just leave behind me a land ruled by the principles of Roman Law and Christian virtue."

Lot hiccuped explosively. "Come now, I thought it was Roman Law that nailed your Christian virtue to a fucking tree."

Suddenly, the room seemed very quiet. *This is it,* I thought; *Arthur will strike him now, or worse.* I'd had just enough wine to be pleased by the prospect. More than ever, if that was possible, I was glad that Lot was not my father.

Arthur's eyes were hard and cold as a frozen loch. "I'll ignore that, lord of Orkney. Some men are born fools; others need strong drink to bring it out."

Once again, Mother saved the situation. She clapped her hands for Cromach, who'd never been formally dismissed and had stood silently by all this time. Now, he began playing again. Arthur and Lot's eyes gradually unlocked while they listened to those soothing melodies. Skillful harpsong can do that to a Briton, and even drunk, Lot was too much a coward to meet Arthur's gaze for long. Arthur's men relaxed, their hands slipping from their hilts, and our own household guard seemed to breathe a sigh of collective relief, except for Beortric and several of his fellow Jutes, who looked sorry that violence was averted. I understand the Saxons think it bad manners to wear steel at the table; considering what could have happened, I can see why.

My memories of the rest of the feast are rather dim. Arthur reaffirmed his oath to hunt down Cado in the morning, to more boisterous hurrahs from his men. Lot glowered and grumbled and finally nodded off in his chair. Mother retired to her tower. As for myself, I sat and brooded on the morrow, half-dreaming of the heroism that I knew was to come. Finally, I paid my respects and trudged up to bed.

My bucktoothed kitchen wench awaited me, Moira's replacement whose name I cannot now recall. I'd never felt any particular passion for her, but she'd warmed my bed quite well enough since Cado's reign of terror had begun. Tonight, though, I wasn't in the mood.

"Go back downstairs," I said. "I have no need of you."

She looked down at her bare feet, her round face veiled by straw-colored hair. "The palace is full of Brits, tonight. Wild, uncouth men. I fear them."

I laughed at that. "Yes, so much baser than Lot's band of Irish reivers and exiled Northmen. Girl, Arthur is a Christian. Do you know what that means?"

She brushed hair out of her eyes and came and sat on the pallet beside me, although I had not bidden her do so. "Oh, aye, Fergus the kitchen steward is a Christian. Sometimes, when he thinks no one is looking, he prays to the Crucified God."

I was surprised. "That will get him flayed alive, if Mother ever finds out."

She nodded. "I don't think the High King would like that."

No, I imagined he wouldn't. Was it shame I suddenly felt, a sense of guilt at my mother's ways? I shook my head to clear it of such thoughts. "The point is, the High King also would take it badly if one of his men tried to stick his wick in you. Mum says Christians don't like it when people fuck. So go downstairs. You'll be quite safe." This was a gross overstatement on my part, of course. Arthur was Christian, though at the time I hardly knew what that meant, but he was also a practical ruler, for all his fervent prayers. Practical rulers don't make a fuss about their best men screwing other people's servants. Still, I wanted her out of my hair.

She rose, but just stood there, looking down at me. "He's why you're sending me away, isn't it?"

I just sat there, dimly irritated but too tired to kick her. "Who is?"

She was smiling, almost in triumph, as if she'd discovered something that gave her a power over me. "The Pendragon. You just said Christians don't like it when people fuck, except when they're married. You don't want to do it when he's here. It's like you're ashamed."

I grabbed a handful of her hair and pulled her face toward mine. "Listen, you stupid cow, you have no idea of what you're talking about. Now leave, and never come near me again."

Choking back tears, she fled the room. I almost called after her, but that would have proved her right, proved that I really was ashamed, and I wasn't, dammit. Instead, I blew out the candle and lay there in the darkness. Eventually, I was able to stop thinking about things and sleep.

I had the damnedest dream. I was standing below the crest of a steep hill, where a tall cross loomed against lowering emptiness. A corpse had been crucified there in the Roman fashion. It was the Christos, just like on the icons. Birds had been at his eyes, and he grinned without lips, or the slightest trace of humor, as if he knew he'd never rise, and didn't like the joke. I trudged closer, drawn by some vague impulse, until I was close enough to see that his ravaged face was Arthur's.

I awoke drenched in sweat and found it hard to sleep again.

Twelve

DESPITE MY ragged night, I managed to wake well before cockcrow. Rising, I splashed my face with cold water from the bedside bucket and donned fresh woolen tunic and breeches and a pair of otterskin boots. To this I added a leather jerkin sewn with protective bronze ringlets, a belted short sword, and a hooded cloak. Would this be enough? On a vague impulse, I also slung my bow and quiver over my shoulder, though I didn't expect to get much use of my skill at archery.

I knew my way about well enough to navigate the pitch-black upper landing and stairwell, but in the great hall I tripped over a sleeping boarhound. The brute gave a brief snarl, but then recognized me and began to wash my face with his huge, rough tongue. After I'd cuffed him on the snout a couple of times, he realized I didn't want to play and allowed me to get up. Not the most auspicious beginning for a heroic adventure.

More careful now, I picked my way through the maze of sleeping forms that lay snoring before the faint embers of the fire, and made it out into the courtyard without further incident. The yard was empty, with servants and livestock still huddled in the barn. My feet crunched on mud still frozen solid in the morning chill. Lowering my breeches so I could piss against the wall proved a bit unpleasant; it was the sort of morning when the air feels sharp enough to take your pecker off.

The dawn was close at hand, with sufficient light

leaking over the horizon for me to see what I was about. Hanging my quiver and bow from a peg on the side of the barn, I squared off in front of the wooden practice post that stood between the barracks and the stables, drew my sword, and began to hack away. Despite the cold and the fierce wind, I'd started to work up a sweat when I heard Arthur's voice behind me.

"Use the point as well as the edge; a good thrust can be worth a dozen cuts."

Like me, he'd dressed for travel in a fur-lined cloak and high boots. Instead of the iron-studded leather he'd worn yesterday, he was clad in a a thigh-length hauberk of inch-wide steel rings, each circlet tightly interlocked with four others. This was the sort of sophisticated modern gear that, along with the stirrup, had made his mounted troops the terror of the Saxon infantry. On his head sat a conical helmet with lacquered leather cheek guards and a metal flange that projected down over his nose. The sword at his side was longer and slimmer than the traditional spatha, and it had a sharpened point like a spearhead, as well as an efficient double edge. He also carried a sturdy iron-headed cavalry lance, and when he turned to survey the yard, I saw the whitewashed shield slung across his back. It was embossed with a crude painting of a woman in a shawl, with some sort of piss-colored hoop floating above her head. "Who is that?" I asked.

"The Holy Virgin Mary, Mother of Our Lord."

Ach, I thought, if his faith allowed virgins to be mothers, then why couldn't a man sire a son upon his own sister? Yes, as I've already said, despite my learning I knew as little of Roman mores as I did of Christian ones, and had no real idea how a man who juggled the spiritual heritages of the Caesars and the carpenter might feel about incest, despite my mother's vague warnings.

I turned my attention back to the post. "Practicing this early," he mused.

"Every day," I gasped between strokes. "Gawain won't be the only warrior in the family."

He leaned on his spear and watched me with a critical eye. "That's it, boyo, that's better. But remember, a swordsman should move like a dancer, not some clod-hopping farmer."

Exhausted, I sat on the cold ground. The post was notched and splintered, and my sword considerably blunted. Didn't matter; it was just a cheap practice weapon, not really fit for battle. Good swords were dear, and Lot had not been inclined to give me one.

"I've made a foolish oversight," Arthur was saying. "I didn't ask if anyone knew where Cado laired."

"I think I know," I panted. "A shepherd who came to us after Cado ate most of his sheep claimed the monster had made a den out of the old burial cairn of Maes Howe, down shore of the Loch of Harray. I can take you there."

He shook his head. "That's brave, but it's too dangerous for you to come along."

I'd expected this argument. "You'll need a guide," I reasoned. "Orkney seems small and bare, but a stranger can get lost for all of that. I know the way; I used to play there when I was little." Time for the baited hook. "Don't you want me to see the power of your god?"

He looked very grave. "Will this deed convince you of the correctness of my faith?"

No. My faith was in him, not his Christos, but I could hardly say that. "It would be something to watch," I said truthfully. "I'd very much like to see a miracle."

His frown finally worked itself into a grin, as I'd known it would. Even then I must have had some unconscious suspicion of just how vain he was of his faith, for all he tried not to show it.

"Saddle horses, then," he said, pointing toward the stable. While I did that, he walked around the great hall and soon returned with bread and smoked cheese from the low stone outbuilding that protected the main hall from fires by serving as the cookhouse. The sun was just peeking over the horizon when we rode across the plank bridge and skirted the nearby village's earth-and-timber palisade.

Beyond lay fallow fields strewn with dung and sea-weed, thatch-roofed stone cottages where the crofters were just rising for their daily toil, and low hills be-decked with grazing sheep and shaggy little cows. The latter shook their horns and ruminated drowsily in pastures protected by nothing more than low dikes of stone and turf, unlike the mainland, where cattle raids were common and one needed better fortification against the avarice of one's neighbors. Fortunately, Cado had not shown any inclination to take his meals from here. I'd have hated to see the reaction if King Lot had been forced to order his men to guard the royal herd.

Keeping in sight of the ocean, we rode between wind-shaped dunes and rolling peaty slopes carpeted with gorse and stubby grass. The rising sun shone on the breakers, golden for a while, then somewhat red past the tip of the headland. It was over six miles down the coast to the Bay of Skail; we soon passed all signs of human settlement. The tireless wind actually seemed fiercer as the morning warmed. My boots became itchy and un-comfortable, for they'd been fashioned with the fur inside for extra warmth, and not being able to scratch was a nuisance. For once I could smell no hint of rain; the great clouds tumbling across the sky were as white as new snow.

"Arthur," I said, breaking a long silence, "were you glad to find out that Uther was your father?"

He took no offense at what could have been an impertinent question. "Yes, though the old sinner wasn't the sort I might have chosen for my da. Still, I'd been conceived in wedlock, and knowing that took many years' weight off my mind."

To hear Lot, "conceived in wedlock" was not exactly accurate, but I wasn't about to mention that. "Why? Is that important to a Christian?"

"It is to this one. Bastardy is a stain that does not wash off easy. Being born in such a fashion only makes the struggle harder."

This was getting rather deep. "What struggle?"

"To keep some part of yourself pure. It's an unclean

world, Mordred. A man has to look beyond the muck he's born in."

I resisted the urge to swing Moira around and look hard into his eyes. "Are there worse stains than bastardy?"

"To be born with, you mean?"

I nodded.

He cleared his throat and spit. "Oh, aye, surely. One could be born of rape, or worse. But there's no profit in that line of thought. A man who's up to his waist in quicksand does himself no favors by considering the plight of another who's sunk up to his neck."

My head felt full of cobwebs from considering these matters. His "or worse" had sounded ominious indeed, but for now I lacked the resolve to press him for clarification. Instead, I took another approach. "But this sin you talk about isn't the child's fault, so why must it be a burden?"

He actually smiled, and my heart lifted to see it. "You dispute these matters well. I can't pretend I'm proud of all your mother must have taught you, but there's no faulting how you've learned to think. Unfortunately, thinking alone can't bring us to salvation."

I didn't particularly want to hear him expound on just what could, or on the nature of this salvation he spoke about so glibly, and my impatience joined with his smile to make me bold. "You're evading me, Uncle. Why is the child to blame?"

His smile became a grin, and I wondered how one could so easily shift between gloom and good-fellowship. "Ach, but you're a sharp one. I could explain myself better had you more theology, something which really must be remedied. One might as well say that none of us are to blame for Adam's sin, or Eve's either. Yet it weighs us all down, just the same. Some of us manage, through the grace of Our Savior and Our Lady, to throw off that weight when we die and thus rise up, light as air. But all are not so fortunate, and spend their lives falling into hell. Forgive me for such grim talk, but I sometimes feel like I'm treading water in heavy boots, and can't quite keep my head above the waves."

I didn't remark on the way he'd switched metaphors from the airy to the aquatic. "Is it always so hard for you?"

He was looking at the ocean, but his gaze seemed fixed on something else entirely. "Yes," he said at last. "Always."

"But sometimes more than others?"

He nodded.

"When was it hardest?"

My head may not have been the only one that felt full of cobwebs, for he shook his before speaking again. "After my first battle. A fog had rolled in, hiding the fighting. Men stumbled out of the mist waving red stumps, or trying to hold in their guts."

Gawain had never spoken of war in such a fashion. "But you won, didn't you?"

I'd never seen such distate on his face before, though I'd later see worse. "The first of many 'glorious victories.' I was green as a March apple, and could no more control my troops than I could command the sea. They burned three Saxon steadings with the men still in them, British slaves and all. The women they crucified upside down against a row of oak trees, after raping them half to death."

I didn't want to hear this, but he kept on. "There was a celebration at Colchester in honor of our triumph. Your parents were there, I think, but my rank was too low for me to sit at the royal table, and I did not meet them. I messed with the junior officers, got more drunk than I've ever been since, and committed all the standard soldier's sins. When I'd sobered up and decided I would live, I made a vow never again to become what I was that day."

I looked at him in puzzled silence, wondering if the bluff, good-humored warrior of the night before would soon be back. Mother was right enough to call him strange past understanding.

Later, we dismounted and devoured the bread and

cheese while taking shelter in one of the stone huts of Skara Brae, the remains of an old Pictish village half-buried in the sandy dunes beside the Bay of Skail. The meal done, Arthur stood beside his gelding and gazed inland, scanning the treeless horizon. Gesturing out at the rolling emptiness, he said "For all its smallness, none could accuse this island of being the most crowded kingdom in the world. Still, you could have a worse inheritance than this."

"Inheritance?"

"The time will come when you must take your father's place on the throne of Orkney."

"I don't know," I said doubtfully. "It's bound to go to Gawain. After all, he's older."

Arthur clapped me on the shoulder. "Not if I have anything to say about it. Your brother's a good man, and I love him dearly, but he doesn't have the makings of a king. All passion and no patience, that's Gawain. The Saxons will rise up again, and when they do I may be too old or too tied down by royal duties to lead the war host into battle. I'll need a good *Dux Bellorum*, and that's one office that will fit your brother like a glove. Lot will proclaim you heir, if he knows what's good for him, and that's the truth of it."

This bothered me, that he'd be judging us so coldly, sizing us up and getting ready to move us into place, like pieces on a board. Besides, the last thing I wanted to do was to remain here, king of the peaty wasteland.

"Maybe not. What if I weren't Lot's son?" I scanned Arthur's face for some hint of his feelings.

He frowned. "You might as well ask, what if Cerdic of the West Saxons became the Pope in Rome? 'What if' is a question that only serves us well when it concerns something we can change."

I mulled this over as we rode inland for the Loch of Harray. With some effort, I was able to turn my thoughts toward the upcoming battle with Cado. Arthur remained outwardly calm, but anticipation was a rat gnawing in my guts. Still, I wasn't worried, for I was confident I'd soon see a deed the like of which hadn't been seen since the days of Hercules himself.

At last, we spied Maes Howe. It was a huge green mound, over a hundred feet in diameter and high as a two-story dwelling. Here and there the great gray stones of the cairn's roof poked their way above their covering of grass and turf. I knew from my boyhood explorations there was an open passage on the other side of the barrow that led to an exposed chamber about fifteen or twenty feet square. If Cado was large as reputed, he obviously did not object to a cramped den. Of course, giants were probably used to things being too small for them.

Arthur reined in his horse at the edge of the broad but shallow ditch that surrounded the mound. "I assume this is it, then."

"Yes. The only entrance I know of is on the other side."

His eyes scanned the great mass of earth and rock. "Keep back. If anything happens, I want you to have time to escape."

Before I could protest that I'd not leave him, Cado walked around from behind the ancient pile.

We gasped in unison, me nearly shitting in my breeches, and Arthur's mount, certainly used to battle but apparently not to monsters, neighed and did a little sideways dance before he managed to control it. One couldn't blame his horse for being frightened. The giant was at least nine feet tall and tremendously broad, with oxlike shoulders and a barrel torso. In fact, he was so stumpy that if seen at a distance he could be mistaken for a dwarf. His filthy, mud-colored hair blended with his equally filthy beard and fell to his knees in matted waves. Woven into this tangled mess were the scalps and facial hair of his victims' severed heads, so that he wore over a dozen skin-covered skulls in a sort of ghastly robe. From this mass of snarled locks and grinning, eyeless faces protruded arms and legs like tree trunks, all brown and leathery and pockmarked with scrapes and scratches that had festered into scabby craters. Even at thirty paces his stench was awful, a uniquely nauseating blend of the smells of the sickroom, the privy, and the open grave. His appearance alone was so formidable that the weapon he held lightly in one gnarled hand, a twenty-foot spear with an arm-length bronze head, seemed virtually superfluous.

Ignoring me, he smiled at Arthur, and raised one spadelike hand in a parody of a formal greeting. "Ho, Centurion," he boomed in surprisingly pure Latin. "How goes the Empire?"

This was the real thing, with no safe gloss of legendary unreality. I found myself wanting to be hunting or fishing, snatching birds' eggs from the cliffs, thrusting away on top of Moira, or even suffering Lot's invective back at the palace, doing anything at all as long as I was doing it somewhere else. It was a shameful feeling, and I did my best to control it. At least Arthur was keeping his cool.

"No more Empire, Cado, not for years. And I'm no Centurion."

Cado squinted at him with red-rimmed eyes the size of goose eggs. "Yes, it's been a long time since I killed stragglers from the legions, and you're wearing different harness. I know as well as you do that the Empire is dead. And so are you, *Artorious Imperator*."

Arthur wasn't taken aback. "You know me, then. Good."

"Oh, I know you, Artorious. How could I not know the man whose soldiers hunted me like a hare across half of Britain. If not for the Mórrígán, you'd have caught me at last, there on the Pictish coast."

"That witch may have saved you then, Cado, but the chase is over now."

Cado ran a few paces forward and leapt nimbly across the broad ditch that surrounded the mound. Although his horse squealed and tried to rear, Arthur didn't even flinch. His only reaction was to lower his lance. "Get back, Mordred," he said softly. "I can't fight him if I'm worrying about you."

Cado paused, maybe sixty feet away, and actually sat on a granite outcropping, his enormous spear propped against one knee. I wasn't reassured; I'd just seen how quickly he could move.

"Witch?" snorted Cado, "The Mother of Ravens is more than just a witch, little man. Do you know, she's the only woman I've had whom I didn't take by force? She actually liked it when I spiked her. In gratitude, she sent me here, and said you would be coming after, and if I was patient, I'd have my chance to meet you without your warband to protect you. I owe her much for this."

Arthur stroked his gelding's neck, calming the beast. "She did not save you, Cado. It was God's plan that we should meet here; by destroying you, I shall bring salvation to these islands."

I was behind Arthur now, and couldn't see his face, but I was disturbed to hear the slightest trace of doubt in his voice. Perhaps he hadn't expected to find Cado such an articulate monster, or perhaps the reference to the Mórrigán unnerved him. Mother had spoken of her on more than one occasion, calling her something between a sorceress and a goddess. So that was the power she'd sensed guarding Cado, the one she couldn't match. Well, I was no longer the child who was once frightened to realize that there were those with greater powers than hers. As for Arthur, maybe he was not as secure in his faith as he'd hoped, and feared it might not be proof against those of the Otherworld.

"Be ready, monster," continued Arthur. "Your vile life is at an end."

"I do not think so, Artorious," said Cado. "She said she was sending me to a place where you'd come after me, with no one with you but your son. And she said that one of us would die, and that you would not kill me."

I was suddenly unable to breathe. *With no one with you but your son.* It was out now, as easily as that. Of course, there were more immediately important things to attend to.

Arthur laughed. "Mordred is not my son, Cado; the witch was wrong about that much. I don't know whether or not you have a soul, but if you do you'd better make your peace with God."

Cado's black-lipped mouth spread out in a face-splitting grin, exposing great square teeth that would have done justice to a plow horse. "Don't you know where giants come from? We're descended from the *nephilim*, the sons of the union between the *Elohim* and the daughters of Adam. I need no peace with any god; my blood is part divine."

Arthur's shield was unslung now, and his lance firmly couched under one arm. "Blasphemy, Cado? You might face your ending with better grace."

Cado growled, a low rumbling sound that made my mare even harder to control. "Tell me one thing. Why have you hounded me this far, even though I am no longer hunting in your lands? What am I to you, Artorious?"

"You know full well what you are," said Arthur grimly. "Your actions have made you an abomination in the eyes of the Lord."

Cado began to laugh, an earsplitting sound like a dozen asses braying all at once. "Oh, that's rich, little man. Don't you know your puking lord fathered all abomination? I see his world as it is, and act accordingly."

They were like that for a moment, a frozen tableau, and then Arthur spurred his gelding forward with what might have been a mumbled prayer and might have been a curse. The sun gleamed on his polished mail as he emerged from the shadow a wind-driven sweep of cloud. Lugh and Dagda, but he looked magnificent in that brief moment.

Coming to his feet with incongruous grace, Cado casually lifted his spear and thrust out with the blunt haft, driving it under Arthur's shield and catching him in the midriff before he was close enough to use his lance. Torn from the saddle, he seemed to sit suspended in the air for a brief eternity. As he crashed to the sward, his horse shied past Cado and went galloping away toward the distant loch.

Cado bent over Arthur, reversing his spear so its tip just touched Arthur's throat. My brain screamed for me to do something, but my body seemed to have no interest in responding. The combatants were frozen, and so was I, and I lost all sense of myself as my awareness shrank to encompass nothing but those two still figures.

At last, Cado spoke. "Now's the time to look me in the eye and say, kill me and be done with it. But you can't, can you?" He laughed even more loudly than before. "They all tell themselves it's victory or death, but in the end, they find those two alternatives not half as attractive as they thought." Saying this, he brushed his head-laden beard away from his crotch, exposing a prick like a gnarled brown root.

Arthur hadn't moved. I was suddenly abnormally aware of my physical sensations: the itchy fur inside my boots, the sting of the cold air on my raw nose, the spreading warmth at my crotch where I'd pissed my breeches, and the mad pounding of my heart. As if the emptying of my own bladder had been his cue, Cado brayed again and urinated on Arthur's prone form, the foul yellow spray gleaming in the fading sun. Arthur groaned and stirred, feebly attempting to cover himself with his shield, which caused the giant's sulphuric pee to splatter off the Virgin's face, smearing the crude paint. I knew that I must do something, and it seemed incredibly unfair for such responsibility to have fallen upon my puny shoulders.

Bless her contrary little heart, Moira had remained calmer than Arthur's spooked charger, and as I urged her forward with my knees, I unslung my bow and drew an arrow from my quiver. The trick was not to think about it, to act smoothly and mechanically. If I thought about it, I'd fumble. Cado was within range now. He looked up just as I pulled the string to my ear and let the arrow fly. Then the feathered shaft was sticking out of his left eye socket. I'd already drawn again, but all the instinctive skill had left me, and the shaft flew wild. Not that it mattered. My impossibly lucky first shot had done the job.

Cado stiffened and groaned. I could smell his bowels let go. He shivered all over, causing the heads in his hair to clack together like dry and hollow gourds. When he fell over backwards, it was like a tower going down.

Suddenly clumsy as a six-year-old, I half fell out of my saddle and ran to Arthur. "Don't be dead," I pleaded like a fool. "Please, Father, don't be dead." As soon as I'd said it, a part of my mind somehow untouched by panic marveled at how easy the word "father" had flown from my lips.

He groaned. "Too big. Sometimes evil's just too damn big. And I'm too old for this."

"Are you all right?"

He sat up painfully. "Rib's broken, I think, and I smell like a giant's chamber pot, but I can still stand." With my help, he did. "Where's my mount?"

I saw no sign of it. Surely, such a seasoned warhorse had not gone far, no matter how much Cado may have spooked it. I pointed to my mare. "Take Moira. I'll search for your gelding."

He clapped me on the shoulder. "You're a good lad. I was an arrogant fool today, and deserved this humiliation. I hope you can forgive me."

I didn't know what he meant. "Of course," I muttered, cupping my hands and helping him to the saddle. From this vantage point, he surveyed Cado's corpse.

"Like Daffyd and Goliath. The Lord works His will; I'm taught humility, and Cado is destroyed."

I looked him in the eye. "Are you saying your god guided my arrow?"

He shrugged. "Perhaps. Not that it takes any of the honor away from you. I'm very proud, Mordred. I pray that one day God will give me as fine a son as the one He gave to Lot. It makes me wish that what Cado claimed was true."

I'd been trying to find an opening all day. My heart was in my mouth; this was more frightening than confronting Cado. "Arthur, there is something you must know."

My tone must have warned him, for he looked at me very oddly. "And what would that be?"

No hope for a smooth tongue; I had to be blunt and open. "You're my father."

"What?"

"You're my father."

I knew it then; I'd blundered. His face wore no expression, but the words hung between us in the heavy air. I tried to laugh, but it was a forced, hollow sound. "I was just joking," I stammered, desperately trying to unsay my revelation. "I didn't mean . . ."

He reached out and gripped my shoulder. I could smell the giant's pee on him, worse than a stable full of goats. His clutch was firm, painful even, and his eyes as hard as Lot's. "You're lying now. I know that much. And Cado called you my son, too. How can that be true?"

I tried to pull away, but he held me fast. Now my terror was of him, of the man himself. This was a side of Arthur I hadn't seen.

"Please, it's all a mistake. I . . ."

He shook me. "What makes you think you are my son? Tell me now, the truth, and all of it."

I could no more refuse that command than I could up and fly away, though I would have been glad to do either. "Mother's familiar told me."

"A demon?" His face relaxed into simple disgust. "And you believed such a creature?"

"I asked Mother, and she said that it was true. Merlin said as much, too, when I came to Cornwall as a boy."

"Ach, Merlin, now there's a trustworthy source." He craned his head up as if to look at the sky, but his eyes were shut. "This is a trick of Satan, it must be, surely." He ran knotted fingers through his foul wet hair. "How? It's impossible. We never . . ." He broke off, then. Did he know, then? Could he have always known, somewhere deep inside?

"At Uther's court after your first battle," I said miserably, knowing this was no good, that I'd already lost him. "She came to your tent in disguise. Merlin helped with that."

The silence that followed that statement was cold and painful as the bitter wind. Arthur mumbled something, another prayer, most likely, and his expression was that of a man kicked by a horse. His hand slipped from my shoulder.

"It's sin," he said at length, his eyes not meeting mine. "It's mortal sin."

This was worse than I'd feared. Bloody gods, why couldn't I have kept my foolish mouth shut? "She didn't know that you were her brother. It's not her fault."

"No, for she's a pagan, and lost anyway. I'm the one to blame."

"It wasn't your fault either. It wasn't anybody's fault."

He shook his head sadly. "Ach, no, it's always someone's fault. Always." Straightening up, he reined the mare toward Cado's still form. "Perhaps you should have killed me, monster. You've stained more than just my shield and clothes." His shoulders slumped, and he looked so old as he sat there, swaying in the saddle. "But then I'd have died in ignorance, unshriven, with no chance at repentance. No wonder I lost today. My own sin rode beside me."

Something was in my hand, his neck cord with the piece of old wood that had supposedly come from his god's cross. I didn't remember picking it up, although I must have done when I helped him to his feet. The cord was broken and must have come free when he was unhorsed. I held it out to him.

He shook his bedraggled head. "No, I'm not worthy, not if it's real, and if it's not, which I now suspect to be true, it was all false vanity anyway. Not that there's any vanity that's not false. I went to battle with a piece of rotting wood at my neck and the fruit of my own sin looking on. My pride mocked Him whom I claimed to serve."

"Don't talk like that!" I shouted, suddenly angry as well as hurt.

He ignored my protest. "Come up behind me. I won't leave you here, no matter what you are."

No matter what you are. Words that have haunted half my life.

"Go on with you," I snapped. "I said I'd find your fucking horse."

He didn't visibly react to my profanity. He just sat there, slumped in his saddle, the wind tugging at his cloak, stinking, piss-plastered bangs falling across his brow. His eyes were focused in my direction, but it was as if he was looking through me at something else. At length, he spoke.

"All right, Mordred, suit yourself."

With that, he spurred the little mare into a gallop. I suppose, in that instant, I became the only thing he ever fled from; the distinction did not make me proud. I stood there, watching him ride away, while the wind whispered in the grass.

"Throw it all away, then," I shouted when he was well beyond hearing. "Damn you, Da, it wasn't my fault, either!"

I never did find his bloody horse. Not that I tried very hard.

Why did I tell him, when even the young fool I was might have guessed how he'd react? I don't know. It's all very well for Socrates to maunder on about how one must know one's self, but sometimes the water's so deep and murky you cannot see the bottom. Remember, the Mordred to whom this tale happened is long dead, and I can't really tell it with his voice or even see it with his eyes. Looking back, I know I didn't hate Arthur, not then, but the love was all dried up. I'd never asked to be made the symbol of his own imagined sin.

It was a long walk home. A storm rolled in from the ocean long before I reached my destination. The rain was curiously warm, as if like Cado, Arthur's god was pissing on his handiwork. Wrapped in my soggy cloak, I trudged back to Lot and Mother's world.

Thirteen

I SAT on the roof of Mother's squat tower and looked down at the crowd shivering in the cold courtyard below. Arthur was addressing everyone—his men, Lot's men, Lot himself, the household slaves, any villagers present—everybody. I was curious as to what he was going to say, but only in a cold, abstracted sort of way. It didn't matter. Nothing mattered.

The tower was less than forty feet high, but in my eyes they all seemed so distant and puny down there, like dolls, or figures on a chessboard, or ants. Yes, ants; that would be nice. I could step on ants.

Arthur spoke in a tired voice. "I wanted to talk to all of you before I left, to confess myself in front of God and everyone. I'd do it in Chapel, if Lot had one. He doesn't, so it's here then, on the cold dirt. That's fitting enough."

Posturing fool, I thought. *If I had a hair shirt, I'd give it to you as a going-away present. Grovel, then, you bastard. Lot and his men should find it very amusing.* Not that they seemed to be laughing.

"Cado's dead," he continued in the same dull voice. "You'll find his corpse down beside Maes Howe. I didn't kill him."

There was much mumbling at that. Arthur raised his hand for silence. Oh, he still knew how to command a crowd, even when full of agonized confession.

"Mordred slew the monster. Or his arrow did, guided by God."

Lot made a barking sound that might have been a laugh. "Mordred? I find that hard to credit."

Arthur looked at the ground. "Nevertheless, the boy's arrow brought the monster down, after I'd failed to do so." He said *the boy* like he'd said *Mordred,* as though it hurt him to make those sounds.

Some members of household and the palace guard seemed to be looking around for me, but no one looked up. Nobody knew I was up here. Since coming back, I'd done my best to avoid everyone.

"I was a fool to think I could bring anyone to the light," continued Arthur. Well, at least he'd said one wise thing. "I am too weighted down with sin. Fifteen years ago, I committed an act for which I'll be atoning all my life. At least God has allowed me some knowledge of how far I have to go. I might have stumbled blindly to the grave, unrepentant and unshriven."

Fuck you too, Arthur. Was he going to confess it all then, the truth of what he was to me, the truth of how he felt, right here in front of everyone? I found myself wishing Cado had killed him.

Arthur didn't say anything else for a few moments. Everyone stood there looking at him, looking uncomfortable. Except Lot, whose expression I couldn't read from where I sat.

"That's all, then," said Arthur finally. "I've nothing else to say, not until I can find a priest. Live your lives, come to God without me. He saved you from Cado, despite my sin. He can save you from yourselves, despite your own."

With that, he turned and trudged off toward the stable. His men followed, looking nonplussed.

I didn't know Mother was behind me until she reached out and touched my shoulder. I whirled around, my right hand a fist. "What do *you* want?"

"To be sure that you're all right," she said softly. "I had some business to attend to in my sanctum, and then I heard you sobbing above me."

I didn't know I'd been crying. I touched my face. Yes, it was wet. It was just the salt wind, I told myself. You could feel it sharp up here. "Oh, I'm fine, just bloody fine. Did you hear him? I killed Cado. Will I be a hero now?"

Then I was crying like a boy again, and she was holding me, very tightly. We held each other on the roof, while the sounds of Arthur's departure drifted up from below.

Later, after we'd stood there for a long time, her arms tight around me and wind rustling her hair about my face, I followed down the ladder that led back into her chamber. There was a sharp, pungent smell, and the air was heavy with a smoke that made my eyes sting. It seemed to emanate from the ceiling directly above her magic circle. I looked up, and saw a black smudge on the beams, a spot two or three feet in diameter where the timbers looked badly scorched. "What happened?" I asked, not really caring.

"Gloam outlived his usefulness," said Mother grimly.

I remembered the day she'd summoned him into being, and how simple things had seemed when I was young. Could I have conceived of such pain and bitterness then? Oh, if only I'd thrown myself wholeheartedly into her magic lessons, and not doomed myself with dreams of Arthur and British glory. I think that was the first "if only" of my life. I'm well stocked in them now.

I trudged to the stairs, Mother following. Our footsteps sounded very hollow on the stairwell. Everything would be hollow from now on, I told myself. Just empty echoes. We emerged from the tower to find the courtyard deserted. Or so it appeared to be, until Lot stepped out from the shadow of the cookhouse.

His face was paler than usual, all of its usual inflamed ruddiness bleached out. The emotion in his mackerel eyes was too cold for anger.

"I knew what he was talking about," he said, his voice like the hiss of the wind in dry gorse. "Everyone knew."

"I don't know what *you're* talking about," said Mother.

"Yes, you do. I've always known you cuckolded me to

get that brat, but I never knew who with. Until now. Bitch."

"Don't talk to her that way," I said, wishing I still had my bow.

Lot didn't even look at me. "Tell the brat to curb his tongue if he wants to keep it. I want him away from here."

"No," said Mother grimly, walking toward him. "It doesn't matter what you want. Mordred is a Prince of Orkney and will remain a Prince of Orkney. In a few months he'll be fifteen and can come or go as he pleases. For now, he stays."

"Don't give me orders," said Lot. "I'm not afraid of you."

Mother was almost upon him now, and sure enough, he shrank back. "Yes, you are," she continued. "You know you are. Do you think this a barren kingdom now? I can blight it. Do you think your life is cold and joyless now? I can blight *you*. You know better than to oppose me. Leave us, Lot. And when you see Mordred again, speak to him as a member of your household."

She stood so close he had to crane his head to lock eyes with her, something he wasn't able to do for very long. With a muffled curse, he turned away and went into the hall without looking back at us.

Mother gently caressed my cheek. "I used to think you didn't look like him. I was wrong."

Him meant Arthur, of course, someone I didn't want to think about ever again. "Lot will try to have me killed, won't he?"

She pulled me to her again, holding me tight, those long arms of hers strong with ropy muscles. I found it difficult to breathe, but I let her hold me. "No, sweet love, he won't hurt you, not ever. Not if he doesn't want a gut full of toads, and spider eggs hatching in his scrotum. The King knows better than to defy me on this. Just keep out of his way for a while, that's all. He's had to learn to deal with much disappointment in his life. An additional helping won't kill him, more's the pity."

And so we stood like that, her holding me, running her

hands down my back, her fingers through my hair. Her soft touch stirred memories of how she'd comforted me as a child, of that lost time when she had been my entire world, and I was suddenly conscious of the womanliness of her, of her warm, hard-muscled body pressing against mine. The sensation, while not entirely new, was not welcome, and the pleasure it brought me was the last thing I wanted now. "No!" I said, shaking off her embrace. "Leave me be!"

"Mordred, sweet love, it's all right," she said soothingly as she reached for my hand.

"No, it's not," I gasped, turning from her as the world seemed to spin vertiginously about me. "Nothing is all right!" All I knew was I had to get away, from her, from the palace, from everything. With a low choking sound I pulled my wrist from her tight grip and fled, her cries fading behind me, through the outer and inner courtyards, under the gatehouse, across the moat, and, stumbling but not stopping, my lungs battering the inside of my chest, toward the welcoming cold solitude of the inland hills.

Sometime later, when the dying sun was leaking redly over the low rise that hid the ocean from my view, I found myself leaning against an outcrop of tumbled limestone. Of how far I'd come, or how long I'd been running, I had no idea. I only knew that my sides ached and my legs were numb, and my breeches were torn at the knee where I'd stumbled against broken rocks. Tired and out of breath, I crouched there, hugging my sore knees, my back to the rough stone, until I got my wind back. My face was sticky with tears, but I didn't know how long I'd been crying, or if I'd stopped yet. "Fuck you, Arthur," I said in a hoarse whisper, "fuck you fuck you fuck you."

That coarse litany seemed to stoke the fires of my anger, and with rage came renewed strength. "That's right, fuck you! I hope you die!" I shouted as I stood up, and heard my voice echo across the low hills. "I hope your ship sinks, I hope the Saxons chop you up for dog meat, I hope you get the pox!" This outburst did not bring release, but a renewed frenzy. With a wordless wail, I turned toward the rock and tried to see Arthur's face in the minute cracks and gullies of its worn surface. "Fucker!" I shouted, punching the worn stone. "Fucker, fucker, fucker." Pain flared up in my hands, but turned to numbness as I continued punching, so I hit harder, desperate to bring the pain back, to feel something sharp and simple, a hurt that was of no one's making but my own. Finally I stopped, wondering if I'd managed to break my hands. I hadn't, but they were a mess, right enough. Even in the dying light, I could see the bloody knuckle prints I'd left on the folded limestone.

brought the hot, colored lamps, which I would not
would I ever showed them a first to get to it. He
felt as sharp, cold, and simple as of his own artist
"pretty" I answered him. Take the art better "No, it
dare I go?" He answered up to my handle. "I am
something of a dangerous painting, so I have been
to get to a place you must be at your own things just
that things. I have neglected of my own condition to
tell. Finally I stopped a moment. "I" she said it
been the man I am it; but they were a time that
know this he quietly felt; and I continued his place
until the point I reflect his pleased her more

The Storming Bone

More love a mother than a father shows,
He *thinks* this is his son; she only knows.

Menander, *Fabulae Incentae*

Fourteen

A WEEK has passed since I first began this testament. I've already gone through one roll of vellum, and the preceding passage seemed a good ending point for the first part of my history. The sun burns low on the horizon and shadows pool in the gaps between the bare Cambrian hills, but there's enough light yet that I don't need my lamp. It's calm now, but a few minutes ago a sudden thrust of wind went rattling through the nearby branches, and white blossoms fell like snow outside my window.

I'll not, I think, be showing this book to Gawain. Oh, as I'll soon reveal, he was not entirely blind to the unnatural intensity of the bond between Mother and me, but I don't think he'd appreciate having it brought up again. As for Guinevere, well, if she wheedles enough, and I'm in my cups, perhaps I'll let her read it. Nothing shocks Gwen very much, for all that she professes to be a Christian.

After that fateful day in Orkney, neither Arthur nor I could ever be the same, blighted as we were by the revealed truth. Something ended then, in that sudden passage into adulthood, a transition that saw the death of one Mordred and the birth of another, a *me* I hardly knew. Something else began as well, my awareness of the knotty convolutions of familial love. Yet as soon as I was aware of the complexity of my mother's feelings for me, I pushed that awareness away, at least for a time, and tried to accept the role of the dutiful son. Really, there was nothing else for me; neither Arthur nor Lot wanted me, and Mother had done a fine job of souring me on the rest of the world. All I could do was wait.

Orkney itself did not fare well during this time. Some dire malady beset our sheep and shaggy little cattle, leaving many dead and others gaunt and listless, with crusty scabs on their mouths and nostrils. A few mules and horses caught it, too, including tough little Moira, who fought the illness for twice as long as any other infected beast before succumbing, which would have broken my heart if it hadn't already seemed past mending. Our fowl proved immune, but there was little solace in that, especially when two bad harvests followed in a row. More than a few of our subjects pulled up stakes and headed for Ireland or Southern Britain, and two of our smaller islands became completely deserted. This did not please Lot, who decreed that anyone caught attempting to leave Orkney without his permission would be hanged, and their family's goods forfeit, but that did not stop the trickle of emigration.

Lot, needless to say, did not bear this with good grace. For the most part, he avoided taking it out on me, except on one occasion late in my bitter seventeenth year, when Orkney was feeling more like a prison than ever, yet the rest of the world seemed to offer nothing better.

I was in the courtyard, dully practicing my swordsmanship, hacking and hacking at the wooden post, soaked in sweat, not entirely sure why I kept on with such exercises, now that my dream of serving at Arthur's court was dead. Well, I told myself, the better my sword arm was, the more hope I had of traveling far in this world, maybe someplace away from Orkney and Britain both, and anyway, it gave me pleasure to cut the post, and imagine it was Arthur's neck. Yes, there was a time then, when I hated him with a raw, fierce hate, which eventually went away, just as my love had.

I heard a dry, hacking sound behind me, and turned,

to see Lot spitting into the dust. "Still want to be the little warrior, eh?"

For two years now he'd known that I was Arthur's son, and that mocking sentence contained more words than he'd directed my way in almost all of that time. I ignored him, and turned back to the post, just as happy to see his face in the wood.

"Don't turn your back on me," he said.

It wasn't a good idea, really, to bait him. Not these days, with him drinking so much, and so prone to rages he did not dare take out on his wife. I turned back, sword arm hanging heavily at my side. "Yes, what is it?"

"Address me as 'Your Highness.'"

Oh, wonderful, it was to be that sort of exchange of pleasantries. "Sorry, Your Highness," I said, putting as much venom into the words as I dared.

He smiled a thin-lipped smile, his face flushed above his tangled beard. "I ask you again: do you still want to be a warrior?"

What was he getting at? "Yes," I said, not sure it was true, but hoping a simple affirmative would shorten our conversation.

He beckoned with one gnarled hand. "Come with me, then."

I followed him out of the courtyard, wondering what was on his nasty mind. We trudged in silence through the gate in the inner palisade, and across the two-acre parade field, to the horseshoe-shaped, thatch-roofed soldiers' barracks. Men in woolen undertunics and leather gambesons lounged in the shadow of the turf-and-timber wall, swilling wine from clay cups and playing at dice. A small joint of unidentified meat roasted over a fire pit, which a swarthy, hook-nosed lout was feeding with lumps of peat and dried dung, a naked sword in one hand.

"Ho, Drustus!" said Lot, hawking more phlegm. "Run fetch Captain Beortric. I have a task for him."

With a regretful look at the sizzling meat, Drustus rose and trudged inside, his posture that of a man mentally cursing the task he's just been given. Sure enough, while he was gone, several of the men lounging against the wall shambled up and seized the spit, to bear their half-cooked prize away across the yard. Lot haughtily ignored this bit of larceny, and one of the thieves nodded his head as they passed us. From inside the barracks came muffled oaths, including colorful descriptions of Lot, which he affected not to hear. Finally, the summoned Beortric emerged into the cold sunlight, a big wide-faced man with thinning red hair and a graying beard, accompanied by Drustus, who seemed unsurprised to find his meal gone.

Beortric ambled toward us. Judging from his walk, he, like Lot, had been drinking. "Yes, Highness?"

Lot pointed at me. "Prince Mordred needs to practice his swordsmanship. Help him do so."

"How so, my lord?"

"Spar with him, dammit. Get a practice sword."

Beortric made no immediate move to do so, but just stared at me incuriously and ran one broad hand through his thinning hair. So this was Lot's game. He was in a sour mood, and in his cups, and desired to see me hurt. I could walk away, of course, but I wasn't sure that wouldn't give him greater pleasure, for then he could call me a coward, and would know I'd fled from whatever it was that he planned for me.

"Get a practice sword, dammit!" repeated Lot, his voice getting shrill. "Or use your real one."

With a look of unconcealed disgust, Beortric turned and hooked a thumb at Drustus, who disappeared back inside the barracks. He soon reappeared with two wooden swords, one of which he tossed to me. I dropped the iron weapon I'd been using on the post, and hefted the one of lead-weighted oak. It had been some time since I'd sparred with anyone from Lot's warband.

"We need shields," said Beortric. "And padded armor."

"No," said Lot sharply. "Are you afraid the boy will hurt you?"

"No, Highness," said Beortric, looking at me with no

discernible emotion. "I'm not afraid he'll hurt me. I just don't want to hurt him, is all."

Lot laughed like a crow mocking human mirth. "Don't worry about the Prince. He's a man now. He can take it. Can't you, Mordred?"

I smiled at him. "Oh, yes. Why don't you try me yourself, and see how much I can take?"

For a moment, he paled under the intensity of my stare, but then he laughed again. "I'm afraid not, Mordred. I'm old and out of breath, not proper sport for a young lad like yourself. No, you and Beortric will engage in a mock combat, and I will stand here and watch."

A crowd of dully curious warriors had come straggling out of the barracks, to lean against the wall or squat on the packed earth, watching us with no more emotion than their chief. A few years ago, many would have smiled at me, and cheered me on, or even wagered on my behalf. Now they just stared.

Best get it over with. I squared off with Beortric, wondering if he could stop me if I turned and ran at Lot. But no, that would give Lot the excuse he'd long craved, to exile me or have me killed, and while neither death nor exile really seemed that terrible, I wasn't about to give him the pleasure.

"Come on, Prince Mordred," said Beortric quietly. "Let's give the King his show."

"No talking!" barked Lot. "Just fight. Fight like it's real."

Suddenly, I welcomed the thought of pain, of hitting something, and being hit back. Snarling, I aimed a cut at Beortric, which he parried easily enough. He in turn swung at me, and I deflected his blow. We went on like that for a minute or more, our swords clacking together, circling and kicking up dust.

"Stop playing, Beortric!" snapped Lot. "Hit him. Hit him hard."

With the look of one bowing to the inevitable, Beortric cut viciously at my head. I parried, but just barely, and the shock numbed my arm.

"Faster!" urged Lot. "Let him feel what it's like. You're not doing him a favor by holding back."

To hell with this, I thought, feeling something of the same impatience. Lunging to stab at Beortric's knee, I caught him on the lower thigh instead, and he cursed and fell back, then launched an attack in earnest. I deflected the first couple of blows, but then one slipped under my wooden blade to catch me on the forearm, and my weapon dropped from numbed fingers.

"Pick it up," said Lot. The angry glint fading from Beortric's eye, he stood back and let me do so.

My arm was still numb, and I could barely clutch the sword. Not surprisingly, it flew from my hand at the first parry. The force of Beortric's swing brought his wooden blade down upon my bicep, and I cried out in pain. Beortric turned back toward Lot.

"I think he's had enough."

Lot's smile was very wide. "Oh, no, I don't think so. Pick it up again, Mordred. Use your left hand if you must."

This time I took a blow in the ribs and another on the head before I was disarmed. I sat there in the dust, holding my head and feeling blood trickle through my fingers.

"I'm sorry, lad," said Beortric under his breath.

"Get up, you whelp!" said Lot, laughing. "You can't sit down on the battlefield."

Enough of this. Oh, I didn't mind the pain; in fact, I'd inflicted worse on myself. It was Lot's jeering that brought the killing rage, the gloating pleasure he took in my humiliation. Not caring if it got me killed, I fumbled at my belt for my dagger, then rose with it in my hand. Beortric was between me and Lot, and I tried to step around him.

Lugh's balls, but he was fast. He chopped down hard on my wrist, and I dropped the knife, tears welling in my eyes no matter how I strove to hold them back. This time he followed through, jabbing me in the pit of the stomach, then bringing the flat of his blade down on my skull as I doubled over.

I lay there, curled up in the dirt, my stomach a knot of pain, and points of light dancing in my eyes. From a long way off, I heard Lot's voice, and Beortric's in reply.

"Imagine that. I believe the brat wanted to kill me, just now. What am I to do with him?"

"Nothing, Your Highness," said Beortric, just the hint of danger in his voice. "He was coming for me."

"Nonsense. He was trying to slip around you."

Beortric shook his head, his eyes full of warning. "I said he was coming for me. Just got a bit worked up, that's all. Isn't that right, men?"

Several dozen voices barked their assent. Sitting up, I looked around through my haze of pain. There were now over a hundred men on the practice field, and they were all gazing coldly at Lot. He visibly wilted under their scornful stare.

"All right then, if you say so. See that he gets cleaned up before he comes back to the palace." With that, he turned on his heel and strode away.

Beortric helped me to my feet. Someone brought me a cup of sour ale, but when I tried to swallow, it wouldn't stay down. That was okay, I could take pleasure in my pain. And in the fact that Lot had disgraced himself in front of his own men.

Beortric looked at me with impassive, wide-set blue eyes. "I am sorry, Prince Mordred," he said, his words slightly slurred by drink. Even after all these years in Lot's service, he spoke with harsh accent of the Northlands. I've never known what accident of fate led him to sell his services to Orkney rather than his Saxon cousins on the mainland.

"It's nothing," I said, spitting out ale and blood.

"I stood up to him and he backed down," continued Beortric. "I would have you remember that."

"Why?" I looked at him closely, perhaps for the first time ever. This was a man, I thought, not just a tool of Lot's. "Do you fear the Queen?"

He grimaced, as near as his face ever came to an expression. "Yes, I fear her, as any man not a fool would.

But that is not what I mean. Someday, I may ask you to remember what happened here."

We stared at each other for a long time. "I see," I said finally, not happy to have to consider such matters with an aching head.

"The King is my master, and I serve him," he continued tonelessly. "But I see the hatred between you and him. Perhaps he will kill you someday. Or perhaps you will kill him. Then you will be master here."

Lugh's balls, but I really didn't want to think of such things now, when I hurt so. Not that the thought of killing Lot wasn't pleasant. "Gawain will be master, not me."

Beortric shook his head. "Your brother is a fine warrior and a noble lord, but he will not be *my* master. Not while he serves Arthur. The Pendragon has killed too many of my people."

"I must consider this," I said, not sure what I felt, and less than grateful for the mention of my father, someone whom I tried very hard to avoid thinking about. "We will speak of this again."

As it happened, we never did, at least not while Lot was still alive.

That night, Mother noticed the scabby knot on my scalp. "What happened?" she asked, as she motioned for me to bend my head and let her wipe it with a damp rag.

"I got it sparring with Beortric," I said, not wishing to spare Lot her rage, but too proud to have my revenge through her.

"Beortric did this? I'll have him flogged."

"No," I replied, shaking off her ministrations. "You most certainly will not. I commanded him to lay on with all his strength, and that's what he did."

Her eyes were hard. "Was Lot any part of this?"

"It's not your concern. I don't need your help."

She followed me to the stairwell. "Mordred, don't treat me like this. Of course it's my concern." There was a quavering weakness in her voice, a hint of hurt. I was detecting more and more of that in her these days. The steely goddess of my boyhood was changing, becoming less than what she'd been, although physically, she looked no older. That can happen, I've discovered. People can just wear away, slowly losing the strongest parts of themselves.

"It's a bruise, that's all. I've gotten worse whacks from Gawain. Now leave me bloody well alone."

She caught my wrist, her arm as wiry strong as ever, and drew me back toward her. "Don't flee from me, Mordred. There's nothing for me here, except you. Please don't flee." Her voice was small and soft, but her grip remained hard. "You used to need me. When you were hurt, I'd hold you until you were better. Let me hold you now."

"Let go of me!"

Instead, she pulled me closer, and before I was realized what she was about, had planted a fierce kiss on my lips. I got my other hand between our foreheads and shoved her roughly away.

"No! I said I don't need you, and I meant it. Now stop it!"

She laughed, and let go of my wrist, which continued to ache from her fierce grip. "All right then, have it your way. Let Lot's bullyboys break your head. I don't care. I really don't."

I was already halfway down the stairs. "Fine. That's exactly what I want." Above me, she made a sound that might have been a sob, might have been choked laughter.

When did Mother start to change? I'm not sure. She'd always been strong and lucid, and then, quite suddenly, she wasn't. It was as if she woke up one day, mislaid something of herself, and never quite got it back. There was no dramatic impetus for the transformation, it just happened, and quite some time passed before I was even aware it had. Maybe it was because I'd been her whole life when I was younger, and now I'd reached my first manhood, but not the way she'd wanted me to, and there was nothing she could do about it. Maybe she'd just been too long in dreary Orkney, and part of her soul

had eroded in the wet, salty wind. It did not surprise
me, if only because nothing much did anymore. but it
pained me, to see my mother slowly diminished. *That*
surprised me, for I thought I was beyond pain. However,
I'm getting ahead of myself again. Things were not so
bad, yet.

I do not mean to exaggerate the extent of the change.
She was still a force to be reckoned with, most especially
by Lot. The morning after my fight with Beortric, Lot
was deathly ill and stayed in bed. When he appeared the
next day, he was noticeably pale and drawn, and moved
as if he was in pain. While passing me in the great hall,
he doubled over and vomited on the floor.

I felt no gratitude toward Mother for this, not even
any real pleasure in his agony. At least, I don't think I
did. Truth to tell, I'm not sure what I felt, for I have little
memory of this period in my life. Thinking back now,
it's all a routine blur, a time of numbness, and sup-
pressed feelings, and mundane toil. Lot and I generally
avoided each other, and on those occasions when I
found him glaring at me, I glared back, and before long
he'd look away. Life gradually gained a certain sem-
blance of normality, for although Mother's decline had
begun, it not yet taken the dramatic turn that was to
come later. I gave fitful if uninspired attention to her
lessons and managed to take some pleasure from
Gawain's visits, even though he usually came on royal
duties from Camelot, a place I no longer enjoyed hearing
about. My seventeenth birthday came and went, but my
brother never spoke of the fact that I was now more than
old enough to take a place at Arthur's court. It was
something we didn't discuss, a gaping hole we skirted in
our conversation.

Finally, three summers and an autumn after the death
of Cado and my love for Arthur, there occurred the next
important chapter in my story, one that ended in more
death. Rather than wasting time with the monotonous
events that led up to it, I'll begin *in medias res,* with
wind and rain and music from a bone.

Fifteen

I STARED out past the tower's crenellated edge, at the muddy courtyard and crumbling curtain wall, the squat hump of bare earth and rock that rose, then sloped down to the steeper slope of the cliff, and beyond that, the sea, all gray-green swells rolling up into ivory streaks of foam. There were no clouds in the iron sky, rusting now at its lower border, where the sun was corroding onto the waves. No wind, either.

I lifted the flute to my lips. It was not very impressive, just a hollow cylinder with two holes drilled near one end and runes scrawled across its lacquered surface. Actually, they only looked scrawled; I'd copied them very carefully from an old black stone in Mother's sanctum.

The bone the flute had been carved from was not immediately identifiable as human, but it was; a radius, to be precise. Two days before, it had been safely sheathed in the fat right arm of Wilf, a household slave who'd pilfered the larder once too often. It had taken me a long time to slice and boil and scrape the fleshy matter from his severed forearm, then whittle the bone down into its present shape.

Now, to see if it worked. I put it to my lips and blew, changing the sound by covering and uncovering the holes and worming my tongue into the hollow where marrow used to be. The notes came clear and muffled, dull and sharp, as I learned to shape them.

No wind started yet, but the stillness felt strained and transient, like a man holding his breath. I blew three sharp notes and three soft ones. They hung in the air, trilling echoes spreading out like ripples in a pool. Out past the sloughing waves, a spot appeared on the horizon, an ink drop in a puddle of spilled wine. It spread through the ruddy smear of the sunset, darkening the stain.

A mottled tern came wheeling up over the lee, coasting on the sudden gust that broke like a wave around the cliff's sheer face, Then I felt it too, gentler at my higher elevation, like a woman running her fingers through my hair. Salt stung my eyes, and I could smell all the miles of ocean that lay between me and the churning blackness where the sea rim met the sky.

"Careful," said Queen Morgawse as she joined me at the parapet's worn edge, the breeze pressing her red linen gown against her tall slim body and catching her unbound hair, spreading it like black wings around the olive triangle of her face. She reached out and plucked the bone flute from my hand. "A wrong note might summon more storm and sea than you'd easily put down again. Carelessness could make another Atlantis of your homeland."

Some homeland, I thought, turning toward the tower's leeward side and looking out across the peaty hills. Her patronizing tone irritated me; I wasn't a child, to be scolded against burning myself on the oven. "Jesus, Mother," I said in a voice of bruised innocence. "I'm not such a fool as that."

"Don't swear by the carpenter, Mordred. You're no Christian yet, I hope."

I was in no mood to argue theology. "Throwing his name about doesn't mean I worship him." Sitting on the crenel, I dangled my feet in empty air. "I don't worship much of anything, really. Except you and King Lot, of course."

"Don't bait me," she snapped, annoyed for once by my guying flattery. "You hated Lot even when you thought he was your father."

For no good reason, this was getting nasty. Good, I hadn't been in the mood for a magic lesson, anyway. "I loved him as much as you ever did," I said sweetly.

I might have regretted that remark if she hadn't pretended to ignore it. "You were pleased to worship something once, you know," she continued lightly. "It's a fine thing you weren't playing with storms then; when your worship stopped, you'd have gladly drowned all Orkney like a bag of unwanted kittens."

Mother had acquired some of her husband's bitterness over the years, and no small skill at salting old wounds. I didn't need to be reminded of what I'd once felt for Arthur, not by her.

"Playing, is it?" I said, drumming my heels against the tower face. "I'm only practicing what you taught me. And what you're talking about is over and done with, isn't it, so why don't you just bloody well leave off?"

Not looking at her, I wasn't conscious of the change until she walked up behind me and gently gripped my shoulders, then bent to kiss the nape of my neck. *Not this again,* I thought, my neck hairs bristling. Now that I was all grown-up, I reminded her too much of the one man she'd wanted and couldn't have, at least not more than once.

"Yes," she said, in the husky, yearning voice she was too wont to use on me these days. "It's long past. You're a man, now, and can be trusted with the art. And with much else, besides."

On the horizon, the storm I'd summoned was breaking up, the black clouds dissipating without my music to sustain them. Mother's fingers stroked the back of my neck. Even if I hadn't been pissed at the mention of Arthur, I would still have sought refuge in the continued fight.

"Oh, fine," I snapped, slipping from the crenel, shaking off her insistent hands, and stalking to the opposite parapet, to look again at the clean sea and feel its salt upon my face. "Toss me another bone; that one's gnawed clean. Magic's a game for women and disillusioned clerics. I can do well enough without it."

She seized me by the upper arm and turned me around with that damnable peasant strength of hers, waving the bone flute so close to my face I thought she'd rap my nose with it. "It's a game that can shape the world. Would you cast that aside?"

"Yes," I replied, emphasizing my point by taking the bone from her hand and tossing it over the tower's edge. "As readily as that. Soldiers shape the world, Mother. Poets and rhetoricians, too, sometimes. Alexander, Aristotle, Homer—they did well enough without your carrion music."

She briefly smiled—I think she was pleased that I could still throw her precious classicism back at her. Then came the stern, matronly look that sat so uneasily upon her earthy Breton face. "This is no age for rhetoricians or for poets, you know that. Soldiers, yes. The age breeds them the way dung breeds flies. Go to my brother and be one, then. He'd not refuse your service, no matter his protested shame."

She turned away, her anger mounting. "Right, then. Forget my 'toys,' leave me to this cold island and its colder lord. Gawain is Arthur's man already, never coming home except to collect the royal taxes. Now that he's got them, he'll be leaving again, tomorrow or the day after. Go back with him. Have your fine squadron of a hundred horse and forget about me. I'll languish here, a Queen of peat and driftwood, while my sons chop up Saxons for pious Arthur and his carpenter god. Go on with you, then. I don't care."

Oh, aye, I thought, as if Arthur would accept me, after having so rejected me three and a half years before. My guts felt all twisted up, and once again I almost hated her for having such a tight grip on my feelings and hated myself for allowing her to tear them this way. I started to accuse her of being maudlin, but my hand was reaching out, acting on its own, and she was hugging me, her arms locked tighter around my ribs than those of a drowning sailor clutching a floating spar. I steadied myself against her fierce, unexpected sobs and wondered what to say.

Sixteen

"**S**HE'S GETTING worse," I said as I cut low at Gawain's legs, a Jutish trick I'd learned from Beortric. He parried with difficulty, and the shock ran up my lead-weighted wooden practice sword. "Her moods vary by the minute," I continued when I'd caught my breath. "She sobs at trifles now."

Gawain spit in the cold dust of the inner courtyard and leaned on his oaken blade. He looked up at mother's slab-sided tower, almost as if he expected her to be watching from the roof. "Losing you isn't a trifle, boyo, and that's what she's scared of. Ignore her tears and get on with your life. It's all you can do."

Too tired to have another go at him, I dropped my sword and sat on the cold ground. "I wish I could. She changes so bloody fast, haughty one minute, weepy the next. I spend half my time wanting to put the boot to her, half feeling like a total shit for wanting to. We're not getting on at all."

I didn't tell him of how she sometimes touched me, or worse, of the feelings stirred in me by that touch. Despite his family background, Gawain was no one to understand how love gets twisted up.

My burly half brother pulled off his padded leather helmet and squatted beside me, shaking coppery bangs out of his deceptively mild brown eyes. There were lines around those eyes, I noticed. That shouldn't have been surprising, for I was two weeks short of eighteen and

Gawain was a decade older than I, making him closer to Arthur's age. Still, it was a shock to realize that my growing up meant my brother was getting old.

"It's not her that's the problem," he said, drawing idly in the dirt with the point of his wooden sword. "It's you. You need to leave this place. Come back to Camelot with me."

I looked at him as if he was mad. Was it something in the air today, that made the only two people I cared about suffer the delusion that I could possibly be welcome at Camelot? "Oh, aye, brother, I'm sure Arthur would greet me with open arms."

"Maybe not, but he'd have you. He's not the way he was when he first found out he was your father. I think the prospect of his upcoming marriage has changed him."

I tried to imagine what sort of woman Arthur could possibly be planning to marry. A pious little would-be nun, maybe, considering his obsession with expunging his past sins. "Oh, yes, marriage is a balm, isn't it? Think of Mother and King Lot."

Gawain rested his chin upon his dusty knees. "That's different. There was never any love there."

True enough. Not for the first time, I tried to picture Morgawse and Lot in bed together, performing the act they must have performed at a few times, only to recoil from the thought. "I hate him, you know."

Gawain looked at me hard. "Arthur?"

"No. There's nothing left for him. Lot. I hate the shriveled old turd. And he hates me. It's a miracle we haven't tried to kill each other in the past three years, since the whole bloody world found out just what Arthur and I am to each other. Even when I was a boy, I often wanted him dead. I'm sorry he's your father."

Gawain stood up. "Let's not talk family here." Shrugging off his padded leather gambeson, he clapped for a servant, who came trotting up with clean, white surtunics for us both. A red dragon wriggled across the front of Gawain's, the symbol of Arthur's united Britain. "Fetch horses," he commanded.

Later, we rode the broken strand beyond the lee, where our hooded otter fur cloaks barely protected us from the salt wind that knifed in across the breakers. Above us, the sheer black palisades of the cliff tumbled upward into a gray sky, all scudding pale cloud and paler, wheeling birds. Pulling ahead, I reined my brindle mare toward the base of the cliff, where a stack of storm-chiseled basalt was undergoing the centuries-long process of becoming a separate pinnacle of rock. A hundred feet above us, it was still attached to the bluff, but here, at sea level, there was a gap of at least a dozen yards between it and the cliff's face, forming a natural arch. This had been our secret place when we were boys.

"Don't hate Father," Gawain said as he joined me in the damp shade. "He's not a bad man, just full of disappointment."

"Full of more than that, I think," I said, relaxing in the saddle and removing my hood, for its inwardly turned fur was making my ears itch. "You don't live with the man."

"And you don't have to," he said, slipping fluidly from the saddle and standing beside his roan gelding, one hand on the uneasy horse's flank while the other caressed the huge column of glistening rock. "That doesn't change what I said. Orkney's to blame, not him. These islands were fine enough for our *Scotti* ancestors, kicked out of Ireland for robbing their neighbors instead of the Brits, but they're no place to build a kingdom. Our cattle die and more and more of our folk slip off to the mainland each year. By the time I'm into my patrimony, I'll be lord of a few hardy crofters and maybe a dozen sheep. Father had his chance for more, once, and lost it. Now Orkney dwindles, and him with it. Three years ago, his kingdom was at least populated and prosperous enough to withstand Cado's depredations. I doubt it could now. It's hard to be a good man when everything is slipping away."

"Including your son," I said with some of the same acid I'd used in arguing with Mother.

"I saw an out, and took it. You can, too. What's the

word—pragmatist? Be a pragmatist. It's the only way to live." There may have been a tinge of sorrow in his voice.

I didn't dismount, though my legs needed stretching. "Mother never had that choice."

Gawain looked at me, his face gone hard. "She made all her choices a long time ago. Now she's stuck with them. Leave her to her boredom and folly. It's not good for you to remain here, now that you're a man. She sees too much of Arthur in you."

I was glad of the dim light, for my face was burning. So simple, stout Gawain didn't understand such things? Well, I was younger then, and people could still surprise me. Suddenly, I needed sunlight and no one near me. Muttering something, I don't know what, I spurred my mare out onto the misty beach. Gawain followed on foot, shouting, but the wind caught his words and carried them away.

Seventeen

LATER, CALM and inside of myself again, I turned back toward the palace. The wind was even fiercer there as I rode over the plank bridge that spanned the great ditch and crossed under the stone-and-timber gatehouse, Lot's addition to the earthwork erected by his father. Dismounting, I let a serf take my horse and entered the inner courtyard, which was surrounded on three sides by the horseshoe-shaped great hall and on the forth by a timber palisade. Mother's tower, where she spent so much of her time these days, was joined to that palisade, but I was too close to that square, sandstone building to see if she was watching from its crenellated roof.

Someone shouted Gawain's name. I looked about, expecting to see him coming up behind me, but he wasn't there. Instead, I saw King Lot approaching from the opposite direction, striding bowleggedly through a flock of hooting geese, his purple robe hiked up almost to his knees in a vain attempt to keep its ermine trim free of the mud and shit of the courtyard. I wanted to laugh out loud at the sight of his sticklike calves and pale, scabby ankles, but the look in his eyes stopped me. Yes, he could rule me like that, with a frosty, fishy glance. I often meant to stare defiantly into his seemingly weak face, only to see the soft, pop-eyed cod mask slip away and reveal the hungry pike beneath.

His vision was not as sharp as it had once been. "Ach,

it's you," he said with bland distaste. "I took you for my son."

"I'm sorry to disappoint you," I said as coolly as I could. "Sometimes it seems my only talent."

He ignored the sarcasm. "Where's Gawain?"

"Out riding." I started to step past him.

"And my wife?"

Now why did he ask that? I shrugged and pointed at her tower. "Where she always is, I suppose."

"Yes, where she always is," he muttered. "I think it time I changed that. Go now and tell her there will be no supper there for her tonight. She must sit at table like a proper Queen." He swayed a bit, and I caught the ale on his breath. It was unusual for him to be drunk this early in the day, but not unheard of.

I bit back my anger at being asked to deliver messages like a servant. "What's the occasion?"

His look turned even more sour. "Gawain sails for Camelot tomorrow morning. It's bad enough he'll have half my treasury in his strongbox; I'll not have him telling his master Arthur that the royal house of Orkney is in disarray. Tonight, my wife will share my table and my bed."

I tried to keep my face calm, not pausing to wonder why I should have trouble doing so. Why was he demanding his conjugal rights now?

"What's the matter, is it Gertruda's time of the month to be bleeding?" Gertruda was the captured Saxon house servant who was his most frequent bedmate.

A flood of color rushed through the gullies of his face. "She died this morning," he said with unaccustomed softness.

Out riding, I hadn't heard the news. I didn't ask how it happened; slaves wore out all the time. "I'm sorry."

I must not have sounded it, for his face quickly hardened again. "I doubt that, but you would be wise to curb your insolence. I'm in no mood."

Any pity I might have felt didn't last long, and the contempt came slinking back in. "Of course, my lord. Anything you wish."

He still blocked my way. "These are hard times, Mordred. Hoofed plague rages among my livestock, driving my herders to the mainland. I've a mad and spiteful wife who'd think Byzantium too mean a kingdom, yet who prefers a cot in an empty tower to the royal bed and who once was randy enough to screw her own brother. My true son devotes his life to that pious usurper, coming home only to collect the imperial taxes. On top of this, I'm saddled with the upkeep of an incestuous bastard with an insolent mouth. This last problem would seem the easiest to solve."

He prodded my sternum with a grubby-nailed finger. "My own father would simply have had you killed. In these more civilized times, exile is still a happy possibility. So, rather than compounding my daily quota of irritation, why don't you go fetch your dear mother down to dinner?"

With that, he turned unsteadily upon his heel and stalked stiffly away. Honking, the flock of geese changed direction and flowed like a river about me, until a swayback dog chased a piglet through their ranks, scattering them. I stood there, hating him, hating myself, wondering why I hadn't provoked him further, as exile would certainly seem a welcome relief from this. Why did I feel so bound to Mother? The wind stirred about me, lifting dust and feathers, then settled, beaten back by a sudden soft drizzle of rain. Walking to the wall, I hit it, several times, hard enough to drive splinters into my bloody knuckles.

I wished I hadn't thrown the bone flute away, wished I had it with me now, so that I could scramble atop the wall and call the waves until they folded over the entire island and scoured it clean, bearing palace, people, and peaty hillsides all down to the cold bosom of the sea.

Eighteen

THE DRIED head of one of Lot's ancestors dangled on a leather cord from the ceiling of Mother's chamber, grinning and swaying in the bar of sunlight that shone in through the single narrow window. Every time I looked at it I could taste cedar oil, a memory of the time when I was five years old and Gawain had dared me to kiss its lipless mouth.

Mother reached out and gave it an idle spin. "If you were Lot's son, you could make strong magic with our smiling friend here, did you know that?" I did, of course, but didn't interrupt her pedantry. "The flesh and bone of one's own kin makes for powerful raw material, and there's plenty of it in the royal cairn. It's too bad I could never interest your brother in the art. What have you done to your hand?"

I was wrapping a strip of linen around my damaged knuckles. "Gawain caught me there with a practice sword." Better change the subject. "I just heard Gertruda died. Did you kill her?"

"What a tedious question." She sat on a three-legged stool and frowned. "That's not for what the draught was intended, no. It was that damned eternal sniffle of hers. You wouldn't expect a Northern girl to be so susceptible to head colds."

"Well, you ended her sneezing, but the other results aren't so happy. Lot now expects you to share his bed tonight."

She smiled absentmindedly, not at all the reaction I'd expected. "Perhaps I'll do that."

I felt obscurely disappointed. "He also requests your presence at dinner. Gawain is leaving in the morning, and Lot thinks we should appear a happy family."

She rose and stretched. "But of course. Now, whatever should I wear?" Unpinning her simple gray linen gown, she let it fall to her ankles and stepped out of it. Her breasts hardly sagged, though her stomach drooped slightly and bore the signs of childbirth. When she turned around I could see that her buttocks were still as firm and flat as a boy's. Coughing, I regained enough control to turn away.

"Now how can you help me find something to wear if you stand there staring at the wall," she said coyly. Cursing under my breath, I fled, leaving her with no audience but the dangling, grinning head.

Nineteen

I MET Gawain at the entrance to the great hall and drew him aside. "Look, I'm sorry I left you behind like that today. You were right. I can't stay here. I'll sail with you in the morning."

His gaze was unreadable, but his embrace seemed warm enough. "Lugh and Jesus be praised. You're well out of this, boyo. Think of the times we'll have together."

I nodded without enthusiasm. "Too bad we can't leave now. Be ready for a turbulent night. Gertruda's died, and now Lot's taken it into his head to want Mother in his bed again. She took the news incredibly well, but I doubt her humor will last."

He shrugged. "Then follow my lead and retire early. There's no need for us to be part of any unpleasantness. Shall we go in? It's cold here, and I'm hungry."

I doubt he found the supper very satisfactory, consisting as it did of seaweed boiled in milk, several salted dogfish, and a few scraps of mutton in jellied ham hocks. It was clear that the meal's niggardliness was intended as a statement, for Lot leaned back in his chair and grinned.

"I'm sorry that I cannot afford a more generous feast, Gawain. What with your uncle's gouging taxes, I'm lucky to be able to provide what you see before you."

Gawain looked embarrassed. I knew he disliked collecting Arthur's levies almost as much as Lot disliked

146

paying them, if that was possible. "Don't worry, Father," he said mildly. "I'm used to campaign rations, so this is luxury indeed."

But Lot was not in a conciliatory mood. "Nonsense. The Saxons have kept within their borders for the past ten years. You've been lounging at Camelot, where I hear Arthur's men live like Romans, stuffing themselves on snails, liquamen, and dormice. Tell me, has he installed a vomitorium yet, or do you just puke it all up in the corner before staggering back to the table to gorge yourselves some more?"

Gawain stiffened. "I don't have to listen to this."

Flickering light from the great hearth played across Lot's bald patch as he bent to pick up a joint of mutton he'd carelessly dropped on the floor. "Ach, but in your father's house you do. Isn't that right, Mordred?"

Mother's entrance prevented me from having to answer. For some reason, she'd decided to be resplendent in a blood-colored linen gown with an ornate collar of raven feathers.

"Ah, dear wife," said Lot. "I was afraid you would be unable to join us. Unfortunately, there's not much left. I was explaining to our son how your sanctimonious brother is depleting the royal treasury."

Ignoring him, she bent to kiss Gawain on the cheek, then me upon the mouth. Lot didn't seem to notice, but Gawain did.

"Hello, Mother," he said, giving her a hard look. "Sorry to be rude, but I must retire early. Father's spoiling for a fight, and I don't much fancy giving him one."

"Run along then, dear," she said as she sat down. "I'm sure the rest of us will do well enough without you. We can quarrel with the King by ourselves, can't we, Mordred?"

"He won't be doing it after tonight," said Gawain testily. "He's coming back to Camelot with me."

Mother didn't make a sound, just sat very straight and began to radiate a chill. I'm not speaking metaphorically; the air around her grew palpably colder. Well, at least this sorcerous hauteur was better than the weeping I'd seen earlier.

For his part, Lot only grunted and picked a piece of gristle from his beard. "And why shouldn't he, then? If my high-and-mighty brother-in-law can command the loyalty of my son, it's about time he commanded it of his own. May you both prosper in his service and rot in hell with him when the Saxons finally rise up to chop you down. The worms and ravens will be grateful, I'm quite sure."

Mother hissed like a snake, and her face went uncustomarily pale, but she still said nothing coherent, just sat there, radiating cold. Lot clapped for one of the serfs, a paunchy, balding lout with a rheumy eye and an old brand on his cheek.

"Ho, Ulrich, fetch out the heart-of-wine. Our dear little Mordred has finally decided to get up off his arse and go soldier with the Brits. Let's drink his health and wish him a glorious career."

Trying to avoid Mother's freezing face, I watched Gawain rise stiffly to his feet. "Forgive me for not staying for the toast, but I'm tired and want my bed."

Lot waved dismissively. "Away with you, then. But your brother must stay and drink. I want him to have pleasant memories of my table." He was clearly enjoying this, and it wasn't hard to figure out why. Anything that upset his wife was likely to please King Lot.

Gawain nodded meaningfully to me as he left. I would have liked to follow him, but somehow Mother's presence stopped me. As much as I did not want to remain there with her, I did not want to leave her alone with Lot, either.

Heart-of-wine is potent stuff, being the fiery liquid left unfrozen in a wine cask that's been buried in a snowdrift for a few days. Lot had already consumed a bucketful of barley ale. Before much longer, he was lolling in his chair, his mouth open and his sweaty red face looking as though it were about to collapse in upon itself at any minute, like a wet, ruddy, half-deflated bladder. Occasionally, he would stir, his head nodding forward and then snapping back with spastic regularity, like some sort of broken-necked doll.

I could no longer avoid Mother's gaze. The frozen mask had cracked and melted at some point, Now, her cheeks were flushed, and a tear trailed from the corner of one eye.

"I don't blame you for leaving," she said at last. "There's no home for you, here, is there?"

"Now, Mother, don't say that."

She shook her head. "It's true. I shouldn't cry. We lose things all our lives. This had to come."

I bowed my head. "I'm sorry."

She drained her cup and stared emotionlessly at her husband. "He can sleep here, I think. Will you help me up to bed, Mordred?"

"Your tower?" Obscurely, I hoped she'd chosen to defy Lot's wishes in that regard. After all, she'd done so often enough before.

She rose, a bit unsteadily, for she had drunk deep of the heart-of-wine, too. (Me, I'd barely touched it.) "No. I think I relish the chance to sleep in the royal bed alone. It is more comfortable than the cot in my tower. Will you help me on the stairs?"

I stood and trudged wearily to her. She gripped me about the waist and rested her head upon my shoulder. As I guided her toward the stairs, she began to whistle an old Breton cradlesong. It was dark on the upper landing, and no serfs appeared with burning tallow to light our way. She seemed to enjoy our stumbling passage, and she interrupted her whistling to giggle and press her self more tightly against me. I was tempted to shove her into the wall, but refrained.

Four candles blazed in the royal bedroom, burned down almost to their holders. Mother stepped away from me and stood in the center of the chamber, no longer swaying. She reached up and untied her hair, swept it forward over her face like a veil, then back again.

"Stay with me in these few hours before your departure, Mordred. There's not much night left, and I'm lonely."

I turned to go. "No, Mother, I can't do that. I'll say good-bye to you in the morning." I'd almost reached the door when a gust of air blew it shut. The candles did not gutter.

She reached out and took my forearms from behind, and I allowed myself to be turned around to face her again. "Remember how you lay with me, when you were small and sick with fever? I feel a fever now, and it's not of the body. Please lie with me again."

I looked at some point on the wall behind her, knowing better than to meet her eyes. "Don't think I don't know what you're asking of me. Stop it now. Just stop."

She reached out, took my chin, and tilted my head till my gaze met hers. "I'm going to die on this island, Mordred. You won't be coming back. Leave me with something, then. Some memory of you, and of your father. Don't deny me that." Then she kissed me. And I let her do it.

I was surprised when she stepped back, a cool Roman smile on the lips that had just touched mine. "See. That wasn't so bad. It's family tradition, after all. I couldn't have him more than once, but he gave me you. Do you hate him? What better way to strike back? At Lot, too, for that matter. Let's try it again."

With that, she unpinned the brooch that fastened her gown at the shoulder. It fell about her feet. Taking my hand, she drew me close again. I felt her nipples against my chest, even through the coarse weave of my tunic. When her teeth closed on my lower lip, I actually became aroused. At that, her tongue wormed its way into mouth and she gripped my buttocks and pulled me into a tighter embrace.

That was the worst of it, that I could feel my arousal, pressing against her through the skirt of my tunic. I think, I hope, I pray (but to whom?) that I would have shoved her away from me, just the same. Maybe. The choice wasn't mine to make, for the door flew open and Lot stepped into the room.

Their was spittle in his beard and his eyes were red and gummy, but his brain was awake and raging. In one hand, he held a long white object, twisty like a unicorn's horn. It was an old gift from some former Saxon ally, the tooth of a narwhal.

"Bitch. Whore. I'm going to kill you."

I'd stepped away from her, not heeding his threat, just wanting to be somewhere else. She faced him, her gown still gathered about her ankles, somehow regal despite her awkward nakedness.

"Go away, you paltry little man. Before I say a word that will enter your brain and burn there like a drop of molten lead. Go!"

She hissed the last word like an angry swan, and he did indeed step back, for he could never stand up to her when she was raging. She might have faced him down, but she made a crucial error. Rather than relying on her magic, or even her mere presence, she took a step toward him. Comically, horribly, her feet tangled in her gown and she stumbled to her knees. He laughed, a dry barking sound, and, taking two steps forward, struck her full in the face with the thick end of the narwhal staff.

Her head snapped back and her arms flailed the air and there was blood coming from her mouth. Jamming the tip of the staff into her midriff, he leaned into it, shoving her backwards as it went into her. Pinned against the floor with her heels beneath her backside, she flailed wildly and drummed her head against the boards. Then she was still and there was blood all over everything.

I'd stood there, paralyzed, watching it all, suddenly aware that my breeches were soiled. My mother had been murdered before my eyes, and my only reaction had been to piss myself.

Maybe before I die I'll do another thing that will shame me as much as that.

Pointlessly, now, the paralysis was gone, and I ran at him, screaming. He wasn't even able to bring up the staff; I smashed into him and we fell across her body and struggled there, both of us rolling about in her blood. My hands were about his throat when the palace guards pulled us apart.

Not much after that is clear. The room was full of guards and servants—I couldn't see Lot for the forest of pop-eyed, candlelit faces. Somewhere, though, I could hear him making hoarse rasping sounds that might have been words. I made for the noise, but Gawain stood in my way. I tried to push past him, only to find myself being half-dragged down the hallway, screaming, by my brother. His lips were moving, and though I couldn't hear anything, some part of me made out that he was saying "Jesus Jesus Jesus Jesus," over and over and over.

He practically threw me into my own room, shut the door behind us, and stood there with his back against it. I threw myself against him, but it was in vain, and at last I sank to my knees at his feet, sobbing.

"It's all right, boyo," he said tonelessly, stupidly, like a man dazed. "There's nothing we can do for her." Squatting clumsily beside me, he held me and we wept together. Sometime later, I remember us standing, facing each other, his face very white, with lines in it like gullies, making him look much older. "Tomorrow we'll be away from this," he kept saying.

I walked to the wall and hit it, hard, several times. He didn't try to stop me. The pain helped, but not enough. So I smashed my forehead against the plaster, with enough force that a chip cracked off to reveal the timber underneath. On my brow's third impact with the wall, my legs crumpled and I slid to the floor. I don't think I'd actually managed to stun myself, but I was all used up and could only swoon. After that, merciful nothing for a time.

Twenty

MAYBE NOT so merciful. In the blackness, I was aware of Mother beside me in my bed, bloody and naked and dead, whispering something in my ear. She whispered it over and over and over again. *Do this,* she said, *If you want to be rid of him and me.* The words were still echoing in my head when I woke up.

Sunlight came in through the window. There was a fresh bandage on my head, and someone had taken my bloody clothing away and wiped me clean. Lot was standing in the doorway, with Gawain between him and me.

At last, the King of Orkney spoke. I heard weariness and a hangover in his voice, but no real emotion.

"It's done with. She's in the cairn now, and there's no help for it. She was mad and now she's at peace. Hate me, if you like, for killing her. I don't care what you think."

I looked at him and didn't feel anything.

"Gawain will be taking you with him when he sails," he continued. "Avoid my sight until then." With that, he turned and left.

Gawain knelt beside me. "Look," he said, stumbling over his words. "I know it must be hard with you. Just remember, soon you'll be someplace away from here and clean."

I sat up, which hurt. He gently pushed me back. "There's something I must do before I go," I said.

"No." He said it softly, his face very close to mine. "Swear you won't. He'll have guards with him at all times until you're gone. If you try to kill him, you'll die. I've lost my mother, Mordred. I don't want to lose my brother, too."

"Bastard," I said. I meant him as much as Lot.

"Swear you won't." His grip on my forearm was painful.

"All right, I swear. Now let go of me."

He did. I shut my eyes. Eventually, he left, shutting the door behind him. I lay there for some time, sleeping and waking. Food was brought to me, and water. After a while, my head didn't hurt so much, and I could move with less difficulty.

Somewhere, I was almost grateful that Lot had killed her. Rage at him was a clean, cool thing, not like the feelings she'd stirred up. I immersed myself in it quietly, feeling it slip over me like the water at the bottom of a well. Gawain visited me to say that the ship would be sailing on the morrow, and to once again ask me not to do anything rash. I said nothing, and eventually he went away.

I'm not sure when it was that I decided what I was going to do. Maybe I'd known since I first awoke after Mother's death.

Twenty-one

THE SUN had set just beneath the lee and the air was full of chittering bats. I stood before the royal cairn, a high, steep-sided mound, overgrown with brown moss and roofed in peat, with stone slabs and heavy timbers projecting here and there like exposed ribs. A hundred yards or so behind me, I could hear the changing of the guard on the palace's landward palisade. If they saw me, no one hailed.

With a leather sack in one hand and an expensive wax candle in the other, I approached the mound. Gnarled faces leered at me from the driftwood posts erected in a circle around the mound. Stepping past those carved sentinels, I put down my burdens and crouched in front of the block of square red sandstone that effectively plugged the entrance.

Grunting with the strain, and splitting a seam in the crotch of my breeches, I finally managed to heave it aside. A dry, dead smell wafted up at me and by the light of the candle I could see a low passage slanting away into the darkness.

Picking up the candle and the sack, I crawled inside. The passage's floor was rough and wet and there was no room to stand erect. I was conscious of the great weight of stone and wood and earth above me, and my stomach clenched like a fist.

The interior of the cairn was a long chamber, perhaps fifty feet in length, at least thirty feet wide, and a good

eight feet high. Standing, I looked about. The stones
were roughly fitted and dripped moisture. Hoards of
spindly, pale crickets fled the candlelight, leaping and
skittering across the uneven floor. Slugs were everywhere, even gleaming like gelid stars from the dark
timbers above my head. Skulls grinned from shadowed
niches set halfway between the floor and dripping ceiling, while more complete remains were carefully laid out
on low slabs that lined the four walls like granite cots. All
except the nearest slab bore bare, desiccated bones and
strips of rotten cloth.

A blanket of fine white ermine covered her from foot
to chin. Small, round spiders and more crickets rustled
in the pale fur and crawled across her bloodless face, to
disappear in her still-luxurious hair. Her eyes already
seemed slightly sunken in her face and her lips were gray,
but she hadn't started to stink noticeably, not even when
I moved the blanket to uncover her right arm.

Gripping her hand, which felt like a glove filled with
cold lard and dry sticks, I took a heavy skinning knife
out of my sack and began to saw away at the crook of her
arm. Slicing through the muscles and tendons, I cut
around to the elbow. Then, putting the knife down, I
produced a small hatchet and chopped away at the
ligaments and bone until I was able to wrench the
forearm free.

More sawing and chopping removed the hand. Shoving the point of the knife into the exposed cross section
of the wrist, I slid the blade down between the ulna and
the radius, separating the two bones. This last took some
effort. I was soon drenched in sweat and gasping in the
musty air.

Still, I was able to make myself do a fairly complete
job of it, whittling most of the soapy flesh away from the
radius in long strips, before wrapping it in calfskin and
putting it back into the sack with the hatchet and the
skinning knife. Gingerly, I tucked the right hand, the
ulna, and the larger strips of sinew back under the con-
cealing blanket, doing my best not to look at her drawn,
dead face. Memorizing the location of the exit, I blew

out the candle and scrambled hurriedly back up into the outer air.

Later, in the top room of her tower, I boiled the remaining flesh away from the bone in a small kettle, carved off the knobby end joints, shoved out the remaining marrow, widened the hollow with an auger, and drilled the necessary holes. Further carving and then the lacquering took me late into the night. I welcomed the exhaustion, for it made it easier not to think.

Twenty-two

THE MONOLITH stood several leagues from the palace, a good hour's ride down the coast and then another twenty minutes' canter up the rising ground inland, not an easy trip in the predawn blackness; but now the sun was coming up, the first gleams highlighting the weathered slab against the brightening sky. There were no nearby traces of the Picts, or whatever other ancient people had reared it; the gorse and bracken-carpeted hills rolled away from me on all sides, bare of everything but clumps of bluebell and horned poppy and the occasional limestone outcropping. I'd come here often as a boy, to pretend I was lord of the peaty wasteland, the crown of the monolith the highest turret of my palace.

One side of the roughly squarish, ten-foot-high pillar of red sandstone had been sculpted into the crude likeness of a frowning visage, which nature had decorated with the scars of wind and rain and pockmarks of greenish lichen. An old, dead god of the harvest or the sea, maybe, though he faced the wrong direction for the latter.

Standing on tiptoe to grip the furrowed brow and using the open mouth for a foothold, I hauled myself atop the monolith and sat cross-legged on its rough, flat crown. Facing away from its stony inland gaze, I looked out toward the invisible ocean and untied the lambskin pouch that hung at my belt. When I gently emptied the bone flute out onto my lap, the fresh lacquer gleamed in the tentative sunlight, while the etched symbols seemed to crawl across its surface like a column of marching ants.

I ran my finger over the polished bone. It was so easy to think of it as something like porcelain or wood, something that had never been sheathed in soft flesh and smooth skin and delicate black hairs. *Damn you, you crazy bitch,* I thought, *that I should think of you this way after you are dead.* Lifting the bone flute to my mouth, I ran my lips across its smooth surface in something like a kiss, then blew into it, producing a single shrill note.

It was audible for a long time, and when it faded it seemed to take all other sounds with it—the rustle of the wind-stirred bracken, the cries of the stirring birds, the snorting of my tethered mare, the dull moan of the distant, unseen sea. No clouds rolled across the rising sun, but the clear brightness faded, giving way to the kind of daylight one sees through dirty glass. The air about me grew cold and heavy and very still, like the waters of a deep pond.

I blew again, repeatedly, varying the notes, building them, weaving them into a textured pattern. The tune was muffled and distant, something heard beyond the next hill or inside a seashell or at the bottom of a well.

Ripples spread through the pond that was the air around me, expanding outward, then crashing in upon themselves, reverberating, swirling into currents and crosscurrents. My mare raised her head and nickered and dug her hooves into the turf. The stubby grass began to bristle and hiss and whisper. With a suddenness that drove my breath back down into my chest, clouds erupted like boils upon the colorless ligament of the sky, coalescing patterns of scudding shadow across the far hillsides. A dozen yards away, a flock of rock pigeons exploded from the short heather and disappeared inland, fleeing the dark turbulence that came beating in from the direction of the sea. The first rumble of thunder was low and distant, but it echoed in the ground beneath my feet.

I stopped trying to form a tune and simply blew shrilly into the bone, but the notes continued, shaping and building upon themselves. Rearing, my horse tore free of the shrub to which I'd tethered her. She paced back and forth for a moment, almost as if she was dancing to the music, rolling her eyes and whinnying, then she wheeled and galloped for the crest of the rise behind me. I didn't even turn my head to watch her go.

The air was full of salt and I could hear the rising cacophony of surf upon the distant rocks. Night seemed to be lingering on the seaward horizon; the sky above the ridge was dark and heaving and folded in upon itself like tumbled layers of billowing wet black cloth. If it looked this bad from here, the view from the palace ramparts was sure to make the sentries piss their breeches. I hoped Lot was on the battlements or looking out a window, anyplace where he could see the approaching storm.

Bracing my feet against the wind, I stood, holding the flute high above my head. The air blew through it and it continued playing, a crazy wild music, fit for the Last Judgment or Ragnarok or the Hunt of the Hounds of Arawn. I shut my eyes and listened and felt the raw tension of the chaos straining to erupt around me.

Thunder crashed deafeningly close, and it was as if a bucket of water had been dashed in my face. There was no transition at all, no preliminary sprinkle; the rain was suddenly falling everywhere in great unbound sheaves, buffeting me, pressing my instantly sopping clothing against my body and threatening to rip my cloak from my back. As the wind increased, the water came sweeping along in near-vertical gusts, carrying with it clods of peat and loamy clay torn from the hills and ridges that lay between me and the surging, unseen ocean. Before I could be hurled off, I half slid, half fell down to the monolith's landward side, where I huddled in the new-made mud and pressed myself against its carved face.

The flute played on by itself, quivering in my clenched fist like a live thing. Impossibly, its tune remained audible above the din; indeed, I could feel it trilling in my bones. Having thought I was past feeling anything, I was surprised to find myself actually frightened of the fury rising about me, of the sheer magnitude of what I'd called up. I thought of great waves surging over the rocks at Brough's Head, of torrents of intermingled water, earth, and air smashing into the palace's frail stone, of the palace servants and the guards and of Gawain, all the people who did not deserve to be smashed or drowned. I'd called up a rage greater than my own, a fury that dwarfed mine and left me powerless to control it. Fear grew inside me, crowding out any catharsis. If the tempest kept on increasing in strength, it would indeed scour the island clean. For all that may have been my crazed intention, I now found myself somewhat unready for the reality.

Without thinking, I'd thrust the flute down into the soft mud between my knees, but its song continued, now apparently originating just above my head. I looked up at the carved face on the monolith. Its features, in the chaotic light, seemed to have sharpened, become more feminine, with Mother's high cheekbones and imperious brow. And its lips were pursed as if it was whistling.

Along with my unexpected fear, I also felt rage. How could she be dead, yet have more power over me than she'd possessed when alive? Would my heart always be so ruled by others? Without really understanding why, I lifted the flute from the mud and smashed it into the graven face, again and again, until I was pummeling the stone with a bloody fist full of shards of polished bone, some of which were driven deep into my palm. The pain felt good and I laughed silently into the howling storm.

The wind roared and beat against the monolith with enough force to make it rock and sway. There was one final crash of thunder, so loud I thought the sky was coming down, and then a silence so sudden and deep I was sure I was deaf, maybe even dead.

After a timeless interval, I rose unsteadily and looked about me. Bare earth showed through where grass and peat and heather had been torn from the battered hillsides, and for as far as I could see, the remaining vegetation was sodden and beaten flat. The sky was still black and low, but it was beginning to be pierced here and there by shafts of ruddy light. There was no trace of rain, and the silent wind was gentle as a caress.

Sometime later, I walked beside the sea, which rolled in upon the strand like a whipped dog creeping back into its kennel. The sand and shingle and even the cliffs were strewn with clumps of glistening weed, with driftwood and dead fish everywhere, while great rocks that had once lain beneath the swells were now scattered beyond the tide line like pebbles tossed by an idle child. I walked aimlessly to and fro and watched the waves and then walked some more, until I finally set my sopping, muddy feet in the direction of the palace.

Long before I got there, a dot rounded the bluff and swelled into an approaching rider. It was Gawain, astride a very nervous gelding. His wet hair hung in his eyes, his harness was in disarray, and his clothes were as soaked as mine, if not so filthy.

He reined in and looked at me. "You're alive, at least," he said with weary relief.

"I am," I answered, still not quite believing it.

"Father's dead."

Three syllables, spoken softly and without apparent emotion.

I did not, I think, feel joy, but something that had been wound very tight now loosened within me. *You got him,* I thought, *you got him after you were dead. Though you had to use me.*

I sat on a weedy rock and looked at my damaged hand. Eventually, the question came.

"How?"

Gawain shifted in his saddle but did not dismount. He didn't look at me, either, but out at the sullen waves. "He'd been drinking constantly, yet hadn't passed out or gone to bed. When he found out that it was time for me to sail and you were nowhere to be found, he started to go into a rage. Then the storm came."

He did look at me then, but I couldn't read his face.

Magic was the world I'd shared with Mother; would he acknowledge its existence?

No. "He began to rave. He said he could hear Mother in the storm, calling to him, mocking him. Everybody went down into the cellar, but not him. He ran out into the courtyard, shouting for her forgiveness. I followed, but got out just in time to see the Queen's tower come tumbling down on top of him. I doubt they've dug out him yet."

I patted his horse, trying to think of what to say. "You're King now."

He shook his head. "Not me. Not here. The Picts can have these islands again for all of me."

"Back to Camelot, then?" As if he'd ever really left.

"Yes. Maybe soon. If either the ship I came in or any of Lot's fleet survived the storm."

I found myself hoping at least one craft had. Someplace clean, and away from all this, he'd said. Good. Maybe Arthur had changed after all. Even if he hadn't, there was nowhere else to go.

We looked at each other. At length, he reached down and pulled me up behind him. There was nothing for it but to ride back, along the ravaged shore.

Twenty-three

NO SENTRIES hailed us from the gatehouse, which was missing its thatched roof. Mother's tower was now just a tumbled pile of sandstone slabs, covering most of the inner courtyard. The storm had collapsed two stables and torn the roof off the great hall. Broken timbers were everywhere, along with soggy thatching from the stables and gatehouse. Here and there water gleamed in dirty pools, and a few bedraggled dogs and chickens picked their way through the rubble. Most of the surviving household had fled inland, leaving fewer than a hundred soldiers and a handful of servants to give us a most-dispirited greeting.

Beortric met us in the yard, flanked by a dozen hard-faced men in mail. "Who's King now?" he asked, no particular deference in his voice.

"No one," said Gawain in an empty voice. "I do not want the office."

"We stayed on here," said Beortric. "When all was going bad, we stayed. We deserve something for our pains." There was a dangerous tone to his voice, and several of his men had a crazed glint in their eyes. Gawain and I exchanged a meaningful glance. The storm was over, but we could still die here, in its emotional aftermath.

Gawain's hand rested on his sword hilt. He looked very tired. "This is no day for dogs to come sniffing about, demanding scraps," he said. "Get out of our way."

"No," said Beortric. "You are not my lord. Your father was, but he's dead now."

I stepped between them, not caring if I got run through. "Enough," I said. "Beortric, you once asked me to remember how you defied Lot, when he gladly would have had you beat me to death with a wooden sword. Yes, you deserve something. Gawain, you said you would not be King here. Am I right?"

"Yes," said my brother, anger slipping off him like a cloak. "This is not my kingdom."

"Then it's mine," I said, sounding more decisive than I felt. "Beortric, I give it to you."

He laughed at that, the first laughter from him I'd ever heard. "I am King of ruins," he said.

"You have warriors," I continued, "whom you can command as you like. Those peasants who have stayed here are your subjects."

Beortric nodded gravely. Behind him, several of his men were smiling. "And what of Lot's treasure?" he asked softly.

"Yes, the treasury," said Gawain tonelessly. "Mordred, do you think we can find it, in all this mess?" That surprised me, that he'd acquiesce so readily, rather than fight. Well, the events of the past two days had been a shock to him, and he was too tired for nobility.

"Yes," I said. "If it's not buried too deep in rubble."

It took the rest of the afternoon, and the light was fading as the remnants of the once-proud warband of Orkney crowded round, to watch me open the stout, iron-banded chest. I palmed a handful of coins, then stood back. "The rest is yours," I said to Beortric. "And those of the warband who follow you. Found your own kingdom here, take service with the Picts, come to Camelot with Gawain and me. It doesn't matter. Orkney died with Lot Mac Conag, and you're welcome to pick the corpse."

"Not to Camelot," said Beortric grimly. "I will not serve the Pendragon."

I took my brother by the arm, and led him away through the bedraggled crowd. Behind us, Beortric's men actually managed a few whoops and cheers as they pawed their way through the contents of the chest.

"We should dig Father out from under that," he said dully as we passed the fallen tower.

Let it be his tomb, I thought. "It's getting dark," I said, "and besides, I don't think anyone would help us right now. Leave him be until tomorrow."

He looked guilty at thought of leaving Lot crushed under stone, but did not argue with me. "You shouldn't have given them that money," he said, pointing back at the rabble behind us.

"Oh, right. They'd have cut our throats, and taken it anyway."

Inside the bedraggled ruins of the hall, he gave a brief, halting speech to the remaining household, telling them that he and I were leaving as soon as Lot was properly buried, and the battered ship listing to one side out in the harbor was capable of making sail. Anyone who wished to return with us to Camelot was welcome, for we'd not be coming back. Anyone who remained behind could not be guaranteed protection from the Picts. "I have not become King upon my father's death," he said in a low, nearly inaudible voice. "There is no Kingdom of Orkney anymore. Beortric is master here." This news was greeted with dull silence.

Along with everyone else, he and I spent that night in one of the outer barracks, a low building whose thick limestone walls had survived the pounding storm, and which had kept its roof timbers and even most of its peat and thatch. Everything around me smelled like the sea, and much of the straw was damp, but we cleared a patch of the earth floor and, after scouring the ruins for dry wood, peat, and charcoal, actually got a fire burning there. Wrapped in our cloaks, we huddled in the smoky gloom, while the small blaze sputtered and popped and threw flickering shadows on the wall, and water dripped through the creaking rafters. Some of the soldiers had brought a wine cask up from the cellars of the ruined hall, and they proceeded to get quietly drunk. Neither Gawain nor I wanted any, but we did not try to stop them from drinking their fill. Using my arm for a pillow, I lay on my side and watched the flames.

Someone was calling my name from a long way off. The next thing I knew, I was standing outside, before the royal burial cairn. The sky over my head was clear and full of stars, with no sign of the previous rain, and the full moon shone down in patches of silvery light. Mother's head was protruding from the mound, as if she'd been planted upright in its loamy surface, and her hair, grown unnaturally long, was draped across its sides in shining ebony waves that reflected the moonlight like black water. She pursed her lips and whistled like the wind in the eaves, like my breath trilling in the bone I'd carved from her dead arm. "Mordred," she said in a low, echoing voice, playfully drawing out my name like a storyteller acting out the part of a ghost: "Mooorrdreed . . ."

"Shut up," I said, furious that she'd invade my dreams like this. "You're dead, so you can just bloody well leave me alone."

She pursed her dark, full lips and whistled again, and the wind sprang up, rustling through the heather and blowing her hair in waves about my feet. "No," she said, "we're not done with each other as easily as that. There's one thing you must do."

I fell to my knees, doubled over, and hid my face in her hair. "Mother, please, let go your hold on me. Let me live my life in peace."

"Ssssh," she trilled, "it's for your own good that I command you to do this thing. Do you think I'd ask you for a trifle, or anything for myself, now that I'm dead? No, all I ask of you is to do what's necessary."

"Necessary" was an ambiguous word, but there was no point in arguing. "And what is that?"

"You must take my head, preserve it in the proper manner, and carry it with you when you go to Britain. You will need its advice before Arthur's wedding day."

I was crying now, and my tears caused her hair to stick to my face as I straightened up. "Don't ask that of me. Can't you leave me alone, now that you and Lot are dead? Just leave me the fuck alone!"

She frowned, and her tresses hissed and coiled across the surface of the mound like angry serpents. "Don't use profanity, Mordred. You should show me proper respect, now that I'm in my grave. I tell you to do this thing because it's for your own good, and you will need to hear from my dead lips what only I can tell you. Cut off my head, pack it with salt and cedar oil, dry it over a smoky fire, and seal it within some small, strong container that will survive being carried in a ship's hold or on a bouncing cart. Then, when you are safe in Arthur's realm, and have found your place there, take out my head, and it shall speak to you. Do this thing, or I will come to you every night, every time you close your eyes. There will be no rest for you, this side of the grave or the other, unless you obey me in this. I'm sorry, but I say this because I love you."

Beaten, I could only bow my head. "All right, Mother. I will do what you ask."

She smiled, and white teeth gleamed in her dark face. "Good. I knew you could not deny me in the end. Now come here and give your mother a kiss."

I trudged forward, wanting to get it over with so I could wake up, and then maybe get back to sleep without her troubling my dreams. The mound was slick with her sleek hair, and I had to crawl up it on my hands and knees, grabbing fistfuls of her tresses for purchase, until my face was level with her own. I saw no corruption there; her eyes were as black and shining and her lips as full and wet as they'd been when she was alive, and even the few lines of age had vanished from her smooth olive skin. Locking my fingers behind her head, I pulled my mouth to hers.

I awoke then, tasting something I couldn't name, and sat up with a groan. "What's that?" said Gawain groggily, from where he lay nearby.

"Nothing," I said. "Just a bad dream." He didn't reply.

I sat there for a while, shivering, then finally made myself stand up. *Best get it over with,* I thought. I only hoped that, despite the palace's half-ruined state, I'd be able to find the salt and cedar oil I'd need.

GUINEVERE

Now Eros has shaken my thoughts,
Like a wind among highland oaks.

Sappho

Twenty-four

PERHAPS I won't be showing this to Gwen, at least not for many years. After all, I will soon come to the part of my story that deals with her, and I doubt she ever envisioned my history becoming *our* history, at least not in such an intimate manner. Maybe I'm too influenced by Catullus, with his unblushing desire to set down the most casual and undignified detail, his direct and confessional desire to grapple with every feeling of the moment. Such an approach is all right, she might say, for that least stately of poets, but an official history needs both distance and dignity. Screw that; I began this testament by renouncing schooled pomposity, for this is no chronicle of wars and grand achievements, but of smaller, more personal things. I do not believe in the Christian heaven, for all that death is quite obviously not the end (I've Mother's posthumous testimony for that). Whatever intangible part of Mordred survives the grave, I can't think that it will include all those mundane, earthy bits that make me so uniquely myself. Perhaps, with these words inscribed on vellum, some part of the Mordred that exists in this particular now will be preserved, when my body is dust and my spirit languishes in some unimaginable other place.

Once again, I find myself entangled in a preamble of excuses. Enough of that. I'll return, then, to where I left off last night, and my last few days in Orkney. Was I really going to Britain? *He'll not deny you,* Gawain had said of Arthur. *Yes,* I thought, *that's well enough for him to say, but what does he know?* He wasn't there on the rainy beach, with the mist rising from Cado's cooling corpse and Arthur's colder gaze looking past me at a lifetime of anguished penance. Did he really think that such an irrevocable moment in our lives didn't matter anymore? Of course it still mattered, but what other choice did I have? Was there any other place for me, in Britain or across the Channel? No, there'd be little enough harm in seeing what Arthur's new court of Camelot was like. Besides, I knew from my dream that Mother wanted me to go there, and I didn't relish having her disturb my sleep again.

We spent the next few days digging through wreckage, burying Lot, and salvaging a few palace goods. Beortric and his men also kept busy, building coracles on the beach, crude craft that would take them to the Caledonian mainland. During this time, the twelve-man crew of the broad little two-masted former corn ship that had been listing in the harbor managed to get their storm-tossed vessel into something approaching seaworthy condition, repairing her foresail and replanking her double hull with wood from the hall. This craft, which had brought Gawain here, was the only one to survive the storm, Lot's paltry fleet having been smashed to driftwood. Fortunately, the fact that it was too small for all of Beortric's men kept him from commandeering it (that and the fact that, despite his distaste for Arthur, he was likely loath to antagonize Arthur directly by taking something that was his). For myself, I took the necessary steps to preserve Mother's head, and got it sealed inside a clay pot that I then locked up in a small oakwood chest from Lot's private chamber.

Nine days after the storm that took Lot's life and made a waste of Orkney, Gawain and I sailed for Britain, along with a handful of dispirited servants, several of whom took sick and did not survive the journey.

It was a dreary trip and took several days, unlike the journey I'd made to Cornwall when I was a child and

Mother's magic had filled our sails, but at least it was an uneventful passage, as we threaded our way past Barra and Jura and Islay and the other western isles, down the Irish Sea, and along the British coast to the narrowing Severn Bay and the southwest tip of Gwent. Our ship had originally been built to carry grain to Gaul in exchange for armor and the big cavalry horses that had made Ambrosius triumphant and his brother Uther the first British High King. It was a broad, round vessel about fourteen meters in length, all of planked oak, with heavy ribs held in place by iron bolts, two sturdy hulls, an outward-leaning forepost, and a high stern with its post bent inward in the shape of a swan's neck. The stern had been built up into a deckhouse containing two cabins, one for the Captain and the other shared by high-ranking human cargo, in this case, Gawain and me. This was cramped, but dryer than the sloshing hold. At least thirty years old, maybe older, the vessel was still seaworthy, despite the beating it had taken from the storm I'd summoned with my carved bone. Maybe something of Mother had actually been part of the wind and the heaving sea, guiding their destructive fury, and that's why the ship was spared, either because she'd known I'd need it or simply because its crew were short, swarthy Bretons, and thus distantly her kin.

We anchored at Cardiff, where the ship was dry-docked for more permanent repair. Exhausted by the voyage, sunk in lethargy, most of the surviving household remained there, to seek what livelihood they could. That was something of a relief, as neither Gawain nor I needed a retinue, having brought so little with us, but we did choose two servants to carry our baggage, and Gawain had enough coins in his purse to purchase two horses and a sturdy if unprepossessing mule. After resting at an inn and recovering our land legs, we set off down the road to Camelot.

During our trip from Orkney, my eighteenth birthday came and went, an occasion neither Gawain nor I marked with comment or ceremony.

Twenty-five

"LUGH'S BALLS," I said when I got a good look at the procession blocking the road ahead of us. "What do they have in that bloody cage?"

"It's not a lion," growled Gawain, who I was pretty sure had never seen a lion in his life. He shook coppery bangs out of his eyes, and for the first time since Orkney there was a look of interest on his face. "The thing's as big as a goddamn ox. Come on, let's get a better look at it."

Spurring our mounts, we left our servants Coel and Fergus behind with the baggage mule and clattered down the Isca Road toward the object of our curiosity. Hearing hoofbeats on flagstone, a dozen footsore-looking warriors turned toward us with lowered spears, forming a defensive line between us and the huge wagon-mounted cage. "Stay back," snapped their apparent commander, a barrel-chested little rooster of a man in a short-sleeved blue tunic that exposed faded tattoos on his muscular forearms. "This is royal property!"

"And aren't we bloody royal, then?" said Gawain with deceptive cordiality. "I'm Gawain Mac Lot, Commander of the King's Horse, and this is my brother Mordred. Just who are you to be talking of royal anything, short-arse? I've not seen any of you lads at Camelot before."

Nodding his head in what might have been a bow, the little man leaned on his spear and tugged at his heavy mustache, one lard-stiffened end of which drooped from the afternoon heat. "Sorry, lord, I took you for common soldiers." Perhaps aware of the insult implicit in that explanation, he continued quickly on. "We're from Cornwall, bearing this gift from King Cador to the Pendragon, in honor of the upcoming nuptials."

"That's fine talk," said Gawain, sounding like his old self for the first time since we'd arrived in Britain, "but if you're Cornish, I'm a buggered saint. Your accent's of the North, as are your tattoos. Or has Cador adopted the markings of the Votadini?"

The little man grimaced, exposing yellow teeth in a gnarled walnut face. "The Lord Gawain is a sharp one. The name's Larcellos, and you're right, I was born the other side of the Wall."

I took my hand off my sword hilt, where it had been resting since Larcellos's first testy command. His eyes caught the movement, and his smile relaxed a bit. "So," I said, hooking my thumb in my belt just above my scabbard, "what brings you to Camelot? And why are you in the service of Cornwall?" Not that there was any mystery about the presence of North Britons in these parts; the South's success at checking the Saxon advance had proved a lure for all sorts of mercenaries, with some even coming from across the Channel.

Larcellos shrugged. "I'd say glory, but I'd be lying. I've knocked about most everywhere, from Strathclyde to the Summer Country, soldiering and trading. It was the latter brought me here. My great-grandfather, see, he was a beast catcher, importing bulls and Caledonian bears to the amphitheaters of the Southern towns. Well, I heard that folk down here are trying to be Roman again, so I thought I'd revive the family trade. Sure enough, Lord Cador paid me nicely for what I've got, and then hired me to haul it across the Severn Sea to Gwent, in honor of the High King becoming his son-in-law and all that." For a moment his squinty eyes had a dreamy look. "'Course, in the old days, I could have gotten a lot more. Caesar himself would have wanted to see this beauty in the arena. Would have paid dearly for it, too."

Gawain looked genuinely shocked, a rare condition

for a member of our family. "You mean Arthur's restored the fort's old amphitheater? He swore he never
would!"

Larcellos shrugged. "I wouldn't know about that, but
it don't matter much, 'cause Camelot's not our destination. We're going on past it, to the civilian amphitheater
at Caerwent. I know *it's* still operating, 'cause I sold 'em
a nice bear two summers ago. Just wait till the townsfolk
see what I've got for them this time; they'll probably
shit!"

Gawain laughed, a sound which I'd not heard in quite
a while, and which I wasn't sure I liked hearing now, still
so soon after our mother's death. He had become a
changed man since we set foot in Britain. "That they
will, but I'm still surprised Arthur approved such a
thing. Let's have a peek at your beastie."

Larcellos clapped his hands for his men. "It's all right
boys, these are the High King's nephews. Let them have
a good long look."

The soldiers parted to let us see what they guarded.
Mounted on a flat wagon and drawn by a quartet of
oxen, the cage was crudely fashioned but impressive for
its stout construction, being made of oak timbers thicker
than my thigh, joined with huge iron spikes and enough
dried strips of cow gut to have emptied the stomach
cavities of a small herd. If not for its occupant, it would
have seemed almost ridiculously sturdy.

The huge bobtailed cat that lay panting on its side
wasn't actually as big as an ox, but it was larger than
any bear I'd ever seen, with wide, splay feet the size of
cushions and a head bigger than that of a yearling calf.
Its shaggy brown-and-cream pelt was mottled with gray
stripes, rather like the pattern of an ordinary tabby, and
reddish pink skin was visible around its yellow eyes and
half-open mouth, making it look like it was wearing
rouge. That mouth did not need to be open for the beast
to display its upper canines; they were almost a foot
long, protruding well below the underslung lower jaw,
and flattened and recurved, with serrated edges, so that

they resembled nothing so much as a pair of carving knives, or even Eastern swords. Great black flies swarmed about its head, becoming especially visible when they crawled over the yellowed tusks. I nearly gagged from the odor of musk and ammonia.

Larcellos took his spear haft and poked the beast in its side. It rose with a low, coughing grunt, growling so deeply I felt the sound as much as heard it, and crouched there, snarling, the wagon creaking with its shifting weight, claws the size of Gawain's index finger extending from their pads and scraping the splintered wood. In some ways, it was built more like a bear than a cat, with short, thick legs, longer in the forequarters than in the rear, and massive humped shoulders. It had no mane, but a thick ruff that was tipped with silver, and the hand-sized tongue that lolled in its panting mouth was a dark, almost royal, purple. I estimated that it was at least nine feet long from the tip of its blue-black nose to its incongruous fluffy white tail, and if we'd been at the same level, its shoulders would have come up to my chest, if not higher.

"Bleeding Jesus," said Gawain, "what is it?"

Larcellos looked very proud of himself, and I could tell he was rehearsing in his mind for a grander audience than us. "In the North, they call the beast Palag Cat, like there's only one, and consider it a fabulous monster. Actually, it's no more fantastical than a badger, just rarer. There's a few here and there in the Caledonian hills, but not many. Never thought I'd catch one."

"How did you?" I asked, looking at him incredulously. He certainly didn't look like a Hercules.

He gave an "oh-it-was-nothing" shrug and grinned more broadly than ever. "I was lucky. A rockslide had trapped it in its cave. I cleared enough rocks that I could shove things inside, but it couldn't get out. When it was hungry enough to be weak, I gave it two cut-up horse haunches that I'd soaked in a cask of wine. By that time, I'd paid the Picts to build me a good stout cage, and when Pussy went to sleep, we dragged him out and shoved him inside. Thought I'd bust a gut doing it, let me tell you, and those Picts were so scared they were nearly pissing in their cowhide breeches."

By this time, the servants and baggage had caught up with us. "Saints preserve us," said Fergus, so startled that he actually crossed himself in my presence, something that would have gotten him whipped back in Orkney, when Mother was still alive. Coel was more phlegmatic. "That's the Palag Cat," he said as he tried to calm the mule. "Bad luck, keeping it in a cage."

"Shut up," I told him. "I'm sure we'll be seeing your monster again," said Gawain, unable to keep his eyes off the beast, which had lain back down on its side.

"Oh, yes," said Larcellos, "come to Caerwent in a week and you'll enjoy quite a show. Lord Rufficius, the town magister, has promised two dozen mastiffs from his private kennel. They're said to be unmatched in Britain for size and fierceness, but we'll see just how well they fare against my kitty. A good journey to you, my lords, and my regards to the High King."

"I don't envy the dogs," I said as we made our way past, for even with two servants on foot leading a well-laden mule, we were faster than the heavy cart, which tended to get bogged down where parts of the road had been dug up for masonry.

"Aye," said Gawain, "but you've not seen them. I was there two years ago, when they went up against the bear Larcellos spoke of. The bear didn't last very long; it only killed or crippled four dogs before they got its belly open."

I'd never seen a beast fight before, for in Orkney the best such sport we managed was with gamecocks. "I hadn't expected to find such civilized niceties here," I said sarcastically.

Gawain took my comment at face value. "Oh, yes. It's a pity Mum never saw what we've built here, with her love for Roman things."

I wondered what he'd say if he knew I'd brought our mother's head with us, preserved in a mixture of salt and cedar oil and sealed in a large clay pot. What was it she'd said in my dream? "You will need my advice again before your father's wedding day." Once again, I thought of Arthur. The memory of the way he'd turned from me in horror when he learned the truth did not hurt much anymore, not after all the more recent turmoil in my life. Nothing did, really. Still, I wondered what I would feel when I met him face-to-face.

Gawain interrupted my reverie. "There she is," he shouted. "Camelot!"

And that's when I first saw Arthur's famous fortress, on green-and-brown slopes that rose above the marshes of the looping Usk, framed by the darker green of the nearby hills, and beyond them, the ragged uplands of Northwest Gwent. The old Roman road ran straight to the southwest gate, so that the civilian settlement to the southeast, between the fortress proper and the river, was mostly out of view. Instead, our way led past squat limestone barracks and the ruined amphitheater, to the ancient ditch and earthworks that had been the primary defense of the original legion camp, and above them, the restored wall that formed the outer boundary of the oblong, fifty-acre enclosure. The eighteen-foot ramparts were much more impressive than the dry-stone-and-timber ones that had protected Lot's Orkney palace. This wall was all of carefully fitted masonry, with no wood visible, pointed with white mortar and picked out with lines of red paint, so spotless and unweathered it might have been built this morning, yet so strong one could imagine it standing for a thousand years. Even when I was boy, dreaming of the glory that Arthur was building in the South, I had not quite imagined this.

Gawain must have read the expression on my face, for he laughed, the second time I'd heard him do so since before Lot and Mother died. "Ach, but it's grand, isn't it? Admit it now, Arthur's made something that will last."

That did indeed appear to be the case. Camelot had been constructed from the old fort of Isca Silurum, which had stood deserted for almost two centuries, since Saxon raids had caused the Second Augustan Legion to be moved to Richboro. Surely even in the old days it had not looked so proud and strong as it did now, with the Red Dragon of Arthur's unified Britain unfurling from the rampart poles that had once flown the Augustan Capricorn.

Sentries on the turreted gatehouse recognized Gawain and waved us through, our footsteps and hoofbeats echoing for a moment in the cool darkness beneath the thick wall, before all sounds were swallowed up by the cacophony inside. Everywhere I heard the tramp of hobnailed boots on tile and cobblestone, the clatter of hooves and the creak of wagon wheels, the ring of hammers on anvils, and the thunk of wooden swords against practice posts, and over everything, all the mingled accents of Britain. The bustling lane ahead of us was paved and culverted, and ran straight through the center of the fortress, giving me my first view of the rectangular, four-story palace that loomed above the orderly grid of barracks, storehouses, workshops, and stables. Rising from the foundation of the old praetorium, its whitewashed walls gleamed in the sun, although not as much so as its gilded roof, and the afternoon light reflected off red-shuttered windows of opaque yellow glass. "Lugh and Jesus," I said, impressed despite myself.

"Smell," said Gawain, straighter now in the saddle and looking younger and less careworn. "Shut your eyes and just smell it all."

Puzzled, and feeling more than a little foolish, I did so. My nostrils detected sweat, burning wood and charcoal in the forges, roasting meat in the cookhouses against the wall, and the usual fragrance of straw and livestock in the stables, not to mention dung. Cocking an eyebrow at Gawain, I said as much.

"Oh, yes," he replied, smiling even more broadly now. "There's dung all right. But is it human dung?"

I smelled again. "Horse shit is all I can make out. What's your point?"

He laughed as he dismounted, and gestured at a low brick building in the southern corner of the wall. "Arthur brought in artisans from the Continent, a few years back. Not only did they repair the aqueduct, but its runoff actually flows through the old legion latrine, flushing all the waste away, so we don't have to make slaves regularly muck it out. Hell, it's even heated, just like the bathhouse and the palace. You'll appreciate that on a cold winter's night, let me tell you."

This, I had to allow, was indeed a wonder, and I was too awestruck to say much else. The sheer bustling crowdedness of the place impressed me as much as anything, for in Orkney the royal household had numbered about fifty, and even in prosperous days Lot's entire warband was less than three hundred strong. Here, according to Gawain, two thousand regular troops were billeted within the fortress proper, while an additional thousand barracked with their families outside the walls, and another three to four thousand men, women, and children occupied the civilian settlement that lined the road from the southeast gate to the riverbank. In the gridiron of narrow, intersecting streets, grizzled veterans with shorn locks and regulation harness rubbed shoulders with wild tribesmen in plaid trousers and gold neck torques, their lime-stiffened hair standing up in spiky quills. Larcellos's tattoos would not have marked him as a stranger here. Dark-haired, dark-eyed men of the Caledonian Border mingled with red-thatched Gaels and strapping, blue-eyed Gauls from across the Channel, and above them towered a few bigger, blonder Jutes, for like the legions of old, Arthur's Company incorporated the peoples it had conquered.

Then there were the buildings. We were still a good distance from the impressive architecture of the headquarters district, but the meanest smithy or workshop was of red brick or fitted limestone masonry, with a roof of tile or slate, so different from Orkney's peat roofs and rough, unmortared walls. Farther on, one entire block was taken up by a huge granary, a long, low structure that bristled with heavy buttresses, making it look like a giant stone caterpillar. Everywhere I looked I saw wonders, even at my very feet, for at each intersection with a side street, there was a stone-built drain leading to underground sewers. None of this was completely alien to me; Mother's library had been quite impressive, if only because no one else had wanted her uncle Ambrosius's books, and so I'd read thorough descriptions of such niceties, and even had some understanding of the craft with which they'd been fashioned. Reading about it, however, was different from actually seeing the reality, and for a moment my cares were forgotten, as I goggled like a farm boy seeing his first whore.

We headed down what had once been the Via Principalia, past parallel rows of barracks and stables, pausing at the final block while Gawain saw to the disposition of our servants and baggage. Coel and Fergus, looking quite cowed by all this, were left under the direction of one of Gawain's captains, a broken-nosed Dobuni who clapped my shoulder like I was a new recruit rather than his commander's brother, and promised to have our belongings safely put away. I didn't like the idea of leaving the amphora containing Mother's head in the hands of two servants and a stranger, but as I wished Gawain to remain ignorant of what it contained, I could make no valid objection. That done, he and I proceeded toward the palace.

In the center of the fortress, the Via Principalia formed a T-junction with the other main street, which ran from the headquarters block and out the southeast gate to the river. We turned the opposite way, past a row of guards in polished conical helmets and full ringmail, who saluted Gawain and allowed us into a paved courtyard with a colonnaded walk, open to the sky and lined with workshops and storerooms. These contained the palace armory and arsenal, for through the open doors I saw stacked spears and lances, piled shields, and rows of glinting mail coats. Opening off the far side of the cross hall were three smaller rooms, and Gawain pointed out the central one as having once served as the legion's Chapel of Standards. Now it appeared to be a chapel in the Christian sense, for on the raised dais formerly reserved for the marble likeness of the emperor was a well-carved but somewhat garishly painted statue of the Virgin, the black enamel outlining the wooden eyes making her look more like some soldier's doxy. Before we passed under the far colonnade, I paused and craned my neck to see the upper stories of the palace, an expanse of white limestone with the dragon banner unfurling above it, the clerestory windows yellow and glinting like the eyes of Larcellos's cat. Oh, I was educated enough to know there were far grander buildings in the world, but I hadn't seen any of them. Indeed, I still haven't.

Inside, the floor was made of slabs of blue-and-white concrete, a building material I'd never seen before, and inlaid with dark gray shale. The plastered walls were painted in bright greens and reds, with floral and architectural designs, and hung with rich tapestries—one depicting a beardless Christ with the Chi-Rho monogram in his halo—as well as a great bearskin. There was a hearth of purple sandstone at one end of the long central hall and a curving stairwell at the other. A burly black-bearded man in long-sleeved woolen tunic and a red cloak was seated in a wicker chair, writing by the yellow light from the translucent east window. The waxed slates on which he scribbled with a bronze pen were hinged face-to-face. Seeing us, he clapped them closed, tied them with a piece of string, and daubed the knot with a lump of soft clay, which he impressed with the seal from his heavy ring. Handing the document to an orderly, he rose and exchanged a brisk salute with my brother.

"Hello, Kay," said Gawain with easy familiarity. "Mordred, this is Lord Kay, Captain of the Palace. Kay, this is my brother Mordred."

Kay and I gave each other a nod that was not quite a bow. I vaguely remembered him from my childhood visit to Cornwall, and knew he was Arthur's foster brother. He took me in at a glance, his hard gray eyes giving nothing away, before turning back to Gawain.

"I'm glad you had a safe journey. How go things in Orkney?" Like many tough and dangerous men I've known, Kay had a soft, high voice.

Much of the carefree easiness drained from Gawain's face. "There is no Orkney anymore, Kay. My mother and father are dead, the palace is a ruin, and many of the islanders have returned to Britain or to Ireland, in the hope of better lives. I'm afraid the Pendragon has one less kingdom to oversee."

From Kay's expression, you might have thought Gawain was commenting on the weather. "A raid, I take it. Picts or Saxons?"

Gawain shook his head. "Neither. Orkney's been dying for decades, with declining crops, diseased livestock, and a dwindling population. We've all known that. The storm that killed King Lot and wrecked the palace just hastened things a bit."

"What happened to Queen Morgawse?" Kay's eyes still registered no emotion, and I knew he was coldly weighing this news. Damn it, I thought, the fall of the house of Orkney was not just another statistic in the governance of Britain. Except, of course, it was, and not a very important one at that.

Gawain looked down at the floor, his right fist clenched on his cloak. I couldn't see his face, but two veins stood out on the back of his hairy hand. "She died before my father," he said softly. "At his hand, it shames me to say. I only want to tell the story once, so I'd best save it for Arthur."

Was that a flicker of compassion in Kay's wintry eyes? "Of course, Gawain. I'm very sorry."

"They made their own ending," said Gawain, and I briefly despised him for the way his tone seemed to indict them both. "May they be happier wherever they are now. Later, maybe Bishop Gerontius can say a prayer for them, if he doesn't mind praying for heathens. Hell, I'm half-heathen myself." He wiped his eye with a corner of his dirty cloak. "Excuse me for rambling, Kay; it's been a long trip, and I'm tired. Where's Arthur?"

"Same as usual, out drilling the new men. He'll be back before sundown."

Gawain nodded. "Always the soldier. I'd go get drunk, if I didn't think it would offend him. I expect we'd best go see him."

"Your baggage is take care of, then?"

Gawain nodded. "Such as it is. We didn't bring much back with us. I'm afraid the Orkney treasury is pretty much lost. If we hadn't distributed it among the surviving members of Lot's warband, they would have cut our throats and taken it anyway."

Kay's expression did not change. "Regrettable, but I'm sure Arthur's main concern will be that you and your brother are safe." He clapped hands with Gawain, then nodded at me. "Welcome to Camelot, Lord Mordred. May your stay here be a pleasant one."

"It's more than a stay," I said truthfully. "I've nowhere else to go."

Twenty-six

T HE GURUS, or horse-training grounds, stood about a mile to the northwest, where the grassy downs leveled off for a bit before rising into bracken-carpeted hills. It was a great wooden ring, with a funneled entrance and double gates, fashioned so that sounds inside were amplified into booming echoes, thus accustoming both the horses and their riders to the din of battle. A new shipment of Gallic chargers was being broken in. Their whinnies reverberated within the enclosure, making conversation impossible, so Arthur accompanied us back outside, where he sat on his cloak in the shadow of the outer timbers and listened to Gawain's tale.

Some way off, a sergeant at arms was instructing new recruits in swordsmanship. Great oaken stakes had been set into the ground at regular intervals, and bare-chested men in woolen breeches attacked the stakes with wickerwork shields and wooden swords. "Heads!" barked the sergeant, and they cut high in unison. "Thighs!" he barked, and they cut lower. "Knees!" and they cut lower still. I pretended to watch the exercise, but my eyes were really on my father.

There was no fat on him yet; at thirty-four, he was still as trim as he'd been the day I first met him, when he was twenty-four and I was eight. There were more lines in his clean-shaven face, but not too many, and only a few streaks of gray in his close-cropped, sandy hair. The eyes under his high brow were clear and piercing; a deep, frosty blue, with just a glint of warmth. A thick, raised scar ran like a jagged lightning bolt under the hairs of his right forearm, a mark he'd not borne the last time I'd seen him, three and a half years before. Was it only that long since that day on the gray beach? I remembered my mare shifting nervously under his unfamiliar weight, the damp wind lifting his cloak like wings, his face pale and suddenly so much older, as he stared, not at me, but at something he'd done years before. Once again, that tired, toneless voice sounded in my head. *"Come up behind me. I'll not leave you here, no matter what you are."* Fuck you Arthur; I hadn't thought about that for a long time, and it stopped mattering to me well before I stopped thinking about it, but fuck you anyway.

He still didn't dress like a king, clad as he was in a patched leather gambeson, the sort worn beneath ringmail, now scuffed and blackened with the marks of that outer armor. The left knee was gone from his woolen breeches, and there was manure on his horsehide boots. He wore no rings, and his brooch was a simple bronze cross. The imperial sword of Maximus was scabbarded in dented brass and scuffed leather, with only the rubies in its hilt as evidence of his royal station. While he listened to Gawain's story, he managed to avoid looking at me. Instead, he rubbed the bridge of his beaky nose between a forefinger and a callused thumb, so that his hand partially covered his face.

Looking at him now, I could scarcely believe there'd been a time when I'd have crawled on my belly over sharpened caltrops to be here, to have been given a place at his glorious court, to have stood beside him at one of his storied battles, to have simply been allowed to bask in his bloody radiance. Oh, Arthur, how many years had it been since last I worshiped at that altar? The temple I built for you inside my heart fell into ruins long ago. All I feel now is an empty, distant nothing.

"I am sorry," he said when Gawain's tale was done. "Gerontius will say a mass for my sister."

"Oh, fine," I said, the first time I'd spoken since we

exchanged awkward greetings. "Be mournful now. What did you do for her when she was alive? If you'd made her welcome in Britain, she would not have gone slowly mad in Orkney. She would have been safe here."

There was nothing kingly about the look he gave me. "I am sorry, Mordred." His lips seemed to struggle to form my name. "I am sorry for what happened to your mother, and for the fact that this conversation should be our first words in such a long, long time. I understand your anger, but you know she would not have come here, even if I had asked her."

He was right, of course, but I took little comfort in that fact. "Yes, I suppose so. All right, then, have your bishop say his mass, if it will make you feel better."

"It's her soul I'm concerned about."

"Yes, I'm sure."

He sat cross-legged, elbows on knees, supporting his chin with a clenched fist. "You still sound bitter. Again, I don't blame you for it. I was wrong, that day in Orkney, to treat you like I did. The sin was mine alone. You had no part of it."

Sin, sin, sin, sin. Did that word resound forever in his head, a single syllable booming back and forth like echoes in the horse ring? Would he go to his grave weighed down by foolish guilt? Let him do so then, and be buried in a hair shirt. Over three years since I'd last heard him prattle on about his sin, I found myself still as heartily sick of it as if it had been yesterday. Still, I couldn't show him that. *He's not really your father,* I told myself, *not in his heart or in yours. But he is a king, one who rules over all the other kings of Britain, and you need his good regard.* I kept my voice calm. "Don't worry about it. It doesn't matter anymore."

He was silent for a moment, and when he spoke again, his voice was low and hoarse. "Gawain has served me well, Mordred. I hope you can, too. I once promised you a place here, when you grew up. Well, that time has come. Your are welcome to join your brother in my service." At last, he was looking me in the eye.

"Thank you, my lord." My voice, like his, was tone-ess. *That's it,* I thought, *he's giving me what was once my heart's desire.* Maybe that's the only way anyone ever attains it, years after they don't want it anymore.

Eager for some distraction from this tension, Gawain was looking past Arthur, at the dirt track that skirted the fortress, branching off from the Roman road a half mile before the southwest gate, then curving to rejoin it another half mile beyond the northeast one. I turned. A small procession laboriously made its way along that detour, kicking up a cloud of orange dust. Even at this distance, I recognized the cage and its escort.

"We passed them on the road," said Gawain to Arthur, who by now had noticed it too. "That cat's a frightful-looking piece of work. Are you really going to allow it to be baited at Caerwent?"

Arthur visibly relaxed, as if he welcomed the turn from personal matters to questions of royal policy. "Half of Gwent's heard about it by now, and I'd have a riot if I didn't. Ruling's a balancing act. Now that we're at peace, the local kings don't feel such a pressing need for my protection, and yearn for their old independence. Many of the men who serve under me are still heathens. I'm not fool enough to deny them their religion, or their entertainment."

I didn't like the way he equated the two. "There's nothing specifically pagan about a beast baiting. Christians do it all the time."

He nodded, grimacing with distaste. "Aye, and they carouse and whore, too, just as much as anybody else. Don't think I don't know that. But if I made a law of my morality, I'd become a tyrant in their eyes. My soldiers would desert me for laxer masters, and before you know it, all the kingdoms of Britain would be fighting among themselves again. Wouldn't the Saxons just love that." He crossed himself. "That's why I let Rufficius run things at Caerwent his way, for the most part, although my close presence here keeps his excesses in check. I say confession for my laxity, and Bishop Gerontius absolves me, and tells me not to let it trouble my conscience; but I fear he flatters me out of undue respect for the throne. In that, he's mistaken. I don't want flattery, or groveling obeisance."

He spoke the truth; I'll grant him that. Few rulers would have tolerated the tone I'd taken with him earlier. Not that it made me like him any the more.

We all rose, and Gawain and I bowed, me more awkwardly than he. I knew, somehow, that if I had not been here, there would have been no bowing; Arthur and my brother would have parted company with clapped hands, or perhaps a hearty embrace. My presence changed that, making things cold and formal.

Arthur returned to the echoing horse ring, while Gawain and I trudged back to the fortress. "Let's go to the baths," he said. "It's been a long time since I've been clean."

Words that could have been spoken by Arthur, I thought, though he would not have been talking about physical cleanliness. For myself, I didn't care about dirt, either material or spiritual. Gawain, however, insisted that the bath would be invigorating, relaxing muscles fatigued by our long journey. Saying that, he kept studying my face, and I knew he was wondering what I was feeling, having just seen Arthur. If he had asked me, and I'd been inclined to honesty, I would have said I felt relief, just relief, that it was over with, quickly and painlessly, with no attempt at a grand reconciliation. He had not embraced me and called me son, nor had I wanted him to do so. Love's a cold, mean thing that leaves little behind when it goes away.

The baths were on the opposite side of the fortress, standing just outside the southeast gate. It was ironic, I thought. With her delusions of Roman grandeur, Mother would have given anything to have had a working bathhouse in Orkney. Now that she was actually near one, she was just a pickled head in a clay jar, and incapable of enjoying it. I laughed.

Gawain looked at me, as we stood in the courtyard outside the changing room, while a dozen or so men in loincloths exercised with lead weights in the fading sunlight, and four officers in scuffed leather undertunics

:ossed a ball in the shadow of the sandstone arch. "It's good to hear you laugh again, boyo. Maybe you can be happy here."

A fat merchant trotted past with a basket of sausages, followed by a young boy, his son from the looks of it, who stumbled under the weight of a tarred goatskin full of wine. Men came padding out of the baths to buy their wares, sharing the wine in red clay cups and making lewd gestures with the sausages. Thinking of what Catullus had written about the panderers who worked the Roman bathhouses, I asked Gawain if the merchant ever sold the boy's favors as well.

Gawain snorted. "He would if he could get away with it, I'm sure, but he knows Arthur would string him from the wall. Eight miles away in Caerwent is a different story, but here Arthur keeps things pretty strict. He does allow a few whores to set up shop between here and the river, but that's because he's no fool, for all his godly ways. Like he said, he knows he can't make saints of his soldiers. Better they should damn themselves by paying for it than he should have to hang them for rape."

Inside, there were geometric mosaics on the floor, and marble steps leading down to a marble-lined pool of waist-deep water. We stripped, an uncomfortable action for me, who was used to washing privately in a wooden tub, when I washed at all. Our bundled cloaks, woolen tunics and breeches, linen shirts, and doeskin boots all went into niches in the wall.

"Lugh and Jesus," I said, seeing my brother naked for the first time I could remember. "You're all hair and scars."

He had already splashed his way to the middle of the pool. "I was born with the hair. The other came later. No matter how good you are, a few cuts and thrusts get through. That's why we call them the soldier's tattoos. Your skin won't stay unmarked for long, so you'd best impress the ladies while you can."

I lowered myself into the water, which was cold enough to make my balls draw up. "Ach, that smarts. Speaking of ladies, what do you know about Arthur's wife-to-be?" I asked, more out of idle conversation than genuine curiosity. I didn't give a shit who became my father's queen.

He actually got all dreamy-eyed, which surprised me, as I'd figured any woman Arthur would marry would be some prim little female anchorite. "Guinevere now, she's a fine one, with flame red hair and milk white skin, and eyes to die for. She's smart, too. Almost as overeducated as you are. I think you'll like her."

"Oh, yes," I said, barely blunting my sarcasm, "I'm sure we'll be great friends."

Our cold plunge done, we clambered out, and followed the tile pathway to the tepid room, where we splashed about in another pool, this one of lukewarm water. After that, we stretched out on wooden benches while attendants rubbed us down with oil. At first I was repulsed by the sensation of having strange men touch me, but under their practiced hands the tension slowly left my shoulders and lower back. When the massage was done, we were given wooden sandals. "What are these for?" I asked.

"The hot room is next," answered Gawain. "It's directly over the furnace, and the floor would burn our feet if we didn't wear them."

The hot room was indeed hot, and so full of steam I could barely see. We sat on benches while it roiled around us, and I felt like I was being cooked. Squinting at the floor, I tried to make out the checkerboard mosaic, imagining the brick-walled tunnels that lay beneath it, where cursing servants stoked wood or charcoal fires under copper boilers, and soft lead pipes twisted everywhere like the tentacles of an octopus. "Lugh's balls," I said. "I'm sweating like a pig."

"That's the idea," coughed the dim form beside me. "It unclogs the pores."

Maybe so, but I was only too glad when it was time to grope our way back to the tepid room, our sandals clacking on the hot tiles. There we lay down again while the attendants scraped us head to foot with blunt iron hooks called strigils, and gave us each a cup of resinated wine. Thus fortified, we plunged our raw bodies back into the cold bath before donning our clothes.

As we left, two drunken soldiers came stumbling in, their arms around a short, buxom woman with crossed eyes and a gap-toothed grin. "Oh shit," said one. "It's Lord Gawain."

Gawain made a clucking sound. "Now, lads, you know how the Pendragon feels about mixed bathing."

"Sorry, sir, we didn't know you were back," said the unsteadier of the two, a broad-shouldered, bowlegged ruffian with a dirty patch over his left eye. "Anyway, Megra here's a whore. It's not like we're going to corrupt her morals."

"Or she ours," snickered his smaller friend.

"Right," said Gawain, not sounding all that disapproving. "It's on your own heads then. I never saw you."

"Mithras bless you, sir," said one of them. "Jesus, too."

"This is my brother Mordred," said Gawain. "Honor him as you would me."

"Of course," said the bigger man.

"Good evening to you, Lord Mordred," hiccuped his companion. They bowed in unison, dipping the woman with them. As she straightened up, she smirked at me speculatively, her round face framed by hair and cleavage. Whore or not, she looked cleaner and more interesting than the kitchen girls I'd tumbled back in Orkney. Evidently there really were pleasures to be found here, for all of Arthur's pious platitudes. Maybe, with enough time, I'd become interested in them.

Outside, it had gotten fairly dark. I didn't comment on the way Gawain had winked at what Arthur would surely consider a serious breach of discipline. Instead, I asked him where we were going next.

He stretched his long arms and brushed his hair out of his eyes. "A tavern, I should think. There's several down the lane. Some good beer will wash the taste of that nasty Greek wine out of my mouth."

I did not yet feel comfortable enough in this strange environment to allow myself to get drunk. Besides, there was some business I had to see to. "I hope it's all right if I don't join you. I think I just want to go back to the barracks."

He clapped me on the shoulder. "God love you, brother. I know it's been hard, all that's happened these last two months, then coming here."

"You're bearing it well enough." I tried not to sound bitter.

He didn't stop smiling. "We were never close, me and Father. Me and Mother, either. I'm sorry for what happened, but I'm back home now. This is my family, Mordred, as much as I've ever had one. This and you. Now they're in the same place, and yes, I'm happy. Is that so bad?"

"No, Gawain, it's not bad at all." I think maybe I meant it.

"Are you sure you won't have one drink?"

"No thank you," I said as I embraced him. "I'm bloody tired."

"Rest easy, then. Are you certain you can find your way?"

"To the barracks, yes." Where I'd go or what I'd do in the days afterward, I had no idea.

Gawain's squadron lodged in the last block on the right, where the road from the civilian settlement intersected the Via Principalia. It was a one-story building, about 250 feet long by forty wide, shaped like a T, with the officers' quarters at one end and the troops bunking in cubicles that opened off the long central hall. Gawain's rooms consisted of a bedroom, an outer chamber furnished with stools, a low table, and several chests and cupboards, and a small antechamber with a paved floor containing stone gullies for ablutions.

Fergus knelt on a sheepskin rug in the outer chamber, praying, something he would not have dared to do in Orkney, at least not where anybody could see him. When I entered, he sprang to his feet.

"Relax," I said. "This is a Christian place, more or less."

He nodded. "The Pendragon is Christian. I'm not sure about his soldiers."

I sat on one of the plain but well-made stools. "The point is, nobody is going to beat you for worshiping your Jesus." Even in Orkney, I'd never cared about such things one way or the other. Mother had always made a fuss, though, even when I unthinkingly followed Gawain's example and swore in Christ's name.

There was a new look in Fergus's eyes, and the little balding Irishman was standing straighter than was his usual wont. "Yes, Lord Mordred." I didn't like the inflection he put on *Lord.* "I've realized that. It's a vindication of my faith." Besides being a Christian, Fergus was apparently better educated than Coel, who would never use a word like vindication. Where was Coel, anyway?

"I'm glad you think so," I said as I pulled off my left boot, something at which he did not offer to help. "Now why don't you go get me some food, before my hunger overrules my good nature. And where the hell is Coel?"

Fergus looked at the floor. "Gone, I think."

"Gone?" Not that it was any great surprise. Even since our ship had rounded the tip of Britain, the taciturn Caledonian had been visibly yearning to go home.

"Yes. He said it wasn't right, these Southerners planning to bait the Palag Cat like it was a common bear. Said there'll be trouble, and he didn't want to be here when it happened."

Truth to tell, Coel and Fergus were not so much servants as slaves. The royal house of Orkney had purchased most of its retainers from Fergus's countrymen, who'd either captured them in raids, or in Fergus's case, reduced him to chattel as punishment for some obscure crime. In Orkney, where a ship docked once every couple of months and no refuge was to be found in the peaty hills, their loyalty had been assured. Here, near a busy port, with roads leading to all of Britain, things were different.

I pulled off my other boot. Damn, but I'd developed a nasty blister. "I expect he just saw a chance to return to

Strathclyde. He couldn't have been that upset about the bloody cat."

"I don't know, lord. You know how superstitious these Northerners are."

I looked at him sharply. His new environment was making him insolent. Well, he'd seen the pagan household in which he'd served fall into literal ruin, its master and mistress dead and its very towers toppled. The bastard was probably feeling a bit smug. If I'd more energy, I might have beaten him. Instead, I tossed him my boots. "Clean them," I said. "And watch your tongue. I'm a Northerner, too. You can't get much more North than Orkney."

He just stood there. "I thought you wanted me to get you some food."

By the Mórrígán's tits, if he kept on with that tone I was going to thrash him, no matter how tired I felt. "Clean them while it's cooking, dammit." I wasn't sure if he could requisition supplies in Gawain's name, so I pulled out my purse and tossed him two coins. "Find out where food is sold at this hour and buy some. Get porridge, lentils, a bit of lamb shank, whatever will make a decent stew, along with a jug of wine." I'd seen stove houses leaning against the inside of the fortress wall, where they wouldn't be a fire hazard, so I told him to take the food there and have it cooked. "There's a couple of clay pots lying about that should serve well enough."

My boots under one arm, he stooped to pick up a large bowl.

"No, not that one, you idiot; that's a chamber pot."

Finally rid of him, I stretched out on the sheepskin and shut my eyes. Through the wall to my left, I could hear sounds from the main wing of the barrack. Soldiers were laughing, making wagers over dice, and swapping bawdy stories in several different British dialects, with both Latin and Irish mixed in. Somebody was singing a song about a girl named Bronwen. Someone else was telling a joke about a priest and a miller's daughter. I thought about going out and telling them to shut up, but was uncertain how much authority I'd have in their eyes, and wasn't yet ready to put it to the test.

Even tired as I was, I also wasn't ready for sleep. Sitting up, I looked around the room, not sure what I was searching for until I saw the wide-mouthed amphora that contained my mother's head, stacked with our other baggage in one corner. Sighing, I rose, got the stoppered jug, and carried it into the tile-floored antechamber.

There I broke it open. The thick mixture of vinegar, salt, and cedar oil in which she'd been preserved made a sludgy mess on the floor, something else for Fergus to take care of when he came back. I washed the head off in the stone trough, then carried it into the bedroom, where I shut and barred the door behind me.

Her features were blackened and leathery, her eyes shut and fallen into their sockets, her shriveled lips drawn back from dull yellow teeth. I balanced the head on my knees, her dank, stringy, oil-soaked hair spilling across my lap. "Well," I said, feeling somewhat ridiculous. "Here we are. This is Camelot, Mother."

Her eyes did not open, but her teeth parted and her mummified lips drew back even farther. The sound that issued from between them was a rasping gurgle that gradually became distinguishable words. This was the first time since her death that she'd spoken to me while I was awake. Despite this, I felt neither surprise nor horror, just a dull pity. Poor Mother, once so vibrant and alive, if crazed and exasperating, was now just this lump of bone and withered flesh, until recently preserved in a jug like a pickled dormouse.

"Camelot," she said, sludge dripping out of the corner of her mouth. "My brother's little citadel of Roman Law and Christian virtue. Hold me to the window so I can see it."

"It's dark, Mother, and the window is covered by opaque glass."

More liquid trickled out of her mouth and nose. "That's all right. I don't want to see his little playground, anyway. Arthur is a fool."

I brushed a strand of soggy hair out of her face. "Maybe so, but he's all I've got. He even welcomed me here, more or less. Everything is forgiven."

Her grimace became more pronounced. "Yes, I'm sure. Christians claim to be as fond of forgiveness as they are of guilt."

Death hadn't changed her much, other than making her somewhat more lucid than she'd been toward the end of her life. "Why did you have me bring you here? You never wanted to come here when you were alive."

It was a moment before she answered, and I wondered if her spirit had withdrawn back to its more usual abode, abandoning the carrion through which it spoke. But no, her black lips moved again. "As you said, there was nowhere else for you to go, and I wished to help you make your way in the world. You will have need of me, before Arthur is married."

I'd heard her say something of the sort before, the first night I lay dreaming in the storm-wracked ruins of Lot's palace. "Yes, yes, that's what you said in my dream, when you made me disinter your head and prepare it this way. Are you going to finally explain what you mean?"

Her eyelids quivered, but did not open, for which I was grateful. "Ah, Mordred, my lovely, lovely boy. Give me a kiss, and maybe then I'll tell you."

I'd had quite enough of that sort of thing when she was alive, and I knew better than to listen to her further, at least right now. So much for the idea that death cures us of all our mortal cares and follies. Looking up, I scanned the room. Gawain, I saw, was something less than neat. Several tunics lay on the floor, as well as assorted breeches and cloaks. Along with other scraps of clothing, there was a pile of rags in one corner. Carrying Mother by her damp hair, I picked up one and stuffed it into her mouth. Then I carried her back to the outer room, wrapped her in my oldest and dirtiest cloak, and shoved her inside a stout cedar trunk which was provided with a well-made brass lock. Turning the lock, I withdrew the key and tied it onto a leather thong which I hung around my neck. Then I lay back down on the sheepskin.

When I was better situated here, and knew my way around, I'd have to make arrangements to dry her head over a low fire, which would complete the preservation process. It wasn't urgent, though. The weather was fairly cool, and she could remain in the trunk for a while without spoiling.

Arthur's wedding; now why was she concerned about that? Once again, I wondered what sort of woman my father would be marrying.

Twenty-seven

THE NEXT day, I found out.

Intent on reestablishing authority with his men, Gawain had taken them out to exercise on the parade grounds. I would have gone with him, to see how such things were done, but Arthur sent word that he wanted to see me.

His private chamber was small and spartan, with a bed that was nothing more than a blanket on a raised slab, a folding iron stool with a leather seat, and a small oak table that served as a desk. The walls were of undecorated plaster, their whitewashed monotony broken by one small window. Yellow light streamed through it, illuminating the room's only ornament, a carved image of the Virgin that was a miniature replica of the one in the chapel. A rather calculated effect, I thought, observing how the shaft of light shone directly on the icon.

Well, I thought, he trusted me enough to allow me into his room unguarded and unsearched. Roman emperors had died that way. Of course, Arthur probably felt that it was all part of God's plan, whether or not I pulled a knife from my boot and attempted to stab him. I suppose there's a certain comfort in predestination.

He motioned for me to seat myself on the stool, a courtesy that made me feel more uncomfortable than I would have been if I'd remained standing. "I need to find a place for you here," he said.

"Yes," I agreed. There had been a time when I

dreamed of having my own company of horsemen, like Gawain.

Perhaps he'd read my thought. "After a while, you may become an officer, and command a squadron of your own. For now, you lack the experience, although Gawain tells me you ride excellently, and can handle a lance. You've no experience at tactics, though, or of handling men."

True enough. Lot had not allowed me any authority over his warband. "I can gain some. Make me Gawain's subaltern."

He paced the room with the rolling, bowlegged stride of one more accustomed to being on horseback than on foot. He wore the same scuffed leather from the day before. I wondered if he'd slept in it. From the smell of him, he did not practice the regular bathing he encouraged in his men. No doubt he found the experience too pleasurable.

"I may do that," he was saying. "For now, though, I have a less military duty. I assume you know I'm getting married."

I said as much. "That's why your bride's father sent you the cat we saw on the road. A nice wedding present, that."

He turned, and for a moment there was anger on his face. "Don't remind me that my nuptials are being celebrated in such a pagan fashion. I've already explained why I can't send the cat back."

I nodded. "Pardon me, Arthur, I meant no offense." He might not like it if I called him father, but I couldn't quite bring myself to address him as *Highness*. The given name would have to do.

He didn't seem to mind the informality. "I know. I'm sorry, but it's still a sore point. The worst part is, I'll have to watch the whole bloody affair tomorrow. Lord Rufficius may have given himself the title of town magister at Caerwent, but in reality he's just another petty despot. If my men are going to be corrupted by his blood sports, I want to be there to keep an eye on things."

Probably he figured his troops would be less inclined to run riot while drunk if he were present in the town. Maybe they would anyway. I found the prospect more exciting than the baiting of the cat. "You were talking about your marriage. Congratulations, by the way. God's blessings on you and you future queen."

He stood before the small window, tracing a line in the dusty opaque glass with his finger. "Don't call on blessings from Him you don't believe in, Mordred. As for my future queen, she's why I called you here."

"I see." Except I didn't, really. What could he be getting at?

He kept his back turned to me. His stance might have been somewhat bowlegged, but his spine and shoulders were as straight as a post. "I've not talked much with Guinevere since she arrived at Camelot. In fact, our only lengthy conversation was the day her father introduced us, in the royal grove at Cadbury."

I felt unexpectedly curious and dared a personal question. "What was it like, meeting her that day?"

He turned to me, and he was actually smiling. "Like falling into an enchanted sleep, and waking up, finding the dreary winter gone, and summer everywhere. She awakened things in me I did not know I could feel."

You got an erection, you mean. Not that I said that. "But you say you've not spent much time with her since then."

He actually blushed. "Well, of course not. It's not proper for us to do before the wedding."

I tried to keep a straight face. Here was a hard-bitten soldier, the bastard son of that old reprobate Uther, and a man who'd once unknowingly lain with his own sister, and he was telling me it was improper to socialize with his bride-to-be before the nuptials. *Idiot,* I thought; *you'll be strangers on your wedding night, and what's the good of that?*

He continued speaking, his face still slightly red.

"Guinevere is bored here, I fear, and feels confined. She'd like to go to the baths, and perhaps to market, but she needs an escort. One man is all that's required. I'm proud of that, that the rule of law is so strong here. A woman can walk about with only one man to protect her."

I didn't want the duty, but I was too curious to protest. "Why me?"

Arthur's expression was unreadable. "Guinevere was educated in a convent, although not a very godly one. As I get older, I'm less and less surprised by just how ungodly so many church folk are, both men and women. Still, she received quite a good education. When I met, she was reading, what's his name, Ovid?"

I nodded in surprise, not bothering to correct his pronunciation.

"Whatever I may think of the arts she practiced, there's no denying the quality of the education my sister gave you. I'll wager you've read more of the old pagan authors than almost anyone else in Britain. Since I exiled Merlin, there's been no such learning here at Camelot."

I shrugged. "It's the legacy of Ambrosius," I said, referring to the last Count of the Saxon Shore, my great-uncle. "Uther inherited his cavalry, but Mother got his books, and took them to Orkney with her. She inflicted most of them on me." Inflicted was the right word. I remembered being ten, and struggling through Seneca.

"Exactly," said Arthur. "You can talk to Guinevere about these things. She'll be so glad of that. Right now, Bishop Gerontius is the only educated person she can talk to, and all they do is argue about Saint Augustine."

Oh, wonderful, I thought. I was being sent to nurse-maid someone who argued theology with bishops. The prospect sounded about as entertaining as an enema. "So I'm to go to the baths with her?" Augustine or no, perhaps she'd want me to scrub her back.

He looked at me sternly. "You will, of course, occupy yourself elsewhere while she's inside. Her lady-in-waiting will accompany her, and see to her needs inside the bathhouse." Suddenly he flushed again, and turned away. Had he suddenly just pictured his bride-to-be naked?

I stood up. It was galling, really, to be given such a duty. The Romans had used eunuchs for such tasks. Still, I didn't let my irritation show. "I'll be happy to escort the Lady Guinevere wherever she may choose to go," I said, trying not to clench my teeth as I smiled.

I found Guinevere in the palace's rear courtyard, which was so big it contained not just a garden but a miniature grove of mulberries and dwarf oaks, as well as the usual fountain and rows of flowers. She matched Gawain's description well enough, with flaming hair cascading over creamy pale skin rather than the freckles typical of redheads. Her face was triangular, with high cheekbones and a full, rather wicked mouth, and she was clad in a shimmering green gown, belted with gold samite, that did not conceal her soft curves. Yes, my brother had been correct; she was piercingly beautiful, and for a moment I was stupidly angry that Arthur should be betrothed to someone so fine and fair, while I'd never had anyone but whores and serving girls. Well, I thought, maybe she's stupid, or shrill, or prone to farting. There has to be some balance in the world.

She reclined sideways in the Continental fashion on cushions strewn across a marble bench, resting on one arm while holding a book with the other. The book was not a scroll, but a bound codex. A large woman in a gray gown and brown shawl sat nearby in a portable wicker chair, knitting with glum concentration and ignoring the small tortoiseshell cat that pawed at her yarn.

"Hello," I said, feeling obnoxious. "Which of you is the Lady Guinevere?"

The knitting woman glared at me with a face like a boiled ham, but her mistress only laughed. "That would be me." Her contralto voice had the lilting accent of someone raised on the summery downs that lay across the Severn Sea. "And this is my maid Regan. Who might you be, my polite and charming lord?"

I gave her an exaggerated bow. "I'm Mordred, Gawain's brother. The Pendragon asked me to escort you to the baths."

She sat up, pulling down her gown to hide her ankles. "From your tone, I'd say you don't like the duty."

I sat beside her, although she hadn't asked me to. "Not at all. Forgive my manners; they breed us this way in Orkney. What are you reading?" Some church twaddle, I guessed.

"Ovid," she replied, which was a surprise, as it was mostly Christian books that got bound that way, with pagans being relegated to scrolls. Unlike Arthur, she pronounced the poet's name correctly. "Do you like him?"

She expected me make some comically rustic answer, I'm sure. Instead, I was truthful. "Yes, well enough. The *Amores* more so than the *Metamorphoses*."

Her eyes widened. They were very green. "You're not like your brother. I don't think he's ever read anything but maps and orders."

I laughed. "I love him, but you're right, we're not much alike." I remembered the scarred torso I'd seen in the baths yesterday. "I doubt he'd appreciate Ovid."

She laughed too, a throaty chuckle. "Regan certainly doesn't. She thinks he's obscene."

I looked at the big woman, who glared and stuck out her long jaw like it was a weapon. "That I do, and not fit for her ladyship's perusal, if I may say so."

Guinevere shook her head chidingly. "But you may not. Anyway, it's passionate, not licentious. Here, listen to what Hero says to Leander:

> *You loiter in the forum or the baths*
> *And your evenings are awash in wine,*
> *while all I do is pine*
> *for him I cannot touch.*
> *This loneliness of mine*
> *Has become my only bliss; I burn*
> *With what you cannot quite return."*

Regan only sniffed, and wrinkled her pitted turnip of a nose. "I still think it indecent, my lady. Hardly the sort of thing to be reciting in front of strange men."

"Oh, I'm not shocked," I said easily, as if that were the point. "I've read racier stuff than that. Catullus, for instance. Let's see, how does his charming little anecdote to Cato go?" Tucking my feet up beside me, I recited from memory.

> "My dear Cato, it was quite funny,
> So bend an ear and hear my tale
> Of the farm boy I found fucking
> His lady love on yonder vale.
> My tunic up, I fell upon him
> Before the lad had yet pulled out
> And thrust myself right up his backside;
> You really should have heard him shout!"

Regan was already on her feet, and for a moment I thought she was going to strike me, a prospect that looked quite painful, considering her powerful shoulders and broad, bony-knuckled hands. Instead, she turned on her heel and lurched away. "I'll fetch help, my lady," she said, her voice choked with outrage.

"Oh, dear," said Guinevere quietly. She was a little flushed herself, but a crooked smile was forming under her emerald eyes. "You certainly routed her."

I was beginning to feel ashamed of myself, a novel sensation. "I'm sorry to have upset her so." At least I hadn't frightened her mistress.

"So you should be. That's hardly a poem to quote at strange ladies. Or their maids. And God save you if Arthur heard you spouting that sort of thing, even if you are his nephew." There was a pause before the word *nephew,* as if she'd almost said something else.

I elaborated on that pause. "More than his nephew, my lady."

She stopped smiling, and her expression was so grave and unreadable it could have been carved in marble. "I know that, Mordred."

"He's told you, then?"

She stood up and turned away, her hair burning in the sunlight. "Yes. Poor man, so eaten up with guilt. His marriage proposal was half confession."

That was no surprise. Arthur was so good at shame. "I hope you absolved him."

Before she could reply, there was a commotion behind us. "There he is!" Regan had returned, accompanied by a big, florid man with beady eyes and a grease-stiffened mustache. He wore a serpentine gold neck torc that marked as him as tribal nobility, and there was a rather plain but quite functional-looking sword at his belt. All I had was my dagger.

"It's all right, Lord Dunvallo," said Guinevere before anything drastic could happen.

"We'll see about that, my lady." said the big man. "Who is this whelp?"

"Lord Mordred of Orkney," I replied, standing up and looking him in the eye. "Who asks?"

"Dunvallo of Gwynnedd, you insolent fool." His hand still on his hilt, he looked me up and down, a sneer twisting his mouth. "*Orkney*, is it? So you're him then, the Pendragon's . . ." His sentence trailed off. Damn, I'd known Arthur liked to make his guilty conscience public, but I'd never realized the extent to which he'd done so.

I finished his sentence for him, albeit with a more tactful slant on his unspoken realization. "*Nephew.* That's right. Arthur is my uncle, and Gawain's my brother. Neither one will like it if you trifle with me, so bugger off."

His grip tightened on his sword. "Hold your tongue, Orkney-boy, or I'll open you like a fish, Pendragon's nephew or no."

"Enough, Dunvallo!" snapped Guinevere, her voice now more steel than velvet. "He has done nothing to offend me, whatever you may have heard from my maid. You, on the other hand, are most unwelcome. Leave, and quickly, unless you want Arthur to hear of my displeasure."

Dunvallo's upper lip quivered, and I thought the big vein in his forehead was going to burst. "Very well, my lady," he said with an outtake of breath. Giving her a curt bow, he turned and strode away, stiff with fury.

Guinevere turned on Regan. "There was no need for such hysteria. You may go, too."

Regan curtseyed, rather clumsily. "I feared for your safety, my lady."

"The fact that Lord Mordred is crude and insolent hardly means he'd rape me in Arthur's own courtyard. For the sake of your own sensibilities, you'd be better off leaving us alone. I'll shout if I need someone."

"Yes, my lady." She lurched off, trailing sniffles.

When Guinevere turned back to me, there was still a glint of amusement in her eyes. "Do you always make friends this easily?"

I slumped back on the marble bench. "Sorry."

She sat beside me and patted my hand. "It's all right. I just didn't want to see Dunvallo carve up the first man I've met with any real learning."

I began to relax. "Secular learning, maybe. There's plenty of educated priests."

She laughed. "Oh, yes, and they're so stimulating to talk to. I'm afraid I'd horrify them."

I looked at her, almost annoyed to be liking her so much. "Not much for Ovid, are they?"

She shook her head. "That's not the problem. To them, I'm a heretic. That's worse than a heathen, you know."

I laughed. "Being heathen myself, the schisms of Christianity are a mystery to me. What do they find offensive in your theology?"

The little cat, which had hidden under the bench during the commotion, now jumped up on it. When Guinevere stroked it, it rolled over on its back and latched playfully onto her hand, claws extended but drawing no blood. She thumped it on its nose, and it let go and began cleaning itself, as if that's what it had intended all along. "I side with Bishop Julian, the Pelagian, who asserted the basic neutrality of human instincts, and preached free will. For me, Augustine's predestination makes moral effort futile. In his theology, unlike Julian's, praise and blame both seem useless, and what's the good of that? Of course, most Churchmen claim not to see it that way."

Most Churchmen couldn't see anything beyond the offering plate, but I didn't say that. There wasn't much I could say, really. These were deep waters, and rather murky ones.

I rose. "We'd better be off, if you're to have your bath."

Not the smoothest attempt at changing the subject, but she didn't seem upset. "All right. Would you mind fetching Regan?"

"Of course." I found myself envying the big, surly maid for the fact that she'd soon be seeing her mistress naked. Well, better her than Arthur, though it would be his turn soon enough. Ach, what a bloody waste.

After Guinevere had her bath, I accompanied her to the rows of shops that lined the road leading from the southeast gate to the river. Past the civilian settlement, I could see tombs with cracked ceremonial vases, a stone-and-timber bridge, and wooden docks where skiffs and barges moored. To the south, the gleaming Usk wound its way through reedy marshes to the Severn Sea.

Regan trudging glumly after us, we wandered past stalls and storefronts. The buildings clustered shoulder to shoulder along the road from the main gate. Most were strip-houses, long and narrow, their gabled ends fronting directly on the street. The fronts were usually open, albeit with carved slots into which wooden shutters could be fitted at night, with the merchant and his family living in the rooms beyond. From the storefronts were sold whetstones from Stratford, mixing bowls from Manchester, and even a few stacks of the fine red Samian pottery from Gaul. From open stalls, other merchants displayed wool combs, loom weights, knives, and iron tools of all descriptions. I eyed a couple of daggers, but Guinevere was more interested in the next block, where clothiers hawked their wares. She bought a bolt of green cloth, and a couple of gold ribbons. Before turning back toward the fortress, she also purchased a small oak chessboard, complete with artfully, if somewhat un-evenly, carved chessmen that had been fashioned from polished river stones.

The sky was overcast as usual, with rain seeming im-minent any moment. I suggested we were pushing our luck if we lingered, for here, unlike inside the fortress, whole sections of the street had been torn up to be used in filling in house foundations, and much of it would quickly turn to mud in a downpour. Guinevere frowned, but nodded in agreement. So we made our way back, through crowds of civilians who stared at us and soldiers who bowed as we passed. Apparently, everyone knew who Guinevere was, even though most of them had surely not seen her before. Well, I doubted there were many women that looked like her around here.

For once, the threatened rain did not come, and by the time we reached the palace, patches of sun were stream-ing through the clouds. Guinevere bade me stay and sit with her for a time in the courtyard, where we played chess. I said that the presence of such an item in a merchant's stall meant that Arthur was succeeding in his dream of making Southern Britain civilized again.

She snorted. "I'll consider Britain truly civilized when each town has its own Bibliopola selling books, with a staff of *librari* to copy them."

I laughed as I laid a trap for her queen. "Oh, right. I don't think they even have those on the Continent anymore, except maybe in Byzantium."

She saw the trap, but I got a bishop anyway. "Maybe so, but I can dream. I can dream of theaters in each town, instead of beast pits. I'd not go to see the death of that poor cat my father sent, even if Arthur were to allow it. Lord knows what possessed Da to make a gift of such a thing."

Probably conspiring with Lord Rufficius, I thought, in order to curry favor with both his warband and Arthur's troops. It was the same game the old Roman magnates had played when they sponsored such events. "What's Lord Cador like?" I asked as she retaliated for the loss of her bishop by taking a knight. "I didn't meet him on my first trip to Britain, when I was eight years old and my mother brought me to Cornwall to see Arthur's coronation. None of the nobility had wanted much to do with King Lot." For the first time in years I thought of Merlin, his ancient eyes staring at me from his boyish face, and how he'd stroked my cheek and called me pretty.

She smiled when I made what I thought was a good move, and positioned her once-threatened queen to take my other knight. Ouch, but my chess was rusty. "I never saw much of him, or of Cornwall, for that matter. My mother was a princess of the Summer Country, and that's where I was raised, directly across the Severn Sea. When she died, I was shipped to Brittany, where my upbringing was completed by nuns."

"Have you any siblings?"

"My half sister Nimüe, whom my father sired on a serving girl. I did not get to meet her until I was summoned back from the convent to Cornwall, so I could be groomed for my introduction to Arthur. She's the only thing about my brief stay in Cador's palace that I miss."

The thought that there might be more like her was a pleasing one. "If she's as lovely as you are, you should send for her."

She actually kicked me. "She's all of four, you rogue, a lovely child indeed, but rather young for you. Not that I'd want your sort sniffing around her even if she was old enough." The teasing affection in her eyes took the sting out of her words.

The tortoiseshell cat suddenly jumped up on the chessboard, scattering several pieces. "Damn it, Deirdre," said Guinevere, "just when I was winning." She picked up the cat and nuzzled its flat little head. It purred and looked at me with eyes nearly as green and mysterious as her own. "First you pester me when I read, always trying to shove yourself between me and the book, now this. If I didn't love you, you horrid beast, I'd have you skinned." She held the cat high. "Yes, cat skin gloves, that's your proper fate." Then she kissed it again, and cradled it in her lap.

I started to rearrange the pieces, deftly repositioning one bishop so he could put her king in check if she moved her queen to take my knight. I didn't get a chance to see if she'd notice my trick, for she waved my hand away. "It's bad luck, to continue a game that's been interrupted this way."

I smiled at her as she put the pieces back in their small leather bag. "I'm surprised you're superstitious."

She cocked an eyebrow. "And I'm surprised you're not, from what Gawain has said about your mother."

Firsthand experience with magic hardly meant that I accepted every folk belief about good and bad luck. Only fools find omens in everything. Not wanting to get into this, I rose.

"That, my lady, is a subject for another day. I thank you for your company and your courtesy." Now why was I sounding so suddenly formal?

She rose too, and took my hand. "Ach, don't 'my lady' me, Mordred. Call me Gwen, if we're to be friends."

I looked into her eyes, which were slightly above the level of my own. *She's taller than me,* I thought. *Like Mother.*

"Friends?"

"Good ones, I hope."

"Yes, I do, too." With a nodding bow, I turned and left. Behind me, I heard her talking softly to the cat, and it meowing back.

Twenty-eight

THE NEXT day I got my chance to see Gawain drill his men on a two-acre stretch of flat green sward, hoof-churned into beaten brown earth that became mud in the drizzling rain. I wore a hooded, coarsely woven coat of oily wool, the kind that Britain had routinely exported throughout the Empire a few centuries before. It itched and made me sweat despite the damp chill, but kept me fairly dry. My brother and I huddled in our saddles, water streaming from our cowls, and watched his troops prepare for the war game they were conducting against a rival squadron commanded by one Geraint, a grizzled, broken-nosed Silure with comically large ears and a mustache that drooped to his collarbone.

Today, Gawain's company were the mounted attackers, while Geraint's wild-eyed hillmen had to play the less exalted role of defending infantry. A shallow trench, about five feet wide and four deep, had been dug along the western end of the trampled field. Beyond it was a turf bulwark, maybe four feet high, and beyond that a row of heavy stakes had been set in the ground at forty-five-degree angles, facing the mock attackers. Their points were sheathed in rag-stuffed horsehide bags, and the stakes were set farther apart than in a real battle, but still presented a formidable obstacle to both horse and rider. Geraint's rowdies crouched behind the picket, clutching long-hafted "spears" tipped with wooden balls

213

that had been wrapped in leather. The "lances" couched
by Gawain's riders were similarly cushioned.

Gawain's horsemen were already in position, and he
leaned toward me and squeezed my arm. "Keep a sharp
eye on my formation, boyo. It's stupid, really; I can't
observe them properly if I'm leading the bloody charge,
but if I don't lead them, I lose their respect. Instead of a
training exercise, it's become a hotheaded competition.
Ach, at least it's fun, and keeps the lads out of trouble."
With that he trotted his gelding forward to its place at
the tip of his squadron's wedge formation.

The rain was falling harder now, and Geraint's men
were gray shapes in the drizzly haze. I'd have to follow
closely behind the charge if I was to see anything, so I fell
into place in back of them and waited with them for
Gawain's signal.

His arm rose and fell. A hundred lance points dipped,
as many horses moved as one, first a trot, then a canter,
finally a full gallop; fortunately, the mud was not quite
deep enough to mire them down, but their hooves tossed
plenty into the air, and I was nearly blinded by the
splatters. Wiping my face on the back of my arm, I
swerved to the left of the formation, which gave me a
clear view past them to the muddy ditch, the turf wall,
the muffled stakes, and the whooping gray-and-brown
forms that crouched behind them, pale oval faces growing larger every second. Rain and dirt in my face, my
horse drumming beneath me, the enemy ahead, I found
myself laughing with a strange, mad joy. *So this is what
it's like,* I thought. *This is what Arthur felt at Badon.*
Suddenly, I wished it was all real, that the men plunging
ahead of me were actually my comrades, and I was
following them into the enemy's bloody embrace.

In front of me, the squadron's wedge spread out into a
line, the experienced riders seeking the path they already
knew lay between the stakes. Even from the rear, it was
thrilling to see a hundred horses leap at once, as they
went over the ditch and up the sloping earthwork. Mud
clods flew everywhere, there were shouts and curses, the
thud of padded spearheads smashing into mail-covered

bodies, the crash of armored men hitting the ground. There would be bruises, broken bones, maybe a few deaths. Caught up in the excitement, I threw back my cloak and tore my scabbarded sword from my belt, then spurred my mare directly toward the gauntlet.

The ditch flashed beneath me; I saw two men and one mount floundering in it, the horse kicking and whinnying, both men drawn up into fetal balls. As my mare topped the sod wall, I nearly went out of the saddle, but I managed to grip her with my knees and steady myself, and then we were plunging down toward the stakes. Unlike Gawain's men, I did not have the benefit of previous experience, and one muffled stake point came perilously close to my face, a padded punching post that could have taken my head clean off. Then I was in the middle of Geraint's men, with cushioned spears thrusting at me. One smashed into my thigh, its oak knob head bruising me despite the leather sheath; another glanced off my horse's ribs, and once again I was nearly thrown, but I hunkered down over her neck, still gripping my sheathed sword, and then right in front of me was Lord Geraint himself, all startled cod eyes staring out from under his walrus mustache, so close I could see the dents in his conical iron helmet.

I squeezed the mare's sides with my knees, straining for the purchase that would let me rise high in the saddle, and brought my scabbarded sword down onto that helmet with all my might. Then there was no horse between my legs, my rump and spine smashed into mud and the hard ground under it, and I found myself sitting in the mire, my sword arm numb and my sword broken in its scabbard; but Geraint stretched out in front of me, unconscious or maybe dead, his eyes closed and mouth open to the rain.

"Shit, he's killed the chief!" shouted someone behind me, "You sneaky little bastard," growled another, and then I was kicked in the small of the back with enough force to knock me forward on my face. *Sore losers,* I thought inanely as I swallowed mud, unable to do anything but draw up into a ball, my hands over the nape of my neck, elbows gripping my head and knees pressed against my chest, and rock with the blows that rained upon me. Somebody kicked me between the shoulder blades, another in the ribs, I don't know how many in the arse, and then I knew I was in trouble, because one clever bastard was aiming for my head, though my arms and elbows took the worst of it.

I lay there, knowing I wouldn't be conscious long, desperate to rise and face my attackers but as helpless as a baby to do so, waiting for the next blow. Instead there was a familiar shout, then the sound that you never forget once you've heard it, nor ever mistake for anything else; the muffled crunch of a sword cutting through mail and into flesh and bone. My ears were ringing, I was choking on mud, and the parts of me that weren't on fire had gone completely numb, but the blows had stopped. Someone was shouting curses, a deep voice I recognized.

"Come on, you bastards, come on! Who's next? Who the fuck is next?"

I rolled over, nearly vomiting as the brown earth and gray sky switched positions, and found myself looking up at Gawain, who stood over me, sword in hand. There was blood on his long blade, and more blood on the upper arm of the bushy-bearded man who knelt a few feet away, moaning as two of his fellows stripped off mail and gambesons in order to tear bandages from their undertunics, then attempted to staunch the wound. They eventually succeeded, and somebody else came running up with a flagon of wine, secured from God knows where, which they tried to pour down the injured man's throat, although most of it ended up spilled over his chest. He sat there, his mouth forming an "o" of pain, his face very pale above his black beard.

Gawain's horsemen crowded around, wanting to protect their leader, but too intermingled with Geraint's company to really do so. Fortunately, there proved to be no need, as my victim began to stir.

"Jesus, Mary, and Judas, but that was a stout thump, wasn't it just!" said Geraint as he sat up. Several of his men ran to him, but he'd already managed to stand, albeit a little unsteadily. Grimacing, he removed his helmet and gingerly ran his hands through his thinning hair. "Easy now, lads," he said as he took in the scene around him. "Don't get so worked up. One way to win the game is to down the opposing captain."

Gawain lowered his sword, but did not put it away. "Are you all right?" he gruffly asked, whether to me or Geraint or the man he'd wounded, I wasn't sure.

The other two didn't answer. I took stock of my injuries. Nothing seemed broken, but I'd hurt for a while. I certainly did right now. "Yes," I said finally, somehow struggling to my feet. "I believe I am."

Somebody, one of Geraint's men, pointed at me. "It's not fair. He's not one of Lord Gawain's."

"He's my brother, damn you!" snapped Gawain.

"I got carried away," I said weakly, wondering if I'd be pissing blood.

"Didn't you just!" Geraint trudged over to embrace me. "Ach, but it was a grand thump, just the same. Good thing for me you kept your sword in its scabbard, otherwise you'd have split my helmet, and head with it!" That was highly unlikely, but I didn't argue, just groaned in his embrace. He squeezed harder and then clapped me on the back, and I wondered if he knew just how much that hurt. Probably.

Their mood changed in an instant; all the gathered men, both Gawain's and Geraint's, sounded a ragged cheer. I could hardly believe it; a few moments ago, I'd nearly been kicked to death, now I was receiving hurrahs. Even the wounded man was grinning, teeth scarcely whiter than his face showing through his beard. It was insane.

Only my brother still looked angry, except now that anger was directed at me. "You idiot!" he snapped. "Stay back and watch, I told you. If you were one of my company, and this had been a battle, I'd have you hanged! You little idiot!"

"Ach, leave off," said Geraint, squeezing my shoulder, which caused me even more pain. "The lad's all right.

Just got excited, that's all. Wish I had a few more with that kind of spirit."

Gawain stalked forward, to glare directly into my face. Then the anger went out of him with his exhaled breath, and he hugged me too, even harder than Geraint had. "Congratulations, boyo. It's not as good as having come through your first battle, but it's close." He squeezed again, and I thought I was going to faint.

Late that afternoon, I joined Gawain and Geraint at the Capricorn, a tavern across the street from the bathhouse. The establishment's name recalled the fortress's imperial history, as did the sign that hung above its entrance, depicting a crudely painted goatfish copied from the Second Augustan's emblem. "Really, Daffyd, you ought to change that placard," said my brother to the tavern's owner, who was pouring a fresh cup of beer from a twin-handled, narrow-mouthed amphora, unglazed so that evaporation would keep its contents cool. "This is Camelot now, not the City of the Legion. You should replace that silly goat-thing with a nice Red Dragon."

The gnomish barkeep struggled to carry the large jug back to the wooden counter, where he set it in a circular hole beside similar containers of wine and mead. "Ach, I couldn't do that," he said when he'd caught his breath. "I honor the Pendragon right enough, but I'd dishonor my da if I changed the name. He served in the Second, you know, when they were stationed here."

"Balls," I said. "It's been nearly two hundred years since there was a legion camp here, and at least eighty since there was one anywhere in Britain."

The little man didn't even blink. "We're a very long-lived family."

I took another sip from my lumpy terra-cotta mug and declined to argue the point, mainly because I was still in pain and lacked the energy. A long soak in the bath had helped some, but I remained quite sore. Indeed, I dreaded what I'd feel like when I woke up the next morning.

Geraint must have noticed the way I grimaced each time I shifted on my stool. He rested his elbows on the scarred oak table and twirled the ends of his enormous mustache, sticky now with mead. "Just think, lad, it could have been worse. Certainly would have been, if you'd tried that trick in a real battle. You ride like you were born to it, but you need to practice your swordsmanship, so you can swing and cut without getting unhorsed."

I drained my cup and banged on the table for another. Fortunately, Geraint was buying. "I've ridden plenty, but haven't been in many fights. Still, I'm pretty good with a lance." I remembered the long hours I'd spent in a dusty Orkney courtyard, tilting at a much-punctured dummy until I could skewer it without being knocked from the saddle.

Geraint was attempting to use the honey in the mead to stiffen the ends of his mustache, but was meeting with little success. "Maybe so, but I bet we can make you better. That right, Gawain?"

My brother's attention had wandered, his expression was clouded by drink and bad memories. "I'm sorry," he said, looking from Geraint's face to mine. "I was thinking of something else."

A tumbled tower in Orkney, I thought, and his father buried under it. Gawain hadn't even brought the crown back with him. What would have been the point? At any rate, the look of melancholy passed. "One more round," he said. "Then we visit Megra!"

"Megra?" The name seemed familiar.

Gawain grinned widely, although to my eye his cheery facade seemed a bit forced. "Remember the buxom little whore we saw the other night? The one Lud and Marcus were sneaking into the bathhouse?"

I nodded, dimly recalling the glimmer of interest I'd felt when I first saw her.

Gawain was positively leering, his tan face gone all ruddy in the fading light. This was an unfamiliar side of him. "Well, it's the last night she'll be readily available, at least for a while. Tomorrow she goes back to Caerwent, to work the crowds come to see the beast baiting. After that, she'll be too sore for a while, I suspect."

"I'm too sore now," I said. Besides, after meeting Guinevere, I was afraid to harbor lusty thoughts, lest they turn in the direction of my father's intended bride.

"And I'm getting too old," said Geraint. He took another swig of mead and looked thoughtful, or as thoughtful as a man can look with fermented honey dripping from his mustache. "No, I'm not," he said with a burp.

"What's so special about Megra?" I asked, intending to store the information away for when I felt better, or at least less distracted by thoughts of Guinevere.

Gawain was suddenly looking embarrassed. "Ach, how much have I drunk? I can't believe I'm having this conversation with my baby brother." I stared at him incredulously, for he was talking as if the last few months hadn't happened. "To think I'm talking whores with a lad I once bounced on my knee."

"You never did," I said. "Anyway, you're the one who brought the subject up. What's so bloody special about her?"

"She's good with her mouth," explained Geraint. "Most whores, see, aren't skilled at that. They have to take you another way, one that hurts, so they try to keep it short. Unless they're barren, and not afraid of doing it in the regular fashion, but most of the barren ones are old, and who wants to pay for an old one?"

"You do, when you're drunk enough," said Gawain.

"I hate to think of Arthur's reaction," I said, "if he overheard two blood relatives and a senior commander having this conversation. God, I remember once hearing him talk about founding a city of virtue, here in Camelot."

Geraint blew mead out his nose. "Ha! Camelot's a city of soldiers, just like when it was a Roman fort. A city of soldiers can't be a city of virtue."

"So my uncle is a hypocrite." *I must be drunk too,* I thought. I'd nearly said "my father."

Geraint's eyes narrowed. "Don't talk about him like

that. Else I'll clout you, if your brother doesn't. Few of us at Camelot may live the way Arthur wants us to, but we all love him, and there's not one of us who wouldn't follow him to Hell. He's two men inside, priest and soldier. The priest half of him would gladly lecture us on scripture, and prescribe abstinence and chastity and all that, until we got bored and marched down the road to sell our services to Rufficius, or shipped across the Severn Sea to Lord Cador, which is exactly what would happen. If the priest half was all of him, he wouldn't care. But it's not, see; he likes leading men, Arthur does. He likes being a soldier. He just doesn't like liking it, that's all."

"Besides," added Gawain, "he knows things would be worse without him. If Camelot wasn't here, nobody could keep Rufficius from turning Caerwent into his own private little stronghold. Same for Cador and all the other local kings. Things may get rowdy under Arthur, a fact which sorely pains him, but they'd get a lot worse under all those others, especially once they started at each other's throats." He drained the last of his beer. "At least half the men here are Christians of a sort. Without them, everything would fall apart, and the Saxons and Picts would roll over us all, and there wouldn't be any Christians anywhere, not in Britain."

"All right," I said, standing up. "So he's not a hypocrite. He's just practical."

"Where are you going?" asked Gawain.

"To bed. Like I said, I'm in no shape for whoring, especially if I'm to ride to Caerwent tomorrow."

"Aye," said Geraint, "I should turn in, too. Much as I'm tempted by Megra's charms, we all need to be up early. I've wagered Kay that the Palag Cat will finish at least ten dogs before they pull it down."

"Bloody pansies," grumbled Gawain. "All right, it's to bed, then. I just don't want to hear anyone complaining tomorrow night, when both Caerwent and Camelot are full of drunken revelers, and there's no pussy to be to found."

Twenty-nine

G AWAIN AND I rose early the next morning and met Kay and Geraint in the palace's outer courtyard. We waited there in the drizzling dawn, under the shelter of the colonnade, keeping a respectful silence while Arthur said his prayers in the small chapel. Feeling vaguely embarrassed, I tried not to hear his imprecations, listening instead to the rain pouring over the awning. My brother and his crony were decked out in flame red cloaks and gold-embroidered tunics, while Kay made up for his plainer gray tunic with a mantle of green-and-orange plaid, with matching breeches. All three of them looked sour at the thought of what a muddy ride might do to their finery.

Arthur finally joined us, looking as dyspeptic as his commanders, although I doubt he was as hung over. Unlike his captains, he wore his usual campaign leather and ragged cloak of plain gray wool. I remembered how he'd looked at his coronation ten years before, when he pulled the imperial sword from its scabbard stone. Then, my eight-year-old eyes had given his dress a ragged, homespun glamour, finding honest nobility in such plainness. Now it just seemed an affectation.

"Thank you for waiting," he said unnecessarily. "I had much to ask forgiveness for. The thought of what will happen today doesn't give me pleasure."

It was early and wet and nasty and my head hurt, and I

was in no mood for this sort of thing. "Then don't let it happen, dammit. You're the High King, after all."

Kay turned toward me, glowering, his hand on his hilt. Gawain got between him and me, while Geraint looked divided as to whose side to take. Arthur, however, brushed through them, to look closely into my face.

"Yes, Mordred, I am the High King," he said softly. "It would do you good to remember that, the next time you're tempted to bait me so." His blue eyes were very cold.

"I am sorry, Arthur; I meant no disrespect. It simply bothered me, to see you flagellate yourself so."

If Arthur detected the irony in my voice, he gave no sign. Instead, he turned away. "Your concern is noted. Let's be off."

Our horses awaited us in the street outside the courtyard, where our escort was already in formation. I would have expected Arthur to have taken a hundred men or more with him to Caerwent, but no, the guard numbered no more than twenty. Commanding them was Dunvallo, the florid lout whom I'd met so unpleasantly in the courtyard garden. His meaty red face hardened when he saw me, and I stuck out my tongue in return.

"Where's everyone else?" I asked Gawain as I climbed astride my mare.

"Already in Caerwent, those that are going. They got off duty yesterday. Of course, those that drew short straws are having to stay behind. We can't abandon the fort." Saying that, he reined his gelding into position at the rear of the column. I followed suit.

If not abandoned, the garrison certainly felt depleted, and our hoofbeats echoed eerily in the empty streets. Outside the northeast gate, the lane was less quiet, as the civilian settlement seemed abuzz with activity. Beyond it, things got even more crowded. A mile past Camelot, the road to Caerwent was packed with carts and mules, slowing traffic so much that I suspected the beast fight would be over and done with before many of the travelers completed their six-mile journey. Of course, we had no trouble skirting the worst of the congestion, leaving the road and plunging our horses across open fields when necessary, although Arthur forbade us to trample anyone's crops.

As we rode, the weather changed dramatically. The rain had stopped before we left the fort, and now the heavy clouds were breaking up, with shafts of sunlight falling through them onto patchwork fields and forested hills, the glittering marshes to the east and black hills to the west, and before us, the straight stone ribbon of the road, broken here and there by patches of fresh green grass. We passed sheep paddocks and granaries that had obviously been quarried from the highway, and beyond them, flower-covered meadows and golden fields where the corn rows gleamed in the brightening sunlight. The land rose and dipped and rose again, into wet meadows where flowers grew; sundew, vetch, bindweed, bog pimpernel, sage, yarrow, their colors so fierce in the changing light that my head hurt to look at them.

A perverse impulse made me pull up beside Arthur. "Ach, but it looks to be a lovely day," I said, baiting him with my gaiety. "Everyone will enjoy themselves, I'm sure.

His expression, needless to say, was quite glum. "Yes, after battening themselves on a dumb beast's painful death, they'll spill out into the streets, to drink and whore and God knows what. My men will be useless for days. Those that left for Caerwent yesterday have likely been carousing ever since. Poor sinful fools, and sinful me for allowing it."

Did the self-recriminations never end? "I take it you could not really forbid them."

His expression became even grimmer. "No, and not just because I've no wish to be a tyrant. It was bad enough as it was, forcing them to draw lots for the one man in six who would have to stay behind. Those who got the short straw will be disgruntled for quite some time, and apt to make trouble in the future."

I doubted that, but kept my peace. It was a strange feeling, seeing a flash of naked insecurity on the face of the most powerful man in Britain. *Ach, Arthur,* I thought, *don't you know how your men worship you? Geraint would have broken my head last night, if I'd gone on disparaging you. The problem is, you refuse to believe yourself worthy of such devotion.*

I dropped back, to ride beside Gawain, who still looked somewhat hung over. For myself, my entire body ached, although not quite as much as it had last night when I lay on a sheepskin on the floor of Gawain's ante-chamber aware of every bruised bone and battered muscle. "How much farther?" I asked him.

He shook hair out of his eyes and grimaced. "Not far, thank God. My stomach is treacherous this morning."

Fortunately for his dignity, and Arthur's good opinion, he did not spew, and before too much longer, we saw the town, rising from the dewy meads. At this distance, Caerwent looked even more impressive than Camelot had, with a high wall defended by great polygonal bastions, which Geraint said had once been mounted with ballistae, so that flanking fire could be directed toward anyone attempting a siege. At first I thought the wall was heavily manned with guards, for its northeast corner was crowded with human forms. The curious thing was, they seemed to be sitting rather than standing, and were facing the wrong way, with their backs to us. As we got closer, I saw these were citizens of the town, men and children and even a few women packed together on the high parapet, the more nimble perched atop the bastions, so that their legs dangled over the crenellated edge. Presumably that corner of the wall gave a clear view down into the amphitheater.

As we got closer, Caerwent proved less impressive. I saw cracks in the battlements, places where the outer stone was rent and the rubble and gravel between it and the inner curtain wall had spilled out. Moreover, when the wind shifted, I detected an odor that had not been so overpowering at Camelot, the smell of sweat and excrement and rotting trash. Having grown up in Orkney, where the royal household was not fastidious but also not large, I was quite unprepared for the stench of several thousand human beings living in close proximity to each other, without the sanitary measures found in Arthur's fortress.

Inside the bronze-and-timber gates, the streets were not paved, just strewn with gravel, with a muddy, trash-filled gutter running through the middle of the main thoroughfare, and standing pools of water visible down side lanes. We passed between the broken foundations of a monumental archway, which I presumed had been dismantled to provide building material for the tower bastions, as they looked newer than the rest of the wall. Past this was a public green, really just a big muddy field, where untended sheep cropped a few tufts of grass and pigs rooted in a garbage heap. On the other side of the green was the old aristocratic district. Many of the houses were half-ruined, and some had collapsed to ground level. Many once-luxurious dwellings now served more plebeian purposes, with stone hearths built on top of tumbled walls and courtyards, and forges, iron smelt-ing pits and tempering troughs dug into mosaic pave-ments. Farther on, in the middle-class residential blocks, two out of three homes were just crumbling shells, occupied by ragged squatters. Nearer the amphitheater, these gave way to shops and stalls, shabbier than the ones that had lined the river road from Camelot. Today, these were mostly boarded up, and no one hawked wares on the street.

In fact, no one did anything on the street, which was almost deserted. We rounded a corner and saw the amphitheater, a wood-and-stone structure like a great tub the size of a city block, with attached stables and other outbuildings. From inside came muffled shouts and laughter, a murmuring sea of excited conversation. From rooftops and the nearby wall, dirty faces peered down at us, shaded by hoods and broad straw hats. Fortunately, the buildings on this block were in better repair than the earlier ones, or they would have col-lapsed from the combined weight of a good portion of the city's population. "Arthur," came the chorus of voices above our heads. "Arthur, Arthur, Arthur." Arthur looked up and waved, his face unreadable, a politician's public mask. *You wear it well,* I thought, *though it would not please you to think so.*

Attendants met us in the street, a dozen blank-faced men in orange tunics decorated with the black boar emblem of Rufficius's household. They took the horses and led them to the stables with ten of Dunvallo's guards following them, while a steward ushered us, not to the amphitheater proper, but in the direction of a low brick building that jutted from its outer wall. There, Dunvallo and the rest of his guards entered before us while we waited in the street. After several minutes they reappeared, short two of their number. Five were posted outside the building, while Dunvallo and the other three preceded us inside. We went down one flight of stairs, to a passage that ran below the level of the street, then up four flights, each more narrow, twisting and steeper than the first. Finally we came out of the gloom into a wide corridor opening on a drapery-shrouded chamber, with cushioned benches, sheepskins on the floor, and colored light streaming through the far curtains.

Ten Caerwent guards stood at attention, facing the pair of Dunvallo's men who'd been posted beside the stairwell. Rufficius's troops wore leather helmets protected by iron bands and cuirasses of leather with metal scales sewn on, poor protection compared to the ringmail worn by Dunvallo and his three lieutenants, who preceded us into the curtained room.

Inside, they took positions beside the door, while the room's occupant rose unsteadily from his bench. Grossly fat, he was stuffed like a sausage into a bright green tunic, his purple cloak pinned at the shoulder with a huge gold brooch shaped like a dragonfly with rubies for eyes. He had curly, rather greasy-looking black hair, and there were red and gold ribbons tied in his graying beard. There was wine and a basket of food on the bench beside him, and even at this distance, his breath smelled of garlic.

"My Lord Arthur," he said, bobbing his head in a token bow. "Greetings and good day!"

"Thank you, Rufficius," said Arthur with little warmth. "I believe you know everyone present except one. This is Prince Mordred."

Rufficius stared at me for a moment, small dark eyes surrounded by crinkles of fat. "Yes," he said, smiling, "I've heard of him. Your nephew, it's said." There had been no actual pause before the word *nephew,* yet he had given it just enough emphasis to make his point. "Please be seated, good sirs." He gestured at the leather-cushioned benches. "I'll have more food and wine brought, if you so desire."

"We want nothing," said Arthur curtly, brushing several pillows from a bench before sitting on it. I started to curse him inwardly, as I was feeling rather peckish, then decided that Rufficius was not someone from whom it would be wise to accept refreshment, not unless you were sure he had partaken of it first.

As I took a seat between Kay and Gawain, the curtains in front of us parted, drawn back by unseen attendants. We were not in a proper room at all, but an open-fronted viewing box, a canopied platform that jutted from the wooden bleachers that lined the inside of the great stone-and-timber circle.

It was an unsettling, vertiginous moment when I first stared out at the bobbing sea of heads, some bare and beribboned for the occasion, others covered by straw hats or shawls, all murmuring in their neighbors' ears, so that the sound reverberated up like the hum of a human beehive. I saw them and heard them and smelled them, the whole packed, seething mass, and despite myself was filled with wonder, for all my cosmopolitan affectations. *Poor backward Orkney boy,* I thought to myself, *there was a time when you'd not have believed there were so many people in the world.* They were all staring down at the sandy floor of the arena, their necks craned, their shoulders hunched with anticipation.

No one spoke as we waited there, blinking in the light reflecting off the arena sand. Then footsteps sounded on the walkway outside, and the left-hand curtains parted as a familiar face peered into the box. I recognized the gnarled brown visage of Larcellos, the beast-catcher we'd met on the road.

"My noble lords," he said, bowing awkwardly with the parted curtain round his shoulders. "All is ready. Shall I make the sign?"

Rufficius giggled like an excited child. "By all means, good sir. And come and join us, don't just peek in like a slave. None of this would have been possible without your effort. I'm sure the Pendragon appreciates that."

Arthur said nothing, but he motioned for Larcellos to come inside. The banty little Caledonian padded to the front rail, leaned over, and waved a strip of red cloth. Someone must have seen his signal, for there was the sound of wood sliding over oiled runners, and a door opened in a recess in the concave wall opposite our box, while from the sound of things, another one was being manipulated directly below us. Around us, the crowd buzzed more loudly, and I thought of hornets rather than bees.

Apparently, the local taste did not run to fire-eaters or acrobats or any other sort of opening performance. No, this was the main event. All conversation stopped, and several thousand people held their collective breath. A low, rumbling growl broke the new silence, and then the Palag Cat stalked out into the light of the midday sun, to stand there blinking, its white bob of a tail twitching as it sniffed the air.

"Bleeding Jesus," gulped Kay.

"Don't blaspheme," said Arthur softly.

It crouched there on the sand, shaking its huge head from side to side, its massive shoulders hunched down and its yellow eyes scanning the bleachers that surrounded it. If the sight of so many people crammed together had proved daunting for me, it should have terrified the cat, but the great beast did not cringe. Instead, it raised its head, affording a good view of its incredible fangs, and gave a full-throated roar, which echoed back and forth within the tiered circle.

"Oh, nice," said Rufficius in a low, crooning voice. "How very, very nice. What a contest this will be for my doggies, oh yes."

As if in response to his thought, I heard barks and growls below us, and a pack of huge woolly gray dogs poured into the ring. Their massive shoulders, deep chests, and big, broad heads marked them as mastiffs, but with the shaggy coats and rangy size of prime wolfhounds. There were over a dozen of them, maybe twenty or more, and when they saw the cat they broke into a baying chorus. The crowd, silent until now, roared as one, whooping and throwing straw hats and sashes into the air, and although I saw Gawain and Geraint's lips moving, I could not hear what they were saying.

As if they had a prearranged strategy, the dogs charged, some leaping directly at the cat while others fanned out to flank it from the sides. Rather than just standing there, it roared again, so loudly it was actually audible above the rest of the din, and sprang forward to meet them. Three dogs went down under its charge, smashed as flat as if they'd been run over by a cart, and then it whirled around, rising on its haunches to box with its great paws, and with a meaty slap, one dog was sent bouncing across the sand, and then another followed it, the first as limp as if it was made of rags, the second curled up in a ball and yelping in pain.

Nearly as fast as the cat, and fiercely, foolishly brave, the other dogs had already closed in, and now they seemed to surge over it, their solid gray pelts mingling with its striped one, and sand was everywhere as the cat rolled beneath them, hissing and spitting under the snarling yelping mass, spinning and twisting and slapping with all four paws, leaving one, two, three, four dead dogs on the bloody sand, and another one dragging itself away on its belly, its hind legs dangling limply. Suddenly, the cat was on its feet with no dogs near it, red smears on its shoulders and sides, and more red on its face and paws, but very little of the blood seemed to be its own. Rather than seeking a defensive position, it launched itself at the nearest cluster of dogs, its paws lashing out to send two more of them flying, and then the great fangs slashed, and one dog was opened up like a sack of blood, and a second was actually speared, until the cat pawed at it, and shook it off its face, and another dog had come up from behind, to worry its rump, but the cat sat down hard, pinning the dog beneath it, and ducked its head with much the same motion as that of a house cat that suddenly decides to wash its own crotch, except it wasn't chewing at its crotch but at the dog under it, and the tusks came up wrapped in guts.

Four dogs were left, and they broke and ran in four separate directions, although obviously none of them could run far. The cat went after them one at a time, its frenzy subsided now, its movements a measured stalk, catching up with each in turn and dispatching it with a casual slap as the poor beast cowered against the wall, or scrabbled at one of the sliding wooden doors. The cat toyed with the last one for a while, loping after it and gently knocking it down, then sitting back while it got up and limped away. Finally, the dog lay on its side, panting, and the cat slapped it twice on head, almost daintily, and became the only living thing in the arena.

Beside me, Gawain was crying. "Those poor dogs," he said. "Those poor, poor dogs. What a fucking waste. I was a bloody-minded fool, to look forward to seeing this."

"Don't blame the cat," I said. "They would have happily pulled out his guts, if they'd been able."

"I know that," said Gawain. "I don't blame the beast." He looked sideways at Rufficius, and I could plainly tell whom he did blame.

Arthur had been kneeling in front of his bench, his head bowed down, and I wondered if he'd been praying since the fight began. Now he rose to his full height, and turned on Rufficius with a look like sharp iron. "You pandering monster," he said very quietly, "if I weren't a godly man, I'd throw you down there with your pet."

Rufficius made an incoherent sound, a yelp that might have come from one of his dogs. Hearing this, several of the Caerwent guards tried to enter the box, but Dunvallo and his men stepped forward, their swords coming out as one, and the rest of us rose, gripping our hilts. Violence seemed imminent, until Rufficius fell to his knees in front of Arthur.

"My lord, you countenanced this! From the start, you allowed it to happen! Surely you don't blame me for it now!"

Arthur glanced back to us. "Sit down, all of you," he said in an even tone. "And put up those swords, everyone." He turned back to Rufficius. "Get up. We'll be leaving now. Tomorrow, I'm coming back here with Bishop Gerontius, who will hold service in this very amphitheater, and pray for all the citizens of Caerwent, and my own troops as well. You will say penance then, and declare your intention to turn one of the city temples into a church. Do you understand me?"

Rufficius never got a chance to answer. At the railing, little Larcellos cleared his throat. "My lords," he said hoarsely, "forgive my interrupting and all, but we've got a problem."

Arthur looked at him with the expression of someone who's just found a bug on his plate. "Yes, what is it?"

Larcellos motioned down at the arena floor, where the great cat was padding back and forth on the bloody sand, making a low coughing sound and glaring up at the bleachers. "Its the Palag Cat. See, I never expected him to dispatch so many dogs. Now they're all dead, and he has some time to think about where he is. This amphitheater was made for bulls and bears and the like, things that don't jump. Cats jump. These walls won't hold him long."

Oh, Jesus, I thought, looking down at the great mottled beast, now crouching to take a piss, to the guffaws of the crowd. In Rome, where they once matched lions and tigers in the arena, they might have taken proper precautions, but here, it hadn't occurred to anyone that the walls weren't high enough.

Arthur turned back to Rufficius. "Get some archers up here. Get them now."

Rufficius gulped, and shouted out the door to one of

his guards, who went racing off down the corridor behind us, his sandals slapping on the stone. We all stood there in silence and watched the cat, who had finished his piss, and now kicked sand over it. Even at this distance, I smelled ammonia.

The crowd below us was not so quiet. Gradually, the laughing murmur became distinguishable words, an idiotic "kitty kitty kitty," and then they were hooting and throwing things, apple cores and peach pits mostly, and other scraps of food.

"They're taunting him!" said Larcellos, who leaned out over the railing and waved his arms. "Stop that, you fools! Stop teasing him!" No one could possibly have heard him, and everyone's eyes were on the arena floor. "Stop it!" he shouted again, pointlessly.

It was then that the cat looked straight up, right at us, or more correctly, right at Larcellos. In order to provide a good view, the box was at the level of all but lowest tier of bleachers, and it projected out past them, which meant that Larcellos, leaning as he was over the railing, was closer to the cat than anyone else in the amphitheater. Still, at fifty feet away, surrounded by more than four thousand human beings, the blood of its kills still on its face, I would never have believed it able to single one man out. Yet it did, and it snarled and stared and crouched, its eyes locked on the little Caledonian who had caught it. Its gaze met that of its former captor, and grizzled beast-catcher though he was, he shrank back.

"He recognizes me, my lords," he said in a choked voice. "The damned cat recognizes me! Please, I think we need those archers."

It was then that ten soldiers with drawn bows tried to crowd through the doorway at once, tripping over each other in their haste. "Kill the poor thing," said Arthur, clucking softly at their incompetence. Finally squeezing into the box, they looked at Rufficius, who nodded in agreement, his eyes not so small and piggy anymore, his face as pale as the underside of a flatfish.

And that was when the cat leapt. One instant it crouched on the sand, the next it was bounding forward,

its roaring charge instantly covering the ten yards to the
wall beneath us, then vaulting up so that it seemed to
hang suspended in the air. I believe that Arthur's best
men might have been able to shoot it in mid-spring, but
the Caerwent archers didn't even have their bows
cocked. The cat slammed into the royal box like it had
been tossed by a siege engine, smashing through the
railing and overturning the bench where Arthur had
been sitting. Larcellos was quick, I'll say that for him,
pushing his way through the archers and past Rufficius
himself, but the cat barreled after him, knocking Gawain
aside as he hacked ineffectually at it with his sword, and
caught him before he'd gone six feet, driving its recurved
tusks into the small of his back. Arthur cut at one of its
flanks, while Dunvallo tried to get his men past the
panicking Caerwent bowmen. Tearing its fangs out of
Larcellos, the great beast lashed out blindly, sending a
stout bench into the air. I saw it coming, tried to duck,
but went down under it anyway.

Fortunately, I'd been struck by its cushioned end and
not badly hurt. The next thing I knew, Gawain had
pulled the bench off me and was helping me to my feet.
His face was pale, and there was blood on his mouth.
Screams were sounding all around us, and a panicky
scrabbling vibration that seemed to shake the whole
amphitheater, as hundreds of onlookers crawled over
each other in their haste to find an exit. To my left, the
partitioning curtain had been torn away, showing the
route the cat had taken out of the box. Besides Larcellos,
two other men lay crumpled on the boards. One of them
was a bowman with a crushed skull, the other was Rufficius himself, no mark visible on him, but his face all
pop-eyed and chalky blue. Apparently, his heart had
given out.

Dunvallo and his men had surrounded Arthur, while
Geraint and Kay stood nearby, obviously unsure of what
to do. I bent to retrieve the dead archer's bow and
quiver. "Where is it?" I shouted. "Where's the bloody
cat?"

"In the town," said Arthur, pushing past his guards to

head for the corridor and the stairs beyond. "I saw it go over the amphitheater wall. It's in the streets somewhere."

We crowded together down the steps, nearly tripping over each other, and I shuddered to think of the panicky crush on the other stairwells, the ones the general public used. The very walls seemed to shake around us, and I could still hear muffled screaming. How many people were dying as they tried frantically to get out?

Gawain was limping, and he cursed when Geraint inadvertently jostled him. I steadied him with my arm. "Are you all right?"

"Damn cat broke one of my ribs, I think. That's what I get for wagering on its death."

The rest of our escort awaited us in the street, horses ready, spears and lances at attention. They were damn good, I thought, keeping their heads in this panic. Apparently, the main entrance was on the other side of the arena, for although we heard the screaming mob, none of them had appeared yet, except for those that had flung themselves over the amphitheater wall, and now lay dead or injured in the street. On the roofs above us, frightened faces peered down. Arthur climbed into his saddle.

"A spear!" he yelled. "Someone give me a spear!"

"My lord," said Kay, "this isn't our problem. Let's get out of here, and rally our men outside. The cat won't stay in the town long, and if we go after it, we're as likely to get trampled by the mob as find it. It can be hunted down later."

Arthur shook his head. Someone had given him a spear. "No. If it gets into the hills, we may never catch it."

"What's so bad about that?" I said. "I'm sure it's had its fill of men."

"Yes," said Arthur, "the poor beast probably has. But there won't be much to feed it in those bare hills, nothing like the stags up north. And our best stud farms are nearby. No, it was my foolish weakness that allowed it to be brought here. I must go after it myself."

"Arthur, this is lunacy!" said Kay, no longer so phlegmatic. "We need to get you out of here."

"The hell you do! This is a judgment on me, on my sin. I command you to get yourselves out of here, and meet the rest of the troops outside the walls. Once you've got them together, you can set about restoring order inside the city. With Rufficius dead, his bullyboys won't be worth much. Get the mob quieted down, do whatever is needed. For me, I'm after the cat." He rode into the center of the street and shouted up at the townspeople above us. "You, up there on the roof, did you see where the cat went?"

Someone on the other side of the building shouted something, and a woman in a red shawl pointed to the north. "There! It's running toward the forum. Save us, my Lord Arthur. Save us from this monster, and we'll all turn Christian!"

He smiled then, actually smiled, but only for an instant, then the mask of saintly suffering came back. Before anyone could stop him, or even think to follow, he spurred his mount down the street, turning the corner in a spray of gravel. "Shit!" said Kay. "Damn you, Arthur, for a pigheaded fool!" Despite the words, there was admiration in his voice.

I still had the bow I'd picked up, and the quiver with a dozen arrows. No one else had a bow, and no one, I wagered, was half the shot I was. Once, a long time ago, my skill had saved Arthur from the giant Cado. If I could kill a giant, I could kill a cat, even such a big one. "I'm going after him," I said, reaching for the nearest reins. "That idiot wants to find his death, but I'm not going to let him."

"He forbade us to follow him," said Geraint.

"Yes, he did," I said as I scrambled up into the saddle, "but he didn't order you to stop anyone else from doing so. Now get out of my way."

Geraint was helping Gawain to his horse. "Go, brother," said Gawain through clenched teeth. "Help him if you can, but don't get yourself killed."

Snarling, I wheeled my gelding around. "I don't intend to. This won't be the first time I saved Arthur's arse, will it? Now get out of here, all of you, like he said." With that, I spurred the horse, who took off nervously down the street.

Around the corner, I saw people pouring along the cross lane ahead, running into houses, slamming shut doors and shutters. I plunged the horse straight into them, no time to stop or be careful, and miraculously managed to get through the crush without trampling anyone or being knocked from the saddle. From the looks of things, relatively few onlookers had yet made it out into the streets. No doubt they'd jammed the exits in their panicked rush, and now the crushed bodies were piling up inside. *Idiots,* I thought, *you're killing more of yourselves than one animal ever could.*

Somewhere ahead of me, I heard a hissing roar, and with it the terrible screaming whinny that's the death cry of a horse, and knew that the stricken mount must be my father's. *Fuck you, Arthur,* I thought, *you're nothing to me anymore, not for years, so be dead already, I don't care.* But then why was I spurring my poor mare so, gripping her sides with my aching knees as I unslung the bow and put an arrow in my mouth? I plunged her down a side street and around another bend, moving toward the center of the town, where the forum lay, where the horse's scream had come from. Shuttered windows flashed past, dilapidated house fronts, pools of mud and filth that were churned up by her hooves, then those hooves were clattering on cobblestones, and we were in the shadow of a crumbling, graffiti-covered marble arch.

Beyond lay the forum, a square some thirty yards wide, surrounded on three sides by colonnades and on the fourth by what had once been the town hall, and now appeared to be a fortified private dwelling, most likely belonging to the late Rufficius. No time to take in details—something big and black was sprawled on the blood-splashed cobblestones, Arthur's dead charger, with something gray and brown and almost as big tearing at it on one side, and Arthur himself pinned by his leg underneath the other, his useless spear a dozen feet away.

My mare shrieked, rearing to a halt, and I slipped from the saddle to avoid being thrown, bow in one hand and an arrow in the other. By all rights, the fight should have been out of the Palag Cat, exhausted as it must have been by its battle with the dogs and flight through the city. That was probably why it hadn't killed Arthur yet, but only crouched there, gnawing idly on the stomach of his fine Gallic charger, ignoring the man trapped a few feet away.

But no, the fight wasn't out of it. It looked up from its prey, spitting blood, and came over the dead horse at me, Arthur slashing with a dagger at its belly as it leapt over him, but I don't think he connected, and I shot it, once in the white patch on its throat and once in the shoulder, then flung myself to the side, tearing open my hand and bruising my forearm on cobblestones as it hurtled blindly past. The cat smashed into a wooden column, which cracked and came loose from its foundation, ripping away part of the awning in a cloud of plaster, then the monster was twisting on its side, shrieking and writhing, trying to chew at the arrows in its flesh and tearing itself with its own tusks in the process.

Arthur had squirmed out from under his gutted horse, and had even picked up the spear, which he used as a crutch as he limped past me, apparently intending to finish off the wounded cat, although he looked in no shape to do so. The beast was rolling, slashing at itself, blood and fur were flying, then its frenzy seemed to pass, and it came unsteadily to its feet, reeling a bit, but focusing back on us, and it coughed, a wet low sound, and came shuffling forward, swaying from side to side like a huge four-legged drunkard. Arthur was now between me and it, and I moved to the left, hoping to draw it away from him. "Here, kitty, kitty, kitty, kitty," I said nonsensically, feeling urine run down my leg and fumbling for another arrow without knowing if there were any left, for some had spilled out in my fall. The cat's charge was a clumsy, lumbering trot, straight at me, and as it passed Arthur, he put his spear into its side and leaned on it, driving it in with all his weight, his boots scraping on the pavement as the cat dragged him with it. It gave another gurgling cough, and as its head snapped convulsively up, I found my one remaining arrow and shot it just under its tufted chin.

Its charge halted, it stood there, stiff on four splayed legs, Arthur still hanging on to the spear, the beast's eyes staring almost straight up, and its curving fangs pointing forward. Drawing my sword, I came around those fangs and drove my blade to the hilt into its other side, so that I actually felt my point glance off what might have been Arthur's buried spearhead. For what seemed a long time we stood braced like that, the cat, Arthur, and me, our weapons married to its flesh, and then, without a sound, it collapsed between us, and we pitched forward on top of it, and there was fur and blood on my face, and the smell of ammoniac feline urine, and I was vomiting, and from the sound of it, so was Arthur.

I lay there, facedown in what felt like a hot, rank, fur-covered hillock, until Arthur's head appeared over the mound that was the cat's body. "Mordred," he said, giving my name an inflection I hadn't heard since I was a boy, "are you all right?"

I wiped my own bile off my mouth and struggled to my feet. "Yes," I said, in a voice that sounded like someone else's. Everything ached, and my head was so light, and what was that pounding in my ears?

Arthur limped forward, steadying himself against the dead cat's flank, and nearly collapsed on top of me. "Merciful God," he said, as we both stumbled to our knees, leaning into each other. "Oh, my son, forgive me."

He would have hugged me, I think, but I twisted away. "Don't touch me," I said. "And don't call me your son. Time's past for that."

He continued to kneel there, beside the cat, as I tottered away from him, waddling on my bruised knees. "It's a miracle," I heard him say. "We should both be dead."

I looked around for my horse, but she'd fled out the archway. Smart beast. "Is that what you wanted, when you went after the cat alone? Were you trying to be a martyr?"

He ran bloody hands through his hair. "I don't know," he said dully.

"Then don't talk about miracles. Sometimes things don't mean anything. They just happen."

Standing, I trudged back to him, intending to help him to his feet, but he was bent in prayer, and I had to wait until he'd finished, trying not to listen to his murmuring drone, the litany of Jesuses and Marys, the imprecations for forgiveness. Finally he looked up at me, his eyes more gray than blue. "No. Everything means something."

There was nothing I could say to that. I helped him up, and together we hobbled out of the square. From a rooftop somewhere, people were cheering. *So that's it,* I thought, *we're both heroes now, and it can't helped. My place at Camelot is assured.* Supporting his weight and trying not to laugh, I led my father under the cracked archway and down the empty, rubbish-strewn street.

Thirty

I WONDER if I'll ever be the subject of a Triad, that verse form so beloved by the bards of Gwynnedd, who like their heroic exploits in triplicate, as an aid to poetic memory. In a generation's time, if the Saxons haven't overrun us all, will harpists commemorate the Three Noble Deeds of Mordred? Possibly yes, and folk still unborn, who know nothing of what I thought and felt, will remember that I slew Cado and the Palag Cat, and rescued Guinevere from the Kingdom of Teeth. Of course, that last deed may yet be my undoing. Don't be impatient. I'll describe it shortly.

The body of the Palag Cat was dragged through the streets of Caerwent, to the steps of the old Temple of Diana, which Arthur ordered consecrated as a church. "Understand what has happened here," he said hoarsely to the crowd. "It is only because of God's grace that Mordred and I were able to slay this monster. You have been saved from its depredations so that your souls may be won to Jesus. This was His victory, not ours." With that he knelt to pray. I stood there, feeling uncomfortable, him kneeling beside me and the intermingled soldiers and townsfolk kneeling before us, and wondered if I should do the same, if only for appearance's sake. Before I'd made my mind up, Arthur was standing again. I can't remember what else he said, only that I was tired and sore and wanted to be somewhere else.

We did not speak, then or later, of how I'd rebuffed his

unexpected attempt at reconciliation, shoving him away
when he'd called me son. Things should have been more
awkward than ever between us, but somehow they
weren't. Killing the cat together had not made us close,
exactly, but certain barricades had crumbled. It was as if
we were now resigned to each other.

Arthur was naturally obliged to reward me for saving
his life, and I was promised the title of Commander of
Horse, as soon as a new squadron could be recruited.
Unfortunately, that took time, and meanwhile there was
little for me to do at Camelot. Arthur decreed that I
should be given new quarters in the palace, and so I
moved into a tower room that had once belonged to
Merlin, and which no one had wanted since his exile. It
was drafty and leaky, but more private than the barracks. Here I had the time and the privacy to finish
preserving Mother's head, curing it like a ham over a low
fire, soaking it in brine and precious oils, then curing it
again, with the process repeated until all the danger of
rot was baked out of it, and it could be safely stored in a
dry place.

Although I will not detail the campaigns here, the
following summer proved quite eventful, with a flurry of
Irish raids and a minor Saxon uprising. Emboldened by
this, and thinking Arthur busy in the South, the Picts
grew restless and sacked several villages this side of the
Wall. In retaliation, Gawain and Geraint were ordered
to Strathclyde, where, with their squadrons and levies
from the local warbands, they ran the insurgents to
ground in the Caledonian hills. Alas, I saw none of that
excitement.

My newfound friendship with Guinevere flourished,
united as we were by useless education and frustrated
boredom. Arthur kept delaying the wedding, and the
strain of waiting had begun to show on her. A winter
passed, and then a spring, and they were still not
married. Arthur was always away somewhere, leading a
host to one tributary kingdom or another, building new
fortifications and restoring old ones, and generally
avoiding Camelot.

I found myself wishing he'd return, and get the wedding over with, and not just for Gwen's sake. I wanted to bury Mother's head, and be done with it, with all memories of my Orkney life, to truly start anew here, and maybe even someday be happy, now that I'd attained everything I'd once desired. Of course, I desired new things now, or one new thing, although I wasn't yet ready to admit that to myself. But I am getting ahead of my story yet again. Here then is the final chapter of my history, as least as it has unfolded so far, the tale of myself and Guinevere.

Thirty-one

I WAS rubbing cedar oil into my mother's head when
someone knocked at the door. Stuffing the rag I'd
been using into her mouth, I put the head back into its
oakwood chest, locked the chest with the bronze key I
kept on a cord about my neck, and threw a sheepskin
over it. That would suffice, I hoped, to keep her quiet, for
I didn't want it known that I'd brought this charming
ancestral custom with me to Camelot. Not that Morgawse would ever have been very welcome here, even
when she was alive.

I opened the door. Sunlight lanced in through a
narrow window set in the tower's stairwell, casting a
dust-filled halo around Guinevere and highlighting her
glorious hair. Over her shoulder loomed her maid, big
cod-faced Regan, whose sour manner and plain gray
gown still made me think she should have been a nun.

"Hello, Gwen," I said, smiling.

"Good morning, Mordred," she said in the lilting
tones of the Summer Country. *Lugh and Jesus,* I
thought, struck afresh by her high-cheeked triangle of a
face, clear pale skin, and magically green eyes, for she
had the sort of beauty that seemed new each time you
saw her. *Marry her, Arthur,* I said to myself, *marry her
and stop tempting me this way.*

"I'd like to talk to you," she said, breaking my reverie.

"Of course." I stepped back and motioned her into the
circular chamber that had once been Merlin's sanctum.

"Not here. Meet me in the amphitheater later. We can play chess, and I'll have Regan bring wine and cheese for us."

The idea seemed not to sit well with Regan, who made a low sound not unlike a mastiff growling in its sleep. She still didn't like me and resented my easy familiarity with her mistress. Guinevere and I both ignored her.

"All right, then. I'll see you there. You owe me a chance to redeem myself." Gwen had proved a wicked chess player, and had humiliated me on more than one occasion since our first abortive match.

"Thanks, love." With that, she was off down the staircase, Regan lumbering after her.

It may seem odd that we were on such good terms. In one month, she'd be Arthur's queen, assuming the wedding didn't suffer yet another delay while he went off to rebuild the Saxon Shore defenses, fight the Picts or Irish, or bully some local king into paying his taxes. As a bastard, my only chance at the crown was for Arthur to directly name me heir, which had never been very likely, but would become even less so if Guinevere bore him a son. Yet friends we were, and had been since almost the first day we met.

Perhaps it was because Guinevere had received a fairly good education after being bundled off to a convent in Brittany. I'd learned the Trivium and Quadrivium from my mother, while Gwen had endured having reading and rhetoric drummed into her by surprisingly literate nuns, but the results were much the same. With Merlin thankfully long gone, I was the only person with whom she could share the burden of her learning.

For all her easy manner, there had been a note of genuine concern in her voice. That did not surprise me. She seemed to be under a cloud these days, and on more than one occasion I'd seen a haunted look creep briefly into those damnably green eyes. Maybe she was finally going to tell me what was wrong.

Restorations to Camelot began in the days of my great-uncle, Ambrosius Aurelianus, Uther's brother and the last Count of the Saxon Shore. Needing a base for his

Severn campaigns, Ambrosius had repaired the outer ramparts of ruined Isca, the Second Augustan's abandoned home. His brother Uther had continued the work, and changed the fort's name to Camelot when he made it his winter palace. After Arthur's coronation, it became the seat of power for all of Britain, with the old summer palace in Cornwall being ceded back to Cador. If Ambrosius were alive today, he'd never recognize his old Severn headquarters, which in his day had been a crumbling ruin.

The amphitheater just outside the southeast wall is still an empty shell, however, with the bleachers and other wooden facilities long gone and the central field now just a circular green meadow. Its dilapidated state is something I've never understood. As the episode with the Palag Cat should indicate, Arthur's not the type for games or blood sports, but it would make a fine parade ground and drilling field. Despite this, he perversely prefers to train his men in the muddied purlieus to the west, saying that they'll have to fight in muck often enough, so they might as well drill in it. And so the amphitheater remains a grassy bowl rimmed by broken gray and brown stones. Pass it on a summer's night and you'd probably hear the low rhythmic sounds of lovemaking coming from the shadowed hollow, for couples often sneak there from the palace or the town, to lie together on the cool grass under a veil of stars; warriors, lords, and commoners screwing within a dozen paces of each other and happily unmindful of the company.

But this was the afternoon, and we were alone except for Regan, who knitted in the sunlight some ways off, sitting on a tumbled piece of masonry and glaring at me when Guinevere wasn't looking. Gwen and I lounged on a blanket in the shade of the crumbly wall, eating pears and smoked goat cheese and dry brown bread, sipping watered wine and playing chess. She was wearing an emerald gown that left her pale arms bare, and there were green and gold ribbons in her flaming hair.

She took my queen with a knight to whom I'd not paid

enough attention, deftly putting me once again in check. "Mate, I think."

"Bloody hell." My position did look grim. If I'd been playing anyone else, I'd have thrown the pretty little oak board against the wall by now. That thought must have shown on my face.

"Ach," she said gently, "now I've done it. I hope your wounded male pride won't keep you from giving me the benefit of your wisdom." Despite her loveliness, her features were slightly irregular, and when she smiled, it turned crooked, becoming what I couldn't help thinking of as a lopsided fuck-me grin.

I cut off a slice of cheese and fruit and handed it to her. "Come on, you know I'm not as graceless as that. If I resented your winning, I'd have stopped playing you long ago. What is it that you need?"

She nibbled daintily on her wedge of fruit and cheese. Her teeth were among the whitest I'd ever seen, second only to those of one of Arthur's warriors, a Spanish mercenary who gargled each morning with his own piss. Her breath was rather better than his, though.

"Advice, really. Do you know much about the Otherworld?"

Now why was she asking that? "A little," I said noncommittally.

"Your mother was a sorceress, wasn't she?"

I stared into those big green eyes, which gave away no more of what she was thinking than a cat's eyes do. "Yes. For all the good it did her."

She sighed. "Mine too, and it didn't do her much good, either. I think it was magic that killed her in the end. Was that what killed yours?"

I plucked a bluebell from the grass and pretended to look at it. "No. Her husband killed her."

She took my hand. "That's why he's dead now, isn't it?"

"Yes. I helped a bit with that." Jesus, I'd never expected to admit it, not to anyone, and certainly not so casually.

She hadn't let go of my hand. Hers was soft, but with a surprisingly firm grip. "You can talk about it, you know. To me, I mean. I know it must be difficult to speak of it around Arthur."

I squeezed her palm. "This isn't what you wanted to talk about. You were asking about the Otherworld."

She let go then, which was a relief, for I found her touch uncomfortably exciting. "When I was a little girl in Castle Cadbury, my mother saved my teeth each time I lost one."

I laughed. "What, for the fairies? I thought only peasants did that."

She frowned. "Everyone in that part of the Summer Country did that. They'd save their children's teeth and bury them, usually in some mound or hillock. It was supposed to bring them good luck and a long life. The practice was so common, the monks at Glastonbury forbade anyone to bury teeth in the tor, saying the place was too holy to be defiled with pagan custom."

I snorted. "Glastonbury was a place of power long before there was a chapel there."

Gwen nodded. "I know. Anyway, my mother was different. She wasn't trying to bring me a long life or good health. She was trying to buy them for herself."

"Oh." This sounded darker than I'd first assumed.

"It's best I just tell the whole story," she continued. "One day when I was little, maybe seven or eight—I'm not sure—my mother took me out riding. It was in late autumn, I think; one of those wet, gray days with a sky like an overturned iron bowl. There were just three of us, me and mother on her fine mare and a tall servant named Sergius on a swaybacked nag. The Saxons were everywhere in those days, but Mother didn't seem worried. I guess she was confident that her magic would protect us.

"The land flattened out, and we rode for hours seeing nothing but low hills and sheep. Finally, a large mound loomed on the horizon. It was nightfall when we reached it. At the top, Mother had Sergius make a fire with the bundle of kindling they'd brought with them. After it had burned for a while, she cut off a lock of my hair with her dagger and then took out a small purse containing every tooth I'd ever lost. She buried the teeth in a circle around the fire, tapping them like seeds into the muddy earth. Kneeling down, she threw the lock of my hair onto the flames and began talking in a voice so low I couldn't make out what she was saying. She did that for a long time, while Sergius and I just stood there watching. Once, he caught my eye and crossed himself. Finally, she stood up and said it was time to go home.

"Later in her chambers, she drew me close to her. 'No men,' she said to me. 'Don't ever lie with a man. Do you understand me? You're to stay a virgin, Guinevere, a virgin always. Don't let a man put his cock in you.'"

"I hardly knew what she meant, but I asked her why. 'Because,' she said, 'you're promised to a fairy king, and he won't want you if your maidenhead is broken. I've bound you to him with your teeth and your hair.' She got a faraway look in her eyes and stopped holding me so tight. 'I don't want to get old,' she said. 'King Melwas is a lord of age and loss; he can make me stay young, if he wishes. If he likes you, you won't get old, either. Your teeth won't fall out, and your hair will keep its color. And the same for me. Except you'll be with him, and I'll be here. Don't fret; you'll feast on sweet apples in the Otherworld, and drink nectar from a silver cup.' I didn't understand what she was talking about, of course, but I didn't ask her to explain. Just thinking about it frightened me."

Guinevere stretched out on her stomach, her chin in her hands. Those hands were rather big for a woman her size, as were her feet, which were bare, for she'd slipped out of her sandals. Like the crooked grin, these deviations from the classical ideal did little damage to her beauty.

"That was that, until I was twelve or so. One day big, shifty-eyed Sergius got me alone in the stable. He said that I should lie with him, that he could save me. He said he knew the bargain that my mother had made, and that it would doom me, but if I lay with him, I'd be free.

Melwas would have no claim on me once my maiden-head was gone."

I thought of her then, seeing her all small and fragile in my head, and I wanted to kill this Sergius, wherever he was now. "What happened?"

Guinevere picked up a small orange beetle with black spots and let it crawl upon her forefinger. She did not speak again until it spread its wings and flew away.

"He tried to force me, but I got away. Mother had him hanged, of course, with his eyes put out first and his nose, fingers and toes all cut off. Soon after that, she sent me across the Channel to the convent. I never saw her again. She was killed the next winter when a horse fell on top of her. Stupid woman. She hadn't asked to stay young, just not to get old. I suppose you could say her wish was granted."

She rested her chin on her hands and looked at me with little girl solemnity. "I'm still a virgin, Mordred, which is surprising. Lots of girls lost their maidenheads at the convent. Novice nuns can be just as wicked as monks, you know. I even joined in some of their love games, but I never let anyone put a candle or carrot inside me. Do I shock you?"

I smiled. "Not likely. So, you kept your mother's wishes in mind?"

She shook her head. "No, I forgot them for a time. The sisters had as many books as some monasteries, and a few of those books were secular, even worldly. They allowed me to read whatever I wanted. There in Brittany, reading the old dead Greeks and Romans with their clear logic and polished grammar, I felt very far away from the superstitions of the Summer Country.

"And then my father brought me back to meet Arthur. Here was a Christian king whose reign had been prophesied by a magician, a magician who claimed to be the son of a Prince of the Otherworld. I never met Merlin, but Arthur has told me about him, and I know my husband-to-be is not a liar. For all that Merlin aided his father, Arthur was terrified of him. Anything that scares Arthur must be very real and very dangerous. Merlin was real enough. Still is, presumably, in his Caledonian exile. Maybe Melwas is real, too."

I lay on my back and looked at the sky, a high blue dome mottled with scudding clouds and wheeling birds, its sweeping arch for once free of any sign of rain. What to tell her that would make her feel better? I couldn't lie, not to her; she was too smart for that.

"It's true; the Otherworld is real enough," I said at last. "It's not just a place to be found over the sea or at the bottom of a lake or inside a hollow hill. It's all around us, inside us even. Believe in it, but don't believe everything you hear about it. Not every superstition is true. People get things wrong, Gwen, all the time, about magic as much as anything else. My mother taught me a lot about the Otherworld and those that dwell there. She never said anything about a prince of that realm named Melwas."

She didn't seem reassured. "Perhaps he's something very old, a god even, one that most people don't remember anymore."

"And perhaps he doesn't exist at all. Soon you'll be married and everything will be all right. If you want to be rid of your maidenhead before then, there's plenty of strapping louts about who can arrange that for you. If Arthur ever asks, tell him that Sergius succeeded in his attempt that time in the stables."

She laughed and threw a piece of cheese at me; she'd never been an easy one to shock. "Right, I could be like one of those old Roman ladies, and have a stream of lovers trooping through my husband's bed. I don't think so, Mordred. I just wish he hadn't postponed the wedding again. You'd think he was scared of me."

Not of you yourself, I thought, *but of what you represent.* That time my mother lay with him in disguise had given him a scar inside, turning him toward God and away from the flesh. He was frightened, if not of marriage, of what went on in the marriage bed. But I couldn't tell her that.

I sat up. "Don't worry, Gwen. You're safe here in Camelot. You'll marry the greatest king this island has ever known, and you're safe in his fortress. Nothing can touch you here."

She sighed. "Except dreams. That's why I brought this up. Last night, I had the same nightmare for the third time in a week. I was running barefoot through a sort of maze. The walls, the floor, the ceiling, everything was made of sharp little stones the color of bone. They cut my feet. Behind me, someone was calling my name in a voice like the sound the wind makes in the eaves at night. I knew it was Melwas, and I was in his power."

I took her hand again. "Dreams are usually just dreams, Gwen. Oh, they can be portents, sometimes, but people put too much stock in that. Usually they tell us more about what we're thinking right now, about the things we want and are scared of, than what's going to happen in the future."

She looked at me without speaking for a long moment, until I felt I might drown in those deep eyes. "Thank you, Mordred," she said at last. "I think I just needed to hear some common sense. You're very good at that, you know."

What she did next surprised me, and even in those days I was not easy to surprise. Bending close, she kissed me. If my head hadn't been slightly tilted, she would have caught me on the mouth instead of the cheek, and even so, our lips brushed for a moment. When I was able to think again, I was glad no one but Regan had seen us.

She put the chessmen back in their little bag and the wine flask back in the basket, which she handed to Regan, and the two of them began the climb up and out of the amphitheater. I remained behind, sitting on the grass, my feet in a warm patch of sunlight and my back against the cool stone. Eventually my erection went away, but when I shut my eyes I could still feel the warm touch of her hand upon my own.

Thirty-two

ARTHUR RETURNED to the palace that afternoon, at the head of a troop of dirty and exhausted soldiers. He'd been drilling them hard, staging mock campaigns with wooden swords and padded armor, pitting squadron against squadron in the mud flats that surrounded the lower reaches of the Usk at low tide. Peacetime would not soften their edge, he liked to say. If the North and South Saxons ever tried to unite, and break the wedge that had been driven between them at Badon, they'd find themselves facing a British army as disciplined and ready as any Roman legion.

That night, when Guinevere and almost everyone else had gone to bed, I found him staring moodily into the dying fire. Disdaining the room's Roman-style couches, he sat cross-legged on a wolf skin in front of the raised hearth, still wearing his ragged harness, a mug of hot ale in his hand and a distant expression on his weathered, clean-shaven face. Studying his fire-limned features, I saw fresh gray streaks in his close-cropped peppery hair, new care lines on his brow and about his wintry eyes.

I remembered that face with fewer lines, and the hair with no gray, as he squinted into the unceasing wind and tried not to look at me. For the hundredth or the thousandth time, the familiar tired words echoed in my head. *Get up behind me; I'll not leave you here, no matter what you are.* The memory no longer had any sting.

"Stop postponing the wedding," I said at last. "It's bothering Guinevere."

"I owe her an apology," he said softly. "And much else besides, considering what sort of husband she's getting. Still, it couldn't be helped. Mark would never have paid his taxes if I hadn't ridden to collect them with a thousand horsemen at my back. Then there was Cormac and his reivers. I can't neglect my duties, no matter how long the land has been at this uneasy peace."

"Yes, but you've more than one sort of duty. You can't just bring her here, then put off marrying her until you're both old and gray. Get it done with, for your sake and hers."

He continued to look at the fire. "What's it to you?"

A good question, that. "I like her, and think she can make you happy. You accepted me here at Camelot when you didn't have to, after Lot and my mother were dead and there was nothing for me in Orkney. I owe you for that, for I know that you'd have been more comfortable if I had gone elsewhere."

He grunted. "If I'd turned you away, I'd have lost Gawain, the best captain I have. My happiness can't be the only reason you want to see me wedded."

I sat beside him on the hearth. "It's a matter of more than happiness. She may be in danger."

He finally looked at me. "What do you mean?"

"Her mother was a sorceress, and not as wise a one as mine. She made a bargain with the Otherworld, pledging her daughter's virginity to a power there. When you wed Guinevere, the terms of that bargain will be broken, and no one will have a claim on her but you. Until that happens, though, I fear for her. Do it before the summer's over. Hell, do it now."

He drained his cup and put it aside. "I'm not grateful for this knowledge, Mordred. I've been too touched by the dark world as it is. This wedding was a way out of that, something clean, with nothing of the stain that has lain upon my life. Now you tell me that it's not clean at all."

Shit, here came his damned guilt again—was there no aspect of his wretched life into which it didn't creep? *Don't be a prat,* I wanted to say to him. *The past is bloody well past; let it rot and be forgotten.* But of course I didn't.

"Clean or unclean, that has nothing to do with this. It's probably just superstition, anyway. Her mother may have been at least as mad as she was magical. But have the wedding soon and you'll allay her fears."

He stood up. "If she has fears, she can confide them to me. I'll not jump at shadows, or be moved by hearsay. Thanks for your concern, but we don't need to speak of this again."

With that he left me, to the dying firelight and myself. Well, I'd tried my best, and if my best wasn't good enough, there was no sense worrying. Besides, was I really so eager to see her wed to him? There was nothing for it but to go to bed.

Trudging back up to Merlin's old room, I was again grateful that I no longer shared the barracks with Gawain. When we were young, he'd teased me often enough for talking in my sleep, and there was no reason to believe I'd lost the habit. If my recent dreams were any indication, I was all too likely to break the stillness of the night by whispering Guinevere's name.

Two weeks later, I was in Caerwent on a cool, clear afternoon, pushing my way through the jostling crowds and trying to keep my prized doeskin boots out of the wide refuse-strewn gutter that ran down the center of the gravel street. I'd dressed in a new cloak with an intricate blue-and-green plaid and my best red woolen tunic, in the hopes that outward finery would improve my mood. If that didn't, there was always food. Word had reached the palace that oyster boats from Cornwall were docked in the harbor, which meant they were already being smoked and sold in the forum, along with trade goods from across the Channel. I was heading that way when I rounded a corner and saw Guinevere coming out of the church that had once been a temple of Diana. She wore a red wool mantle over a gown of green-and-gold linen, and there were silver pins in her braided hair.

"Hello," I said, squeezing my way through a small flock of confused-looking sheep. "Don't tell me you've come here alone, dressed in such finery. Where's your shadow?"

She laughed. "Regan has a cold. It was too nice a day to stay cooped up in the palace, so I bullied Kay into letting me come to town. Unfortunately, you weren't to be found, and the only available bodyguard was Dunvallo, who doesn't seem to much appreciate the duty. I left him in the stable, playing dice with the grooms. If you care to join me for the day, you'll spare me having to ride back with him."

I bristled at the thought of her in Dunvallo's company. We'd barely spoken to each other since he'd tried to eject me from the palace garden, but we'd glared at each other on more than one occasion. "I'll be glad to join you. There are oysters in the market."

"Aye, and merchants from Gaul. I've a mind to buy a new brooch, and maybe fine cloth for my wedding gown."

I laughed. "What, it's not made yet?"

For a moment, her expression was grim. "Oh, it's made, but I've had too long to get used to it; perhaps a new one will cheer me up."

I looked up at the stone-and-plaster facade of the church, where the image of the Goddess had rather crudely been transformed into that of the Virgin. "Why pray here when you have the chapel in the palace?"

A donkey nearly bumped into her, but the beast's owner rapped the animal with his staff and tugged his forelock in deference. She patted the donkey's flank as it ambled past.

"I pray wherever I can, Mordred. Bishop Gerontius is a good man, and gives me some comfort. The bloody nightmares have been troubling me again."

We moved toward the forum, me staying slightly ahead of her to keep her from being jostled into the gutter. I was troubled by this news. Even if her dreams weren't portents, they indicated a state of mind that did not bode well for the marriage.

"Can I ask you a blunt question?" I said, frowning at a whore whom I did not want to recognize me just then.

"Of course."

The woman grinned at me, but said nothing as we passed her. "Do you love Arthur?"

"Love him? I hardly know the man. It's been nearly a year since he brought me to Camelot, and in that time he's not spent two continuous weeks here."

That was true enough. Arthur had never been one to lounge at court, but he'd become even more restless since Gwen had arrived, and the wedding had been postponed four times in eighteen months. My abortive attempt at discussing the matter with him had done no good at all.

"What was it like? When you met him, I mean?"

"Oh, God, was I surprised. I'd known something was up when my father brought me out of that wretched convent, for he'd never shown any interest in me before. I suppose if I'd thought about it, I'd have realized some sort of prearranged marriage was in the air, for what else does one do with eligible daughters? But I hadn't thought about it. So there I was in the orchard, sitting under a tree and reading Ovid, when my father came walking down the lane with a man I might have taken for a common soldier."

She smiled warmly, and I felt a pang of jealousy. "Arthur was his usual roughneck self, dressed in worn leather and smelling like a horse, and I could hardly credit it when father introduced him as the Pendragon. Still, when I rose from bowing, I saw depths in those blue eyes, like looking at the sea from high up, or the sky on a bright clear morning."

Oh yes, I knew that gaze; winter, but with just a hint of May. I tried to sound nonchalant. "So, what did you talk about, that first time?"

She sighed. "Not much. He was shy around women, and blushed when I took a bite out of an apple and handed it to him. Then he asked me to read aloud from my book, but when I did he blushed even redder and bade me stop. He must have liked me, though, for the next thing I knew, the arrangements had been made and it was off to Camelot."

I steered her away from a beggar, an ex-soldier who'd lost his arm in some campaign and his nose to the clap. "Were you happy?"

"I was . . . surprised. And nervous, of course. And relieved, for now I knew what the future held for me." She laughed, a full throaty sound, not at all a giggle. "And it's not a bad future, is it, becoming Queen of all the Britons? There were times when I'd thought I'd been forgotten after Mother's death and would grow old among nuns."

I smiled at the thought of her in the convent, a lark cooped up with puffins. We were in the forum now, a big open square, paved in flagstones rather than gravel, walled by open-fronted shops of wood and whitewashed plaster. These were manned by the merchants who actually lived here, and made their homes on the second floor above their goods. Other sellers worked from wooden stalls in the center of the square, or simply stood beside open barrels, or laid their goods out on cowhides or plank-and-trestle tables.

Gwen ended up buying two brooches, both of silver, and a string of white pearls. Then, after haggling with a cloth dealer like any village wife, she purchased a bolt of green-and-gold linen. I bought two dozen smoked oysters from a balding one-eyed Cornishman, then a wicker basket to put them in from a dark little gap-toothed girl with hair even blacker than mine. Gwen helped me devour the oysters before we were out of the forum. She ate more daintily than I did, and scolded me for getting their dark juice on my chin, which she then wiped with one corner of her fine new cloth.

We found her temporary bodyguard in the stable. Red-faced and unpleasant as ever, Dunvallo was lying on his back on the straw, his head on the lap of Megra, the whore I'd seen earlier. Fortunately, she gave no sign that she knew me, but continued to twirl the pointed ends of Dunvallo's mustache.

Dunvallo greeted us with an explosive belch. Rising, he smiled and gave Gwen a bow I thought far too casual. "Here now, Lady Guinevere, I see you've found yourself a new escort. Will you not be needing me, then?"

"No thank you, Lord Dunvallo. Mordred will see me safely back to the palace."

Dunvallo grinned at me, exposing more stumps than whole teeth. "I'm sure he will, for the boy's a good lad, despite everything." The condescending tone was nothing new; he and I had never gotten along.

"You can go now," I said coldly.

"Don't mind if I do," he snickered. "Megra here has been keeping me company, and since I've had a fumble, I'm craving a tumble. She's a fine one in the sack, and she doesn't charge much. Say good-bye to little Mordred, Megra. I believe you two know each other." Megra remained silent, but gave me a smirking curtsy.

Anger flared on Gwen's cheeks. "Lord Dunvallo, you bring dishonor to yourself and to your High King, consorting with a whore in front of his Queen-to-be. I shall speak of this with Arthur, when he returns from Chichester."

That brought a change in Dunvallo's manner. He blanched and fell to one knee, all his arrogance gone at the mention of Arthur's name. "Lady, don't; I didn't mean any disrespect. There's no need to trouble the Pendragon about this; I'll say penance in the chapel tonight and mind my manners in the future. Please forgive me."

There was sweat on his brow. Was it Arthur's rage he feared? No, I knew better than that; it was his disapproval. That was my father's genius, to inspire something like worship even in a sodden, ill-tempered lout like this one.

Guinevere turned to me. "Do you forgive him, Mordred? I believe that you were the one he was trying to insult."

I was starting to enjoy this. "Well, Dunvallo," I said smugly, "is it my forgiveness you crave as well?"

He tilted his head lower, probably to keep Gwen from seeing the expression on his face. "Lord Mordred," he said through what certainly sounded like clenched teeth, "I beg your pardon also."

"You have it, then," I said airily. "Now off with you."

He left, not looking back. After a moment, Megra, who'd watched all this while we ignored her, followed him. She paused at the entrance of the stable long enough to flash a quick grin. "Good day to you, your ladyship," she said to Guinevere. "And one to you also, Mordred." I'd have thrown something at her if she hadn't moved quickly on.

"Whores, is it then?" said Guinevere as I saddled her dappled mare. "The ladies of the palace aren't good enough for you?"

My face felt very warm. Damn her, how could she have this effect on me; I usually didn't give a fart what anybody thought. "A man has needs, my lady."

She snorted. "Don't 'my lady' me, Mordred. We women have needs, too, but we don't go sneaking off to some lusty farm boy or smith's apprentice each time we feel them, do we?"

Enough of this nonsense. I turned from the horse and walked toward her. "Look at me, Gwen; I'm no saint, nor even a proper Christian. My mother once lay with her own brother, and her husband later murdered her in front of me. I may be young, but I've killed men, and not all of them honorably. I get drunk from time to time. I blaspheme a god I don't even believe in. I cheat at games, except for chess. I have a foul temper. And I lie with whores. Accept me as I am, like me or don't like me, be my friend or not, but don't expect me to change."

Damn those unreadable eyes of hers. "Not even for me?"

I turned away from her. "Not even for you, lady. If it was me you were going to marry, maybe I could manage it. But for my father's bride, no, I'm not that perfect, nor do I want to be. I'm satisfied with myself, and that's enough. It's better than some people can claim." It was Arthur I was thinking of.

"I'm sorry," she said softly. "I didn't mean to judge you like that." She tugged at my sleeve until I faced her again, and brushed a strand of hair out of my eyes.

"We better go," I said, looking down at the straw, at her feet, at the delicate tracery of veins in one exposed ankle, at anything but her face.

She didn't say anything else. Neither did I, not in the stable or out of it, or on the road back to the palace. In the courtyard, though, she thanked me, and bade me a good day. There was a sadness in her eyes I'd never noticed there before. Lord knows what was in mine.

The wedding was postponed yet again. There was talk of an alliance forming between Aelle of the South Saxons and Oesc of Kent, with Cunedag of the Picts possibly joining them as well. Nothing came of it, at least not then, but it was a tense summer. Arthur spent much time in the East Midlands, drilling his men with the local warbands and making sure no ambitious petty king would sell him out the way Cerdic had done three years before. Guinevere seemed resigned. "It's become comic," she said. "He *is* older than me, you know; if we go on like this, I'll be a widow before we're even married."

Despite the mordant joking, I could tell she was becoming somewhat depressed and withdrawn, and we spent less time in each other's company. When I did see her, she had circles under her eyes and looked like she wasn't sleeping much. I asked her if she was still having bad dreams. She said no, but I knew she was lying.

Bored and restless, I even thought about visiting Gawain up North, but couldn't quite pull myself away from court, from her, though I knew I'd feel even less comfortable here once she was married. Instead, I started avoiding the fortress, spending my available time riding the broken hills of West Cambria, where the land was higher and rockier than my native Orkney, but just as barren. When I was in the palace, I tended to keep to my chamber. Sometimes, I talked to Mother.

Thirty-three

ERLIN'S OLD sanctum was as spartan as any
monk's cell, just a circular wall of undressed
stone with a floor and ceiling of rough timbers. There
was a trapdoor in the ceiling, which opened on the roof
and leaked during rainstorms. The floor was still covered
with scuffed chalk marks and dried bloodstains and the
crushed stubs of tallow candles. The only other relic of
the chamber's former occupant was the big oak trunk
that I used as a table, which was full of rat-gnawed books
and scrolls. I'd skimmed some of them, but the depredations of the rats, as well as water damage from the leaky
ceiling, had left most unreadable. There had been another trunk, even bigger and rimmed with iron bands and
locked with a heavy padlock. Soft, muddy voices had
whispered from it when I was trying to sleep at night, so
I'd given it to two servants with instructions that it
should be buried somewhere far from the palace.

The timbers in the low ceiling were irregularly set with
small bronze hooks. I took Mother's head from its chest
and hung it from the stoutest hook by a loop I tied in her
dull black hair. Then I sat on the stool that was the
room's only furnishing, other than a tin basin and the
wooden box filled with straw and covered with sheepskins that was my bed. My lamp burned low on top of
the big oak chest, sending shadows dancing across the
shriveled brown face that hung in front of me, smelling
of cedar oil and preservative spices.

"Why did you want me to bring you with me?" I asked it.

The sunken eyes did not open, but the gray lips moved. The voice that issued from between them was faint and full of echoes, as though it was coming from the bottom of a deep well.

"Why do you think I wanted you to do anything?"

So, it would be that sort of conversation. The night before we sailed for Camelot, when Gawain and I slept in a hut beside the collapsed ruin of Lot's palace in Orkney, she'd come to me in a dream, naked and bloody as on the night she'd died. I reminded her of that. "You told me not to leave you there, that I should keep your head with me until the day of Arthur's wedding."

The head actually chuckled, a dry, raspy, disconcerting sound. "Perhaps you had that dream because you could not bear to part with me. Do you love me, Mordred? If so, give me a kiss."

Even dead, she would jab at me like this. "I loved you when you were alive. Now you're just a skull and leathery skin, through which your spirit can speak. Such a thing has no business speaking to me of love. Or should I just bury you, and love your memory?"

She hissed like the wind in dry, dead grass. "Don't do that yet. You need me."

Why had I even begun this conversation? I should have left her locked up in her chest. "I don't need anybody, Mother."

The drawn lips pulled back from yellow teeth, forming what might have been a smile. "Oh? Have you attained your heart's desire?"

This was pointless. I rose to remove the head from the hook, then sat down again. There was one thing I'd been meaning to ask her. "Who is Melwas?"

She was silent for so long I thought she wasn't going to answer. "A lord who is less than he once was," she said at last.

"Less than he once was?"

Her eyes opened then, unnaturally soft and dark and alive in that dead face. "His realm is much diminished.

Ages ago, he warred with the other Fair Folk and lost, to suffer blight and banishment. Now he rules alone in a wasted, barren corner of the Otherworld. Only the offerings given him by the folk of the Summer Country sustain him at all."

I related what Guinevere had told me. "What would this creature want with her?"

Her rictus spread wider. "What does a magpie want with a shiny bauble? He takes pretty things, when they are offered him, though he can get no pleasure from them, and forgets them almost as soon as they are his."

I did not like what I was hearing. "Is she in danger, then?"

She chuckled again. "Why would you care?"

I hated her for enjoying this. "Just answer the question."

"Not if Arthur marries her before Samhain, when the Old Powers are strongest. And not if he lies with her before that. But he is probably unwilling to do such a thing before marriage, and maybe not even after it. That's a pity, for he was a good lay once."

I suddenly wanted to tear her from her hook and dash her against the wall, until her withered brains spilled out upon the floor. Instead, I put her back in her chest and covered her up again.

The autumn came without incident, and it seemed unlikely that the Saxons and Picts would start any trouble before the next summer. Arthur announced that he would definitely marry Guinevere in November, right after Samhain. I tried to tell him something of what Mother had told me, without revealing the source of my information, but it was to no avail. In fact, I wondered if my previous warnings were why he'd kept postponing the wedding throughout the summer, for he could be bloody contrary at times. I also wondered if, perversely, that had been what I'd really wanted, him putting off the marriage so I had more time alone with Guinevere. And I thought these twisty, knife-in-the-gut feelings had died with my mother.

My posting was not to come until after Christmas. It had become too wet and dreary in the hills, so when I wanted to get away from the palace, my only alternative was the town. I tried to forget Guinevere in taverns and in the beds of whores. One such whore in particular was the aforementioned Megra, after I'd gotten over my irritation at how she and Dunvallo had embarrassed me in front of Guinevere. Megra had a room above a smithy near the forum, which one reached via a ladder set against the alley wall after the smithy was locked at night.

The festivities began well before the wedding itself, with the fortress and the whole town turning out for days of games and nights of drunken revelry, to such an extent that one would have thought it was May, with Beltane rather than Samhain coming up. The day before the ceremony, it all became too much, and I got very drunk, then sought solace in Megra's bed. Our fumbling did not go well.

"Never mind, love," she said, sitting up and searching for a flea in her pubic hair, "it happens all the time. Rest a bit, think of something nice, and in no time at all the old Maypole will be tall and straight again, won't it, and we'll have our fun, down the rabbit hole with your old badger, yes we will."

"You're mixing metaphors," I said as I turned over on my back.

"What's that?" she asked, rolling the flea between her thumb and forefinger.

"Metaphors. Maypoles and badgers. Never mind."

Megra hadn't stopped talking. "Oh, you're wrong, love," she continued cheerfully, "it's you who should be paying me no mind, babbling on like I do. I can't help it, though, I'm just a talkative sort; words, words, words and seldom a lick of sense, Fergus used to say. Fergus, now, he was a sweet one. Couldn't stand my chatter, though, not at all. He got to stopping his ears with tallow before coming to my chamber. Tallow, can you believe that? One time, it was a hot summer's night and all, and we'd rolling about for almost an hour, Fergus being able to keep it up like a goat—no offense, love—and wouldn't you know it, the plugs in his ears began to melt, and there he was with yellow goo dripping down the sides of his head, and didn't I just scream and scream. Thought he'd caught some horrible disease, I did; I mean, he *was* Irish."

I padded to the opening in the wall that served as both door and window to Megra's loft. Torches were lit in the street, and there was a bonfire in the square, with warriors and townspeople cavorting about, breaking off in pairs to go screw in the shadows or singly to pass out or puke in some dark corner. At least everyone else was having fun.

"You're thinking of someone else, aren't you?" asked Megra, the lamplight sending shadows dancing across the pink and fleshy landscape of her body.

"No."

"Yes, yes you are. Believe me, I know men. All of you are always thinking of someone else all the time, and you're always bringing them to bed with you. Fergus was like that. In his head, he was with a dozen different women or twenty dozen, I don't know. Not that we women don't do the same. Tell you what, let's play Let's Pretend. Shut your eyes, and tell me who you want me to be, and I'll be her, all night long, as many times as you want. 'Course, you have to be who I want *you* to be, too, it's only fair."

I actually smiled. "No. I don't think so."

"Come on, love, think of it. I could be anyone you want. Helen of Troy, Theodosa–whatever her name is, Iseult of Cornwall. You can even call me Guinevere, if you like."

I turned at that. "What?"

"You can call me Guinevere, and I'll call you Arthur. We can be the King and Queen, here in our heads and bed, and who's to know, and we'll do it better now than they'll be doing it tomorrow, won't we just? Are you for it, then? Grab my tits and call me Gwennie."

Before I knew it, I was on top of her, not in any loving

or lustful way, but with one hand twisting her hair and the other clutching her under the chin.

"Don't say that. And don't bring her into this. I mean it."

Her eyes were popping, and she was gasping like a landed carp, and then I had control of myself again and let her go, for relations with Arthur would be even worse if I committed murder on the night before his wedding. No dead whores for the dowry. Still, it might do me good to kill someone.

I donned my wool breeches and tunic, pulled on my boots and picked up my belted sword. Megra huddled on her sheepskin, her broad, flat face all frightened eyes staring out from under her disheveled hair. "I'm sorry," I said as I stood up.

"Fine," she mumbled. "I just didn't know you were like the rest, that's all."

"Like the rest of what?"

"Men. Always ready to hurt."

"Yes, Megra," I said gently. "We're all alike. Bastards, bloody bastards all. I wish we weren't." I kissed her on the cheek and left.

When I clambered down the ladder, I found half a dozen or so palace warriors waiting in the alley, hunkered down and throwing dice by the light of a small pile of burning manure. Available girls were in short supply this night, so they were waiting their turns with Megra. One of them, bigger than the others, starting laughing when he saw me. I recognized the braying voice as Dunvallo's.

"Done already, Mordred?" he asked with a boozy leer. "The salt air of Orkney must breed limp manhood."

I stopped and looked at him, and actually found myself smiling. This was the sort of trouble Gawain usually kept me out of, but he had been delayed up North. Bad luck for me, maybe, but worse for this idiot.

The firelight made Dunvallo even more red-faced than usual, and as he lurched closer I smelled the ale on his breath and saw fresh, unidentified crusty stains all tan-

gled in his filthy beard. He was not a fastidious sort, even
sober. More to the point, he was one of those men who
seem bigger when they're drunk. If I did fight him, I'd be
a fool to fight fair.

"Arthur won't have any such trouble tomorrow," he
continued, turning back to his cronies. "Not with a
handful like Guinevere. The Pendragon, bless him, has
been too solemn of late. It'll do him good to lie with that
tasty piece of work. Maybe it'll make him forget his past
troubles, like the time a certain witch tricked him into
siring this whelp here. Or is that just a story the bitch
made up?"

He turned back to me. "It's a lie, isn't it, Orkney-boy,
the claim that the Dragon is your father. I mean, how
could he be? You're short and dark as a Pict. That's what
really happened, isn't it? You mother screwed a Pict,
then told everybody she'd lain with her own brother."

Dunvallo was obviously extremely drunk, and his
comrades seemed a bit taken aback by this, shocked
even. Oh, they didn't like me much, but even if they
didn't believe me Arthur's son, they knew he was my
uncle, and that made me blood kin to a man they worshiped, a relationship not to be spoken of in such coarse
terms. For myself, I'd made my mind up to kill Dunvallo when he made his crude reference to Gwen, and
his cheap insults only gave me a pretext. Still smiling, I looked him straight in the eye, my thumb resting on the hilt of my sword. "I'll have an apology for that.
Or your blood."

"Oh, what's this?" he said, sneering. "I think I should
be the one to take offense, Mordred. What was it you
called me the other night?"

"A cretinous rat-faced git who smells like a pig's arse
and looks like somebody who would fuck one," I said
loudly and clearly. Actually, I'd only called him half of
that, the part before the word "who," but since he was
already drunk, I might as well make him really mad, too.
That way he might not fight so well. Oh, yes, a wise
strategy indeed, like asking someone to piss on your
head when your breeches are on fire.

His sword was out and glittering in the torchlight. "I'm going to cut you, Orkney-boy; I'm going to open you up and feed your guts to my dogs. How's that?"

Instead of drawing my own sword, I turned and walked out into the middle of the street, then wheeled to face him. "Maybe you will, Dunvallo. It's in God's hands now. Will you let me kneel and pray before we fight?"

He laughed as he came after me. "You, pray?"

"Arthur will take it better if he hears you let him pray first," said one of his companions.

The logic was specious, but Dunvallo paused a moment. Arthur's displeasure was something he'd apparently not considered. "All right, then; kneel away. But be quick, or I'll chop you before you're up again."

I knelt. My right hand was beside my calf, out of his line of sight. I felt for a handful of gravel and found a fresh horse turd instead. Well, that would do. When I was a boy in Orkney, I could bring birds down from cliffs with just a stone and my throwing arm.

I stood up and threw the turd in one motion. My sword was out a half second after it smacked him in the face, and he was bellowing and scraping it from his eyes when I lunged and cut low at his legs. My blade caught him on the right thigh just below the hem of his woolen tunic, and I felt it bite down into bone. I pulled it out and skipped back.

"You bastard," he yelled in a high-pitched voice. "I'm going to kill you!"

"You'll have to catch me first," I said, still dancing backwards. With such a wound he'd be much slower, and all I had to do was stay out of his way until blood loss took its toll.

He came lurching forward, his face very pale now; the blood soaking through his cross-gartered breeches was black in the firelight. If he'd had any brains, he would have called upon his comrades to protect him while he staunched his wound, but instead he just stumbled after me, groaning and cursing. He didn't take more than ten paces before falling to his knees.

I walked up to him. He tried to use his sword to help himself stand. I knocked it away with mine. "Mercy," he gasped. "I yield."

"Too late for that, Dunvallo," I said. I cut at his neck, but he put up his arm. Only in stories do you cut someone's arm clean off with one blow. My sword got stuck in the bone just above his elbow. His eyes rolled up as I put my foot on his chest and pulled the blade out. He flopped backwards and lay there bleeding. After a while, he didn't breathe anymore. None of his friends had made a move to help him.

"You didn't fight fair," said one of them, sounding for all the world like a petulant child. Despite this, he was a hard-looking oaf, nearly as big as Dunvallo and rather lighter on his feet. Drawing his sword, he advanced on me, with several of his comrades following suit.

"Come on, shitheads," I said with a careless laugh. I heard hoofbeats in the street behind me, the sound of several riders, but did not turn around. "You want some of what your friend got? Come on, then." Flight would have been prudent; although quite drunk, they were all hardened veterans, with years of experience in cutting up armed men, whereas all I had to my name was a couple of minor skirmishes. I didn't care; the thought of getting wounded or even killed on the night before Arthur and Guinevere's wedding was perversely attractive.

"Enough of this nonsense," snapped a voice behind me. "Put away those goddamn swords, all of you, or I'll stick them up your bums." I didn't sheathe my sword, but I did lower it as I turned around, for even in those circumstances I was not stupid enough to raise a weapon without knowing whom I faced.

There were five riders, four holding torches that glittered off their polished mail. The fifth, a great bear of a man with a long black beard, struck the butt of his long spear against the ground and glared at me.

"Hello, Lord Kay," I said. "What brings you to town on this fine night?"

"We've been searching for you," he growled, looking at the corpse beside me. "It that Dunvallo?"

I put my sword away. "It was a fair fight." One should always temper lies with a little truth, so I pointed at Dunvallo's friends. "Even they'll admit he started it."

He didn't give them time to respond. "Nobody cares about that right now. Arthur wants you."

I was in no mood to be summoned like a lackey. "Why?"

Kay hooked a thumb at one of his men, who quickly dismounted. "It's the Lady Guinevere," he said with unaccustomed softness. "She's been abducted."

"What?" Lugh and Jesus, while I'd been whoring and brawling. "Abducted? How? And by whom?"

He motioned for Dunvalo's friends to leave, which they did, lugging the deceased with them. "No one knows. She disappeared from her chamber, with no witness but her maid, who's having hysterics. When Arthur sorted out what had happened, he sent us to find you. Lucky for you we came when we did, or you'd have been chopped up like dog meat."

Oh, yes, I'd just been drowned in good fortune lately. "Why does Arthur want me?"

He shook his head. "No time for talk. Take Riderch's horse and come with us."

I started to protest that I wanted to get my own horse from the stable three blocks away, but thought better of it. If Arthur felt my help was needed, then maybe it was, and time was indeed crucial. Riderch boosted me to his saddle and we were off without further ceremony.

Jesus, Lugh, and a dozen buggered saints. Was this what Gwen had feared, the work of the mysterious Melwas, or was it something more mundane, a move by Picts or Saxons looking for concessions? Nobody had any time for answers. We rode in silence, through dark streets, some still crowded with revelers, and out the town gates and down the road that ran beside the sighing river. When we reached the fortress, there was a double guard at the gatehouse and the outer courts were a blaze of torchlit activity, men running and yelling, riders and whole squadrons galloping in or pounding away into the night, sentries shouting back and forth on the high walls. Kay hustled me through the confusion and into the great hall.

Arthur was pacing in front of the fire. I'd apparently missed the worst of his rage. Couches, stools, and benches were scattered about, some in several pieces, and the imperial sword of office, the sword of Maximus that Arthur once pulled from its block at Tintagel, was wedged in an overturned table, like a butcher's cleaver in a chopping block. An old woman in a familiar-looking gray gown huddled beside the raised hearth, sobbing hysterically. There was a bloody gash on her forehead.

"Here he is," said Kay, "though I still don't know why you wanted him. When we found him, he'd just killed Dunvallo in some sort of drunken squabble."

"That can be sorted out later," said Arthur. "If she is where I think she is, he may be the only one who can help."

My fears were confirmed. He wouldn't be asking for my aid if her abduction was the work of human enemies. "What's happened?"

Arthur turned toward me. His face was drawn and pale, and there was a crazed gleam in his eyes, but his voice was calm. "Guinevere's gone, by Jesus and Our Lady, and I fear that it's no mortal man who's taken her." He nodded at the old woman in black. "Tell Mordred what happened."

"It was a devil," shrieked the crone. "A devil has taken my lady. I was brushing her hair before she went to bed, just like every night, when there he was, out of nowhere!"

I stared at the old woman. Why did she look so damned familiar? "There *who* was?"

"The devil, I said! He was horribly tall, and thin, and gray and wrinkled like leather, and naked under his cloak, which was made of teeth. Teeth! There were teeth in his staff, too, and when he struck me with it, I fell down in a swoon." That explained the gash in her forehead. "When they found me, I was like this. God and Jesus, help me! Help her, but help me!"

"Be quiet, Regan," snapped Arthur. "You do yourself no credit, and her no good."

I walked toward the old woman with horrified fascination. It was Regan all right, but much changed, her face drawn and gray and mapped with wrinkles. Her hair was white as snow, and when she opened her mouth, there didn't seem to be any teeth in her shriveled gums.

I wheeled on Arthur. "It was Melwas. I warned you about this. A lord of the Otherworld has her now."

Arthur wrenched his sword from the hacked table. Its long blade swept through the air above his head, reflecting the roaring fire. "Where can I find him? Just tell me where, Otherworld or Hell itself, I'll kill him and bring her back. Tell me where to find him."

Easy, I told myself, we both needed to stay calm. "All right," I said, "but control yourself. Let me think on this."

Arthur put his sword back in its scabbard. There was more color in his face, and his voice softened again. "I need you, Mordred. I needed you when I faced Cado, and you did not fail me, though I failed you. I needed you when I went after the Palag Cat. And now I need you more than ever, and for the sake of someone better than myself. Unlike my father, I have no pet magician to help me understand such things. But you understand them, don't you? My sister taught you much, I think. For the first time in my life, I hope she did. I would rather have your aid in this than Merlin's, even if he could be summoned from the Caledonian wood."

Any other time I would have been thunderstruck to hear him admit to needing me, or to acknowledge that I'd twice saved his life. Right now, however, I could not allow myself to be distracted by such thoughts, and I made my face hard when I looked at him. "You find me preferable to Merlin. How flattering."

He met my gaze with an odd, resolute acceptance, and

I felt momentary shame, actual shame, for baiting him. "I would rather have your help than anyone's. I'll give you whatever you want."

I had to turn my back on him, so he couldn't see the emotions fighting themselves in my face. *I'll settle for your wife,* I thought, and for one crazed moment almost said as much. *Oh, Arthur, you bloody, noble-minded fool, too much has passed between us for that.* "The first time I saved your life, you didn't want me at all."

His voice was strong and sincere. "I know. That was my true sin, not in siring you, but in abandoning you like that. I'd change it, if I could."

Oh would you now? But I resisted further brittle gibes, and instead turned a toppled bench upright and sat down on it, throwing my cloak down to warm on the stones before the fire. "Mother taught me some things about the Otherworld. And what she didn't teach me, I can ask her about. I brought her head with me."

Arthur looked at me as if he thought me mad. "Her head? God preserve us." He sat on the bench beside me. "First, Kay tells me you've killed a man; now you say you have my sister's head with you, like the pagan trophies the Votadini still keep in their brochs. God's blood, Mordred, at another time I would be angry with you."

"Perhaps, but at this time you ought to be bloody grateful, since I think she can help us. The head is in my room."

He buried his face in his hands. "Get it, then," he said quietly.

When I returned with the oakwood chest, the hacked table and the other bench had been turned upright again, and Arthur was seated, a cup of wine in his hand. Kay and several servants stood about, their faces pale in the gloom left by the dying fire, and Regan still squatted before the hearth, running her withered hands through her hair and muttering to herself. Nobody was paying any attention to her.

"Tell me one thing," I said to Arthur as I walked past

him, to put the chest down and sit cross-legged on my cloak, my back to him.

"Yes?"

I unlocked the chest, but did not open it yet. "Do you love her?"

There was a silence. For some reason I was glad I could not see his face. "Yes," he finally said. "I believe I do."

Idiot. "Then why did you keep putting off the bloody wedding? You might have prevented this."

His voice was so soft now I had to strain to hear him. "I don't know. I wanted her, more than anything. It was the first time I'd wanted a woman since . . . since your mother came to my tent in disguise, when I was just a soldier. Every night, I think of her, when I'm alone in bed, and every morning when I rise, and every day." *Bastard,* I thought; *puking, Christ-ridden, stupid, sanctimonious bastard. Why couldn't you have listened to me, then?*

"But I was frightened," he continued. "I suppose that is the right word. Me, frightened of a girl, a girl who'd given her consent to become my Queen. It was all right when Cador first proposed the idea, when it was just practical politics, a way to make sure that Cornwall and the Summer Country and the other kingdoms of the Southeast would not ally themselves with their Saxon neighbors, the way Cerdic did. I was getting older; it was time for me to marry, to sire an heir."

And to think he'd once spoken of bestowing that honor upon me, back when I was a boy and he thought me simply his nephew. Not that I cared anymore. "Go on," I said. "Tell me all, if you want my help."

"Things changed when I met her," he continued haltingly. "When I came to know her, I wanted her, and that wanting frightened me. So I put off the wedding, once, and then again and again. I don't know whether it's her I fear, or what she may think of me after our wedding night. It doesn't matter now; just get her back. I was a fool, but I do love her."

"Love's a knife, right enough," I said with strained lightness. "I found that out when I was a boy, and again since. Now you know it, too."

I opened the box and took out my mother's head. Her eyes were open and staring, glittering like polished brown stones in the firelight, living eyes in a dead face. I heard loud gasps and curses. Beside me, Regan gave a choked scream and collapsed, to lie twitching on the hearthstones. Since she wasn't actually in the fire, I ignored her.

"Hello, brother," said my mother's head, her unnatural gaze fixed over my shoulder. I did not turn around to see his reaction, for this would take all my concentration. He said nothing, but I heard the intake of his breath.

"I'm not in hell, in case you've been wondering," continued the head. "What does that say about your faith?"

This was no time for theology or acrimonious family bickering. "How can I find her?" I demanded of the head.

The withered features drew up into even more of a grimace. "I will not tell you that. You may find your death there. I don't want you to die, Mordred."

"I don't care what you want, Mother. You'll tell me. You know you will. It's why you wanted me to bring you with me, isn't it?" Oh yes, it was clear enough now. "You knew all this would happen, and you knew I'd go after her, with your help or without it." As before, I'd said "I" rather than "Arthur," for I already knew that only I could go where she was now.

Behind me, Arthur muttered a prayer. I bit down on my own tongue, hard, then I kissed her dry lips and spit my own blood into her mouth. More curses and gasps sounded from behind me, and above them, I could hear Kay saying "Jesus" over and over.

"With this kiss I bind you," I said in a thick voice. "By my blood I command you. Answer now. Tell me how to find Guinevere. Tell me how to defeat Melwas."

"Turn your ear this way," she said tonelessly, "and I will whisper what you must do." The room grew very quiet, as if they were all straining to hear what she was saying, but I doubt any of them did, or they would have reacted with even greater horror. When she was done, she shut her eyes and became a dead thing again, just so much preserved flesh and bone.

I stood up and faced the assembly, the head dangling from my fist by its long hair. Everyone recoiled from it, as though I was Perseus holding the trophy he took from Medusa. "Everybody must go," I said to Arthur. "Except you. You can stay, if you want. I'll need a knife and a chisel and a carpenter's mallet. And have someone bring me a bucket of water. But first I'll need some bread, and a jug of wine as well." The last were for my stomach, not the magic I was about to attempt.

Arthur turned to pale-faced Kay and nodded. The food and wine were brought, and then we were alone while Kay went out to fetch the tools and water. Arthur silently watched me eat and drink, giving no outward sign of the impatience I'm sure he felt. After I'd done, I held my mother's head in front of me and kissed her again on her leathery mouth. "Good-bye," I said. She didn't say anything back.

Kay came back with the tools and a tin bucket full of water. He handed them to me without looking at me, and hurriedly went out again. Before he shut the door behind him, I glimpsed soldiers and servants gathered in the courtyard. Several pointed at me and crossed themselves. I tossed the head on the floor, where it rolled like a cabbage before coming to a stop, faceup and eyes still closed. Arthur couldn't seem to stop looking at it.

"Still want Guinevere back, even at this price?"

"Yes," he said softly. "Even at the price of my soul."

Somehow, I couldn't taunt him further. Instead, I walked toward him. "Listen to me," I said, surprised at the unexpected and rather unwanted traces of compassion I was feeling for him. "You once said that your defeat by Cado was a lesson from your God."

"Yes," he said, sounding nothing like the man I'd met when I was eight and full of wonder at him and his world.

"Then he must work through all we do. Everything that lives, everything that *is,* is his instrument, and everything that happens is his plan. If a soul will be lost here, it's mine."

He looked me strangely, as if seeing something in me he'd not seen before. "I don't think . . ."

I shook my head. "No, just listen to me. If I'm to get her back, I want you to promise me one thing, that you won't blame her for this, or yourself either." Bloody gods, could such prattle be coming from my own lips?

"I won't blame her," he said.

Time to give him something to do. "Regan said Gwen was combing her hair when Melwas took her. I need that comb. Will you go get it for me?" I felt like I was speaking to a child.

There was something that might have been relief in his eyes as he left the room. Fortifying myself with a swallow of wine, I picked up the mallet that Kay had brought me and knelt beside my mother's head.

Her eyes opened again. "This will bind you to him more than you ever were before," she said. "Do you really want that."

I stroked Mother's leathery cheek and twirled a strand of her lank hair, befuddled to realize that I was actually going to miss her, even in this form. "I want Guinevere back."

Her gnarled face twisted into what could have been a mocking grin. "For you or him?"

"For herself." But did I really believe that?

When Mother next spoke, her voice was so much that of her old, live self that I might have wept, had there been any tears in me. "Even now, I can't see all that will happen. I do know that if I had not told you how to do this thing, you would have tried anyway, and died in trying it. You may still die because of it. Not in the Otherworld, I think, and not for a while, but in doing this, you may be assuring your own death. And Arthur's."

"We'll all die soon enough, Mother." My hand tightened on the mallet.

"Do you love her?"

I stayed my hand for a moment. "Yes."

"Him, too, I think, even after so many years of hating him."

I didn't want to argue that point. "Enough of this. I love you, Mother, even now. May you find peace."

She shut her eyes before the first blow, and made no sound nor sign of life when I smashed her in the mouth with the mallet, striking several times until her jaw was well broken. That done, I got the knife and chisel and used them to extract all her teeth, Once they were all in a little pile on the rushes-strewn floor, I threw the ruined head in the fire. It burned with loud pops and cracks and foul black smoke.

After a while, Arthur returned with Gwen's comb. It had taken him a long enough time, but I repressed the urge to chide him. Indeed, I wondered if coming back into that room was one of the hardest things he'd ever done.

I watched the head burn. It was a charred skull now, without a lower jaw. I dully wondered where the spirit that animated it was now. Guinevere's comb, which Arthur silently handed to me, was fine silver, with an ivory handle. There were several long red hairs in it. Just what I needed. I took the hairs and put them in my purse, along with my mother's teeth. The fire was burning low. I looked at Regan's crumbled form. She seemed to have stopped breathing.

An idea came to me. Mother had told me what to do, but not how to get everything I would need. Perhaps this was a grim opportunity. "Is she dead?"

Arthur walked to her and knelt at her side. "Yes," he said tonelessly, after checking her pulse. "Poor woman. We need a priest."

"Later. You better go now."

He shook his head. "I am going to come with you."

I walked over and looked him in the eye. "Only I can go where I shall have to go, Arthur. You know that. And before I go, I must do things that you do not need to watch." I pointed down at Regan. "I'll need some of her blood, before it clots in her veins."

He blanched. "Are you mad? I'll not let you desecrate this poor creature's body, not even for Guinevere."

Still looking him directly in the eye, I spoke very softly. "Arthur, listen to me. She's dead, and what I do to her body can't harm her in heaven." Or wherever she was. "She can have full rites soon enough, but for now she can help us save her mistress. Please go, and let me do what I must."

He turned away, his posture that of a much older man. "I thought I'd never be like Uther, and have dealings with such dark matters. Will you be able to get Guinevere back?"

I wished I knew. "Yes. I swear I will." At least I managed to sound certain.

He turned and quite unexpectedly embraced me. "If you can do that, my son, I'll be in your debt forever."

My son. Twice he'd called me that now, me whom he once called his sin. At another time, I might have felt something, to hear those two words from his lips. Not tonight.

"Go to the chapel and pray. For me as well as her." It was not likely to help, but at least it would make him feel better.

He left without saying anything else. I crouched beside Regan. This could only work if she was a virgin. It would take a lot of blood, and getting it from a live one wasn't practical, even if I were capable of such a murderous deed. I'd always thought that Regan resembled a very large nun; now was the time to find out if she'd lived like one. Grimacing, I slipped my hand under her gown and up between her withered legs. Well, I'd done worse things tonight. Good, she was intact.

Poor Regan; despite her weathered peasant looks and

her big bones, she'd been little older than Gwen. I'd disliked her, but she deserved better than this.

She might have lost a lot of her body fat when Melwas stole her youth, but she was still very large, and it was with some difficulty that I got her up onto one of the benches, laying her out so that her head lolled off the end. I lifted it by the hair and placed the bucket under it, then let it go. Her head splashed back into the bucket. I picked up the knife and cut her throat.

After a few minutes, I lifted her head out of the red water and carried the bucket to the hearth. There I poured the water out onto my cloak. When it was soaked, I picked it up and carefully wrung it out. Then I threw the damp garment over the remains of the fire, smothering the flames and extinguishing their light.

Darkness rushed in. "With virgin's blood and my mother's ashes," I chanted, "I command this cloak to keep me from the sight of Melwas." A blue flame played over the cloak for a moment, so briefly that it might have been a trick of my eyes as they adjusted to the sudden blackness. No, it was more than that, for the air about me became very cold, and I could feel hairs stirring all over my body. I'd managed some sort of magic. I'd know soon enough whether it would help me.

I drank my wine and tried, with little success, not to think too much about what I would have to do. Damn everything to fucking hell, why was I doing this? I'd lived a bitter enough life for most of my twenty years, but not so bitter that the losing of it would be sweet. Did I love Gwen enough to do this thing I was contemplating, to follow her to a place I could not even imagine, where I might well die, despite Mother's assurances? And if I did succeed, then Arthur would have her again, and there'd be only pain ahead.

For that matter, was it even Gwen I was doing this for? Perhaps in some manner I still had to prove myself to my father. No, Mother was wrong, it wasn't his love I wanted, not for years, but there was a certain harsh pleasure in the thought he might torment himself with further guilt, guilt that this time would be founded on how he'd treated me in the past rather than on the simple fact of my existence. Oh fuck, I didn't know why I was doing what I was about to do; all I knew was that I had no choice. "Here's to you, my king and father," I said with mock solemnity at I hoisted the wine jug. "And to you, Sweet Gwen. Fortuna has somehow bound me to both of you, and I doubt I'll ever be free again."

In that moment I found myself almost hating Gwen, for needing something only I could do. In some nebulous way, the thought of success was almost as terrible as that of failure, and I wished I could just walk out of the room and away from Camelot. Gulping down the wine, I tried to put such thoughts out of my head, and to turn to practical consideration of the long trip that lay before me, not all of which would be in this world.

Thirty-four

THREE DAYS later and nearly a hundred miles away, I rode alone under a gray afternoon sky with rain drizzling on the horizon. The landscape was dank, sedgy, and treeless, a low heath rimmed with stony mountains. Over everything hung the sweetish smell of bracken, moss, and sheep droppings. Since I'd passed the last farm a few miles back, there'd been no living things in sight but moor birds and scattered groups of ewes. I'd been drenched twice by sudden flurries of rain, and my cloak and tunic were soaked. If it had been colder, I'd have been forced to stop and try to make a fire, or huddle for warmth amongst the sheep.

I'd come alone. Arthur would have given me as many men as I'd wanted, and come himself, of course, if I'd consented to his help, but I'd known somehow that the part of my journey that lay in this world would proceed without mishap, and I couldn't take anyone else to where I'd be going from here. Besides, when I'd left Camelot I'd not been in the mood for any sort of company.

The mound loomed in front of me, a great steep-sided hill over a hundred feet high, covered in stubby grass except where outcroppings of bare limestone showed through like weathered bones. At its summit were two upright menhirs supporting a horizontal granite slab. Turning my horse loose to graze as best he could, I scrambled my way wearily to the top and took shelter in the comparatively dry shadow of the huge stones. Hunching there, I wrapped myself in my wet cloak and waited for nightfall. Surprisingly, I was actually able to sleep.

I dreamed of summer, a landscape of blooming furze and bluebells and green, green grass. I lay on my back in the cool shadow of an apple tree, my head in Guinevere's lap, listening to the sweet-smelling breeze whispering in the branches and feeling her fingers in my hair. "My love," she was saying, "my sweet, sweet love. Sing me that song they sing in Orkney, when it's a bright calm day and the men are putting out to sea."

Then I awoke, and the night was all about me, dull and dark and wet, with no moon or stars visible against the soggy black curtain of the sky. I rose and stretched, then climbed atop the horizontal slab that had been my shelter. Somewhere below me was my horse, if he'd not wandered off. Damn, but I should have tethered him. No time for that now, though.

Jumping down upon the spongy ground, I found a flat stretch of earth. I'd carried my mother's teeth with me, of course, and the strand of Guinevere's hair. Fumbling in the darkness, I finally managed to tie the hair around one finger. Then I tapped the teeth down into the mud, spreading them out to form a circle. All the time, I kept repeating Guinevere's name.

That done, I stood up. "Open the way," I said. "Open the way to the realm of Melwas. By these teeth, I say it. Teeth of my mother, open the way to the Kingdom of Teeth."

Where each of the teeth had been buried, there appeared a little point of blue flame. The ground seemed to shift a bit beneath my feet, there was a rumbling deep within the mound, and then the circle of earth marked by the points of flame fell away, revealing a narrow opening like a large rabbit hole. A wind blew out of it, and I felt colder.

Not to hesitate, that was the key, but plunge on in unthinking. Sinking to my hands and knees, I scrambled there, squeezing my way through the opening. Dunvallo mocked my lack of height, but my shoulders are broad enough, and it was a bloody tight fit. I couldn't see, could barely breathe. There was dirt in my eyes, and slick clay; the passage widened, then narrowed again, and I went on scrambling and burrowing like a badger. Down, down and down I went, sometimes at an angle, sometimes at a near-vertical plummet. I could no longer tell if I was following a preexisting passage or creating one; the earth seemed to be simultaneously opening before me and closing behind me, so I couldn't have backed out now if I tried, wedged deeply as I was. My arms were stuck tightly at my sides and all I could do was wriggle, no longer a badger, but a snake or a worm, writhing my way deeper within the hill. My lungs were starved for air, there was dirt in my mouth and nose, the crushing weight of the mound all about me. How did worms and grubs and moles endure this? My brain screamed for release from the loamy weight, the smothering darkness, the feeling of the whole world pressing down on me as I was sucked into its bowels. I felt I was crawling into my own grave, or back into Mother's womb, or both at once. The reality of what I was doing was scarcely less terrible than such a fancy. I'd failed, I thought, expecting to die there, enfolded in the earth.

Mother, I thought, not daring to open my mouth. *If you can still hear me, wherever you are, aid me now.* I felt like I was miles beneath the ground, too exhausted to wiggle my way deeper, the blood roaring in my head, my lungs collapsing, and me calling for my mother and to any gods that might listen, wishing I'd walked away from all this, that I'd never met Guinevere or come to Camelot, not knowing why I clung so to life but sure that any other death was preferable to this, when there was a vertiginous shift, the feeling of an entire universe tilting on its axis, and then, with strength I didn't know I had, I was scrambling blindly *upward* into stale, cold air. My hands were free, then my arms and head, with something like grass or reeds about me, as I squeezed my way up and out like a baby being born.

I lay on my back and gasped in the strange still air, like that of an unheated but long boarded-up room in winter. Finally, I was able to rise, weary and filthy and sore, my heavy cloak plastered to my body by mud and wet clay. The sky overhead was gray and featureless, like a roof of fog, and there was a dull, colorless light everywhere, not sunlight or moonlight, but a pale, flat illumination that came from nowhere and left no shadows. As far as I could see, the low rolling landscape was carpeted by clumps of unfamiliar vegetation that looked less like stalks of grass or reed than hanks of human hair. Walking to the nearest clump, I pulled a handful free from the pebbly soil, or whatever it was rooted in. Yes, it *was* hair, some fine and straight, some coarse and curly, some fair, some dark, most of it a dull gray. All around me, the land was an enormous scalp, of varying textures and shades, with patches of bare earth showing through like scabby skin. I crossed myself, a quite uncharacteristic and pointless gesture from me no matter where I was, but doubly meaningless in such a place, and for the first time in my life wished I believed in something besides power, that I could have the comfort of praying to something. But no, I'd never worshiped anything or anyone but Arthur, a faith which would hardly have served me here even had I still possessed it, and I knew I was even more on my own than in the human world, with nothing to call upon but my own resources. And perhaps the help that Mother had given me. Such musings, of course, were a way of avoiding the next stage in my journey, so I pushed them aside and began to walk, wincing at the feel of the hair beneath my bare right foot, for I'd lost that boot in my tortuous scramble through the earth.

I'd also left my sword belt there, which left me unarmed except for the dagger still stuck inside my other boot. Even invisible, I did not relish the prospect of fighting Melwas with just a knife. Well, maybe I wouldn't have to. Mother had been vague on details, but she'd indicated that I should be able to get Gwen out of this place without fighting its lord at all. First, though, I had to find his dwelling.

I walked for what seemed like hours over rolling fields of hair, some fine, some coarse, but all of it dry and dead. Where this covering thinned out, the bare ground beneath it did not just look like skin; when I trod upon it, that's what it proved to be, scabby and wrinkled and dry except where yellow pools of what smelled like sweat lay in shallow depressions that pitted the fleshy landscape. If the air had seemed stale when I first arrived in this place, it now positively reeked, and at times the sour stench was overpowering, and I wanted to gag. Indeed, I think that the only thing that stopped me from vomiting was the determination to leave no part of myself behind there, not even the contents of my stomach. Bury your nose in the armpit of a very old man who's been laboring all day in the hot sun, and you'll have some concept of what that place smelled like.

The clumps of hair became less and less frequent, and the folded landscape seemed more withered. I was relieved that there were no more pools or rivulets of sweat, but now my eyes stung from what I took to be dust, which swirled before me despite the stillness of the dead air, the motes getting larger as I progressed, until it seemed like I was walking through a desiccated blizzard, for the small pale particles hung in the air less like dust than snowflakes. And flakes were what they proved to be when I brushed them from my eyes, not of snow, but of skin, as if the landscape was sloughing away.

Eventually, the air cleared, and the low rolling hills ahead of me seemed covered in pebbles, which crunched beneath my feet. Closer inspection revealed that these were not stones but teeth and fragments of teeth, hundreds or thousands or millions of them. Guinevere's mother had struck a foul bargain indeed. This was not the Otherworld of the Blessed Heroes, the Happy Lands, the Realm of Always Summer. There were no sweet apples here, or silver goblets filled with nectar. This was a lost place, a realm of exile for an immortal being who'd offended his fellows in some unimaginable way. I trudged onward under that low sunless sky, crunching painfully over broken teeth, looking for the habitation of the one who ruled this unnatural land.

My walking was not aimless. The strand of Guinevere's hair that I'd tied around my finger tightened like an unbreakable wire, digging into my flesh whenever I strayed from the right course. I held my hand outstretched before me and stumbled in whatever direction brought the least pain, my cloak dragging behind me like soggy wings. Finally, something large and pale and shapeless loomed on the low horizon.

The building, if I can call it a building, seemed to grow out of the landscape, a huge tumbled edifice the color of bone and ivory. It grew slowly in size as I walked, and kept on growing, until I thought I'd never reach it, or be driven mad by its sheer immensity when I did. Finally, I stood before it, and craned my head up at the structure that loomed over me like a mountain. It had no plan or design; it was just an artificial hill, like the mound I'd burrowed into in our world, but much larger, and made of teeth rather than of earth, unimaginable numbers of teeth all mortared together into a kind of cement, with the only feature a great doorless entrance like the mouth of the Cyclops's cave.

In tales of Annwn, that aspect of the Otherworld that lies over the western sea, those who displease the Fair Folk are imprisoned in the dreadful dungeon called Oeth and Anoeth, which is made from human bones. I doubted that Oeth and Anoeth could be more terrible than the mountain of teeth that stood before me now. This was the Palace of Melwas, his stronghold, the place where he held Gwen. There was no point in waiting. I drew my damp, dirty cloak about me, hoping its magic still worked.

"Come out, Melwas," I yelled in a hoarse voice. "Come out if you dare."

Nothing stirred for a long time, so long that I thought I might have to go in after him, when I heard a dull, dragging tread from within the dark entrance, and the air about me grew perceptively colder. Those slow, heavy footsteps crunched closer, echoed by the dull thumping of my heart. This was it, the first time I'd ever confronted one of the Old Powers face-to-face, and I desperately wished I'd paid closer attention to Mother's lessons. Would she have been so stricken with terror in this situation, I wondered. Probably. Had she been a more powerful magician, she'd not have ended up with nothing in her life but bare Orkney, a sour husband, and me. Merlin himself, clearly her superior, might have felt ill at ease here. Had I anything to tempt him from his solitude in the Caledonian wood, I would have sought his aid, but no, there'd have been no help from that quarter. Besides, I couldn't change the past. There was nothing for it but to stand and wait and hope that Mother knew more about these matters now that she was no longer alive, and that her advice could be trusted.

Melwas emerged into the pale light. I immediately wished he had not, for his appearance was even worse than I'd imagined. Think of one of the shriveled, leathery corpses that are sometimes dug out of peat bogs, only *stretched* like a piece of unrendered suet and imbued with unnatural life. Though he could not have weighed much more than me, he tottered forward on stiltlike legs that gave him twice my height, and he had equally long arms and a long, thin, wattled neck, the latter somehow supporting a huge round head that resembled a withered gourd. His exposed scrotum was a tiny shriveled pouch, and I could count every rib in his gaunt sides, for his only garment was a kind of cloak or mantle made from teeth, strung together like a beaded curtain, which rattled when he walked. In one hand he held a long crooked staff, the end of which was decorated with discolored molars, their roots driven into the wood and their crowns pointing outward to form knobby spikes.

Oh Jesus, I said to myself, calling upon the carpenter for the second time in my life, *I'll believe in you and be yours always, if you don't let this thing see me.* Silently, I directed similar pleas to Lugh, Mithras, and even the Odin of the Saxons. *And you, Mother, it was your dark*

*skills that brought me here; don't fail me now, smirking
ghost that you are. If you ever loved me, don't fail me
now.*

The magic must have worked, for he looked right at
me with eyes like flat black buttons and did not see me. I
steadied myself as he came closer, and marveled at the
intricate web of wrinkles that creased his scrawny frame,
for he was as shriveled as a prune. Every part of him
except his eyes was covered in dust, and he smelled, not
like carrion as I would have expected, but of nothing so
much as dust, so much so that I had to pinch my nose to
keep from sneezing. As he stalked past me, his staff
swung very close to where I stood, but I did not flinch,
for fear I'd make some sound and give myself away. The
very proximity of the staff made my bones ache, and I
could only imagine what its touch might do to me.

Two yards from me, he paused and stood there, his
black eyes looking at nothing in particular, his slit of a
mouth hanging slackly open, exposing a toothless cavity
the color of old meat. It seemed ironic that the Lord of
Teeth would have none of his own, but I managed to
keep myself from laughing. He stood there for a long
time, his head tilting to one side, and then he began to
shuffle slowly and aimlessly forward into the fields of
hair.

Slowly, carefully, I moved toward the entrance to his
palace. It wasn't so much a hall or a corridor as a tunnel,
walled and floored in the inevitable teeth. The bare sole
of my right foot was cut and bleeding, and I was limping
after ten steps, but I hurried on, surprised that I didn't
have to grope my way in darkness. Fortunately, the same
colorless light suffused everything as it had outside, and
I had no problem seeing where I was going.

The passage branched out, then branched out again, I
passed low-ceilinged chambers and the entrances to
other passages, but the hair wrapped so tightly around
my finger did not fail me, and I always knew what fork to
take, which passage to choose. Soon, I was deep within
that terrible palace. I don't remember much of it, just
corridor after corridor, irregular chamber after cham-

ber, like cells in a honeycomb. How did Melwas make his gangling way through such cramped space?

Abruptly, I rounded a corner and was in a vast open space, a room so large that Arthur's palace could have fitted inside. Great columns of teeth shot up to a rough ceiling a hundred feet or more above my head. In the center of this huge chamber was a sort of crude throne, also made of teeth, and covered with a blanket woven from different-colored strands of hair. All about the throne, pits were sunk in the floor, like silos for storing grain. I limped among them and peered down, barely conscious of the growing pain in my right foot.

Many of the pits had occupants. Here a woman huddled, nude and gaunt, thin arms wrapped around scarred and scabby knees, downturned face veiled by dusty, colorless hair. Here were two children in rags, clutching each other and looking up at nothing with a mindless, frightened stare. Here something pale moved feebly on the toothed floor, a spindly, big-headed thing no larger than a kitten. A miscarriage, perhaps? I passed more women, most of them of indeterminate age, either naked or in rags, all of them covered with sores, all seemingly leeched of life and color. Above several pits, I paused and hissed. Only two of the occupants looked up, and neither had any awareness in her eyes. Most were covered in dust, and some looked as though they had not moved in a long time, yet they all appeared alive. Well, it was probably impossible to die here, no matter how long one went without food or drink. Who were they? Had they all been promised to the lord of this place, the way Guinevere had? I never found out.

However they'd come here, Melwas had collected them in much the same way that a magpie collects shiny baubles. They were not slaves or concubines, or even livestock, just pretty trinkets to be carried off, then thrown into pits and forgotten. Christians believe that devils will torment them in Hell, but is torment worse than mindless neglect?

Suddenly, the hair tied round my finger loosened and fell away. Looking into the pit directly in front of me, I saw Guinevere. Even covered with dust and cobwebs, her hair stood out like a flame. She crouched there in a plain woolen shift, obviously what she'd been wearing when Melwas had taken her, her head resting on her knees. "Thank you," I said aloud, to all the gods I'd prayed to, and Mother's ghost besides.

Guinevere looked up, green eyes streaked with red. "Mordred!"

Well, my cloak was not supposed to make me invisible to human eyes. I almost wished it did, for I must have looked a sight. "Aye, love," I whispered, "it's me. I've come to take you home."

That was easier said than done, of course. To do the thing that Mother said would break the spell binding Guinevere to this place would require me to get down in the pit with her. I was sure that I loved her, and was of course overjoyed to have found her, yet something in me balked at the thought of scrambling down into that tooth-studded hole, no matter how much I wanted to hold her in my arms.

I was still thinking it over when I heard a rattling sound behind me and turned, to see Melwas standing there, vacant black eyes tracking the bloody footprints I'd left upon the jagged floor. His staff snaked out, not so much toward me as toward the red smear beside my right foot, but that proved near enough. I ducked forward like an idiot, overbalanced, and toppled into the pit.

My cloak caught on the edge and for a moment I hung there, dashed against the pit's side, gasping and twisting and feeling roots and broken crowns scraping into my thigh and shoulder. Then my brooch tore loose and I fell, leaving the cloak behind me. Fortunately, the drop was only about twelve feet, and I landed bruised and cut but not seriously injured. Scrambling painfully to my feet, I drew my dagger and I glared up at Melwas.

He looked down at us with his black shark's eyes. The slit that was his mouth spread and spread, becoming a wound that split his face. He began to make a high, keening sound that I finally recognized as laughter.

"What, you think I'm funny?" I snarled, no longer quite in my right mind. "Come on down here and I'll show you how funny I am!"

His only response was to rasp deep in his throat, as if attempting hawk up phlegm or spittle. Then he coughed, a dry explosion of dust and stale air. Giving us a grin and a cock of his head, he then shambled out of view. What, that was all, he was just going to leave us here? Well, why not; it wasn't as if we'd be able to climb out, unless Gwen stood on my shoulders.

"You came after me," she said, and then she was in my arms, and it was so good to be holding her, even under these circumstances, that all I could do was stand there, and feel my arms about her and her body pressed against mine, and take pleasure in that feeling. For the second time, I was ashamed of what a filthy mess I was, but she seemed not to mind. "You came," she said again. "I knew that if anybody could, it would be you."

My heart skipped a beat at that, and suddenly I wished to be a better person than I was, to be worthy of her. Not the sort of emotion I was accustomed to, but here, in this placeless place, all defenses were down, and there was no help for it.

"Aye, all will be well now," I murmured, feeling foolish as I said it. "We'll be back in Camelot before you know it."

She hugged me tighter. "Is Regan all right? That monster struck her with his staff. After that, I don't remember anything, until I woke up here."

"She's fine," I lied. Letting go of her, I stepped back and gave her a closer look. There were dark hollows under her eyes, and her hair was a tangled rat's nest. Her shift was torn and dirty, and she stank of sweat and urine and was covered in dust. God, but she looked beautiful for all of that.

She actually smiled, a smile that, in such a place as the Realm of Melwas, may have been the bravest thing I've ever seen, and I've seen much courage in my life. "Aye, I'm a sight, I'm sure. I'd have fixed myself up if I'd known for sure you'd be coming." Her finger traced a line in the grime of my cheek. "Forgive my eagerness, but how is it that we're getting out of here?"

I took her hand. "Listen to what I have to say, Gwen. Don't think me mad, and don't get angry." Saying what was on my mind, which should have been the easiest part of this, was proving harder than I would have imagined.

She nodded, with just the barest hint of impatience. "Tell it to me straight, Mordred. What must we do to leave this place."

"You mentioned being a virgin, once. I assume you still are."

She crossed her arms and regarded me with eyes that reminded me of those that had once stared at me from the cage of the Palag Cat, albeit greener, and without the languorous hate.

"My maidenhood is intact, yes. Why does it matter?"

"It is what binds you here. Your virginity, I mean. When your maidenhood breaks, so does the spell."

Her expression did not change, but remained a lovely mask beneath dust and cobwebs. "How do you know this?"

I turned, in that narrow space, and fingered the teeth set in the wall, wondering if we'd be able to climb out if this did not work, now that there were two people in the pit and one could boost the other. "I consulted Mother's spirit." There was no reason to explain how. "She told me certain things. Your mother made a pact with an ancient power, one so old that, from the look of things, it's senile. The pact is sealed by your virginity, which was pledged to Melwas, even though it's as useless to him as any of his other magpie trinkets, as he has no ability to take it. If Arthur had not postponed the wedding, this most likely could not have happened, but he let things drag on, into that time of year when the Old Powers are strongest, and Melwas could come for you."

Gwen walked up behind me and hugged me, her cheek warm between my shoulder blades, her hands meeting on my breastbone. It was good to stand like that, feeling her presence, oblivious to the teeth I felt beneath my feet and the palms of my hand where I leaned against the wall. It was a while before she spoke. When she did, her voice was clear and resolute, with an unexpected note that might have been muted pleasure.

"I understand. If we do something that means life and the flesh, in this place that is so far from either, the bargain my mother made will be broken. Let's do it, then."

I hadn't expected it to be this easy. "I am sorry to ask this of you, Gwen."

Her cheek was warm against the nape of my neck. "It's not much to ask, Mordred, and wouldn't be if it were only the price of my freedom. I've been thinking of you. Both since I found myself here, and well before. I've wanted you."

On hearing that, I could almost believe myself not in the Realm of Melwas, but some Faerie domain where all wishes come true, and the world reshapes itself to your need. Her hands were clasped on my chest. I took one of them in my own and kissed it, sucking gently for a moment on her finger, which tasted sweet despite all its grime. At this, she pressed her hips against me and I felt a shudder run through her tall frame.

She finally broke the silence. "Oh, Mordred, perhaps it shames to me to say this, but it's true. Fucking you is more than just a price I'd gladly pay for my freedom from this realm. You're a bitter enough piece of work, with more prickles than a hedgehog, but in my contrary heart, I've been a wanton for quite some time." She actually laughed. "Oh, God, what a place to so reveal ourselves to each other."

I turned around, to stare once again into those eyes which, with the dust on her skin and hair, were the only color in this place. The word *fucking* had sounded so strange, coming from her lips. *Ah, Arthur,* I wanted to say, *don't you see, she's my sort after all, not yours.* But before I could say anything at all, she kissed me. We pressed together, our arms locked around each other, tasting each other's bad breath and not caring, our tongues fumbling past the barriers of our teeth, time

measured in the beating of our hearts. Through my tunic
and her shift and our mutual filth, I felt her nipples
harden. Yet there came no corresponding hardness from
my cock. Oh shit, I thought, would I prove too self-
aware, too much inside my own head and heart, to lose
myself here, to abandon my body to the actions it must
perform, that I had wanted it to perform for so long. It
would be pathetically laughable if my rescue should fail
because I couldn't get it up.

Taking my hand, she sat down, gently pulling me
toward her. "Lie here, with me."

"Not that most comfortable bed," I said with more
lightness than I felt. "I wish we had a chance to do this
on a better one."

She lay back, pulling me down on top of her. "We will,
I hope. And then, I'll know more of what to do. For now,
you'll have to show me, for I'm better at the theory than
the practice. But I do know these have to come off."

She fumbled clumsily with my filthy breeches. What
I'd wanted in my dreams, what I saw behind my eyelids
when I lay in bed at night, was actually about to happen.
It was insane, of course, but there was nothing else to do.
Mother had said it would work, and I had no recourse
but to take that advice. And if it didn't, it would make
death easier to face. At least, that's what I told myself.

She'd gotten my breeches down. I kissed her, probed
once more with my tongue, found hers again as she
pulled her shift up about her waist. The roots and
broken crowns of the teeth set in the floor must have
hurt her backside even more than they hurt my knees,
but she gave no sign of discomfort. Our mouths sepa-
rated to let her pull the shift over her head. Normally,
she seemed very pale, but naked here in this pale place,
there was a ruddy glow about her, for the radiance of life
itself shone from her soft skin, and the hair on her
armpits, legs, and crotch burned like copper fire. She'd
undone my belt. I threw off my sodden tunic and kicked
off the breeches that were about my ankles.

She spread her legs. "In me," she said, breathing more
rapidly now. "Oh, God and Mary, I want you in me."

Her attempts at guiding my cock, even had they been more expert, came to naught. "Isn't it supposed to be hard?" she asked.

"I'm trying," I said through gritted teeth. "Ach, Gwen, I've wanted this for so long. But there's one thing I must know."

I didn't give much thought to it then, but now, eight years later, I find myself wondering anew as I write these words at her single-mindedness. My weight must have been driving the broken teeth of the cell floor into her, biting her buttocks, thighs, and shoulders in a dozen places, yet she showed all the signs of real passion. "What is that, sweet love?" At those words from her lips, did I feel my cock stir?

"You said we'd do this again. If it works, I mean, and we return to the world."

"Yes." More stirring, and genuine stiffness setting in.

"But you'll be married to Arthur."

"I don't care," she gasped, "I really don't. I'll be yours, if you'll have me."

An insane thought, that, or maybe not so insane. Suppose we told Arthur the truth of what we did to free her from this place. He could hardly execute us, or punish us in any way. She'd be sent back to Cador, most likely. I wouldn't be welcome at Camelot, but that didn't matter, I hadn't wanted that for over six years. I could follow her. I was all hard readiness now, and she guided me in, and I thrust, and thrust again, and her moan grew higher pitched as her maidenhead gave way, my cock wet now with blood rather than just her juices, yet she kept heaving under me, matching my thrusts. I must have hurt her badly, and would have done so even if we weren't making love on a bed of teeth, teeth that were now surely leaving her back and buttocks as bloody as her cunt, but after that first cry, she gave no sigh of discomfort, but locked her arms around me and drew me tight, her mouth clamped shut on the spot where my neck met shoulder blade, her fingernails in my back, drawing blood there to match her own.

I remembered what I'd told her, in the amphitheater

so long ago. The Otherworld wasn't just a place. It was a part of us, of everyone. If we changed ourselves, we could change it, or at least this aspect of it.

Above the roaring in my head, and the sound, wetter now, of our stomachs smacking together, I heard her voice. I hadn't told her what to say, but she was of sorcerous blood, too, and somehow, she found the words. "Melwas," she gasped, "with this act I renounce my mother's bargain. You've no claim on me, or on this man who came after me!"

As I came, as we came, I heard a sound from above us, like rusty metal screaming. Rolling off her, I looked up, to see Melwas perched on the edge of the pit, glaring down at us, his mouth twisted open like a hole torn in a leather bag. "No," he said, the only word I ever heard him speak. Then the floor of teeth lurched beneath us, and the air grew dark, and Melwas and the circle of pale light around him were getting smaller and smaller, and I realized that the bottom of the pit had fallen away, and we were falling with it, falling and falling. Then it was just black vertigo and loose teeth all around us; I could still feel Gwen's hand and I tried to call her name, but there were teeth and bits of teeth in my mouth and a great weight on me, and then I didn't know anything else.

Thirty-five

WHEN I awoke, aching but alive, we were back in our world, lying atop the mound in the cold rain, naked, our clothes beside us and dawn breaking on the horizon. We were both cut and bruised all over, and half-buried in a great wash of mud and teeth, as if the hill itself had vomited us out. Perhaps it had. *Can it really have been so easy,* I thought groggily, *to be freed by a mere fucking?* Foolish me; everything has consequences, and its own dear price, and I don't just mean magic.

Guinevere sat up before I did, looking like someone who'd just clawed her way out of a grave. "Oh God," she said finally. "We're alive!" Then she was on top of me, hugging me again, which was torture on my bruised ribs. "Jesus and the Saints, Mordred, we did it!" Our mouths locked together, her hair was a damp, dirty veil across my face, and we sat like that, her legs around my face and her hands knotted in my hair, until our mutual laughter forced our lips apart. I ran my fingers over the skin of her back and rejoiced in the feel of it, real living skin on the sweetest real living body in the world, nothing like the skin that had covered the land in the Realm of Melwas. I wanted to get someplace warm and dry and explore every glorious inch of her, to rejoice in my victory, in our victory, to continue feeling this pure unsullied joy, which I knew could not last long, for in my life it never did.

Mother had given me better advice than had ever come from her lips when she was alive. The spell had been broken, and that aspect of the Otherworld that was the Realm of Melwas had spat or shat us out. I'd never seen a cold and rainy morning look so bloody lovely. It was over, I told myself, all over, except for the long walk home. I hugged her to me again, and we sat there, wrapped in each other, and let the rain wash us clean.

After a while, we stood. I pointed at the ancient stones. "There's shelter there, until the rain stops."

She shook her head, tangled hair in her eyes. "No. We'll leave now."

"Jesus, Gwen, we'll catch our deaths!" It was stupid, to risk letting the weather kill us, after what we'd been through. Besides, I wasn't sure how far I could walk. "The nearest farm is at least four miles back." There was no sign of my horse, but then, I had no real idea of how long I'd been gone.

Naked there, in the dawning of that dreary November day, she was like a goddess. And goddesses are not to denied. "I'll not stay here," she said through clenched teeth. "This mound is his, and I want to be away from it. We can rest in a ditch, if need be." She cupped her hands for rainwater, which she drank in thirsty gulps. I imagined she was hungry, too. I knew I was, and not been in Melwas's realm nearly as long.

I held up her shift and my tunic. "Well, these won't be much comfort, but they're better than being naked. Perhaps the farmer can spare some clothes."

We looked for my horse, but eventually had to give up, and I silently cursed myself for refusing to bring an escort. That had been bloody stupid, but I'd no thoughts at the time for the aftermath of my return from the Otherworld; indeed, I'd not been entirely convinced we would return. Well, at least we had our privacy, and walking through rain on mud was better than standing in dusty air with teeth underfoot.

Still, it was a limping, painful journey, and I managed the better part of it with my arm around Gwen's shoulders, as she steadied me and helped take the weight off my injured foot. In Orkney or the North, we'd have probably caught a chill and died, walking in wet rags at that time of year, but the weather is mild in the South lands, even in November. The farmer turned out to sympathetic, or at least afraid of my knife, and he gave us a sack and an old, much-mended cloak, and the use of his barn until the rain stopped.

It rained until late in the day, but we kept warm in the loft, lying naked together on the cloak, which I'd spread across the hay. "Let's do it again," said Gwen. "What we did to break the spell. We can take our time, and it won't hurt so much." Not an unappealing prospect, although I was surprised that she had the strength. I kissed her, and was completely, ineffably happy, there in the warm, sneeze-inducing hay, with things scurrying about us and rainwater dripping here and there through the timbers of the roof. A bedchamber in the finest palace in Byzantium could not have been more comfortable.

Not that such euphoria could last. Does it ever? "We can go to Brittany," I finally said, once I could speak again. "That is, if you don't want to go back to your father's kingdom."

"No." She sat up, brushing hay out of her hair. "We must return to Camelot."

I started to pull on my clothes, which, if not clean, were drier than they had been. "You're not still marrying Arthur," I bleated in a tone that I'm ashamed to think of, eight years later. "You don't love him!"

She rested her chin on her lovely knees. "No, I don't. And maybe I do love you."

I looked at her. "That's my point. Damn it, Gwen, you've been rescued from the Otherworld. Live now for yourself in this one. Do what will make you happy." And me, too, of course, but I'd long since learned the folly of asking anyone for that.

She looked down at her feet, her toes curling in the straw, her hair cascading over her face and shoulders. "That's what I'm doing, Mordred. I'm not some noble lady in a story, like Deirdre of the Sorrows, ready to renounce my worldly position for the sake of love. There's not much for a woman in this life, and I've a chance to be a queen. I've been hurt and frightened, offered like a sacrifice to Old Powers, a tool first of my mother's vanity and then my father's political ambitions. Now I want something for myself, some comfort and control, some power, damn it. Is that selfish? You can't imagine what it gives you, that thing between your legs that you used to free me from my bondage. Full of sorrow as your life has been, you've owned more of yourself than I ever have. What would you do, if you were me?"

I shook my head sadly. "I don't know." My daydream of us telling Arthur and him renouncing his claim on her seemed very foolish now.

She stretched out her leg and hooked her foot around my ankle. "Even though I don't love Arthur, I cherish what he's built in Camelot. I want something of the same world that he wants, even if less tinged with his variety of faith. The only way I can share in that and shape it, the only way I can build a better world, is by marrying him. I once joked about wanting a Bibliopola on every corner. Maybe I can make that happen. Probably not, but I can at least try, an attempt that will give some sort of meaning to my life."

Despite my mood, I reached out and gently squeezed her toe. "More meaning than I could give it?" I asked wryly, flashing her my best, most self-deprecating smile.

She smiled back, and my heart tumbled over to see the sadness in her face, and I wanted to hate her, or at least myself, for the power she had over me, but I couldn't.

"I once said I wouldn't be like one of the old Roman ladies, and have a troop of lovers in my bed. I will have one, though, if he'll have me. Lord knows, we're sure to get the opportunity. Arthur won't let himself get tied down at court."

That was dangerous. If we went to Arthur now, and told him what had transpired, his honor would keep him from vengeance, no matter what he felt. But if we cuckolded him after the wedding, that would be a different story. Besides, there were less tangible considerations.

"I don't want to share you, Gwen. With him least of all. My life has been too much bound to his already."

She came toward me, uncannily graceful even when clumping forward on her knees, and reached out and stroked my cheek. "I'm sorry, then. You came after me, when no one else could. And I've wanted you for many months. You deserve better of me, I know. But this is the world, and we are in it. What would you have me do? If I could, I'd tell you that your love was enough of a kingdom for me, but I can't live up to such a pretty phrase, or help the thing I am. Does wanting to be Queen of all the Britons make me vile in your eyes?"

I gently kissed her finger, then pulled back. "I'm not sure anything could do that."

She smiled, and brushed a piece of straw from the corner of her crooked, lovely mouth. "Fie on that. I'm glad to see there's still a human heart beneath those hedgehog prickles, but don't make me empty promises. I'm sure you would once have said the same thing about Arthur. We both know how love can turn upside down."

I met her gaze with all the bravery I'd used in facing Melwas, or the Palag Cat, or Cado before him. "Think of what we do here, Gwen. If we go back to Camelot, and do not tell Arthur of what's transpired between us, we set things in motion that we may not yet imagine. Besides, what if he inquires about your maidenhead?"

She shrugged. "What indeed? For all we know, he's only lain with one woman, and she was no virgin. If he asks, I'll tell him more than he wants to hear about what goes on when young women are locked up in convents, of their games with candles and vegetables and the like. That will make him sorry enough he asked, I'm sure."

I had to laugh at the thought, despite my quiet despair. Knowing that I could do nothing brought passivity, and an odd fatalistic relief. "Ach, Gwen, I don't know where we'll end up, I really don't, but I can't pretend I'm not glad we've come this far." Saying that, I tried very hard to tell myself I meant it.

Unbidden, she crawled into my arms and we lay there again, her head on my chest. "Think on this," she murmured, her mouth just above my heart. "When you were a boy, what did you want in all the world, or out of it?"

Running my fingers through her hair, I resisted the urge to grip her tresses tightly as I spoke. "I wanted to serve at Arthur's right hand, to be his man, to live with honor and glory at Camelot."

"And that will happen, love," she said as soothingly as Mother used to speak to me. "Tell me one thing more. When last we spoke in this world, before Melwas came for me, what did you want more than anything?"

My hand was now a fist in her hair, but I did not twist the strands, and she did not protest the tightening of my grip. "You, Gwen, just you, nothing but you."

She kissed my chest. "Well then, love, there's your heart's desire twice over. Who could ask for so much as that?"

I laughed for the second time, but colder this time. "Oh, yes, nothing but happiness lies before me, I'm sure of it."

Her voice was softer, and she sounded sleepy. "I'll see that Arthur proclaims you his heir, for what you've done in bringing me back to him. You will have that claim before any son I give him, which is only right, as that child is as likely to be yours as his. We've but to wait long enough, and all Britain will be ours. Arthur is not an old man, but his youth is near gone. You're sixteen years younger than him, and I'm two years younger than you. Let him live a good full life, and we'll still have decades after he's gone, and the kingdom besides. Isn't that enough?"

"Maybe it is, Gwen," I murmured, my grip loosening and my hand stroking her head. "Maybe it is at that."

She didn't say anything else. I lay there for a long time,

holding her close in the warm straw and listening to the rain.

We did not speak of it again on the way back, but of other, smaller things, favorite meals, old songs and stories, childhood memories, palace gossip, dead authors we wished we'd known when they were still alive. The next farmer down the road had a mule he didn't seem to need, a swaybacked animal with rheumy eyes. He also had two tough-looking sons, who leaned on their staves and glared, while Gwen knelt to make friends with their shaggy, suspicious dog. I stood my ground, knife in hand, insisting I was royal, dammit, and they'd be compensated for their mule once I was back at Camelot. Incredibly, they finally gave in, although I had to trade my filthy tunic for the farmer's even filthier one, and swap my good knife for the rusty, blunt-edged dagger that belonged to his largest son. The mule limped, and it took us another three days to get back to Camelot, with nights spent in two more barns and the stable of a church, where the priest gave me a hard look, but smiled at Gwen's green eyes and piety. It was a dirty, tiresome, and wet journey, but Gwen didn't seem to care. She greeted each dreary morning as if it were her first, as if the gray sky and heavy clouds and briefly glimpsed sun were strange wonders, and the world itself was unfolding newly born around her. I would have been amazed at her resiliency, except that I was trying very hard to think and feel nothing at all, so I simply listened to her talk, the sound of her voice washing over me like the rain that wouldn't stop. Indeed, it was going strong when we arrived at Camelot.

We looked bedraggled and ridiculous, begrimed from the road, Gwen astride the swaying, scab-kneed mule and me a ragged, footsore scarecrow. If she'd been pregnant, which thank all the gods she wasn't, we could have passed for Mary and Joseph, searching for a manger. We ambled under the gatehouse and down the fortress streets, so narrow and crowded compared to the wide and empty countryside. Mounted warriors jostled past, frequently cursing me and the slow mule, and as we passed the barracks, a small crowd whistled and leered at Gwen, not recognizing her, but woman-conscious enough to see loveliness beneath the dirt.

Guards glared at us when we dismounted in front of the palace's outer courtyard. Their captain approached, a broad, anvil-chinned Caledonian I vaguely recognized from the night I'd killed Dunvallo. "You there!" he barked, hawking a glob of phlegm up onto the wet cobblestones. "What the hell do you want? You can't leave that mule there! Take it and your slut out of here."

I threw back the hood of my filthy cloak. The cold drizzle felt good, running through my hair, streaming down my face. "Fuck off, you stupid git. This is the Lady Guinevere, and I'm Lord Mordred."

His massive jaw dropped, exposing a cavernous mouthful of square yellow teeth. "It can't be."

"It bloody well can. I expect you remember when I killed your predecessor. Let us by, or I'll do the same to you." I was being stupid, really, risking our lives on this lunkhead's comprehension. With two strokes, he could have cut us down on the palace doorstep, a mad peasant and his drab. I didn't care, was past all caring. "Get out of the bloody way!"

Before he could respond, someone shouted from behind him. "What's this? You there, man, let them pass!" The command had the bite of a good blade, cutting through the guard's thick-witted befuddlement. He stiffened at his sovereign's order, and stood aside.

Arthur appeared in the arched colonnade. I assume he'd been in the chapel, and had heard my voice. "Mordred!" he yelled as he came bounding forward. "Guinevere, is she . . . ?"

"He saved me, Arthur," she said softly as she came up beside me. "He came after me, when no one else could, and brought me back. We both owe him our thanks."

Arthur barreled into us, grinning, the smile so alien to his weathered face. "Oh, yes, praise Jesus, yes!" he said, his ropy arms, so long for a man who wasn't tall, encircling us, hugging us both to his hard chest. There we were, me and Gwen shackled by his embrace, the rain pouring now, plastering my hair, more and more soldiers clattering into the courtyard, their murmurs rising in pitch, turning into cheers. "My bride, my son," said Arthur in an inane litany, "my son, my bride, my son, my bride, my son!" *Oh shut up,* I thought, *just let me go off somewhere and be alone,* but those damned arms were strong, and I was conscious of Gwen's hip pressing into my side, the scent of her grimy body, Arthur's sweat, the smell of soggy leaves and autumn rainstorms. There was yet another shout, this one in Gawain's familiar baritone. "Mordred! Strike me dead, lads, it's my goddamn lovely brother!" I hadn't expected him back from the North yet, but there he was, trying to embrace us too, and I wondered if it would stop, if all the soldiers were going to join in, crushing us to death in an orgy of hugging. Guinevere was laughing, her throaty chuckle nearly as deep as Gawain's, and kissing all three of us indiscriminately, and Arthur was actually whooping, long deep guffaws that shook his body like a bucking horse, no trace of gloom or guilt in his manner now. Maybe I'd been that happy, when I first met him. I remembered that day, as clear as this one was overcast, the swells lapping beneath the Cornish dock, the spinning blue sky, Gawain roaring with merriment and Arthur a grinning young god in dull iron and scuffed leather. Here it was, everything I wanted then, and I wondered where my old joy was, once surging and transcendent, now memory's cold ashes. Then I was weeping, my sobs easily mistaken for choked laughter, tears streaming down my dirty face, and me telling myself it was the rain, just the rain, nothing but the rain.

There's not much else left to say, really. Various tedious ceremonial honors were bestowed. Geraint and even dour Kay treated me with awe and respect, and Gawain kept embracing me at awkward moments, squeezing so hard I thought my ribs would be caved in. There was another feast, one that lasted three whole

days, and with Arthur blissfully smiling the whole time,
ignoring the gluttony and drunken excess raging around
him. After that they were married, and the celebration
grew even more riotous. That was the hardest thing I've
done, I think; cheerfully carousing downstairs, and while
she and Arthur fucked. At least, I assume they fucked.
She hasn't spoken of her wedding night, not in the nine
and a half years I've known her now, and I haven't
asked.

Anyway, it wasn't long after the wedding that we
resumed what we had started, Guinevere and I, first on a
floor of teeth and later in a pile of straw. Don't misun-
derstand when I tell you the truth of it. Arthur hurt me
once, a long time ago, and nothing much has hurt me so
much since. When love happened between her and me it
happened *because* of her and me, not because of him.
Don't think otherwise. This was not revenge for the way
he'd rejected me, that long-gone day in Orkney. Early in
this testament I said I would not be a star in Arthur's
firmament, although that's the first thing I can remember wanting. Now I conclude with another denial. I'm
not acting out an incestuous tragedy by Sophocles or
some other long-dead boy-loving Greek. I'm just me,
Mordred, my own self, and not part of any story.

Rest you on that knowledge, as I rest me now. My
hand is sore, there's no more vellum, and in the sun-
shower afternoon I see yarrow and cow parsley gleaming
on the meadows outside the fortress wall. Perhaps I'll
stroll there before the light fails, musing on the feelings
I've conjured up, while my tired fingers weave a garland
for Gwen's brow.

Author's Note

I first became interested in King Arthur's incestuous offspring when, at the age of seventeen, I auditioned for the part of Mordred in the Fayetteville Little Theater production of *Camelot* (in which future special effects goremeister Tom Savini played Arthur), and again six years later, when I actually performed the role semi-professionally in a dinner theater production. Shortly after that, Mordred helped me make my first fiction sale, although in that nascent incarnation he was little more than Harry Flashman in greaves. My stint in the MFA Writing Program at the University of North Carolina at Greensboro inspired me to try something more ambitious, and the novella "Son of the Morning," which I wrote for the workshop and subsequently sold to *Isaac Asimov's Science Fiction Magazine,* was the seed from which this novel grew. That seed was planted in 1983, and looking back with no little chagrin at over a decade of stalls and false starts, I find the myth of the tormented artist a pernicious lie, having discovered the hard way that one is more productive when reasonably sane and happy.

At some point before beginning this work in earnest, and thus finding myself unable to read anyone else's take on the material, I devoured no few quasi-historical Arthurian novels, from the sublime achievements of Rosemary Sutcliffe and Parke Godwin to rather drearier thud and blunders that discretion forbids me to name.

Many such books include a foreword or afterword in which the author sallies forth in favor of Arthur's historical reality. I'm not sure I buy that, despite the diligent efforts of Geoffrey Ashe and other scholars. Maybe it's just my glib cynicism at work, but arguments about how Arthur was "really" the Riothamus named by the sixth-century historian Jordanes, or that the renovated Iron Age fort at Cadbury was "really" Camelot, leave me as unconvinced as the claims of the charming cranks who believe that Edward DeVerre wrote *Hamlet* or that Richard III was a paragon of kingly virtue. I'd like to believe that Arthur, or someone like him, really existed, just as I'd like to believe that there are large, undiscovered aquatic animals living in Loch Ness, but for now I must remain an affectionate skeptic.

Which is why I'm not overly concerned with historical reality. This is, after all, a fantasy, and my Dark Ages Britain is no more "real" a place than Middle Earth, Gormenghast, or The Dreaming. I have tried to place my characters against a backdrop that at least hints at the gritty specificity of real history and the earthy flavor of the earliest versions of the legend before it was prettified by High Chivalry and Courtly Love, but I make no serious claim on authenticity. There are anachronisms here, some committed deliberately and others in ignorance. Readers will note that I generally use the most familiar names for my principal characters, calling my hero and heroine Mordred and Guinevere even when taking my inspiration from sources in which they are known as Medraut or Gwynhwyfar. For the same reason, I generally opt for familiar place names rather than purely Roman or Celtic ones, though I am no more consistent about this than I am about anything else in my often disorderly life.

Ah, yes, Mordred and Guinevere; their relationship here is rather different from that depicted in familiar treatments of the legend, and some readers may be surprised to find the saga's "villain" taking on the role famously assigned to Lancelot. That worthy was a later Continental addition to the story, and does not seem to predate Chrétien de Troyes's twelfth century *Le Cheva-lier de la charette*. The tradition of Guinevere's infidelity goes back much further than that, and I thought it only proper to pair her with the one character whose name appears in the legend almost as early as that of Arthur himself.

Not that I don't also take a cue from later writers. Mordred may have originally simply been one of Ar-thur's comrades and was his nephew before becoming his son. The theme of incest first appears in the Vulgate *Mort Artu* of the early thirteenth century, where Guine-vere is very much the object of Mordred's passion, although she rejects his advances. I also found inspira-tion in the alliterative *Morte Arthure* of the late four-teenth century. That work, which predates Malory by about seventy years, treats Mordred more sympatheti-cally than any other pre-twentieth century source, and even names him as the father of Guinevere's children (all but the earliest Welsh sources claim that Arthur himself was unable to sire offspring). Significantly, there is no Lancelot in the alliterative *Morte*.

My debt to that unknown North Midlands poet and to Geoffrey of Monmouth (his lesser known *Vita Merlini* as well as his pseudo-history) will be more apparent in the forthcoming *Merlin's Gift,* which concerns the fall of Camelot, among other things. Although the present novel, having always been conceived of as a bildungs-roman, ends with Mordred riding high atop Fortuna's Wheel, and does not deal with his descent, I'd like to think that it stands well enough alone, just as *The Sword in the Stone* can be profitably read apart from *The Once and Future King* (indeed, I prefer the earlier, separate version of White's masterpiece). At any rate, there will be only one sequel, for this genre presently suffers from far too many five- and six-volume "trilogies."

But I've probably said too much. So let us rest a while before we take up the tale again. Thanks for coming this far with me.

AVONOVA PRESENTS
MASTERS OF FANTASY AND ADVENTURE